The Conquest of Joiry

A little light kindled behind Guillaume's eyes as he swept the long, strong lines of Jirel with a practiced gaze. "By the Nails!" he roared. "I'll wager your mouth is sweeter than your words."

Jirel drove a spurred heel into the shin of one guard and twisted from his grip, bringing up an iron knee into the abdomen of the other. She had made three long strides toward the door before Guillaume caught her. She felt his arms closing about her from behind, and she lashed out with both spiked heels, twisting like a maniac, straining hopelessly at the ropes which bound her arms.

Guillaume laughed and whirled her around, grinning down into the blaze of her yellow eyes. Then deliberately he set a fist under her chin and tilted her mouth up to his.

"By heaven, that's like kissing a sword blade," said Guillaume, lifting his lips at last.

Jirel choked something that was mercifully muffled as she darted her head sidewise and sank her teeth into his neck. She missed the jugular by a fraction of an inch!

Watch for all the volumes in Ballantine's Classic Library of Science Fiction—big, definitive collections by the true masters in the field. Each book in the series is introduced by a well-known science fiction writer or by a distinguished critic.

NOW AVAILABLE IN A BALLANTINE EDITION:

The Best of Stanley G. Weinbaum
Introduction by Isaac Asimov

The Best of Fritz Leiber
Introduction by Poul Anderson

The Best of Frederik Pohl
Introduction by Lester del Rey

The Best of Henry Kuttner
Introduction by Ray Bradbury

The Best of Cordwainer Smith
Introduction by J. J. Pierce

VOLUMES IN PREPARATION:

The Best of John W. Campbell
Introduction by Lester del Rey

The Best of L. Sprague de Camp
Introduction by Poul Anderson

The Best of Raymond Z. Gallun
Introduction by Frederik Pohl

The Best of Edmond Hamilton
Introduction by Leigh Brackett

The Best of Murray Leinster
Introduction by J. J. Pierce

The Best of Philip K. Dick
Introduction by John Brunner

The Best of Cyril Kornbluth
Introduction by Frederik Pohl

COMING SOON FROM BALLANTINE BOOKS

THE BEST OF
C. L. Moore

Edited and with an introduction by
LESTER DEL REY

Afterword by
C. L. MOORE

BALLANTINE BOOKS • NEW YORK

ACKNOWLEDGMENTS

"Shambleau," copyright © 1933 by Popular Fiction Publishing Co., for *Weird Tales*, November 1933; copyright renewed 1961 by C. L. Moore.

"Black Thirst," copyright © 1934 by Popular Fiction Publishing Co., for *Weird Tales,* April 1934; copyright renewed 1961 by C. L. Moore.

"The Bright Illusions," copyright © 1934 by Street & Smith Publications, Inc., for *Astounding Stories,* October 1934; copyright renewed 1961 by C. L. Moore.

"Black God's Kiss," copyright © 1934 by Popular Fiction Publishing Co. for *Weird Tales,* October 1934; copyright renewed 1961 by C. L. Moore.

"Tryst in Time," copyright © 1936 by Street & Smith Publications, Inc., for *Astounding Stories,* December 1936; copyright renewed 1964 by C. L. Moore.

"Greater Than Gods," copyright © 1939 by Street & Smith Publications, Inc., for *Astounding Science Fiction,* July 1939; copyright renewed 1966 by The Condé Nast Publications, Inc.

"Fruit of Knowledge," copyright © 1940 by Street & Smith Publications, Inc., for *Unknown,* October 1940; copyright renewed 1968 by C. L. Moore.

"No Woman Born," copyright © 1944 by Street & Smith Publications, Inc., for *Astounding Science Fiction,* December 1944; copyright renewed 1971 by The Condé Nast Publications, Inc.

"Daemon," copyright © 1946 by All-Fiction Field, Inc., for *Famous Fantastic Mysteries,* October 1946; copyright renewed 1974 by C. L. Moore.

"Vintage Season," copyright © 1946 by Street & Smith Publications, Inc., for *Astounding Science Fiction,* September 1946; copyright renewed 1973 by C. L. Moore.

Contents

Forty Years of C. L. Moore

Back in the fall of 1933, I opened the November issue of *Weird Tales* to find a story with the provocative but meaningless title, "Shambleau," by an unknown writer named C. L. Moore—and life was never quite the same afterwards. Up to that time, science-fiction readers had accepted the mechanistic and unemotional stories of other worlds and future times without question. After the publication of Moore's story, however, the bleakness of such writing would never again be satisfactory.

Almost forty years later, I sat in the audience at a World Science Fiction Convention banquet, listening to Forrest J. Ackerman announce a special award that was about to be presented to a writer. As is customary, Ackerman was saving the name of the recipient for the climax. But he mentioned a story called "Shambleau" and never got to finish his speech. As one, the 2,000 people in the audience came instantly to their feet in unanimous tribute—clapping, shouting, and craning to see a gracious and lovely lady blushingly accept the applause.

Many in that audience had never read the story. But everyone knew about it. And everyone knew that Catherine Moore was one of the finest writers of all time in the field of science fiction.

It is probably impossible to explain to modern readers how great an impact that first C. L. Moore story had. Science fiction has learned a great deal from her many examples. But if you could go back to the old science-fiction magazines of the time and read a few issues, and then turn to "Shambleau" for the first time, you might begin to understand. The influences of that story were and are tremendous.

Here, for the first time in the field, we find mood, feeling, and color. Here is an alien who is truly *alien*— far different from the crude monsters and slightly-altered humans found in other stories. Here are rounded and well-developed characters. Northwest Smith, for instance, is neither a good guy nor a bad guy—he may be slightly larger than life, but he displays all aspects of humanity. In "Shambleau" we also experience as never before both the horror at what we may find in space and the romance of space itself. And—certainly for the first time that I can remember in the field—this story presents the sexual drive of humanity in some of its complexity.

"Black Thirst" was Moore's next story, and it continued the exploits of Northwest Smith. In this story, something new was brought to our tales of the far planets: a quality of beauty as a thing a man must strive for, even when it is perverted to wrong ends. There were other stories of Northwest Smith, but these first two stand out as the most moving and original.

Many of Moore's early stories appeared in *Weird Tales,* though they were basically science fiction. Apparently, some of the editors of the sf magazines of the day were afraid of such extreme deviation from the more standard stories. But in October, 1934, *Astounding Stories* published her "Bright Illusion." Now in those days, as countless letters to the editor indicated, the one thing readers of the science-fiction magazines did not want was a love story. Yet here was a tale of the pure quintessence of love that transcended all limits! Nevertheless, the readers raved about it and clamored for more.

A few years ago, Larry Janifer was putting together an anthology of the favorite stories of a number of leading writers in the field. I sent him three titles, including "Bright Illusion." He wrote back to say that he had never read it before, that he was deeply grateful to me for suggesting it, and that it was an absolute *must* for the book. Somehow, in spite of advances and changes in our writing, the stories of C. L. Moore remain as fresh and powerful now as they were back when the field was groping through its beginnings.

Meanwhile, in *Weird Tales,* Moore was beginning a new series of stories about Jirel, the warrior maid of the mythical kingdom of Joiry. In those days, the sf magazines were all intensely male oriented. Most of the readers were male, and the idea of sexual equality had never been considered—certainly not for the protagonist of an adventure story. For such fiction, it followed axiomatically, one used a male hero. But in "Black God's Kiss" the intensely feminine Jirel was a woman equal in battle to any swashbuckling male hero who ever ruled over the knights of ancient valor.

Jirel of Joiry was no imperturbable battler, however. She loved and hated, feared desperately to the core of her superstitious heart—and yet dared to take risks that no man had ever faced. Every male reader loved the story, forgot his chauvinism, and demanded more stories about Jirel. More were quickly forthcoming, though to my mind, the first one remained marginally the best and most original. "Black God's Kiss" was simply too good to be surpassed in later episodes of the series.

"Tryst in Time" was another love story that greatly pleased the readers of *Astounding Stories.* Once again Moore captured the ultimate sense of romance that could be accepted only in a world of fantasy. Here was a love that swept through time—roving among the ages and building slowly to a climax of full realization. Yet "Tryst in Time" was more than a love story—it was also an exposition of both the fallibility and the glory of man.

During these early years, C. L. Moore had been a fairly prolific writer of stories which dealt almost exclusively with the most emotional elements of fiction. But after 1938, changes came about that may or may not have been caused by a change in her personal life. Her biographers disagree, and she makes few comments that provide us with any real answer. My own suspicion is that the changes occurred because of greater maturity on the part of the writer. Certainly, however, the alteration of her fictional interests coincide with a major event in her life.

When her first story was published, she was just twenty-two years old and was employed as a secretary in a bank in Indianapolis. By all accounts, she was a lovely and very popular young lady. But there had been many years of ill health before, during which she had turned to fiction as an escape. She says that she had been writing for fifteen years before submitting anything for publication. That would explain the "escapist" nature of her early fiction, though hardly the vigor of the stories.

In 1938, Catherine Moore met Henry Kuttner, a young writer of great promise, who was then just becoming recognized. She gave up her job in Indianapolis and moved to New York, where she and Kuttner were married in 1940. From then until 1958, when Kuttner died of a heart attack, after becoming one of the leading writers of science fiction, her interests were strongly focused on writing as a way of life.

Kuttner and Moore were an unusual mating of talents. Her fiction was noted for its sensitivity and emotional coloration. His was essentially intellectual in its creation, based upon a firm understanding of plot structure and, initially, often more clever than moving in its developments. Somehow, the couple managed to merge their talents, so that a story by either one would display both an intellectual base and a richly colored background.

They often worked together upon a single story; indeed, few stories produced during their marriage seem to be the work of either one alone. They used a great number of pseudonyms, some of which they seemed to share or exchange. And generally, the authorship of many of the stories is something of a puzzle, even today. A tale credited to Kuttner in one compiler's list may be ascribed to Moore in another list. Internal evidence isn't always much help, either. I'm told that the novel *Fury* was written by Kuttner, based upon a novelette entitled "Clash by Night," by Moore; yet of the two, the novel seems to have more of the richness of emotional tone one might expect from Moore.

The change in Moore's fiction began before her marriage, however. "Greater than Gods" appeared in the July, 1939, issue of *Astounding Science Fiction* (the magazine having changed its title slightly). In this story, love again plays a key role—but hardly in its old, romantic fashion. Here love is no longer some unbreakable tie between man and woman that can defy time and the gods. Now the conflict lies in a choice between duty and a man's desire for love. The problem and the resolution of the story are clearly intellectual in their development. Only the power of the writing remains unchanged from the preceding "Tryst in Time."

Moore's next story also must have been written before her marriage, though it appeared afterward, in the October, 1940, issue of *Unknown*. "Fruit of Knowledge" is straight fantasy with none of the trappings of science fiction. And here it is difficult to determine whether emotion or intellect is the stronger element. The basic idea—the ancient myth of Lilith—is one that almost forces a writer to fall back on the emotionalism usually associated with this strangely undying bit of folklore. Moore's refusal to accept the obvious in telling of this conflict of love and Divine Power indicates clearly the deeper insight she was gaining in the handling of the elements of fiction.

Unfortunately, the years of marriage resulted in very few stories that can be credited with any certainty to C. L. Moore alone. As time went on, her stories became increasingly more rare in the magazines. Yet when one did appear, it was generally so outstanding that the quality of this later work almost makes up for the lack in number.

Of these later stories, my favorite is "No Woman Born," which appeared in the December 1944 issue of *Astounding Science Fiction*. This is a nearly perfect blend of emotion and intellect. The conflict of the story lies in the problem of discovering what the basis of true humanity may really be—a problem that has baffled philosophers for centuries. Quite rightly, Moore sees the problem also as encompassing the need to know the basis and nature of human emotions. The resulting portrait of a great artist and marvelously feminine woman struggling to be true to her inner self is unforgettable.

Perhaps the least typical Moore story included here is "Daemon," which appeared in the October, 1946, issue of *Famous Fantastic Fiction*. This is a straight fantasy about a "simpleton" with a strange gift. The idea seems slight, and it could easily lead to an excess of sentimentality. Yet the story is told simply and calmly—but very effectively. It's an excellent example of Moore's developed craftsmanship as a writer.

At about the same time, in the September, 1946, issue of *Astounding Science Fiction,* "Vintage Season" appeared. This is the story which most seem to consider Moore's masterpiece. Certainly it has been included in more of the great anthologies than her other stories. C. L. Moore seems to have posed a problem for most anthologists; her stories are never less than 10,000 words in length, and most are much longer. The editor of an anthology is usually compelled to include as many stories as possible, which means that novelettes tend to be passed up in favor of shorter stories. But "Vintage Season" proved to be so good that it could hardly be left out!

Certainly the story is a showpiece for all the talents of C. L. Moore. It blends the disparate elements of horror and beauty, alien culture and human feelings, and progress and decadence. And it has the sense of inevitability needed for great fiction, skillfully combined with the uncertainty of a fine suspense story. I refuse to describe the story further, since it must be read to be truly appreciated.

During the following years, C. L. Moore wrote a few stories and a novel, *Doomsday Morning*. But most of her time seems to have been spent in collaborating with her husband and in finishing her college education, which was interrupted by financial difficulties during the Depression.

After the tragic death of Henry Kuttner, she remained in California, where she turned to the lucrative field of television writing. She has married again, this time to Thomas Reggie, who is not a writer.

There have been no new science-fiction or fantasy stories from C. L. Moore for almost twenty years now. But her reputation among readers and editors has never diminished. She remains preeminent in the field. And recently she has begun to talk about trying her hand again at science fiction. 'Tis a consummation devoutly to be wished!

Lester del Rey
New York
1975

Shambleau

Man has conquered space before. You may be sure of that. Somewhere beyond the Egyptians, in that dimness out of which come echoes of half-mythical names—Atlantis, Mu—somewhere back of history's first beginnings there must have been an age when mankind, like us today, built cities of steel to house its star-roving ships and knew the names of the planets in their own native tongues—heard Venus' people call their wet world "Sha-ardol" in that soft, sweet, slurring speech and mimicked Mars' guttural "Lakkdiz" from the harsh tongues of Mars' dryland dwellers. You may be sure of it. Man has conquered Space be-fore, and out of that conquest faint, faint echoes run still through a world that has forgotten the very fact of a civilization which must have been as mighty as our own. There have been too many myths and legends for us to doubt it. The myth of the Medusa, for instance, can never have had its roots in the soil of Earth. That tale of the snake-haired Gorgon whose gaze turned the gazer to stone never originated about any creature that Earth nourished. And those ancient Greeks who told the story must have remembered, dimly and half believing, a tale of antiquity about some strange being from one of the outlying planets their remotest ancestors once trod.

"SHAMBLEAU! HA . . . SHAMBLEAU!" The wild hysteria of the mob rocketed from wall to wall of Lakkdarol's narrow streets and the storming of heavy boots over the slag-red pavement made an ominous undernote to that swelling bay, "Shambleau! Shambleau!"

Northwest Smith heard it coming and stepped into the nearest doorway, laying a wary hand on his heat-gun's grip, and his colorless eyes narrowed. Strange sounds were common enough in the streets of Earth's latest col-ony on Mars—a raw, red little town where anything might happen, and very often did. But Northwest Smith, whose name is known and respected in every dive and wild outpost on a dozen wild planets, was a cautious man, despite his reputation. He set his back against the wall and gripped his pistol, and heard the rising shout come nearer and nearer.

Then into his range of vision flashed a red running figure, dodging like a hunted hare from shelter to shelter in the narrow street. It was a girl—a berry-brown girl in a single tattered garment whose scarlet burnt the eyes with its brilliance. She ran wearily, and he could hear her gasping breath from where he stood. As she came into view he saw her hesitate and lean one hand against the wall for support, and glance wildly around for shelter. She must not have seen him in the depths of the doorway, for as the bay of the mob grew louder and the pounding of feet sounded almost at the corner she gave a despairing little moan and dodged into the recess at his very side.

When she saw him standing there, tall and leather-brown, hand on his heat-gun, she sobbed once, inarticulately, and collapsed at his feet, a huddle of burning scarlet and bare, brown limbs.

Smith had not seen her face, but she was a girl, and sweetly made and in danger; and though he had not the reputation of a chivalrous man, something in her hopeless huddle at his feet touched that chord of sympathy for the underdog that stirs in every Earthman, and he pushed her gently into the corner behind him and jerked out his gun, just as the first of the running mob rounded the corner.

It was a motley crowd, Earthmen and Martians and a sprinkling of Venusian swampmen and strange, nameless denizens of unnamed planets—a typical Lakkdarol mob. When the first of them turned the corner and saw the empty street before them there was a faltering in the rush and the foremost spread out and began to search the doorways on both sides of the street.

"Looking for something?" Smith's sardonic call sounded clear above the clamor of the mob.

They turned. The shouting died for a moment as they took in the scene before them—tall Earthman in the space-explorer's leathern garb, all one color from the burning of savage suns save for the sinister pallor of his no-colored eyes in a scarred and resolute face, gun in his steady hand and the scarlet girl crouched behind him, panting.

The foremost of the crowd—a burly Earthman in tattered leather from which the Patrol insignia had been ripped away—stared for a moment with a strange expression of incredulity on his face overspreading the savage exultation of the chase. Then he let loose a deep-throated bellow, "Shambleau!" and lunged forward. Behind him the mob took up the cry again, "Shambleau! Shambleau! Shambleau!" and surged after.

Smith, lounging negligently against the wall, arms folded and gun-hand draped over his left forearm, looked incapable of swift motion, but at the leader's first forward step the pistol swept in a practiced half-circle and the dazzle of blue-white heat leaping from its muzzle seared an arc in the slag pavement at his feet. It was an old gesture, and not a man in the crowd but understood it. The foremost recoiled swiftly against the surge of those in the rear, and for a moment there was confusion as the two tides met and struggled. Smith's mouth curled into a grim curve as he watched. The man in the mutilated Patrol uniform lifted a threatening fist and stepped to the very edge of the deadline, while the crowd rocked to and fro behind him.

"Are you crossing that line?" queried Smith in an ominously gentle voice.

"We want that girl!"

"Come and get her!" Recklessly Smith grinned into his face. He saw danger there, but his defiance was not the foolhardy gesture it seemed. An expert psychologist of mobs from long experience, he sensed no murder here. Not a gun had appeared in any hand in the crowd. They desired the girl with an inexplicable bloodthirstiness he was at a loss to understand, but toward himself he sensed no such fury. A mauling he might expect, but his life was in no danger. Guns would have appeared before now if they were coming out at all. So he grinned in the man's angry face and leaned lazily against the wall.

Behind their self-appointed leader the crowd milled impatiently, and threatening voices began to rise again. Smith heard the girl moan at his feet.

"What do you want with her?" he demanded.

"She's Shambleau! Shambleau, you fool! Kick her out of there—we'll take care of her!"

"I'm taking care of her," drawled Smith.

"She's Shambleau, I tell you! Damn your hide, man, we never let those things live! Kick her out here!"

The repeated name had no meaning to him, but Smith's innate stubbornness rose defiantly as the crowd surged forward to the very edge of the arc, their clamor growing louder. "Shambleau! Kick her out here! Give us Shambleau! Shambleau!"

Smith dropped his indolent pose like a cloak and planted both feet wide, swinging up his gun threateningly. "Keep back!" he yelled. "She's mine! Keep back!"

He had no intention of using that heat-beam. He knew by now that they would not kill him unless he started the gunplay himself, and he did not mean to give up his life for any girl alive. But a severe mauling he expected, and he braced himself instinctively as the mob heaved within itself.

To his astonishment a thing happened then that he had never known to happen before. At his shouted defiance the foremost of the mob—those who had heard him clearly—drew back a little, not in alarm but evidently surprised. The ex-Patrolman said, "Yours! She's *yours?*" in a voice from which puzzlement crowded out the anger.

Smith spread his booted legs wide before the crouching figure and flourished his gun.

"Yes," he said. "And I'm keeping her! Stand back there!"

The man stared at him wordlessly, and horror, disgust and incredulity mingled on his weather-beaten face. The incredulity triumphed for a moment and he said again, *"Yours!"*

Smith nodded defiance.

The man stepped back suddenly, unutterable contempt in his very pose. He waved an arm to the crowd and said loudly, "It's—his!" and the press melted away, gone silent, too, and the look of contempt spread from face to face.

The ex-Patrolman spat on the slag-paved street and turned his back indifferently. "Keep her, then," he advised briefly over one shoulder. "But don't let her out again in this town!"

Smith stared in perplexity almost open-mouthed as the suddenly scornful mob began to break up. His mind was in a whirl. That such bloodthirsty animosity should vanish in a breath he could not believe. And the curious mingling of contempt and disgust on the faces he saw baffled him even more. Lakkdarol was anything but a puritan town—it did not enter his head for a moment that his claiming the brown girl as his own had caused that strangely shocked revulsion to spread through the crowd. No, it was something more deeply rooted than that. Instinctive, instant disgust had been in the faces he saw—they would have looked less so if he had admitted cannibalism or *Pharol*-worship.

And they were leaving his vicinity as swiftly as if whatever unknowing sin he had committed were contagious. The street was emptying as rapidly as it had filled. He saw a sleek Venusian glance back over his shoulder as he turned the corner and sneer, "Shambleau!" and the word awoke a new line of speculation in Smith's mind. Shambleau! Vaguely of French origin, it must be. And strange enough to hear it from the lips of Venusians and Martian drylanders, but it was their use of it that puzzled him more. "We never let those things live," the ex-Patrolman had said. It reminded him dimly of something . . . an ancient line from some writing in his own tongue . . . "Thou shalt not suffer a witch to live." He smiled to himself at the similarity, and simultaneously was aware of the girl at his elbow.

She had risen soundlessly. He turned to face her, sheathing his gun, and stared at first with curiosity and then in the entirely frank openness with which men regard that which is not wholly human. For she was not. He knew it at a glance, though the brown, sweet body was shaped like a woman's and she wore the garment of scarlet—he saw it was leather—with an ease that few unhuman beings achieve toward clothing. He knew it from the moment he looked into her eyes, and a shiver of unrest went over him as he met them. They were frankly green as young grass, with slit-like, feline pupils that pulsed unceasingly, and there was a look of dark, animal wisdom in their depths—that look of the beast which sees more than man.

There was no hair upon her face—neither brows nor lashes, and he would have sworn that the tight scarlet turban bound around her head covered baldness. She had three fingers and a thumb, and her feet had four digits apiece too, and all sixteen of them were tipped with round claws that sheathed back into the flesh like a cat's. She ran her tongue over her lips—a thin, pink, flat tongue as feline as her eyes—and spoke with difficulty. He felt that that throat and tongue had never been shaped for human speech.

"Not—afraid now," she said softly, and her little teeth were white and pointed as a kitten's.

"What did they want you for?" he asked her curiously. "What had you done? Shambleau . . . is that your name?"

"I—not talk your—speech," she demurred hesitantly.

"Well, try to—I want to know. Why were they chasing you? Will you be safe on the street now, or hadn't you better get indoors somewhere? They looked dangerous."

"I—go with you." She brought it out with difficulty.

"Say you!" Smith grinned. "What are you, anyhow? You look like a kitten to me."

"Shambleau." She said it somberly.

"Where d'you live? Are you a Martian?"

"I come from—from far—from long ago—far country——"

"Wait!" laughed Smith. "You're getting your wires crossed. You're not a Martian?"

She drew herself up very straight beside him, lifting the turbaned head, and there was something queenly in the poise of her.

"Martian?" she said scornfully. "My people—are—are—you have no word. Your speech—hard for me."

"What's yours? I might know it—try me."

She lifted her head and met his eyes squarely, and there was in hers a subtle amusement—he could have sworn it.

"Some day I—speak to you in—my own language," she promised, and the pink tongue flicked out over her lips, swiftly, hungrily.

Approaching footsteps on the red pavement interrupted Smith's reply. A dryland Martian came past, reeling a little and exuding an aroma of *segir*-whisky, the Venusian brand. When he caught the red flash of the girl's tatters he turned his head sharply, and as his *segir*-steeped brain took in the fact of her presence he lurched toward the recess unsteadily, bawling, "Shambleau, by *Pharol!* Shambleau!" and reached out a clutching hand.

Smith struck it aside contemptuously.

"On your way, drylander," he advised.

The man drew back and stared, blear-eyed.

"Yours, eh?" he croaked. *"Zut!* You're welcome to it!" And like the ex-Patrolman before him he spat on the pavement and turned away, muttering harshly in the blasphemous tongue of the drylands.

Smith watched him shuffle off, and there was a crease between his colorless eyes, a nameless unease rising within him.

"Come on," he said abruptly to the girl. "If this sort of thing is going to happen we'd better get indoors. Where shall I take you?"

"With—you," she murmured.

He stared down into the flat green eyes. Those ceaselessly pulsing pupils disturbed him, but it seemed to him, vaguely, that behind the animal shallows of her gaze was a shutter—a closed barrier that might at any moment open to reveal the very deeps of that dark knowledge he sensed there.

Roughly he said again, "Come on, then," and stepped down into the street.

She pattered along a pace or two behind him, making no effort to keep up with his long strides, and though Smith—as men know from Venus to Jupiter's moons—

walks as softly as a cat, even in spacemen's boots, the girl at his heels slid like a shadow over the rough pavement, making so little sound that even the lightness of his footsteps was loud in the empty street.

Smith chose the less frequented ways of Lakkdarol, and somewhat shamefacedly thanked his nameless gods that his lodgings were not far away, for the few pedestrians he met turned and stared after the two with that by now familiar mingling of horror and contempt which he was as far as ever from understanding.

The room he had engaged was a single cubicle in a lodging-house on the edge of the city. Lakkdarol, raw camp-town that it was in those days, could have furnished little better anywhere within its limits, and Smith's errand there was not one he wished to advertise. He had slept in worse places than this before, and knew that he would do so again.

There was no one in sight when he entered, and the girl slipped up the stairs at his heels and vanished through the door, shadowy, unseen by anyone in the house. Smith closed the door and leaned his broad shoulders against the panels, regarding her speculatively.

She took in what little the room had to offer in a glance—frowsy bed, rickety table, mirror hanging unevenly and cracked against the wall, unpainted chairs— a typical camp-town room in an Earth settlement abroad. She accepted its poverty in that single glance, dismissed it, then crossed to the window and leaned out for a moment, gazing across the low roof-tops toward the barren countryside beyond, red slag under the late afternoon sun.

"You can stay here," said Smith abruptly, "until I leave town. I'm waiting here for a friend to come in from Venus. Have you eaten?"

"Yes," said the girl quickly. "I shall—need no—food for—a while."

"Well—" Smith glanced around the room. "I'll be in sometime tonight. You can go or stay just as you please. Better lock the door behind me."

With no more formality than that he left her. The door closed and he heard the key turn, and smiled to himself. He did not expect, then, ever to see her again.

He went down the steps and out into the late-slanting sunlight with a mind so full of other matters that the brown girl receded very quickly into the background. Smith's errand in Lakkdarol, like most of his errands, is better not spoken of. Man lives as he must, and Smith's living was a perilous affair outside the law and ruled by the ray-gun only. It is enough to say that the shipping-port and its cargoes outbound interested him deeply just now, and that the friend he awaited was Yarol the Venusian, in that swift little Edsel ship the *Maid* that can flash from world to world with a derisive speed that laughs at Patrol boats and leaves pursuers floundering in the ether far behind. Smith and Yarol and the *Maid* were a trinity that had caused the Patrol leaders much worry and many gray hairs in the past, and the future looked very bright to Smith himself that evening as he left his lodging-house.

Lakkdarol roars by night, as Earthmen's camp-towns have a way of doing on every planet where Earth's outposts are, and it was beginning lustily as Smith went down among the awakening lights toward the center of town. His business there does not concern us. He mingled with the crowds where the lights were brightest, and there was the click of ivory counters and the jingle of silver, and red *segir* gurgled invitingly from black Venusian bottles, and much later Smith strolled homeward under the moving moons of Mars, and if the street wavered a little under his feet now and then—why, that is only understandable. Not even Smith could drink red *segir* at every bar from the *Martian Lamb* to the *New Chicago* and remain entirely steady on his feet. But he found his way back with very little difficulty—considering—and spent a good five minutes hunting for his key before he remembered he had left it in the inner lock for the girl.

He knocked then, and there was no sound of footsteps from within, but in a few moments the latch clicked and the door swung open. She retreated soundlessly before him as he entered, and took up her favorite place against the window, leaning back on the sill and outlined against the starry sky beyond. The room was in darkness.

Smith flipped the switch by the door and then leaned back against the panels, steadying himself. The cool night air had sobered him a little, and his head was clear enough—liquor went to Smith's feet, not his head, or he would never have come this far along the lawless way he had chosen. He lounged against the door now and regarded the girl in the sudden glare of the bulbs, blinding a little as much at the scarlet of her clothing as at the light.

"So you stayed," he said.

"I—waited," she answered softly, leaning farther back against the sill and clasping the rough wood with slim, three-fingered hands, pale brown against the darkness.

"Why?"

She did not answer that, but her mouth curved into a slow smile. On a woman it would have been reply enough—provocative, daring. On Shambleau there was something pitiful and horrible in it—so human on the face of one half-animal. And yet . . . that sweet brown body curving so softly from the tatters of scarlet leather —the velvety texture of that brownness—the white-flashing smile. . . . Smith was aware of a stirring excitement within him. After all—time would be hanging heavy now until Yarol came. . . . Speculatively he allowed the steel-pale eyes to wander over her, with a slow regard that missed nothing. And when he spoke he was aware that his voice had deepened a little. . . .

"Come here," he said.

She came forward slowly, on bare clawed feet that made no sound on the floor, and stood before him with downcast eyes and mouth trembling in that pitifully human smile. He took her by the shoulders—velvety soft shoulders, of a creamy smoothness that was not the texture of human flesh. A little tremor went over her, perceptibly, at the contact of his hands. Northwest Smith caught his breath suddenly and dragged her to him . . . sweet yielding brownness in the circle of his arms . . . heard her own breath catch and quicken as her velvety arms closed about his neck. And then he was looking down into her face, very near, and the green animal eyes met his with the pulsing pupils and the flicker of—something—deep behind their shallows—and through the rising clamor of his blood, even as he stooped his lips to hers, Smith felt something deep within him shudder away—inexplicable, instinctive, revolted. What it might be he had no words to tell, but the very touch of her was suddenly loathsome—so soft and velvet and unhuman —and it might have been an animal's face that lifted itself to his mouth—the dark knowledge looked hungrily from the darkness of those slit pupils—and for a mad instant he knew that same wild, feverish revulsion he had seen in the faces of the mob. . . .

"God!" he gasped, a far more ancient invocation against evil than he realized, then or ever, and he ripped her arms from his neck, swung her away with such a force that she reeled half across the room. Smith fell back against the door, breathing heavily, and stared at her while the wild revolt died slowly within him.

She had fallen to the floor beneath the window, and as she lay there against the wall with bent head he saw, curiously, that her turban had slipped—the turban that he had been so sure covered baldness—and a lock of scarlet hair fell below the binding leather, hair as scarlet as her garment, as unhumanly red as her eyes were unhumanly green. He stared, and shook his head dizzily and stared again, for it seemed to him that the thick lock of crimson had moved, *squirmed* of itself against her cheek.

At the contact of it her hands flew up and she tucked it away with a very human gesture and then dropped her head again into her hands. And from the deep shadow of her fingers he thought she was staring up at him covertly.

Smith drew a deep breath and passed a hand across his forehead. The inexplicable moment had gone as quickly as it came—too swiftly for him to understand or analyze it. "Got to lay off the *segir*," he told himself unsteadily. Had he imagined that scarlet hair? After all, she was no more than a pretty brown girl-creature from one of the many half-human races peopling the planets.

No more than that, after all. A pretty little thing, but animal. . . . He laughed a little shakily.

"No more of that," he said. "God knows I'm no angel, but there's got to be a limit somewhere. Here." He crossed to the bed and sorted out a pair of blankets from the untidy heap, tossing them to the far corner of the room. "You can sleep there."

Wordlessly she rose from the floor and began to rearrange the blankets, the uncomprehending resignation of the animal eloquent in every line of her.

Smith had a strange dream that night. He thought he had awakened to a room full of darkness and moonlight and moving shadows, for the nearer moon of Mars was racing through the sky and everything on the planet below her was endued with a restless life in the dark. And something . . . some nameless, unthinkable *thing* . . . was coiled about his throat . . . something like a soft snake, wet and warm. It lay loose and light about his neck . . . and it was moving gently, very gently, with a soft, caressive pressure that sent little thrills of delight through every nerve and fiber of him, a perilous delight —beyond physical pleasure, deeper than joy of the mind. That warm softness was caressing the very roots of his soul with a terrible intimacy. The ecstasy of it left him weak, and yet he knew—in a flash of knowledge born of this impossible dream—that the soul should not be handled. . . . And with that knowledge a horror broke upon him, turning the pleasure into a rapture of revulsion, hateful, horrible—but still most foully sweet. He tried to lift his hands and tear the dream-monstrosity from his throat—tried but half-heartedly; for though his soul was revolted to its very deeps, yet the delight of his body was so great that his hands all but refused the attempt. But when at last he tried to lift his arms a cold shock went over him and he found that he could not stir . . . his body lay stony as marble beneath the blankets, a living marble that shuddered with a dreadful delight through every rigid vein.

The revulsion grew strong upon him as he struggled against the paralyzing dream—a struggle of soul against sluggish body—titanically, until the moving dark was streaked with blankness that clouded and closed about him at last and he sank back into the oblivion from which he had awakened.

Next morning, when the bright sunlight shining through Mars' clear thin air awakened him, Smith lay for a while trying to remember. The dream had been more vivid than reality, but he could not now quite recall . . . only that it had been more sweet and horrible than anything else in life. He lay puzzling for a while, until a soft sound from the corner aroused him from his thoughts and he sat up to see the girl lying in a catlike coil on her blankets, watching him with round, grave eyes. He regarded her somewhat ruefully.

"Morning," he said. "I've just had the devil of a dream. . . . Well, hungry?"

She shook her head silently, and he could have sworn there was a covert gleam of strange amusement in her eyes.

He stretched and yawned, dismissing the nightmare temporarily from his mind.

"What am I going to do with you?" he inquired, turning to more immediate matters. "I'm leaving here in a day or two and I can't take you along, you know. Where'd you come from in the first place?"

Again she shook her head.

"Not telling? Well, it's your own business. You can stay here until I give up the room. From then on you'll have to do your own worrying."

He swung his feet to the floor and reached for his clothes.

Ten minutes later, slipping the heat-gun into its holster at his thigh, Smith turned to the girl. "There's food-concentrate in that box on the table. It ought to hold you until I get back. And you'd better lock the door again after I've gone."

Her wide, unwavering stare was his only answer, and he was not sure she had understood, but at any rate the lock clicked after him as before, and he went down the steps with a faint grin on his lips.

The memory of last night's extraordinary dream was slipping from him, as such memories do, and by the time he had reached the street the girl and the dream and all of yesterday's happenings were blotted out by the sharp necessities of the present.

Again the intricate business that had brought him here claimed his attention. He went about it to the exclusion of all else, and there was a good reason behind everything he did from the moment he stepped out into the street until the time when he turned back again at evening; though had one chosen to follow him during the day his apparently aimless rambling through Lakkdarol would have seemed very pointless.

He must have spent two hours at the least idling by the space-port, watching with sleepy, colorless eyes the ships that came and went, the passengers, the vessels lying at wait, the cargoes—particularly the cargoes. He made the rounds of the town's saloons once more, consuming many glasses of varied liquors in the course of the day and engaging in idle conversation with men of all races and worlds, usually in their own languages, for Smith was a linguist of repute among his contemporaries. He heard the gossip of the spaceways, news from a dozen planets of a thousand different events. He heard the latest joke about the Venusian Emperor and the latest report on the Chino-Aryan war and the latest song hot from the lips of Rose Robertson, whom every man on the civilized planets adored as "the Georgia Rose." He passed the day quite profitably, for his own purposes, which do not concern us now, and it was not until late evening, when he turned homeward again, that the thought of the brown girl in his room took definite shape in his mind, though it had been lurking there, formless and submerged, all day.

He had no idea what comprised her usual diet, but he bought a can of New York roast beef and one of Venusian frog-broth and a dozen fresh canal-apples and two pounds of that Earth lettuce that grows so vigorously in the fertile canal-soil of Mars. He felt that she must surely find something to her liking in this broad variety of edibles, and—for his day had been very satisfactory—

he hummed *The Green Hills of Earth* to himself in a surprisingly good baritone as he climbed the stairs.

The door was locked, as before, and he was reduced to kicking the lower panels gently with his boot, for his arms were full. She opened the door with that softness that was characteristic of her and stood regarding him in the semi-darkness as he stumbled to the table with his load. The room was unlit again.

"Why don't you turn on the lights?" he demanded irritably after he had barked his shin on the chair by the table in an effort to deposit his burden there.

"Light and—dark—they are alike—to me," she murmured.

"Cat eyes, eh? Well, you look the part. Here, I've brought you some dinner. Take your choice. Fond of roast beef? Or how about a little frog-broth?"

She shook her head and backed away a step.

"No," she said. "I can not—eat your food."

Smith's brows wrinkled. "Didn't you have any of the food tablets?"

Again the red turban shook negatively.

"Then you haven't had anything for—why, more than twenty-four hours! You must be starved."

"Not hungry," she denied.

"What can I find for you to eat, then? There's time yet if I hurry. You've got to eat, child."

"I shall—eat," she said softly. "Before long—I shall —feed. Have no—worry."

She turned away then and stood at the window, looking out over the moonlit landscape as if to end the conversation. Smith cast her a puzzled glance as he opened the can of roast beef. There had been an odd undernote in that assurance that, undefinably, he did not like. And the girl had teeth and tongue and presumably a fairly human digestive system, to judge from her human form. It was nonsense for her to pretend that he could find nothing that she could eat. She must have had some of the food concentrate after all, he decided, prying up the thermos lid of the inner container to release the long-sealed savor of the hot meat inside.

"Well, if you won't eat you won't," he observed philo-sophically as he poured hot broth and diced beef into the dishlike lid of the thermos can and extracted the spoon from its hiding-place between the inner and outer receptacles. She turned a little to watch him as he pulled up a rickety chair and sat down to the food, and after a while the realization that her green gaze was fixed so un-winkingly upon him made the man nervous, and he said between bites of creamy canal-apple, "Why don't you try a little of this? It's good."

"The food—I eat is—better," her soft voice told him in its hesitant murmur, and again he felt rather than heard a faint undernote of unpleasantness in the words. A sudden suspicion struck him as he pondered on that last remark—some vague memory of horror-tales told about campfires in the past—and he swung round in the chair to look at her, a tiny, creeping fear unaccountably arising. There had been that in her words—in her un-spoken words, that menaced. . . .

She stood up beneath his gaze demurely, wide green eyes with their pulsing pupils meeting his without a fal-ter. But her mouth was scarlet and her teeth were sharp. . . .

"What food do you eat?" he demanded. And then, after a pause, very softly, "Blood?"

She stared at him for a moment, uncomprehending; then something like amusement curled her lips and she said scornfully, "You think me—vampire, eh? No—I am Shambleau!"

Unmistakably there were scorn and amusement in her voice at the suggestion, but as unmistakably she knew what he meant—accepted it as a logical suspicion— vampires! Fairy tales—but fairy tales this unhuman, outland creature was most familiar with. Smith was not a credulous man, nor a superstitious one, but he had seen too many strange things himself to doubt that the wildest legend might have a basis of fact. And there was something namelessly strange about her. . . .

He puzzled over it for a while between deep bites of the canal-apple. And though he wanted to question her about a great many things, he did not, for he knew how futile it would be.

He said nothing more until the meat was finished and another canal-apple had followed the first, and he had cleared away the meal by the simple expedient of tossing the empty can out of the window. Then he lay back in the chair and surveyed her from half-closed eyes, colorless in a face tanned like saddle-leather. And again he was conscious of the brown, soft curves of her, velvety —subtle arcs and planes of smooth flesh under the tatters of scarlet leather. Vampire she might be, unhuman she certainly was, but desirable beyond words as she sat submissive beneath his low regard, her red-turbaned head bent, her clawed fingers lying in her lap. They sat very still for a while, and the silence throbbed between them.

She was so like a woman—an Earth woman—sweet and submissive and demure, and softer than soft fur, if he could forget the three-fingered claws and the pulsing eyes—and that deeper strangeness beyond words. . . . (Had he dreamed that red lock of hair that moved? Had it been *segir* that woke the wild revulsion he knew when he held her in his arms? Why had the mob so thirsted for her?) He sat and stared, and despite the mystery of her and the half-suspicions that thronged his mind—for she was so beautifully soft and curved under those revealing tatters—he slowly realized that his pulses were mounting, became aware of a kindling within . . . brown girl-creature with downcast eyes . . . and then the lids lifted and the green flatness of a cat's gaze met his, and last night's revulsion woke swiftly again, like a warning bell that clanged as their eyes met—animal, after all, too sleek and soft for humanity, and that inner strangeness. . . .

Smith shrugged and sat up. His failings were legion, but the weakness of the flesh was not among the major ones. He motioned the girl to her pallet of blankets in the corner and turned to his own bed.

From deeps of sound sleep he awoke much later. He awoke suddenly and completely, and with that inner excitement that presages something momentous. He awoke to brilliant moonlight, turning the room so bright that he could see the scarlet of the girl's rags as she sat up on her pallet. She was awake, she was sitting with her shoulder half turned to him and her head bent, and some warning instinct crawled coldly up his spine as he watched what she was doing. And yet it was a very ordinary thing for a girl to do—any girl, anywhere. She was unbinding her turban. . . .

He watched, not breathing, a presentiment of something horrible stirring in his brain, inexplicably. . . . The red folds loosened, and—he knew then that he had not dreamed—again a scarlet lock swung down against her cheek . . . a hair, was it? a lock of hair? . . . thick as a thick worm it fell, plumply, against that smooth cheek . . . more scarlet than blood and thick as a crawling worm . . . and like a worm it crawled.

Smith rose on an elbow, not realizing the motion, and fixed an unwinking stare, with a sort of sick, fascinated incredulity, on that—that lock of hair. He had not dreamed. Until now he had taken it for granted that it was the *segir* which had made it seem to move on that evening before. But now . . . it was lengthening, stretching, moving of itself. It must be hair, but it *crawled;* with a sickening life of its own it squirmed down against her cheek, caressingly, revoltingly, impossibly. . . . Wet, it was, and round and thick and shining. . . .

She unfastened the fast fold and whipped the turban off. From what he saw then Smith would have turned his eyes away—and he had looked on dreadful things before, without flinching—but he could not stir. He could only lie there on his elbow staring at the mass of scarlet, squirming—worms, hairs, what?—that writhed over her head in a dreadful mockery of ringlets. And it was lengthening, falling, somehow growing before his eyes, down over her shoulders in a spilling cascade, a mass that even at the beginning could never have been hidden under the skull-tight turban she had worn. He was beyond wondering, but he realized that. And still it squirmed and lengthened and fell, and she shook it out in a horrible travesty of a woman shaking out her unbound hair—until the unspeakable tangle of it—twisting, writhing, obscenely scarlet—hung to her waist and

beyond, and still lengthened, an endless mass of crawling horror that until now, somehow, impossibly, had
been hidden under the tight-bound turban. It was like a
nest of blind, restless red worms . . . it was—it was like
naked entrails endowed with an unnatural aliveness, terrible beyond words.

Smith lay in the shadows, frozen without and within
in a sick numbness that came of utter shock and revulsion.

She shook out the obscene, unspeakable tangle over
her shoulders, and somehow he knew that she was going
to turn in a moment and that he must meet her eyes.
The thought of that meeting stopped his heart with
dread, more awfully than anything else in this nightmare
horror; for nightmare it must be, surely. But he knew
without trying that he could not wrench his eyes away
—the sickened fascination of that sight held him motionless, and somehow there was a certain beauty. . . .

Her head was turning. The crawling awfulnesses rippled and squirmed at the motion, writhing thick and wet
and shining over the soft brown shoulders about which
they fell now in obscene cascades that all but hid her
body. Her head was turning. Smith lay numb. And very
slowly he saw the round of her cheek foreshorten and
her profile come into view, all the scarlet horrors twisting ominously, and the profile shortened in turn and her
full face came slowly round toward the bed—moonlight
shining brilliantly as day on the pretty girl-face, demure
and sweet, framed in tangled obscenity that crawled. . . .

The green eyes met his. He felt a perceptible shock,
and a shudder rippled down his paralyzed spine, leaving
an icy numbness in its wake. He felt the goose-flesh rising. But that numbness and cold horror he scarcely realized, for the green eyes were locked with his in a long,
long look that somehow presaged nameless things—not
altogether unpleasant things—the voiceless voice of her
mind assailing him with little murmurous promises. . . .

For a moment he went down into a blind abyss of
submission; and then somehow the very sight of that obscenity in eyes that did not then realize they saw it, was
dreadful enough to draw him out of the seductive dark-

ness . . . the sight of her crawling and alive with unnameable horror.

She rose, and down about her in a cascade fell the
squirming scarlet of—of what grew upon her head. It
fell in a long, alive cloak to her bare feet on the floor,
hiding her in a wave of dreadful, wet, writhing life. She
put up her hands and like a swimmer she parted the
waterfall of it, tossing the masses back over her shoulders to reveal her own brown body, sweetly curved. She
smiled exquisitely, and in starting waves back from her
forehead and down about her in a hideous background
writhed the snaky wetness of her living tresses. And
Smith knew that he looked upon Medusa.

The knowledge of that—the realization of vast back-
grounds reaching into misted history—shook him out of
his frozen horror for a moment, and in that moment he
met her eyes again, smiling, green as glass in the moonlight, half hooded under drooping lids. Through the
twisting scarlet she held out her arms. And there was
something soul-shakingly desirable about her, so that all
the blood surged to his head suddenly and he stumbled
to his feet like a sleeper in a dream as she swayed toward him, infinitely graceful, infinitely sweet in her
cloak of living horror.

And somehow there was beauty in it, the wet scarlet
writhings with moonlight sliding and shining along the
thick, worm-round tresses and losing itself in the masses
only to glint again and move silvery along writhing tendrils—an awful, shuddering beauty more dreadful than
any ugliness could be.

But all this, again, he but half realized, for the insidi-
ous murmur was coiling again through his brain, promising, caressing, alluring, sweeter than honey; and the
green eyes that held his were clear and burning like the
depths of a jewel, and behind the pulsing slits of darkness he was staring into a greater dark that held all
things. . . . He had known—dimly he had known when
he first gazed into those flat animal shallows that behind
them lay this—all beauty and terror, all horror and delight, in the infinite darkness upon which her eyes
opened like windows, paned with emerald glass.

Her lips moved, and in a murmur that blended indistinguishably with the silence and the sway of her body and the dreadful sway of her—her hair—she whispered—very softly, very passionately, "I shall—speak to you now—in my own tongue—oh, beloved!"

And in her living cloak she swayed to him, the murmur swelling seductive and caressing in his innermost brain—promising, compelling, sweeter than sweet. His flesh crawled to the horror of her, but it was a perverted revulsion that clasped what it loathed. His arms slid round her under the sliding cloak, wet, wet and warm and hideously alive—and the sweet velvet body was clinging to his, her arms locked about his neck—and with a whisper and a rush the unspeakable horror closed about them both.

In nightmares until he died he remembered that moment when the living tresses of Shambleau first folded him in their embrace. A nauseous, smothering oder as the wetness shut around him—thick, pulsing worms clasping every inch of his body, sliding, writhing, their wetness and warmth striking through his garments as if he stood naked to their embrace.

All this in a graven instant—and after that a tangled flash of conflicting sensation before oblivion closed over him. For he remembered the dream—and knew it for nightmare reality now, and the sliding, gently moving caresses of those wet, warm worms upon his flesh was an ecstasy above words—that deeper ecstasy that strikes beyond the body and beyond the mind and tickles the very roots of the soul with unnatural delight. So he stood, rigid as marble, as helplessly stony as any of Medusa's victims in ancient legends were, while the terrible pleasure of Shambleau thrilled and shuddered through every fiber of him; through every atom of his body and the intangible atoms of what men call the soul, through all that was Smith the dreadful pleasure ran. And it was truly dreadful. Dimly he knew it, even as his body answered to the root-deep ecstasy, a foul and dreadful wooing from which his very soul shuddered away—and yet in the innermost depths of that soul some grinning traitor shivered with delight. But deeply, behind all this, he knew horror and revulsion and despair beyond telling, while the intimate caresses crawled obscenely in the secret places of his soul—knew that the soul should not be handled—and shook with the perilous pleasure through it all.

And this conflict and knowledge, this mingling of rapture and revulsion all took place in the flashing of a moment while the scarlet worms coiled and crawled upon him, sending deep, obscene tremors of that infinite pleasure into every atom that made up Smith. And he could not stir in that slimy, ecstatic embrace—and a weakness was flooding that grew deeper after each succeeding wave of intense delight, and the traitor in his soul strengthened and drowned out the revulsion—and something within him ceased to struggle as he sank wholly into a blazing darkness that was oblivion to all else but that devouring rapture. . . .

The young Venusian climbing the stairs to his friend's lodging-room pulled out his key absent-mindedly, a pucker forming between his fine brows. He was slim, as all Venusians are, as fair and sleek as any of them, and as with most of his countrymen the look of cherubic innocence on his face was wholly deceptive. He had the face of a fallen angel, without Lucifer's majesty to redeem it; for a black devil grinned in his eyes and there were faint lines of ruthlessness and dissipation about his mouth to tell of the long years behind him that had run the gamut of experiences and made his name, next to Smith's, the most hated and the most respected in the records of the Patrol.

He mounted the stairs now with a puzzled frown between his eyes. He had come into Lakkdarol on the noon liner—the *Maid* in her hold very skillfully disguised with paint and otherwise—to find in lamentable disorder the affairs he had expected to be settled. And cautious inquiry elicited the information that Smith had not been seen for three days. That was not like his friend—he had never failed before, and the two stood to lose not only a large sum of money but also their personal safety by the inexplicable lapse on the part of Smith. Yarol could think of one solution only: fate had at last caught up with his friend. Nothing but physical disability could explain it.

Still puzzling, he fitted his key in the lock and swung the door open.

In that first moment, as the door opened, he sensed something very wrong. . . . The room was darkened, and for a while he could see nothing, but at the first breath he scented a strange, unnameable odor, half sickening, half sweet. And deep stirrings of ancestral memory awoke him—ancient swamp-born memories from Venusian ancestors far away and long ago. . . .

Yarol laid his hand on his gun, lightly, and opened the door wider. In the dimness all he could see at first was a curious mound in the far corner. . . . Then his eyes grew accustomed to the dark, and he saw it more clearly, a mound that somehow heaved and stirred within itself. . . . A mound of—he caught his breath sharply—a mound like a mass of entrails, living, moving, writhing with an unspeakable aliveness. Then a hot Venusian oath broke from his lips and he cleared the door-sill in a swift stride, slammed the door and set his back against it, gun ready in his hand, although his flesh crawled—for he *knew*. . . .

"Smith!" he said softly, in a voice thick with horror. "Northwest!"

The moving mass stirred—shuddered—sank back into crawling quiescence again.

"Smith! Smith!" The Venusian's voice was gentle and insistent, and it quivered a little with terror.

An impatient ripple went over the whole mass of aliveness in the corner. It stirred again, reluctantly, and then tendril by writhing tendril it began to part itself and fall aside, and very slowly the brown of a spaceman's leather appeared beneath it, all slimed and shining.

"Smith! Northwest!" Yarol's persistent whisper came again, urgently, and with a dreamlike slowness the leather garments moved . . . a man sat up in the midst of the writhing worms, a man who once, long ago, might have been Northwest Smith. From head to foot he was slimy from the embrace of the crawling horror about him. His face was that of some creature beyond humanity—dead-alive, fixed in a gray stare, and the look of terrible

ecstasy that overspread it seemed to come from somewhere far within, a faint reflection from immeasurable
distances beyond the flesh. And as there is mystery and
magic in the moonlight which is after all but a reflection
of the everyday sun, so in that gray face turned to the
door was a terror unnameable and sweet, a reflection of
ecstasy beyond the understanding of any who have
known only earthly ecstasy themselves. And as he sat
there turning a blank, eyeless face to Yarol the red
worms writhed ceaselessly about him, very gently, with a
soft, caressive motion that never slacked.

"Smith . . . come here! Smith . . . get up . . .
Smith, Smith!" Yarol's whisper hissed in the silence,
commanding, urgent—but he made no move to leave the
door.

And with a dreadful slowness, like a dead man rising,
Smith stood up in the nest of slimy scarlet. He swayed
drunkenly on his feet, and two or three crimson tendrils
came writhing up his legs to the knees and wound themselves there, supportingly, moving with a ceaseless caress that seemed to give him some hidden strength, for
he said then, without inflection,

"Go away. Go away. Leave me alone." And the dead
ecstatic face never changed.

"Smith!" Yarol's voice was desperate. "Smith, listen!
Smith, can't you hear me?"

"Go away," the monotonous voice said. "Go away.
Go away. Go—"

"Not unless you come too. Can't you hear? Smith!
Smith! I'll—"

He hushed in mid-phrase, and once more the ancestral prickle of race-memory shivered down his back, for
the scarlet mass was moving again, violently, rising. . . .

Yarol pressed back against the door and gripped his
gun, and the name of a god he had forgotten years ago
rose to his lips unbidden. For he knew what was coming
next, and the knowledge was more dreadful than any ignorance could have been.

The red, writhing mass rose higher, and the tendrils
parted and a human face looked out—no, half human,

with green cat-eyes that shone in that dimness like lighted jewels, compellingly. . . .

Yarol breathed "Shar!" again, and flung up an arm across his face, and the tingle of meeting that green gaze for even an instant went thrilling through him perilously.

"Smith!" he called in despair. "Smith, can't you hear me?"

"Go away," said that voice that was not Smith's. "Go away."

And somehow, although he dared not look, Yarol knew that the—the other—had parted those worm-thick tresses and stood there in all the human sweetness of the brown, curved woman's body, cloaked in living horror. And he felt the eyes upon him, and something was crying insistently in his brain to lower that shielding arm. . . . He was lost—he knew it, and the knowledge gave him that courage which comes from despair. The voice in his brain was growing, swelling, deafening him with a roaring command that all but swept him before it —command to lower that arm—to meet the eyes that opened upon darkness—to submit—and a promise, murmurous and sweet and evil beyond words, of pleasure to come. . . .

But somehow he kept his head—somehow, dizzily, he was gripping his gun in his upflung hand—somehow, incredibly, crossing the narrow room with averted face, groping for Smith's shoulder. There was a moment of blind fumbling in emptiness, and then he found it, and gripped the leather that was slimy and dreadful and wet —and simultaneously he felt something loop gently about his ankle and a shock of repulsive pleasure went through him, and then another coil, and another, wound about his feet. . . .

Yarol set his teeth and gripped the shoulder hard, and his hand shuddered of itself, for the feel of that leather was slimy as the worms about his ankles, and a faint tingle of obscene delight went through him from the contact.

That caressive pressure on his legs was all he could feel, and the voice in his brain drowned out all other sounds, and his body obeyed him reluctantly—but somehow he gave one heave of tremendous effort and swung Smith, stumbling, out of that nest of horror. The twining tendrils ripped loose with a little sucking sound, and the whole mass quivered and reached after, and then Yarol forgot his friend utterly and turned his whole being to the hopeless task of freeing himself. For only a part of him was fighting, now—only a part of him struggled against the twining obscenities, and in his innermost brain the sweet, seductive murmur sounded, and his body clamored to surrender. . . .

"*Shar! Shar y'danis . . . Shar mor'la-rol*—" prayed Yarol, gasping and half unconscious that he spoke, boy's prayers that he had forgotten years ago, and with his back half turned to the central mass he kicked desperately with his heavy boots at the red, writhing worms about him. They gave back before him, quivering and curling themselves out of reach, and though he knew that more were reaching for his throat from behind, at least he could go on struggling until he was forced to meet those eyes. . . .

He stamped and kicked and stamped again, and for one instant he was free of the slimy grip as the bruised worms curled back from his heavy feet, and he lurched away dizzily, sick with revulsion and despair as he fought off the coils, and then he lifted his eyes and saw the cracked mirror on the wall. Dimly in its reflection he could see the writhing scarlet horror behind him, cat face peering out with its demure girl-smile, dreadfully human, and all the red tendrils reaching after him. And remembrance of something he had read long ago swept incongruously over him, and the gasp of relief and hope that he gave shook for a moment the grip of the command in his brain.

Without pausing for a breath he swung the gun over his shoulder, the reflected barrel in line with the reflected horror in the mirror, and flicked the catch.

In the mirror he saw its blue flame leap in a dazzling spate across the dimness, full into the midst of that squirming, reaching mass behind him. There was a hiss and a blaze and a high, thin scream of inhuman malice and despair—the flame cut a wide arc and went out as the gun fell from his hand, and Yarol pitched forward to the floor.

Northwest Smith opened his eyes to Martian sunlight streaming thinly through the dingy window. Something wet and cold was slapping his face, and the familiar fiery sting of *segir*-whisky burnt his throat.

"Smith!" Yarol's voice was saying from far away. "N. W.! Wake up, damn you! Wake up!"

"I'm—awake," Smith managed to articulate thickly. "Wha's matter?"

Then a cup-rim was thrust against his teeth and Yarol said irritably, "Drink it, you fool!"

Smith swallowed obediently and more of the fire-hot *segir* flowed down his grateful throat. It spread a warmth through his body that awakened him from the numbness that had gripped him until now, and helped a little toward driving out the all-devouring weakness he was becoming aware of slowly. He lay still for a few minutes while the warmth of the whisky went through him, and memory sluggishly began to permeate his brain with the spread of the *segir*. Nightmare memories . . . sweet and terrible . . . memories of—

"God!" gasped Smith suddenly, and tried to sit up. Weakness smote him like a blow, and for an instant the room wheeled as he fell back against something firm and warm—Yarol's shoulder. The Venusian's arm supported him while the room steadied, and after a while he twisted a little and stared into the other's black gaze.

Yarol was holding him with one arm and finishing the mug of *segir* himself, and the black eyes met his over the rim and crinkled into sudden laughter, half hysterical after that terror that was passed.

"By *Pharol!*" gasped Yarol, choking into his mug. "By *Pharol,* N. W.! I'm never gonna let you forget this! Next time you have to drag me out of a mess I'll say—"

"Let it go," said Smith. "What's been going on? How—"

"Shambleau." Yarol's laughter died. "Shambleau! What were you doing with a thing like that?"

"What was it?" Smith asked soberly.

"Mean to say you didn't know? But where'd you find it? How—"

"Suppose you tell me first what you know," said Smith firmly. "And another swig of that *segir,* too, please. I need it."

"Can you hold the mug now? Feel better?"

"Yeah—some. I can hold it—thanks. Now go on."

"Well—I don't know just where to start. They call them Shambleau—"

"Good God, is there more than one?"

"It's a—a sort of race, I think, one of the very oldest. Where they come from nobody knows. The name sounds a little French, doesn't it? But it goes back beyond the start of history. There have always been Shambleau."

"I never heard of 'em."

"Not many people have. And those who know don't care to talk about it much."

"Well, half this town knows. I hadn't any idea what they were talking about, then. And I still don't understand, but—"

"Yes, it happens like this, sometimes. They'll appear, and the news will spread and the town will get together and hunt them down, and after that—well, the story doesn't get around very far. It's too—too unbelievable."

"But—my God, Yarol!—what was it? Where'd it come from? How—"

"Nobody knows just where they come from. Another planet—maybe some undiscovered one. Some say Venus—I know there are some rather awful legends of them handed down in our family—that's how I've heard about it. And the minute I opened that door, awhile back —I—I think I knew that smell. . . ."

"But—what *are* they?"

"God knows. Not human, though they have the human form. Or that may be only an illusion . . . or maybe I'm crazy. I don't know. They're a species of the vampire—or maybe the vampire is a species of—of them. Their normal form must be that—that mass, and in that form they draw nourishment from the—I suppose the life-forces of men. And they take some form—usually a woman form, I think, and key you up to the highest pitch of emotion before they—begin. That's to work the life-force up to intensity so it'll be easier. . . . And they give, always, that horrible, foul pleasure as they—feed. There are some men who, if they survive the first experience, take to it like a drug—can't give it up—keep the thing with them all their lives —which isn't long—feeding it for that ghastly satisfaction. Worse than smoking *ming* or—or 'praying to *Pharol*.' "

"Yes," said Smith. "I'm beginning to understand why that crowd was so surprised and—and disgusted when I said—well, never mind. Go on."

"Did you get to talk to—to it?" asked Yarol.

"I tried to. It couldn't speak very well. I asked it where it came from and it said—'from far away and long ago'—something like that."

"I wonder. Possibly some unknown planet—but I think not. You know there are so many wild stories with some basis of fact to start from, that I've sometimes wondered—mightn't there be a lot more of even worse and wilder superstitions we've never even heard of? Things like this, blasphemous and foul, that those who know have to keep still about? Awful, fantastic things running around loose that we never hear rumors of at all!

"These things—they've been in existence for countless ages. No one knows when or where they first appeared. Those who've seen them, as we saw this one, don't talk about it. It's just one of those vague, misty rumors you find half hinted at in old books sometimes. . . . I believe they are an older race than man, spawned from ancient seed in times before ours, perhaps on planets that have gone to dust, and so horrible to man that when they are discovered the discoverers keep still about it—forget them again as quickly as they can.

"And they go back to time immemorial. I suppose you recognized the legend of Medusa? There isn't any question that the ancient Greeks knew of them. Does it mean that there have been civilizations before yours that set out from Earth and explored other planets? Or did one of the Shambleau somehow make its way into Greece three thousand years ago? If you think about it long enough you'll go off your head! I wonder how many other legends are based on things like this—things we don't suspect, things we'll never know.

"The Gorgon, Medusa, a beautiful woman with—with snakes for hair, and a gaze that turned men to stone, and Perseus finally killed her—I remembered this just by accident, N. W., and it saved your life and mine—Perseus killed her by using a mirror as he fought to reflect what he dared not look at directly. I wonder what the old Greek who first started that legend would have thought if he'd known that three thousand years later his story would save the lives of two men on another planet. I wonder what that Greek's own story was, and how he met the thing, and what happened. . . .

"Well, there's a lot we'll never know. Wouldn't the records of that race of—of *things,* whatever they are, be worth reading! Records of other planets and other ages and all the beginnings of mankind! But I don't suppose they've kept any records. I don't suppose they've even any place to keep them—from what little I know, or anyone knows about it, they're like the Wandering Jew, just bobbing up here and there at long intervals, and where they stay in the meantime I'd give my eyes to know! But I don't believe that terribly hypnotic power they have indicates any superhuman intelligence. It's their means of getting food—just like a frog's long tongue or a carnivorous flower's odor. Those are physical because the frog and the flower eat physical food. The Shambleau uses a—a mental reach to get mental food. I don't quite know how to put it. And just as a beast that eats the bodies of other animals acquires with each meal greater power over the bodies of the rest, so the Shambleau, stoking itself up with the life-forces of men, increases its power over the minds and the souls of other men. But I'm talking about things I can't define—things I'm not sure exist.

"I only know that when I felt—when those tentacles closed around my legs—I didn't want to pull loose, I felt sensations that—that—oh, I'm fouled and filthy to the very deepest part of me by that—pleasure—and yet—"

"I know," said Smith slowly. The effect of the *segir* was beginning to wear off, and weakness was washing back over him in waves, and when he spoke he was half meditating in a low voice, scarcely realizing that Yarol listened. "I know it—much better than you do—and there's something so indescribably awful that the thing emanates, something so utterly at odds with everything human—there aren't any words to say it. For a while I was a part of it, literally, sharing its thoughts and memories and emotions and hungers, and—well, it's over now and I don't remember very clearly, but the only part left free was that part of me that was all but insane from the —the obscenity of the thing. And yet it was a pleasure so sweet—I think there must be some nucleus of utter evil in me—in everyone—that needs only the proper stimulus to get complete control; because even while I was sick all through from the touch of those—things—there was something in me that was—was simply gibbering with delight. . . . Because of that I saw things—and knew things—horrible, wild things I can't quite remember—visited unbelievable places, looked backward through the memory of that—creature—I was one with, and saw—God, I wish I could remember!"

"You ought to thank your God you can't," said Yarol soberly.

His voice roused Smith from the half-trance he had fallen into, and he rose on his elbow, swaying a little from weakness. The room was wavering before him, and he closed his eyes, not to see it, but he asked, "You say they—they don't turn up again? No way of finding—another?"

Yarol did not answer for a moment. He laid his hands on the other man's shoulders and pressed him back, and then sat staring down into the dark, ravaged face with a new, strange, undefinable look upon it that he had never seen there before—whose meaning he knew, too well.

"Smith," he said finally, and his black eyes for once were steady and serious, and the little grinning devil had vanished from behind them, "Smith, I've never asked your word on anything before, but I've—I've earned the right to do it now, and I'm asking you to promise me one thing."

Smith's colorless eyes met the black gaze unsteadily. Irresolution was in them, and a little fear of what that promise might be. And for just a moment Yarol was looking, not into his friend's familiar eyes, but into a wide gray blankness that held all horror and delight—a pale sea with unspeakable pleasures sunk beneath it. Then the wide stare focused again and Smith's eyes met his squarely and Smith's voice said, "Go ahead. I'll promise."

"That if you ever should meet a Shambleau again— ever, anywhere—you'll draw your gun and burn it to hell the instant you realize what it is. Will you promise me that?"

There was a long silence. Yarol's somber black eyes bored relentlessly into the colorless ones of Smith, not wavering. And the veins stood out on Smith's tanned forehead. He never broke his word—he had given it perhaps half a dozen times in his life, but once he had given it, he was incapable of breaking it. And once more the gray seas flooded in a dim tide of memories, sweet and horrible beyond dreams. Once more Yarol was staring into blankness that hid nameless things. The room was very still.

The gray tide ebbed. Smith's eyes, pale and resolute as steel, met Yarol's levelly.

"I'll—try," he said. And his voice wavered.

Black Thirst

NORTHWEST SMITH LEANT his head back against the warehouse wall and stared up into the black night-sky of Venus. The waterfront street was very quiet tonight, very dangerous. He could hear no sound save the eternal slap-slap of water against the piles, but he knew how much of danger and sudden death dwelt here voiceless in the breathing dark, and he may have been a little homesick as he stared up into the clouds that masked a green star hanging lovely on the horizon—Earth and home. And if he thought of that he must have grinned wryly to himself in the dark, for Northwest Smith had no home, and Earth would not have welcomed him very kindly just then.

He sat quietly in the dark. Above him in the warehouse wall a faintly lighted window threw a square of pallor upon the wet street. Smith drew back into his angle of darkness under the slanting shaft, hugging one knee. And presently he heard footsteps softly on the street.

He may have been expecting footsteps, for he turned his head alertly and listened, but it was not a man's feet that came so lightly over the wooden quay, and Smith's brow furrowed. A woman, here, on this black waterfront by night? Not even the lowest class of Venusian street-walker dared come along the waterfronts of Ednes on the nights when the space-liners were not in. Yet across the pavement came clearly now the light tapping of a woman's feet.

Smith drew farther back into the shadows and waited. And presently she came, a darkness in the dark save for

the triangular patch of pallor that was her face. As she
passed under the light falling dimly from the window
overhead he understood suddenly how she dared walk
here and who she was. A long black cloak hid her, but
the light fell upon her face, heart-shaped under the little
three-cornered velvet cap that Venusian women wear,
fell on ripples of half-hidden bronze hair; and by that
sweet triangular face and shining hair he knew her for
one of the Minga maids—those beauties that from the
beginning of history have been bred in the Minga
stronghold for loveliness and grace, as race horses are
bred on Earth, and reared from earliest infancy in the
art of charming men. Scarcely a court on the three planets lacks at least one of these exquisite creatures, long-
limbed, milk-white, with their bronze hair and lovely
brazen faces—if the lord of that court has the wealth to
buy them. Kings from many nations and races have
poured their riches into the Minga gateway, and girls
like pure gold and ivory have gone forth to grace a
thousand palaces, and this has been so since Ednes first
rose on the shore of the Greater Sea.

This girl walked here unafraid and unharmed because
she wore the beauty that marked her for what she was.
The heavy hand of the Minga stretched out protectingly
over her bronze head, and not a man along the wharf-
fronts but knew what dreadful penalties would overtake
him if he dared so much as to lay a finger on the milk-
whiteness of a Minga maid—terrible penalties, such as
men whisper of fearfully over *segir*-whisky mugs in the
waterfront dives of many nations—mysterious, unnameable penalties more dreadful than any knife or gun-flash
could inflict.

And these dangers, too, guarded the gates of the Minga castle. The chastity of the Minga girls was proverbial,
a trade boast. This girl walked in peace and safety more
sure than that attending the steps of a nun through slum
streets by night on Earth.

But even so, the girls went forth very rarely from the
gates of the castle, never unattended. Smith had never
seen one before, save at a distance. He shifted a little
now, to catch a better glimpse as she went by, to look
for the escort that must surely walk a pace or two be-

hind, though he heard no footsteps save her own. The slight motion caught her eye. She stopped. She peered closer into the dark, and said in a voice as sweet and smooth as cream,

"How would you like to earn a goldpiece, my man?"

A flash of perversity twisted Smith's reply out of its usual slovenly dialect, and he said in his most cultured voice, in his most perfect High Venusian,

"Thank you, no."

For a moment the woman stood quite still, peering through the darkness in a vain effort to reach his face. He could see her own, a pale oval in the window light, intent, surprised. Then she flung back her cloak and the dim light glinted on the case of a pocket flash as she flicked the catch. A beam of white radiance fell blindingly upon his face.

For an instant the light held him—lounging against the wall in his spaceman's leather, the burns upon it, the tatters, ray-gun in its holster low on his thigh, and the brown scarred face turned to hers, eyes the colorless color of pale steel narrowed to the glare. It was a typical face. It belonged here, on the waterfront, in these dark and dangerous streets. It belonged to the type that frequents such places, those lawless men who ride the spaceways and live by the rule of the ray-gun, recklessly, warily outside the Patrol's jurisdiction. But there was more than that in the scarred brown face turned to the light. She must have seen it as she held the flash unwavering, some deep-buried trace of breeding and birth that made the cultured accents of the High Venusian not incongruous. And the colorless eyes derided her.

"No," she said, flicking off the light. "Not one goldpiece, but a hundred. And for another task that I meant."

"Thank you," said Smith, not rising. "You must excuse me."

"Five hundred," she said without a flicker of emotion in her creamy voice.

In the dark Smith's brows knit. There was something fantastic in the situation. Why—?

She must have sensed his reaction almost as he realized it himself, for she said,

"Yes, I know. It sounds insane. You see—I knew you in the light just now. Will you?—can you?—I can't explain here on the street. . . ."

Smith held the silence unbroken for thirty seconds, while a lightning debate flashed through the recesses of his wary mind. Then he grinned to himself in the dark and said,

"I'll come." Belatedly he got to his feet. "Where?"

"The Palace Road on the edge of the Minga. Third door from the central gate, to the left. Say to the door-warden—'Vaudir.' "

"That is—?"

"Yes, my name. You will come, in half an hour?"

An instant longer Smith's mind hovered on the verge of refusal. Then he shrugged.

"Yes."

"At the third bell, then." She made the little Venusian gesture of parting and wrapped her cloak about her. The blackness of it, and the softness of her footfalls, made her seem to melt into the darkness without a sound, but Smith's trained ears heard her footsteps very softly on the pavement as she went on into the dark.

He sat there until he could no longer detect any faintest sound of feet on the wharf. He waited patiently, but his mind was a little dizzy with surprise. Was the traditional inviolability of the Minga a fraud? Were the close-guarded girls actually allowed sometimes to walk unattended by night, making assignations as they pleased? Or was it some elaborate hoax? Tradition for countless centuries had declared the gates in the Minga wall to be guarded so relentlessly by strange dangers that not even a mouse could slip through without the knowledge of the Alendar, the Minga's lord. Was it then by order of the Alendar that the door would open to him when he whispered "Vaudir" to the warden? Or would it open? Was the girl perhaps the property of some Ednes lord, deceiving him for obscure purposes of her own? He shook his head a little and grinned to himself. After all, time would tell.

He waited a while longer in the dark. Little waves lapped the piles with sucking sounds, and once the sky lit up with the long, blinding roar of a spaceship splitting the dark.

At last he rose and stretched his long body as if he had been sitting there for a good while. Then he settled the gun on his leg and set off down the black street. He walked very lightly in his spaceman's boots.

A twenty-minute walk through dark byways, still and deserted, brought him to the outskirts of that vast city-within-a-city called the Minga. The dark, rough walls of it towered over him, green with the lichenlike growths of the Hot Planet. On the Palace Road one deeply-sunk central gateway opened upon the mysteries within. A tiny blue light burned over the arch. Smith went softly through the dimness to the left of it, counting two tiny doors half hidden in deep recesses. At the third he paused. It was painted a rusty green, and a green vine spilling down the wall half veiled it, so that if he had not been searching he would have passed it by.

Smith stood for a long minute, motionless, staring at the green panels deep-sunk in rock. He listened. He even sniffed the heavy air. Warily as a wild beast he hesitated in the dark. But at last he lifted his hand and tapped very lightly with his fingertips on the green door.

It swung open without a sound. Pitch-blackness confronted him, an archway of blank dark in the dimly seen stone wall. And a voice queried softly, *"Qu'a lo' val?"*

"Vaudir," murmured Smith, and grinned to himself involuntarily. How many romantic youths must have stood at these doors in nights gone by, breathing hopefully the names of bronze beauties to doormen in dark archways! But unless tradition lied, no man before had ever passed. He must be the first in many years to stand here invited at a little doorway in the Minga wall and hear the watchman murmur, "Come."

Smith loosened the gun at his side and bent his tall head under the arch. He stepped into blackness that closed about him like water as the door swung shut. He stood there with quickened heartbeats, hand on his gun, listening. A blue light, dim and ghostly, flooded the place without warning and he saw that the doorman had crossed to a switch at the far side of the tiny chamber wherein he stood. The man was one of the Minga eunuchs, a flabby creature, splendid in crimson velvet. He carried a cloak of purple over his arm, and made a splash of royal colors in the dimness. His sidelong eyes regarded Smith from under lifted brows, with a look that the Earthman could not fathom. There was amusement in it, and a touch of terror and a certain reluctant admiration.

Smith looked about him in frank curiosity. The little entry was apparently hollowed out of the enormously thick wall itself. The only thing that broke its bareness was the ornate bronze door set in the far wall. His eyes sought the eunuch's in mute inquiry.

The creature came forward obsequiously, murmuring, "Permit me—" and flung the purple cloak he carried over Smith's shoulders. Its luxurious folds, faintly fragrant, swept about him like a caress. It covered him, tall as he was, to the very boot-soles. He drew back in faint distaste as the eunuch lifted his hands to fasten the jeweled clasp at his throat. "Please to draw up the hood also," murmured the creature without apparent resentment, as Smith snapped the fastening himself. The hood covered his sun-bleached hair and fell in thick folds about his face, casting it into deep shadow.

The eunuch opened the bronze inner door and Smith stared down a long hallway curving almost imperceptibly to the right. The paradox of elaborately decorated simplicity was illustrated in every broad polished panel of the wall, so intricately and exquisitely carved that it gave at first the impression of a strange, rich plainness.

His booted feet sank sensuously into the deep pile of the carpet at every step as he followed the eunuch down the hall. Twice he heard voices murmuring behind lighted doors, and his hand lay on the butt of the ray-gun under the folds of his robe, but no door opened and the hall lay empty and dim before them. So far it had been amazingly easy. Either tradition lied about the impregnability of the Minga, or the girl Vaudir had bribed with incredible lavishness or—that thought again, uneasily —it was with Alendar's consent that he walked here unchallenged. But why?

They came to a door of silver grille at the end of the curved corridor, and passed through it into another hallway slanting up, as exquisitely voluptuous as the first. A flight of stairs wrought from dully gleaming bronze curved at the end of it. Then came another hall lighted with rosy lanterns that swung from the arched ceiling, and beyond another stairway, this time of silvery metal fretwork, spiraling down again.

And in all that distance they met no living creature. Voices hummed behind closed doors, and once or twice strains of music drifted faintly to Smith's ears, but either the corridors had been cleared by a special order, or incredible luck was attending them. And he had the uncomfortable sensation of eyes upon his back more than once. They passed dark hallways and open, unlighted doors, and sometimes the hair on his neck bristled with the feeling of human nearness, inimical, watching.

For all of twenty minutes they walked through curved corridors and up and down spiral stairs until even Smith's keen senses were confused and he could not have said at what height above the ground he was, or in what direction the corridor led into which they at last emerged. At the end of that time his nerves were tense as steel wire and he restrained himself only by force from nervous, over-the-shoulder glances each time they passed an open door. An air of languorous menace brooded almost visibly over the place, he thought. The sound of soft voices behind doors, the feel of eyes, of whispers in the air, the memory of tales half heard in waterfront dives about the secrets of the Minga, the nameless dangers of the Minga. . . .

Smith gripped his gun as he walked through the splendor and the dimness, every sense assailed by voluptuous appeals, but his nerves strained to wire and his flesh crawled as he passed unlighted doors. This was too easy. For so many centuries the tradition of the Minga had been upheld, a byword of impregnability, a stronghold guarded by more than swords, by greater dangers than the ray-gun—and yet here he walked, unquestioned, into the deepest heart of the place, his only disguise a velvet cloak, his only weapon a holstered gun, and no one challenged him, no guards, no slaves, not even a passer-by to note that a man taller than any dweller here should be strode unquestioned through the innermost corridors of the inviolable Minga. He loosened the ray-gun in its sheath.

The eunuch in his scarlet velvet went on confidently ahead. Only once did he falter. They had reached a dark passageway, and just as they came opposite its mouth the sound of a soft, slithering scrape, as of something over stones, draggingly, reached their ears. He saw the eunuch start and half glance back, and then hurry on at a quicker pace, nor did he slacken until they had put two gates and a length of lighted corridor between them and that dark passage.

So they went on, through halls half lighted, through scented air and empty dimness where the doorways closed upon murmurous mysteries within or opened to dark and the feel of watching eyes. And they came at last, after endless, winding progress, into a hallway low-ceiled and paneled in mother-of-pearl, pierced and filigreed with carving, and all the doors were of silver grille. And as the eunuch pushed open the silver gate that led into this corridor the thing happened that his taut nerves had been expecting ever since the start of the fantastic journey. One of the doors opened and a figure stepped out and faced them.

Under the robe Smith's gun slid soundlessly from its holster. He thought he saw the eunuch's back stiffen a little, and his step falter, but only for an instant. It was a girl who had come out, a slave-girl in a single white garment, and at the first glimpse of the tall, purple-robed figure with hooded face, towering over her, she gave a little gasp and slumped to her knees as if under a blow. It was obeisance, but so shocked and terrified that it might have been a faint. She laid her face to the very carpet, and Smith, looking down in amazement on the prostrate figure, saw that she was trembling violently.

The gun slid back into its sheath and he paused for a moment over her shuddering homage. The eunuch twisted round to beckon with soundless violence, and Smith caught a glimpse of his face for the first time since their journey began. It was glistening with sweat, and the sidelong eyes were bright and shifting, like a hunted ani-

mal's. Smith was oddly reassured by the sight of the
eunuch's obvious panic. There was danger then—danger
of discovery, the sort of peril he knew and could fight.
It was that creeping sensation of eyes watching, of unseen things slithering down dark passages, that had
strained his nerves so painfully. And yet, even so, it had
been too easy. . . .

The eunuch had paused at a silver door half-way
down the hall and was murmuring something very softly, his mouth against the grille. A panel of green brocade was stretched across the silver door on the inside,
so they could see nothing within the room, but after a
moment a voice said, "Good!" in a breathing whisper,
and the door quivered a little and swung open six inch-
es. The eunuch genuflected in a swirl of scarlet robes,
and Smith caught his eye swiftly, the look of terror not
yet faded, but amusement there too, and a certain respect. And then the door opened wider and he stepped
inside.

He stepped into a room green as a sea-cave. The
walls were paneled in green brocade, low green couches
circled the room, and, in the center, the blazing bronze
beauty of the girl Vaudir. She wore a robe of green velvet cut in the startling Venusian fashion to loop over
one shoulder and swathe her body in tight, molten folds,
and the skirt of it was slit up one side so that at every
other motion the long white leg flashed bare.

He saw her for the first time in a full light, and she
was lovely beyond belief with her bronze hair cloudy on
her shoulders and the pale, lazy face smiling. Under
deep lashes the sidelong black eyes of her race met his.

He jerked impatiently at the hampering hood of the
cloak. "May I take this off?" he said. "Are we safe
here?"

She laughed with a short, metallic sound. "Safe!" she
said ironically. "But take it off if you must. I've gone
too far now to stop at trifles."

And as the rich folds parted and slid away from his
leather brownness she in turn stared in quickened interest at what she had seen only in a half-light before. He
was almost laughably incongruous in this jewel-box
room, all leather and sunburn and his scarred face keen

and wary in the light of the lantern swinging from its silver chain. She looked a second time at that face, its
lean, leathery keenness and the scars that ray-guns had
left, and the mark of knife and talon, and the tracks of
wild years along the spaceways. Wariness and resolution
were instinct in that face, there was ruthlessness in every
line of it, and when she met his eyes a little shock went
over her. Pale, pale as bare steel, colorless in the sun-
burnt face. Steady and clear and no-colored, expressionless as water. Killer's eyes.

And she knew that this was the man she needed. The
name and fame of Northwest Smith had penetrated even
into these mother-of-pearl Minga halls. In its way it had
spread into stranger places than this, by strange and devious paths and for strange, devious reasons. But even
had she never heard the name (nor the deed she con-
nected it with, which does not matter here), she would
have known from this scarred face, these cold and
steady eyes, that here stood the man she wanted, the
man who could help her if any man alive could.

And with that thought, others akin to it flashed
through her mind like blades crossing, and she dropped
her milk-white lids over the sword-play to hide its dead-
liness, and said, "Northwest . . . Smith," in a musing
murmur.

"To be commanded," said Smith in the idiom of her
own tongue, but a spark of derision burned behind the
courtly words.

Still she said nothing, but looked him up and down
with slow eyes. He said at last,

"Your desire—?" and shifted impatiently.

"I had need of a wharfman's services," she said, still
in that breathing whisper. "I had not seen you, then. . . .
There are many wharfmen along the seafront, but only
one of you, oh man of Earth—" and she lifted her arms
and swayed toward him exactly as a reed sways to a lake
breeze, and her arms lay lightly on his shoulders and her
mouth was very near. . . .

Smith looked down into the veiled eyes. He knew
enough of the breed of Venus to guess the deadly

sword-flash of motive behind anything a Venusian does, and he had caught a glimpse of that particular sword-flash before she lowered her lids. And if her thoughts were sword-play, his burnt like heat-beams straight to their purpose. In the winking of an eye he knew a part of her motive—the most obvious part. And he stood there unanswering in the circle of her arms.

She looked up at him, half incredulous not to feel a leather embrace tighten about her.

"Qu'a lo'val?" she murmured whimsically. "So cold, then, Earthman? Am I not desirable?"

Wordlessly he looked down at her, and despite himself the blood quickened in him. Minga girls for too many centuries had been born and bred to the art of charming men for Northwest Smith to stand here in the warm arms of one and feel no answer to the invitation in her eyes. A subtle fragrance rose from her brazen hair, and the velvet molded a body whose whiteness he could guess from the flash of the long bare thigh her slashed skirt showed. He grinned a little crookedly and stepped away, breaking the clasp of her hands behind his neck.

"No," he said. "You know your art well, my dear, but your motive does not flatter me."

She stood back and regarded him with a wry, half-appreciative smile.

"What do you mean?"

"I'll have to know much more about all this before I commit myself as far as—that."

"You fool," she smiled. "You're in over your head now, as deeply as you could ever be. You were the moment you crossed the door-sill at the outer wall. There is no drawing back."

"Yet it was so easy—so very easy, to come in," murmured Smith.

She came forward a step and looked up at him with narrowed eyes, the pretense of seduction dropped like a cloak.

"You saw that, too?" she queried in a half-whisper. "It seemed so—to you? Great Shar, if I could be *sure. . . ."* And there was terror in her face.

"Suppose we sit down and you tell me about it," suggested Smith practically.

She laid a hand—white as cream, soft as satin—on his arm and drew him to the low divan that circled the room. There was inbred, generations-old coquetry in the touch, but the white hand shook a little.

"What is it you fear so?" queried Smith curiously as they sank to the green velvet. "Death comes only once, you know."

She shook her bronze head contemptuously.

"Not that," she said. "At least—no, I wish I knew just what it is I do fear—and that is the most dreadful part of it. But I wish—I wish it had not been so easy to get you here."

"The place was deserted," he said thoughtfully. "Not a soul along the halls. Not a guard anywhere. Only once did we see any other creature, and that was a slave-girl in the hall just outside your door."

"What did she—do?" Vaudir's voice was breathless.

"Dropped to her knees as if she'd been shot. You might have thought me the devil himself by the way she acted."

The girl's breath escaped in a sigh.

"Safe, then," she said thankfully. "She must have thought you the—the Alendar." Her voice faltered a little over the name, as if she half feared to pronounce it. "He wears a cloak like that you wore when he comes through the halls. But he comes so very seldom. . . ."

"I've never seen him," said Smith, "but, good Lord, is he such a monster? The girl dropped as if she'd been hamstrung."

"Oh, hush, hush!" Vaudir agonized. "You mustn't speak of him so. He's—he's—of course she knelt and hid her face. I wish to heaven I had. . . ."

Smith faced her squarely and searched the veiled dark eyes with a gaze as bleak as empty seas. And he saw very clearly behind the veils the stark, nameless terror at their depths.

"What is it?" he demanded.

She drew her shoulders together and shivered a little, and her eyes were furtive as she glanced around the room.

"Don't you feel it?" she asked in that half-whisper to which her voice sank so caressingly. And he smiled to himself to see how instinctively eloquent was the courtesan in her—alluring gestures though her hands trembled, soft voice huskily seductive even in its terror. "—always, always!" she was saying. "The soft, hushed, hovering menace! It haunts the whole place. Didn't you feel it as you came in?"

"I think I did," Smith answered slowly. "Yes—that feel of something just out of sight, hiding in dark doorways . . . a sort of tensity in the air. . . ."

"Danger," she whispered, "terrible, nameless danger . . . oh, I feel it wherever I go . . . it's soaked into me and through me until it's a part of me, body and soul. . . ."

Smith heard the note of rising hysteria in her voice, and said quickly,

"Why did you come to me?"

"I didn't, consciously." She conquered the hysteria with an effort and took up her tale a little more calmly. "I was really looking for a wharfman, as I said, and for quite another reason than this. It doesn't matter, now. But when you spoke, when I flashed my light and saw your face, I knew you. I'd heard of you, you see, and about the—the Lakkmanda affair, and I knew in a moment that if anyone alive could help me, it would be you."

"But what is it? Help you in what?"

"It's a long story," she said, "and too strange, almost, to believe, and too vague for you to take seriously. And yet I *know*. . . . Have you heard the history of the Minga?"

"A little of it. It goes back very far."

"Back into the beginning—and farther. I wonder if you can understand. You see, we on Venus are closer to our beginnings than you. Life here developed faster, of course, and along lines more different than Earthmen realize. On Earth civilization rose slowly enough for the —the elementals—to sink back into darkness. On Venus—oh, it's bad, *bad* for men to develop too swiftly! Life rises out of dark and mystery and things too strange and terrible to be looked upon. Earth's civilization grew slowly, and by the time men were civilized enough to look back they were sufficiently far from their origins not to see, not to know. But we here who look back see too clearly, sometimes, too nearly and vividly the black beginning. . . . Great Shar defend me, what I have seen!"

White hands flashed up to hide sudden terror in her eyes, and hair in a brazen cloud fell fragrantly over her fingers. And even in that terror was an inbred allure as natural as breathing.

In the little silence that followed, Smith caught himself glancing furtively over his shoulder. The room was ominously still. . . .

Vaudir lifted her face from her hands, shaking back her hair. The hands trembled. She clasped them on her velvet knee and went on.

"The Minga," she said, and her voice was resolutely steady, "began too long ago for anyone to name the date. It began before dates. When Far-thursa came out of the sea-fog with his men and founded this city at the mountain's foot he built it around the walls of a castle already here. The Minga castle. And the Alendar sold Minga girls to the sailors and the city began. All that is myth, but the Minga had always been here.

"The Alendar dwelt in his stronghold and bred his golden girls and trained them in the arts of charming men, and guarded them with—with strange weapons— and sold them to kings at royal prices. There has always been an Alendar. I have seen him, once. . . .

"He walks the halls on rare occasions, and it is best to kneel and hide one's face when he comes by. Yes, it is best. . . . But I passed him one day, and—and—he is tall, tall as you, Earthman, and his eyes are like—the space between the worlds. I looked into his eyes under the hood he wore—I was not afraid of devil or man, then. I looked him in the eyes before I made obeisance, and I —I shall never be free of fear again. I looked into evil as one looks into a pool. Blackness and blankness and raw evil. Impersonal, not malevolent. Elemental . . . the elemental dreadfulness that life rose from. And I know very surely, now, that the first Alendar sprang from no mortal seed. There were races before man. . . . Life goes back very dreadfully through many forms and evils, before it reaches the wellspring of its beginning. And the Alendar had not the eyes of a human creature, and I met them—and I am damned!"

Her voice trailed softly away and she sat quiet for a space, staring before her with remembering eyes.

"I am doomed and damned to a blacker hell than any of Shar's priests threaten," she resumed. "No, wait—this is not hysteria. I haven't told you the worst part. You'll find it hard to believe, but it's truth—truth—Great Shar, if I could hope it were not!

"The origin of it is lost in legend. But why, in the beginning, did the first Alendar dwell in the misty sea-edge castle, alone and unknown, breeding his bronze girls? —not for sale, then. Where did he get the secret of producing the invariable type? And the castle, legend says, was age-old when Far-thursa found it. The girls had a perfected, consistent beauty that could be attained only by generations of effort. How long had the Minga been built, and by whom? Above all, why? What possible reason could there be for dwelling there absolutely unknown, breeding civilized beauties in a world half-savage? Sometimes I think I have guessed the reason. . . ."

Her voice faded into a resonant silence, and for a while she sat staring blindly at the brocaded wall. When she spoke again it was with a startling shift of topic.

"Am I beautiful, do you think?"

"More so than any I have ever seen before," answered Smith without flattery.

Her mouth twisted.

"There are girls here now, in this building, so much lovelier than I that I am humbled to think of them. No mortal man has ever seen them, except the Alendar, and he—is not wholly mortal. No mortal man will ever see them. They are not for sale. Eventually they will disappear. . . .

"One might think that feminine beauty must reach an apex beyond which it can not rise, but this is not true. It can increase and intensify until—I have no words. And I truly believe that there is no limit to the heights it can reach, in the hands of the Alendar. And for every beauty we know and hear of, through the slaves that tend them, gossip says there are as many more, too immortally lovely for mortal eyes to see. Have you ever considered that beauty might be refined and intensified until one could scarcely bear to look upon it? We have tales here of such beauty, hidden in some of the secret rooms of the Minga.

"But the world never knows of these mysteries. No monarch on any planet known is rich enough to buy the loveliness hidden in the Minga's innermost rooms. It is not for sale. For countless centuries the Alendars of the Minga have been breeding beauty, in higher and higher degrees, at infinite labor and cost—beauty to be locked in secret chambers, guarded most terribly, so that not even a whisper of it passes the outer walls, beauty that vanishes, suddenly, in a breath—like that! Where? Why? How? No one knows.

"And it is that I fear. I have not a fraction of the beauty I speak of, yet a fate like that is written for me —somehow I know. I have looked into the eyes of the Alendar, and—I know. And I am sure that I must look again into those blank black eyes, more deeply, more dreadfully. . . . I know—and I am sick with terror of what more I shall know, soon. . . .

"Something dreadful is waiting for me, drawing nearer and nearer. Tomorrow, or the next day, or a little while after, I shall vanish, and the girls will wonder and whisper a little, and then forget. It has happened before. Great Shar, what shall I do?"

She wailed it, musically and hopelessly, and sank into a little silence. And then her look changed and she said reluctantly, "And I have dragged you in with me. I have broken every tradition of the Minga in bringing you here, and there has been no hindrance—it has been too easy, too easy. I think I have sealed your death. When you first came I was minded to trick you into committing yourself so deeply that perforce you must do as I asked to win free again. But I know now that through the simple act of asking you here I have dragged you in deeper than I dreamed. It is a knowledge that has come to me somehow, out of the air tonight. I can feel knowledge beating upon me—compelling me. For in my terror to get help I think I have precipitated damnation upon us both. I know now—I have known in my soul since you entered so easily, that you will not go out alive —that—*it*—will come for me and drag you down too. . . . Shar, Shar, what have I done!"

"But what, what?" Smith struck his knee impatiently. "What is it we face? Poison? Guards? Traps? Hypnotism? Can't you give me even a guess at what will happen?"

He leaned forward to search her face commandingly, and saw her brows knit in an effort to find words that would cloak the mysteries she had to tell. Her lips parted irresolutely.

"The Guardians," she said. "The—Guardians. . . ."

And then over her hesitant face swept a look of such horror that his hand clenched on his knee and he felt the hairs rise along his neck. It was not horror of any material thing, but an inner dreadfulness, a terrible awareness. The eyes that had met his glazed and escaped his commanding stare without shifting their focus. It was as if they ceased to be eyes and became dark windows— vacant. The beauty of her face set like a mask, and behind the blank windows, behind the lovely set mask, he could sense dimly the dark command flowing in. . . .

She put out her hands stiffly and rose. Smith found himself on his feet, gun in hand, while his hackles lifted shudderingly and something pulsed in the air as tangibly as the beat of wings. Three times that nameless shudder stirred the air, and then Vaudir stepped forward like an automaton and faced the door. She walked in her dream of masked dreadfulness, stiffly, through the portal. As she passed him he put out a hesitant hand and laid it on her arm, and a little stab of pain shot through him at the contact, and once more he thought he felt the pulse of wings in the air. Then she passed by without hesitation, and his hand fell.

He made no further effort to arouse her, but followed after on cat-feet, delicately as if he walked on eggs. He was crouching a little, unconsciously, and his gun-hand held a tense finger on the trigger.

They went down the corridor in a breathing silence,

an empty corridor where no lights showed beyond
closed doors, where no murmur of voices broke the live
stillness. But little shudders seemed to shake in the air
somehow, and his heart was pounding suffocatingly.

Vaudir walked like a mechanical doll, tense in a
dream of horror. When they reached the end of the hall
he saw that the silver grille stood open, and they passed
through without pausing. But Smith noted with a little
qualm that a gateway opening to the right was closed
and locked, and the bars across it were sunk firmly into
wall-sockets. There was no choice but to follow her.

The corridor slanted downward. They passed others
branching to right and left, but the silver gateways were
closed and barred across each. A coil of silver stairs
ended the passage, and the girl went stiffly down without
touching the rails. It was a long spiral, past many floors,
and as they descended, the rich, dim light lessened and
darkened and a subtle smell of moisture and salt invad-
ed the scented air. At each turn where the stairs opened
on successive floors, gates were barred across the out-
lets; and they passed so many of these that Smith knew,
as they went down and down, that however high the
green jewel-box room had been, by now they were descending deep into the earth. And still the stair wound
downward. The stories that opened beyond the bars like
honeycomb layers became darker and less luxurious,
and at last ceased altogether and the silver steps wound
down through a well of rock, lighted so dimly at wide
intervals that he could scarcely see the black polished
walls circling them in. Drops of moisture began to appear on the dark surface, and the smell was of black salt
seas and dank underground.

And just as he was beginning to believe that the stairs
went on and on into the very black, salt heart of the
planet, they came abruptly to the bottom. A flourish of
slim, shining rails ended the stairs, at the head of a hallway, and the girl's feet turned unhesitatingly to follow
its dark length. Smith's pale eyes, searching the dimness,
found no trace of other life than themselves; yet eyes
were upon him—he knew it surely.

They came down the black corridor to a gateway of wrought metal set in bars whose ends sank deep into the stone walls. She went through, Smith at her heels raking the dark with swift, unresting eyes like a wild animal's, wary in a strange jungle. And beyond the great gates a door hung with sweeping curtains of black ended the hall. Somehow Smith felt that they had reached their destination. And nowhere along the whole journey had he had any choice but to follow Vaudir's unerring, unseeing footsteps. Grilles had been locked across every possible outlet. But he had his gun. . . .

Her hands were white against the velvet as she pushed aside the folds. Very bright she stood for an instant—all green and gold and white—against the blackness. Then she passed through and the folds swept to behind her—candle-flame extinguished in dark velvet. Smith hesitated the barest instant before he parted the curtains and peered within.

He was looking into a room hung in black velvet that absorbed the light almost hungrily. That light radiated from a single lamp swinging from the ceiling directly over an ebony table. It shone softly on a man—a very tall man.

He stood darkly under it, very dark in the room's darkness, his head bent, staring up from under level black brows. His eyes in the half-hidden face were pits of blackness, and under the lowered brows two pinpoint gleams stabbed straight—not at the girl—but at Smith hidden behind the curtains. It held his eyes as a magnet holds steel. He felt the narrow glitter plunging bladelike into his very brain, and from the keen, burning stab something within him shuddered away involuntarily. He thrust his gun through the curtains, stepped through quietly, and stood meeting the sword-gaze with pale, unwavering eyes.

Vaudir moved forward with a mechanical stiffness that somehow could not hide her grace—it was as if no power existing could ever evoke from that lovely body less than loveliness. She came to the man's feet and stopped there. Then a long shudder swept her from head to foot and she dropped to her knees and laid her forehead to the floor.

Across the golden loveliness of her the man's eyes met Smith's, and the man's voice, deep, deep, like black waters flowing smoothly, said,

"I am the Alendar."

"Then you know me," said Smith, his voice harsh as iron in the velvet dimness.

"You are Northwest Smith," said the smooth, deep voice dispassionately. "An outlaw from the planet Earth. You have broken your last law, Northwest Smith. Men do not come here uninvited—and live. You perhaps have heard tales. . . ."

His voice melted into silence, lingeringly.

Smith's mouth curled into a wolfish grin, without mirth, and his gun-hand swung up. Murder flashed bleakly from his steel-pale eyes. And then with stunning abruptness the world dissolved about him. A burst of coruscations flamed through his head, danced and wheeled and drew slowly together in a whirling darkness until they were two pinpoint sparks of light—a dagger stare under level brows. . . .

When the room steadied about him as he was standing with slack arms, the gun hanging from his fingers, an apathetic numbness slowly withdrawing from his body. A dark smile curved smoothly on the Alendar's mouth.

The stabbing gaze slid casually away, leaving him dizzy in sudden vertigo, and touched the girl prostrate on the floor. Against the black carpet her burnished bronze curls sprayed out exquisitely. The green robe folded softly back from the roundness of her body, and nothing in the universe could have been so lovely as the creamy whiteness of her on the dark floor. The pit-black eyes brooded over her impassively. And then, in his smooth, deep voice the Alendar asked, amazingly, matter-of-factly,

"Tell me, do you have such girls on Earth?"

Smith shook his head to clear it. When he managed an answer his voice had steadied, and in the receding of that dizziness even the sudden drop into casual conversation seemed not unreasonable.

"I have never seen such a girl anywhere," he said calmly.

The sword-gaze flashed up and pierced him.

"She has told you," said the Alendar. "You know I have beauties here that outshine her as the sun does a candle. And yet . . . she has more than beauty, this Vaudir. You have felt it, perhaps?"

Smith met the questioning gaze, searching for mockery, but finding none. Not understanding—a moment before the man had threatened his life—he took up the conversation.

"They all have more than beauty. For what other reason do kings buy the Minga girls?"

"No—not that charm. She has it too, but something more subtle than fascination, much more desirable than loveliness. She has courage, this girl. She has intelligence. Where she got it I do not understand. I do not breed my girls for such things. But I looked into her eyes once, in the hallway, as she told you—and saw there more arousing things than beauty. I summoned her—and you come at her heels. Do you know why? Do you know why you did not die at the outer gate or anywhere along the hallways on your way in?"

Smith's pale stare met the dark one questioningly. The voice flowed on.

"Because there are—interesting things in your eyes too. Courage and ruthlessness and a certain—power, I think. Intensity is in you. And I believe I can find a use for it, Earthman."

Smith's eyes narrowed a little. So calm, so matter-of-fact, this talk. But death was coming. He felt it in the air —he knew that feel of old. Death—and worse things than that, perhaps. He remembered the whispers he had heard.

On the floor the girl moaned a little, and stirred. The Alendar's quiet, pinpoint eyes flicked her, and he said softly, "Rise." And she rose, stumbling, and stood before him with bent head. The stiffness was gone from her. On an impulse Smith said suddenly, "Vaudir!" She lifted her face and met his gaze, and a thrill of horror rippled over him. She had regained consciousness, but she would never be the same frightened girl he had known. Black knowledge looked out of her eyes, and her face was a strained mask that covered horror barely —barely! It was the face of one who has walked through a blacker hell than any of humanity's understanding, and gained knowledge there that no human soul could endure knowing and live.

She looked him full in the face for a long moment, silently, and then turned away to the Alendar again. And Smith thought, just before her eyes left his, he had seen in them one wild flash of hopeless, desperate appeal. . . .

"Come," said the Alendar.

He turned his back—Smith's gun-hand trembled up and then fell again. No, better wait. There was always a bare hope, until he saw death closing in all around.

He stepped out over the yielding carpet at the Alendar's heels. The girl came after with slow steps and eyes downcast in a horrible parody of meditation, as if she brooded over the knowledge that dwelt so terribly behind her eyes.

The dark archway at the opposite end of the room swallowed them up. Light failed for an instant—a breath-stopping instant while Smith's gun leaped up involuntarily, like a live thing in his hand, futilely against invisible evil, and his brain rocked at the utter blackness that enfolded him. It was over in the wink of an eye, and he wondered if it had ever been as his gun-hand fell again. But the Alendar said across one shoulder,

"A barrier I have placed to guard my—beauties. A mental barrier that would have been impassable had you not been with me, yet which—but you understand now, do you not, my Vaudir?" And there was an indescribable leer in the query that injected a note of monstrous humanity into the inhuman voice.

"I understand," echoed the girl in a voice as lovely and toneless as a sustained musical note. And the sound of those two inhuman voices proceeding from the human lips of his companions sent a shudder thrilling along Smith's nerves.

They went down the long corridor thereafter in silence, Smith treading soundlessly in his spaceman's boots, every fiber of him tense to painfulness. He found himself wondering, even in the midst of his strained watchfulness, if any other creature with a living human soul had ever gone down this corridor before—if frightened golden girls had followed the Alendar thus into blackness, or if they too had been drained of humanity and steeped in that nameless horror before their feet followed their master through the black barrier.

The hallway led downward, and the salt smell became clearer and the light sank to a glimmer in the air, and in a silence that was not human they went on.

Presently the Alendar said—and his deep, liquid voice did nothing to break the stillness, blending with it softly so that not even an echo roused,

"I am taking you into a place where no other man than the Alendar has ever set foot before. It pleases me to wonder just how your unaccustomed senses will react to the things you are about to see. I am reaching an—an age"—he laughed softly—"where experiment interests me. Look!"

Smith's eyes blinked shut before an intolerable blaze of sudden light. In the streaked darkness of that instant while the glare flamed through his lids he thought he felt everything shift unaccountably about him, as if the very structure of the atoms that built the walls were altered. When he opened his eyes he stood at the head of a long gallery blazing with a soft, delicious brilliance. How he had got there he made no effort even to guess.

Very beautifully it stretched before him. The walls and floor and ceiling were of sheeny stone. There were low couches along the walls at intervals, and a blue pool broke the floor, and the air sparkled unaccountably with golden light. And figures were moving through that champagne sparkle. . . .

Smith stood very still, looking down the gallery. The Alendar watched him with a subtle anticipation upon his face, the pinpoint glitter of his eyes sharp enough to pierce the Earthman's very brain. Vaudir with bent head brooded over the black knowledge behind her drooping lids. Only Smith of the three looked down the gallery and saw what moved through the golden glimmer of the air.

They were girls. They might have been goddesses—angels haloed with bronze curls, moving leisurely through a golden heaven where the air sparkled like wine. There must have been a score of them strolling up and down on the gallery in twos and threes, lolling on the couches, bathing in the pool. They wore the infinitely graceful Venusian robe with its looped shoulder and slit skirt, in soft, muted shades of violet and blue and jewel-green, and the beauty of them was breath-stopping as a blow. Music was in every gesture they made, a flowing, singing grace that made the heart ache with its sheer loveliness.

He had thought Vaudir lovely, but here was beauty so exquisite that it verged on pain. Their sweet, light voices were pitched to send little velvety burrs along his nerves, and from a distance the soft sounds blended so musically that they might have been singing together. The loveliness of their motion made his heart contract suddenly, and the blood pounded in his ears. . . .

"You find them beautiful?" The Alendar's voice blended into the humming lilt of voices as perfectly as it had blended with silence. His dagger-glitter of eyes was fixed piercingly on Smith's pale gaze, and he smiled a little, faintly. "Beautiful? Wait!"

He moved down the gallery, tall and very dark in the rainbow light. Smith, following after, walked in a haze of wonder. It is not given to every man to walk through heaven. He felt the air tingle like wine, and a delicious perfume caressed him and the haloed girls drew back with wide, amazed eyes fixed on him in his stained leather and heavy boots as he passed. Vaudir paced quietly after, her head bent, and from her the girls turned away their eyes, shuddering a little.

He saw now that their faces were as lovely as their bodies, languorously, colorfully. They were contented faces, unconscious of beauty, unconscious of any other existence than their own—soulless. He felt that instinctively. Here was beauty incarnate, physically, tangibly; but he had seen in Vaudir's face—before—a sparkle of daring, a tenderness of remorse at having brought him here, that gave her an indefinable superiority over even this incredible beauty, soulless.

They went down the gallery in a sudden hush as the musical voices fell silent from very amazement. Apparently the Alendar was a familiar figure here, for they

scarcely glanced at him, and from Vaudir they turned
away in a shuddering revulsion that preferred not to recognize her existence. But Smith was the first man other
than the Alendar whom they had ever seen, and the surprise of it struck them dumb.

They went on through the dancing air, and the last
lovely, staring girls fell behind, and an ivory gateway
opened before them, without a touch. They went downstairs from there, and along another hallway, while the
tingle died in the air and a hum of musical voices sprang
up behind them. They passed beyond the sound. The
hallway darkened until they were moving again through
dimness.

Presently the Alendar paused and turned.

"My more costly jewels," he said, "I keep in separate
settings. As here—"

He stretched out his arm, and Smith saw that a curtain hung against the wall. There were others, farther
on, dark blots against the dimness. The Alendar drew
back black folds, and light from beyond flowed softly
through a pattern of bars to cast flowery shadows on the
opposite wall. Smith stepped forward and stared.

He was looking through a grille window down into a
room lined with dark velvet. It was quite plain. There
was a low couch against the wall opposite the window,
and on it—Smith's heart gave a stagger and paused—a
woman lay. And if the girls in the gallery had been like
goddesses, this woman was lovelier than men have ever
dared to imagine even in legends. She was beyond divinity—long limbs white against the velvet, sweet curves
and planes of her rounding under the robe, bronze hair
spilling like lava over one white shoulder, and her face
calm as death with closed eyes. It was a passive beauty,
like alabaster shaped perfectly. And charm, a fascination all but tangible, reached out from her like a magic
spell. A sleeping charm, magnetic, powerful. He could
not wrench his eyes away. He was like a wasp caught in
honey. . . .

The Alendar said something across Smith's shoulder,
in a vibrant voice that thrilled the air. The closed lids

rose. Life and loveliness flowed into the calm face like a tide, lighting it unbearably. That heady charm wakened and brightened to a dangerous liveness—tugging, pulling. . . . She rose in one long glide like a wave over rocks; she smiled (Smith's senses reeled to the beauty of that smile) and then sank in a deep salaam, slowly, to the velvet floor, her hair rippling and falling all about her, until she lay abased in a blaze of loveliness under the window.

The Alendar let the curtain fall, and turned to Smith as the dazzling sight was blotted out. Again the pinpoint glitter stabbed into Smith's brain. The Alendar smiled again.

"Come," he said, and moved down the hall.

They passed three curtains, and paused at a fourth. Afterward Smith remembered that the curtain must have been drawn back and he must have bent forward to stare through the window bars, but the sight he saw blasted every memory of it from his mind. The girl who dwelt in this velvet-lined room was stretching on tiptoe just as the drawn curtain caught her, and the beauty and grace of her from head to foot stopped Smith's breath as a ray-stab to the heart would have done. And the irresistible, wrenching charm of her drew him forward until he was clasping the bars with white-knuckled hands, unaware of anything but her compelling, soul-destroying desirability. . . .

She moved, and the dazzle of grace that ran like a song through every motion made his senses ache with its pure, unattainable loveliness. He knew, even in his daze of rapture, that he might hold the sweet, curved body in his arms for ever, yet hunger still for the fulfilment which the flesh could never wring from her. Her loveliness aroused a hunger in the soul more maddening than the body's hunger could ever be. His brain rocked with the desire to possess that intangible, irresistible loveliness that he knew he could never possess, never reach with any sense that was in him. That bodiless desire raged like madness through him, so violently that the room reeled and the white outlines of the beauty unattainable as the stars wavered before him. He caught his breath and choked and drew back from the intolerable, exquisite sight.

The Alendar laughed and dropped the curtain.

"Come," he said again, the subtle amusement clear in his voice, and Smith in a daze moved after him down the hall.

They went a long way, past curtains hanging at regular intervals along the wall. When they paused at last, the curtain before which they stopped was faintly luminous about the edges, as if something dazzling dwelt within. The Alendar drew back the folds.

"We are approaching," he said, "a pure clarity of beauty, hampered only a little by the bonds of flesh. Look."

One glance only Smith snatched of the dweller within. And the exquisite shock of that sight went thrilling like torture through every nerve of him. For a mad instant his reason staggered before the terrible fascination beating out from that dweller in waves that wrenched at his very soul—incarnate loveliness tugging with strong fingers at every sense and every nerve and intangibly, irresistibly, at deeper things than these, groping among the roots of his being, dragging his soul out. . . .

Only one glance he took, and in the glance he felt his soul answer that dragging, and the terrible desire tore futilely through him. Then he flung up an arm to shield his eyes and reeled back into the dark, and a wordless sob rose to his lips and the darkness reeled about him.

The curtain fell. Smith pressed the wall and breathed in long, shuddering gasps, while his heart-beats slowed gradually and the unholy fascination ebbed from about him. The Alendar's eyes were glittering with a green fire as he turned from the window, and a nameless hunger lay shadowily on his face. He said,

"I might show you others, Earthman. But it could only drive you mad, in the end—you were very near the brink for a moment just now—and I have another use for you. . . . I wonder if you begin to understand, now, the purpose of all this?"

The green glow was fading from that dagger-sharp gaze as the Alendar's eyes stabbed into Smith's. The Earthman gave his head a little shake to clear away the vestiges of that devouring desire, and took a fresh grip on the butt of his gun. The familiar smoothness of it brought him a measure of reassurance, and with it a re-awakening to the peril all around. He knew now that there could be no conceivable mercy for him, to whom the innermost secrets of the Minga had been unaccountably revealed. Death was waiting—strange death, as soon as the Alendar wearied of talking—but if he kept his ears open and his eyes alert it might not—please God—catch him so quickly that he died alone. One sweep of that blade-blue flame was all he asked, now. His eyes, keen and hostile, met the dagger-gaze squarely. The Alendar smiled and said,

"Death in your eyes, Earthman. Nothing in your mind but murder. Can that brain of yours comprehend nothing but battle? Is there no curiosity there? Have you no wonder of why I brought you here? Death awaits you, yes. But a not unpleasant death, and it awaits all, in one form or another. Listen, let me tell you—I have reason for desiring to break through that animal shell of self-defense that seals in your mind. Let me look deeper —if there are depths. Your death will be—useful, and in a way, pleasant. Otherwise—well, the black beasts hunger. And flesh must feed them, as a sweeter drink feeds me. . . . Listen."

Smith's eyes narrowed. A sweeter drink. . . . Danger, danger—the smell of it in the air—instinctively he felt the peril of opening his mind to the plunging gaze of the Alendar, the force of those compelling eyes beating like strong lights into his brain. . . .

"Come," said the Alendar softly, and moved off soundlessly through the gloom. They followed, Smith painfully alert, the girl walking with lowered, brooding eyes, her mind and soul afar in some wallowing darkness whose shadow showed so hideously beneath her lashes.

The hallway widened to an arch, and abruptly, on the other side, one wall dropped away into infinity and they stood on the dizzy brink of a gallery opening on a black, heaving sea. Smith bit back a startled oath. One moment before the way had led through low-roofed tunnels deep underground; the next instant they stood on the shore of a vast body of rolling darkness, a tiny wind touching their faces with the breath of unnameable things.

Very far below, the dark waters rolled. Phosphorescence lighted them uncertainly, and he was not even sure it was water that surged there in the dark. A heavy thickness seemed to be inherent in the rollers, like black slime surging.

The Alendar looked out over the fire-tinged waves. He waited for an instant without speaking, and then, far out in the slimy surges, something broke the surface with an oily splash, something mercifully veiled in the dark, then dived again, leaving a wake of spreading ripples over the surface.

"Listen," said the Alendar, without turning his head. "Life is very old. There are older races than man. Mine is one. Life rose out of the black slime of the sea-bottoms and grew toward the light along many diverging lines. Some reached maturity and deep wisdom when man was still swinging through the jungle trees.

"For many centuries, as mankind counts time, the Alendar has dwelt here, breeding beauty. In later years he has sold some of his lesser beauties, perhaps to explain to mankind's satisfaction what it could never understand were it told the truth. Do you begin to see? My race is very remotely akin to those races which suck blood from man, less remotely to those which drink his life-forces for nourishment. I refine taste even more than that. I drink—beauty. I live on beauty. Yes, literally.

"Beauty is as tangible as blood, in a way. It is a separate, distinct force that inhabits the bodies of men and women. You must have noticed the vacuity that accompanies perfect beauty in so many women . . . the force so strong that it drives out all other forces and lives vampirishly at the expense of intelligence and goodness and conscience and all else.

"In the beginning, here—for our race was old when this world began, spawned on another planet, and wise and ancient—we woke from slumber in the slime, to feed on the beauty force inherent in mankind even in cave-dwelling days. But it was meager fare, and we studied the race to determine where the greatest prospects lay, then selected specimens for breeding, built this stronghold and settled down to the business of evolving mankind up to its limit of loveliness. In time we weeded out all but the present type. For the race of man we have developed the ultimate type of loveliness. It is interesting to see what we have accomplished on other worlds, with utterly different races. . . .

"Well, there you have it. Women, bred as a spawning-ground for the devouring force of beauty on which we live.

"But—the fare grows monotonous, as all food must without change. Vaudir I took because I saw in her a sparkle of something that except in very rare instances has been bred out of the Minga girls. For beauty, as I have said, eats up all other qualities but beauty. Yet somehow intelligence and courage survived latently in Vaudir. It decreases her beauty, but the tang of it should be a change from the eternal sameness of the rest. And so I thought until I saw you.

"I realized then how long it had been since I tasted the beauty of man. It is so rare, so different from female beauty, that I had all but forgotten it existed. And you have it, very subtly, in a raw, harsh way. . . .

"I have told you all this to test the quality of that— that harsh beauty in you. Had I been wrong about the deeps of your mind, you would have gone to feed the black beasts, but I see that I was not wrong. Behind your animal shell of self-preservation are depths of that force and strength which nourish the roots of male beauty. I think I shall give you a while to let it grow, under the forcing methods I know, before I—drink. It will be delightful. . . .

The voice trailed away in a murmurous silence, the pinpoint glitter sought Smith's eyes. And he tried half-heartedly to avoid it, but his eyes turned involuntarily to the stabbing gaze, and the alertness died out of him, gradually, and the compelling pull of those glittering points in the pits of darkness held him very still.

And as he stared into the diamond glitter he saw its brilliance slowly melt and darken, until the pinpoints of light had changed to pools that dimmed, and he was looking into black evil as elemental and vast as the space between the worlds, a dizzying blankness wherein

dwelt unnameable horror . . . deep, deep . . . all about
him the darkness was clouding. And thoughts that were
not his own seeped into his mind out of that vast, elemental dark . . . crawling, writhing thoughts . . . until he had a glimpse of that dark place where Vaudir's soul
wallowed, and something sucked him down and down into
a waking nightmare he could not fight. . . .

Then somehow the pull broke for an instant. For just
that instant he stood again on the shore of the heaving
sea and gripped a gun with nerveless fingers—then the
darkness closed about him again, but a different, uneasy
dark that had not quite the all-compelling power of that
other nightmare—it left him strength enough to fight.

And he fought, a desperate, moveless, soundless struggle in a black sea of horror, while worm-thoughts coiled
through his straining mind and the clouds rolled and
broke and rolled again about him. Sometimes, in the
instants when the pull slackened, he had time to feel a
third force struggling here between that black, blind
downward suck that dragged at him and his own sick,
frantic effort to fight clear, a third force that was weakening the black drag so that he had moments of lucidity
when he stood free on the brink of the ocean and felt
the sweat roll down his face and was aware of his laboring heart and how gaspingly breath tortured his lungs,
and he knew he was fighting with every atom of himself,
body and mind and soul, against the intangible blackness sucking him down.

And then he felt the force against him gather itself in a
final effort—he sensed desperation in that effort—and
come rolling over him like a tide. Bowled over, blinded
and dumb and deaf, drowning in utter blackness, he
floundered in the deeps of that nameless hell where
thoughts that were alien and slimy squirmed through his
brain. Bodiless he was, and unstable, and as he wallowed there in the ooze more hideous than any earthly
ooze, because it came from black, inhuman souls and
out of ages before man, he became aware that the
worm-thoughts a-squirm in his brain were forming slowly into monstrous meanings—knowledge like a formless
flow was pouring through his bodiless brain, knowledge
so dreadful that consciously he could not comprehend it,

though subconsciously every atom of his mind and soul sickened and writhed futilely away. It was flooding over him, drenching him, permeating him through and through with the very essence of dreadfulness—he felt his mind melting away under the solvent power of it, melting and running fluidly into new channels and fresh molds—horrible molds. . . .

And just at that instant, while madness folded around him and his mind rocked on the verge of annihilation, something snapped, and like a curtain the dark rolled away, and he stood sick and dizzy on the gallery above the black sea. Everything was reeling about him, but they were stable things that shimmered and steadied before his eyes, blessed black rock and tangible surges that had form and body—his feet pressed firmness and his mind shook itself and was clean and his own again.

And then through the haze of weakness that still shrouded him a voice was shrieking wildly, "Kill! . . . kill!" and he saw the Alendar staggering against the rail, all his outlines unaccountably blurred and uncertain, and behind him Vaudir with blazing eyes and face wrenched hideously into life again, screaming "Kill!" in a voice scarcely human.

Like an independent creature his gun-hand leaped up —he had gripped that gun through everything that happened—and he was dimly aware of the hardness of it kicking back against his hand with the recoil, and of the blue flash flaming from its muzzle. It struck the Alendar's dark figure full, and there was a hiss and a dazzle. . . .

Smith closed his eyes tight and opened them again, and stared with a sick incredulity; for unless that struggle had unhinged his brain after all, and the worm-thoughts still dwelt slimily in his mind, tingeing all he saw with unearthly horror—unless this was true, he was looking not at a man just rayed through the lungs, and who should be dropping now in a bleeding, collapsed heap to the floor, but at—at—God, what *was* it? The dark figure had slumped against the rail, and instead of blood gushing, a hideous, nameless, formless black poured sluggishly forth—a slime like the heaving sea below. The whole dark figure of the man was melting,

slumping farther down into the pool of blackness forming at his feet on the stone floor.

Smith gripped his gun and watched in numb incredulity, and the whole body sank slowly down and melted
and lost all form—hideously, gruesomely—until where
the Alendar had stood a heap of slime lay viscidly on
the gallery floor, hideously alive, heaving and rippling
and striving to lift itself into a semblance of humanity
again. And as he watched, it lost even that form, and the
edges melted revoltingly and the mass flattened and slid
down into a pool of utter horror, and he became aware
that it was pouring slowly through the rails into the sea.
He stood watching while the whole rolling, shimmering
mound melted and thinned and trickled through the
bars, until the floor was clear again, and not even a stain
marred the stone.

A painful constriction of his lungs roused him, and he
realized he had been holding his breath, scarcely daring
to realize. Vaudir had collapsed against the wall, and he
saw her knees give limply, and staggered forward on uncertain feet to catch her as she fell.

"Vaudir, Vaudir!" he shook her gently. "Vaudir,
what's happened? Am I dreaming? Are we safe now?
Are you—awake again?"

Very slowly her white lids lifted, and the black eyes
met his. And he saw shadowily there the knowledge of
that wallowing void he had dimly known, the shadow
that could never be cleared away. She was steeped and
foul with it. And the look of her eyes was such that involuntarily he released her and stepped away. She staggered a little and then regained her balance and regarded him from under bent brows. The level inhumanity of
her gaze struck into his soul, and yet he thought he saw
a spark of the girl she had been, dwelling in torture
amid the blackness. He knew he was right when she
said, in a faraway, toneless voice,

"Awake? . . . No, not ever now, Earthman. I have
been down too deeply into hell . . . he had dealt me a
worse torture than he knew, for there is just enough humanity felt within me to realize what I have become,
and to suffer. . . .

"Yes, he is gone, back into the slime that bred him. I

have been a part of him, one with him in the blackness
of his soul, and I know. I have spent eons since the
blackness came upon me, dwelt for eternities in the
dark, rolling seas of his mind, sucking in knowledge . . .
and as I was one with him, and he now gone, so shall I
die; yet I will see you safely out of here if it is in my power,
for it was I who dragged you in. If I can remember—if I
can find the way. . . ."

She turned uncertainly and staggered a step back
along the way they had come. Smith sprang forward and
slid his free arm about her, but she shuddered away
from the contact.

"No, no—unbearable—the touch of clean human
flesh—and it breaks the cord of my remembering. . . .
I can not look back into his mind as it was when I dwelt
there, and I must, I must. . . ."

She shook him off and reeled on, and he cast one last
look at the billowing sea, and then followed. She staggered along the stone floor on stumbling feet, one hand
to the wall to support herself, and her voice was whispering gustily, so that he had to follow close to hear, and
then almost wished he had not heard,

"—black slime—darkness feeding on light—everything wavers so—slime, slime and a rolling sea—he rose
out of it, you know, before civilization began here—he
is age-old—there never has been but one Alendar. . . .
And somehow—I could not see just how, or remember
why—he rose from the rest, as some of his race on other
planets had done, and took the man-form and stocked
his breeding-pens. . . ."

They went on up the dark hallway, past curtains hiding
incarnate loveliness, and the girl's stumbling footsteps
kept time to her stumbling, half-incoherent words.

"—has lived all these ages here, breeding and devouring beauty—vampire-thirst, a hideous delight in drinking in that beauty-force—I felt it and remembered it
when I was one with him—wrapping black layers of pri-
mal slime about—quenching human loveliness in ooze,
sucking—blind black thirst. . . . And his wisdom was
ancient and dreadful and full of power—so he could
draw a soul out through the eyes and sink it in hell, and
drown it there, as he would have done mine if I had not

had, somehow, a difference from the rest. Great Shar, I wish I had not! I wish I were drowned in it and did not feel in every atom of me the horrible uncleanness of—what I know. But by virtue of that hidden strength I did not surrender wholly, and when he had turned his power to subduing you I was able to struggle, there in the very heart of his mind, making a disturbance that shook him as he fought us both—making it possible to free you long enough for you to destroy the human flesh he was clothed in—so that he lapsed into the ooze again. I do not quite understand why that happened—only that his weakness, with you assailing him from without and me struggling strongly in the very center of his soul was such that he was forced to draw on the power he had built up to maintain himself in the man-form, and weakened it enough so that he collapsed when the man-form was assailed. And he fell back into the slime again—whence he rose—black slime—heaving—oozing. . . ."

Her voice trailed away in murmurs, and she stumbled, all but falling. When she regained her balance she went on ahead of him at a greater distance, as if his very nearness were repugnant to her, and the soft babble of her voice drifted back in broken phrases without meaning.

Presently the air began to tingle again, and they passed the silver gate and entered that gallery where the air sparkled like champagne. The blue pool lay jewel-clear in its golden setting. Of the girls there was no sign.

When they reached the head of the gallery the girl paused, turning to him a face twisted with the effort at memory.

"Here is the trial," she said urgently. "If I can remember—" She seized her head in clutching hands, shaking it savagely. "I haven't the strength, now—can't —can't—" the piteous little murmur reached his ears incoherently. Then she straightened resolutely, swaying a little, and faced him, holding out her hands. He clasped them hesitantly, and saw a shiver go through her at the contact, and her face contort painfully, and then a shudder communicated itself through that clasp and he too

winced in revolt. He saw her eyes go blank and her face
strain in lines of tensity, and a fine dew broke out on her
forehead. For a long moment she stood so, her face like
death, and strong shudders went over her body and her
eyes were blank as the void between the planets.

And as each shudder swept her it went unbroken
through the clasping of their hands to him, and they
were black waves of dreadfulness, and again he saw the
heaving sea and wallowed in the hell he had fought out
of on the gallery, and he knew for the first time what torture she must be enduring who dwelt in the very deeps
of that uneasy dark. The pulses came faster, and for moments together he went down into the blind blackness
and the slime, and felt the first wriggling of the worm-
thoughts tickling the roots of his brain. . . .

And then suddenly a clean darkness closed around
them and again everything shifted unaccountably, as if
the atoms of the gallery were changing, and when Smith
opened his eyes he was standing once more in the dark,
slanting corridor with the smell of salt and antiquity
heavy in the air.

Vaudir moaned softly beside him, and he turned to
see her reeling against the wall and trembling so from
head to foot that he looked to see her fall the next moment.

"Better—in a moment," she gasped. "It took—nearly
all my strength to—to get us through—wait. . . ."

So they halted there in the darkness and the dead salt
air, until the trembling abated a little and she said,
"Come," in her little whimpering voice. And again the
journey began. It was only a short way, now, to the barrier of black blankness that guarded the door into the
room where they had first seen the Alendar. When they
reached the place she shivered a little and paused, then
resolutely held out her hands. And as he took them he
felt once more the hideous slimy waves course through
him, and plunged again into the heaving hell. And as
before the clean darkness flashed over them in a breath,
and then she dropped his hands and they were standing
in the archway looking into the velvet-hung room they
had left—it seemed eons ago.

He watched as waves of blinding weakness flooded

over her from that supreme effort. Death was visible in her face as she turned to him at last.

"Come—oh, come quickly," she whispered, and staggered forward.

At her heels he followed, across the room, past the great iron gateway, down the hall to the foot of the silver stairs. And here his heart sank, for he felt sure she could never climb the long spiral distances to the top. But she set her foot on the step and went upward resolutely, and as he followed he heard her murmuring to herself,

"Wait—oh, wait—let me reach the end—let me undo this much—and then—no, no! Please Shar, not the black slime again. . . . Earthman, Earthman!"

She paused on the stair and turned to face him, and her haggard face was frantic with desperation and despair.

"Earthman, promise—do not let me die like this! When we reach the end, ray me! Burn me clean, or I shall go down for eternity into the black sinks from which I dragged you free. Oh promise!"

"I will," Smith's voice said quietly. "I will."

And they went on. Endlessly the stairs spiraled upward and endlessly they climbed. Smith's legs began to ache intolerably, and his heart was pounding like a wild thing, but Vaudir seemed not to notice weariness. She climbed steadily and no more unsurely than she had come along the halls. And after eternities they reached the top.

And there the girl fell. She dropped like a dead woman at the head of the silver spiral. Smith thought for a sick instant that he had failed her and let her die uncleansed, but in a moment or two she stirred and lifted her head and very slowly dragged herself to her feet.

"I will go on—I will, I will," she whispered to herself. "—come this far—must finish—" and she reeled off down the lovely, rosily-lit hallway paneled in pearl.

He could see how perilously near she was to her strength's end, and he marveled at the tenacity with which she clung to life though it ebbed away with every breath and the pulse of darkness flowed in after it. So with bulldog stubbornness she made her wavering way past door after door of carven shell, under rosy lights that flushed her face with a ghastly mockery of health, until they reached the silver gateway at the end. The lock had been removed from it by now, and the bar drawn.

She tugged open the gate and stumbled through.

And the nightmare journey went on. It must be very near morning, Smith thought, for the halls were deserted, but did he not sense a breath of danger in the still air? . . .

The girl's gasping voice answered that half-formed query as if, like the Alendar, she held the secret of reading men's minds.

"The—Guardians—still rove the halls, and unleashed now—so keep your ray-gun ready, Earthman. . . ."

After that he kept his eyes alert as they retraced, stumbling and slow, the steps he had taken on his way in. And once he heard distinctly the soft slither of—something—scraping over the marble pavement, and twice he smelt with shocking suddenness in this scented air a whiff of salt, and his mind flashed back to a rolling black sea. . . . But nothing molested them.

Step by faltering step the hallways fell behind them, and he began to recognize landmarks, and the girl's footsteps staggered and hesitated and went on gallantly, incredibly, beating back oblivion, fighting the dark surges rolling over her, clinging with tenacious fingers to the tiny spark of life that drove her on.

And at long last, after what seemed hours of desperate effort, they reached the blue-lit hallway at whose end the outer door opened. Vaudir's progress down it was a series of dizzy staggers, interspersed with pauses while she hung to the carven doors with tense fingers and drove her teeth into a bloodless lip and gripped that last flicker of life. He saw the shudders sweep over her, and knew what waves of washing dark must be rising all about her, and how the worm-thoughts writhed through her brain. . . . But she went on. Every step now was a little tripping, as if she fell from one foot to the other, and at each step he expected that knee to give way and pitch her down into the black deeps that yawned for her. But she went on.

She reached the bronze door, and with a last spurt of effort she lifted the bar and swung it open. Then, that tiny spark flickered out like a lamp. Smith caught one flash of the rock room within—and something horrible on the floor—before he saw her pitch forward as the rising tide of slimy oblivion closed at last over her head. She was dying as she fell, and he whipped the ray-gun up and felt the recoil against his palm as a blue blaze flashed forth and transfixed her in midair. And he could have sworn her eyes lighted for a flickering instant and the gallant girl he had known looked forth, cleansed and whole, before death—clean death—glazed them.

She slumped down in a huddle at his feet, and he felt a sting of tears beneath his eyelids as he looked down on her, a huddle of white and bronze on the rug. And as he watched, a film of defilement veiled the shining whiteness of her—decay set in before his eyes and progressed with horrible swiftness, and in less time than it takes to tell he was staring with horrified eyes at a pool of black slime across which green velvet lay bedraggled.

Northwest Smith closed his pale eyes, and for a moment struggled with memory, striving to wrest from it the long-forgotten words of a prayer learned a score of years ago on another planet. Then he stepped over the pitiful, horrible heap on the carpet and went on.

In the little rock room of the outer wall he saw what he had glimpsed when Vaudir opened the door. Retribution had overtaken the eunuch. The body must have been his, for tatters of scarlet velvet lay about the floor, but there was no way to recognize what its original form had been. The smell of salt was heavy in the air, and a trail of black slime snaked across the floor toward the wall. The wall was solid, but it ended there. . . .

Smith laid his hand on the outer door, drew the bar, swung it open. He stepped out under the hanging vines and filled his lungs with pure air, free, clear, untainted with scent or salt. A pearly dawn was breaking over Ednes.

The Bright Illusion

THROUGH THE BLINDING shimmer of sun upon sand, Dixon squinted painfully at the curious mirage ahead. He was reeling with thirst and heat and weariness, and about him the desert heaved in long, blurred waves, but through the haze of his own weakness, and through the sun haze upon the desert, he peered anxiously at the thing and could not make it out.

Nothing he had ever seen or heard of could cause such a mirage as this. It was a great oval of yellow light, bulging up convexly from the earth like some translucent golden egg half buried in the sand. And over its surface there seemed to be an immense busyness, as if it was covered with tiny, shimmering things that moved constantly. He had never seen anything remotely resembling it before.

As he toiled through the sand toward the bright illusion, he became aware of darker specks around it haphazardly, specks that as he approached took on the aspect of men grotesquely sprawled in attitudes of death. He could not make it out. Of course it was a mirage, yet it did not recede as he advanced, and the details of those sprawled bodies became clearer and clearer, and the great translucent oval loomed up against the sky mystifyingly.

He thought he must be dreaming, or perhaps a little unbalanced by the heat and thirst. He had been struggling through this burning sand under this burning sun for a long while now, and there were times when the rush of illusion swallowed him up, and he could hear water splashing and fountains tinkling in the empty desert about him. This must be a hallucination, then, for it could scarcely be a mirage. He was almost upon it, and it had so real a look—those bodies, sprawling—

He stumbled over the first, for somehow his muscles did not co-ordinate very well now. It was the sun-withered body of an old man in the Legion uniform, his kepi fallen forward over his face. The next was that of an Arab in a tangle of dirty white garments, and beyond him was the almost-fresh corpse of a boy in khaki shorts and sun helmet.

Dixon wondered dully what had happened to them and why the bodies were in such varying stages of decomposition. He lifted a dragging head and peered at the great egg-shape thing bulging up from the sand. It reminded him of a huge bubble of golden water, save that bubbles were round, and—

Belatedly, caution returned to him. These dead men must have met their deaths somehow through the presence of the great egg. He had better advance more cautiously or— And then the pull seized him. He had come too near. Something inexorable and slow was dragging him forward—or was it that the great bubble was advancing toward him?

Sky and sand reeled. And the distance between him and the great egg-shaped thing lessened and lessened and—and somehow he found himself flat against a great golden translucency that shivered against him with the strangest motion, as if it was alive and hungry for—

He felt that he should be afraid, yet somehow he was not aware of fear at all. The golden light was closing over him and around him with a queer, engulfing motion. He shut his eyes and relaxed utterly in the impassive grip of the thing.

Dixon was lying motionless in the midst of a golden radiance that seemed crystal clear, yet so obstructed his vision that he could see only a few yards away, and the desert landscape outside was as unreal as a dream. The most delicious sensation of rest and well-being was surging through him in slow waves that succeeded one another like ripples on a shore, each leaving an increasing residue of serenity and luxurious comfort. Thirst and hunger and weariness had vanished in a breath. He knew no fear or anxiety. In a trancelike calm he lay there, feeling the waves flow through him unbroken, staring up into the lucid golden light without wonder or surprise.

How long he lay there he never knew. In the perfect peace of the glow enfolding him, he was very dimly aware that the all-penetrating waves were washing through him in a way which queerly suggested searching. They permeated every atom of him, flooding his brain with light and calmness.

In his tranced quiet he knew, without actually realizing, that memory in lightning flashes was reeling through his mind. Abstract memories of things he had learned in college and in afterlife. Snatches of literature, fragments of sciences. Mathematical problems solved in breathtaking speed and supplanted by chemical formulas that melted into the bits of psychology remembered from schooldays. Impassively he lay there, scarcely realizing the flashing reviews that passed through his light-flooded brain.

And then the tempo of the ripples that went over him began to change. His mind awoke by degrees from its pleasant coma, though his body still lay relaxed. And now the wavelets in the queerest way were beating upon his brain tantalizingly. Little fragments of thoughts not his own blew through his mind and faded.

He struggled to grasp them. He clutched at the vanishing tags, striving to weld them together, feeling obscurely that if he could retain each small flutter as it wavered through his mind, if he could put them together and fuse them in a unit, he might understand.

Very slowly he succeeded. Very slowly the waves as they flowed through him began to surrender their meanings to his clutching mind: meanings that solidified and amplified with each succeeding wave, building themselves up slowly as ripple after ripple washed serenely through the straining brain that was learning so painfully to comprehend their significance.

By degrees Dixon realized that some intelligence was striving to communicate with him. The knowledge did not come in words or even word forms introduced into his brain. But it came, slowly and inexorably, building up and up as wave after measured wave flowed through him and vanished, leaving a residue of knowledge to be increased by the next.

And the vast, the almost divine, impersonality of it staggered him. This being—intelligence, presence—was so utterly abstract a thing that even in the knowledge it imparted to him there was no hint of personality or consciousness of individual being. There could have been no "I" in its supervocabulary of thought ripples. Divinely serene, divinely abstract, it allowed knowledge to flow through the brain of the man suspended in its heart. And by measured degrees that knowledge built itself up in his mind.

He had been chosen. For a long while this being had been waiting here, trapping the men who came near enough, sending its light waves in floods through their minds to illuminate their thoughts and their capacity for knowledge, probing their intelligences. All those others lying outside had been found wanting. The being had discarded them and waited, in its serene passivity, until the right man came by.

This much flowed through his brain. Then there was a hiatus, to permit him to absorb the knowledge, to understand. After a while the wavelets began to beat through him again in their measured slowness. He became aware of vast, dim voids, blank stretches empty of space or time or any of the myriad dimensions. He knew that through these, while long periods elapsed which yet had no relation to the time he understood, the great light-bubble had traveled from some origin unthinkably far away, on a quest. He realized that it had at last emerged from those gray, formless voids into the interstellar space of his own universe; that it had made its way here, driven by a vast purpose he could not grasp, and had come to rest upon the desert sands, to lie in wait.

Again there was a gap in the thought waves, and again Dixon lay still, assimilating that stunning knowledge. And yet, somehow, he was not greatly surprised or in the remotest way skeptical. He waited.

Presently the flow began again. There was, in another part of space, a world which this being desired—or no, not desired; there was nothing so human or personal a thing as desire about it. A world which it meant to have; a very alien world, he gathered, from the sort he knew. Peopled by alien creatures and built in other dimensions than those which formed his own universe.

These people worshiped a powerful god. And it was this worship—this godhood—which the being that enfolded him meant to possess. It tried to give him a glimpse of why, but the thought waves which flowed through his brain were incomprehensible and remote—not knowledge, but a jumble of unrelated impressions, without coherence. After a few vain attempts to instill the reason for its purpose into his mind, the being apparently dismissed the point as unnecessary and went on.

This god which it meant to dispossess was very powerful; so powerful that of itself the being could do nothing to overthrow it, could not even pass the barriers set up to guard the strange world. It had need of an intelligent, animate creature from a world different enough in structure so that the god's peculiar powers would have no effect upon him.

Gradually the measured beats made it clear to Dixon that he was the chosen envoy. He was to be transported there, armed in potent ways, sent out into the new world to overthrow the god's domain and make way for his sponsor to take possession.

There was a long hiatus after that. Dixon lay quiet, rather stunned by the magnitude of the thing. The being which engulfed him must have sensed the growing rebellion in his mind, for after a while the beats began again. And Dixon knew that the proposition was not a compulsory one. But—the knowledge flowed casually through him—though he was free to be released and set back upon his journey if he refused the plan, he would inevitably die soon, die very unpleasantly.

There was no water within any possible reach, and a band of veiled Tuaregs was scouring the desert nearby in search of that Arab who lay in a huddle of dirty white robes outside the egg-shaped bubble. If he did not die of thirst before they caught him, he would die in a manner infinitely more undesirable at their hands. But, of course, if he so desired, he was free to go.

Dixon digested this information thoughtfully. hesitatingly, though he knew he had no choice. His blind stumbling through the desert could have no other end than slow death, as he had been aware even before he came upon the great bubble. And if there were Tuaregs near— Even in the bodily trance that cradled him he shuddered. He had seen victims of Tuareg tortures, miraculously alive after days and days of— He turned his mind from that. No; he had no choice.

And gradually a little spark of excitement began to burn in him. What an adventure! And though death might lie at the end of it, there was at least a hope for life, and he knew he had not even that if he refused. Consent was forming in his mind, but, even before it crystallized, the being must have known, for about him the lucid radiance suddenly began to cloud and change. Milkiness flooded through it and through his body and his brain. Oblivion swallowed him up.

When realization returned to Dixon it came slowly. Layer by layer the oblivion melted from his mind. He had a vague impression of vast spaces traversed and barriers surmounted, and somehow he sensed an indefinable difference in the space that surrounded the bubble, though it was indefinite how he knew it. A little beat quivered through him, and another, clearing away the fogs of his consciousness. Then knowledge began to pulse again through him in measured flow.

They had crossed gulfs greater than he could comprehend. They were suspended now above the world of their destination. He was to look briefly upon it, for even through the protecting walls of the light-bubble the thing that he would see was so alien to him that in his present form he could not bear to gaze upon it long.

Then the light about Dixon cleared to translucence, and somehow he was looking out and down upon a scene that stunned his eyes with its violence. He had an instant's impression of a land that shrieked and raved with maniacal color beyond any conception of color as he knew it. He turned his eyes wincingly away and stared down at the scene immediately below. And though in point of actual space it must have been very far away, he could see everything quite clearly and with a wider radius of vision than he was accustomed to. It was as if in one glance he encompassed the whole circle of the horizon.

The world below was one vast city that reeled away in terrace below crazy terrace out to a skyline that shimmered with white dazzle. And the colors that blazed and howled and agonized over the insane angles of the place turned him sick and dizzy. They were incredible angles and impossible colors, the tints and the tilts of madness —wild, staggering lines and arcs and jagged peaks, crazy inclines broke by ridges of eruptive color, zigzag bridges, buildings that leaned out in gravity-defying angles.

All these incredible terraces mounted up and up in diminishing arcs to the topmost tier of all. This was small and smooth, though over its pavement the insane colors sprawled blotchily. And in the very center a mighty column rose, blacker than any darkness he had ever seen before. On its height burned a pale flame.

But the inhabitants! Dixon could see them quite clearly despite the distance. They were sinuous and surpentine, and their motions were blurs of swiftness, poems of infinite grace. They were not men—they had never been men in any stage of their evolution. And if the colors of the buildings were agony to his eyes, the living, unstable hues that writhed and crawled over the beings below were so frightful that his gaze rebelled. For this reason he never knew just how they were shaped.

There was one standing just below the great black pillar whereon burned the flame, and of this he had the clearest view. It was boneless and writhing, livid with creeping color. Its single great eye, lucid and expressionless, stared from an unfeatured, mouthless face, half scarlet and half purple, between which two shades a wedge of nameless green broadened as he looked away.

He had seen this much before the pellucid crystal began to cloud about him once more and the slow knowledge began its beat through his brain. He must look no longer, or something disastrous might happen to his benumbed senses. He understood by now that it was not in his own form that he was to go out into the crazy land. He was sure, even without that seeping knowledge, that his own body could never endure the colors of the place, nor could his own material feet tread the dizzy angles. Many of the streets and bridges were too steep for human feet to walk.

And he was understanding, as the slow waves flowed on, how different these people were from his own kind. Not only in appearance; their very substance was different from flesh and blood, the atoms arranged in different patterns. They obtained nourishment in an incomprehensible way from some source he could not understand. Their emotions and habits and purposes were alien to all his experience, and among them even the sexes were not those he knew. They were more numerous than mankind's two, and their functions were entirely different. Reproduction here was based on an utterly alien principle.

When the pause came in the waves of knowledge, Dixon was a little dizzy with the complete strangeness of this place and with wonder how he would be enabled to enter it. He lay still, wondering, until the flow began again.

Then the knowledge of the way he was to be introduced into the strange god's domain began to surge in deliberate beats through his brain. It seemed simple, yet the magnitude of it was staggering. A sort of veil of illusion was to be dropped between him and these alien beings. To them, his form would seem one of their own. Through the veil his speech would be filtered and changed into their indescribable mode of communication. And to him they would have the appearance of humanity, their speech would be understandable, their curious emotions translated into familiarity.

Even their multiple sexes would be resolved arbitrarily into two. For though this being could not approach any nearer the strange god whose flame burned upon the pillar, it seemed to have immense power even from this distance in the crazy world below.

The slow-beating waves made him aware that during his sojourn in the strange place he would be guided and in a measure protected, and that this knowledge would still flow through his brain. All this was possible, he understood, because of his own complete difference from anything in this world—such a difference that he would not cause even a ripple upon the surface of the god's consciousness until the time came for his overthrow.

Then again the cloudiness began to clear, until Dixon was looking out through crystal walls upon that reeling city below. For an instant it shuddered with mad colors before his aching eyes. And then over the whole crazy panorama the queerest blurring came. He looked down upon a changing world wherein the wild colors faded and ran together and the staggering angles of that mighty vista below were obscured in structural changes whose purpose he began to understand.

Before his eyes a splendid and stately city was taking shape. Out of the ruin of eye-wrenching color rose tier beyond tier of white pillars and translucent domes. Roofs of alabaster formed themselves under a sky whose pallor was deepening into blue.

When he tore his eyes away from that magnificent vista, terrace dropping away below terrace, crowned with domes and spires and columns wreathed in green, far out to the distant horizon, he saw that over the crowded streets with their swarms of multicolored horrors a stranger change was falling. Out of the mingling indistinctnesses of those colors without name, the semblance of humanity grew. People of noble stature and stately bearing, robed in garments of shining steel, took form before his eyes.

In less time than it takes to tell, a metropolis of familiar aspect stretched invitingly under his gaze. That nightmare of colors was gone as a nightmare goes, leaving no faintest trace behind. Yet he knew as he looked down that in reality nothing was changed. The writhing people still flashed with infinite speed and grace through tiptilted streets of gravity-defying angles. He blinked and looked again, but the illusion held steady—a stupendous city, smiling under a blue, familiar sky.

Slowly through his consciousness beat the realization

that, once down there in the metamorphosed world, he must search out the temple of the god, find its vulnerable spot, provide as it were a window, so that through his eyes the being which had brought him here could see its enemy's weakness and instruct Dixon further. And it was impressed upon him, too, that all possible speed must be made, for though there was little danger that the god would realize the inimical presence, yet his very safeguard was his greatest danger. Dixon was so alien to the ultimate particles of his being that, though this protected him from the god, it made his maintenance in the strange world very difficult. It was a strain even upon the vast powers of the light-bubble being to keep that veil of illusion stretched protectingly between him and this world, the very sight and touch of which would send him mad if he was exposed to it long unguarded.

There was a little pause after this, and Dixon lay still, awed by the unthinkable difference between his own structure of mind and body and that of the strange place and people below. Then with breathtaking abruptness, darkness dropped over him. One instant he lay serenely cradled in golden radiance, the next he was dropping through blackness with a queer, high scream in his ears as if he fell through some resisting atmosphere which was not air. Physically he was protected, but he could hear the thin sound of it in varying intensities.

And then without warning the darkness broke, and he found his feet upon solid ground without any hint of jar. He was simply standing upon a marble pavement under a clear blue sky and looking out over a breath-stopping vista of world-city, dropping away in terrace below shining terrace to a distant skyline, out and away in broadening tiers. Light shimmered dazzlingly upon faraway steel figures moving through the streets below, away and away until they were no more than tiny pinpricks of shimmer on the horizon's edge. From each broad circular terrace a marble ramp led down to the next beneath, and over these the steel-bright people were swarming in busy hordes.

And Dixon knew, even as he stared with caught breath at the magnificence of it, that in reality he stood at the apex of a city of madness that reeled away below him in tier after crazy tier, a nightmare of meaningless angles and raving color, through whose streets things writhing and dreadful and acrawl with living hues were flashing with movements of blurring speed. All this splendor was a veil across his eyes. What unknowable activities were really taking place below? On what nameless errands were these busy crowds bound? Then a little sound at his side turned him from the dizzy thoughts tormenting his brain, and he flashed an abrupt glance sidewise, alert for danger. Then he caught his breath and stared.

She was slim as a sword blade in her steel robe, standing under the mighty tower of the black pillar, and she was lovelier than a dream. Her hair swung in black page-boy curls to her shoulders, and from under the darkness of it eyes as blue as steel met his unwaveringly. She was all bright metal to his first glance, steel-molded curves of her under the armored robe, steel lights upon her burnished hair, steel-bright eyes shining. All steel and brightness—but Dixon saw that her mouth was soft and colored like hot embers. And for an instant he wanted to burst into crazy song. It was an inexplicable feeling that he had never known before, a heady delight in being alive. But even through the exultation, he knew that he looked upon an illusion. He knew that she was a faceless, crawling thing, without sex, without any remotest kinship to anything he knew. And yet this illusion was very lovely and—

She was looking up at him with startled eyes, and now she spoke, a little breathlessly, in a sweet, tinkling voice. "You—you have come? Oh, whence have you come?" And he thought that she was striving hard not to believe something which she wanted with all her soul to think true.

There was no answer he could give. He glanced around helplessly at the blue, empty sky, at the great pillar rising behind her, at the pale flame burning so steadily upon its summit. The blaze held him for an instant, and in the instant he stood with eyes uplifted the girl must have thought she had her answer, for she caught her breath in a gasp that was half a sob, and in one swift motion she fell to her knees before him, a miracle of sliding grace in that close gown of steel, so that the light rippled all down her sweet, slim body and lay bluely on the wings of her hair that swung forward as she bent her head.

"I knew it! I knew!" she breathed. "I knew my god would send you! Oh, praise great IL, who has sent me such an envoy!"

Dixon looked down upon the bent black head, his eyes troubled. If she believed him a messenger from the god, it would simplify his task enormously. And yet . . . He had entertained no scruples about displacing the god of a maniacal world peopled with writhing monstrosities, but this was different, somehow. This girl . . .

"I am the high priestess of our god," she murmured, as if in answer to his half-formed query. "I have served IL with all my heart for many cycles now, but only he knows who I have prayed for the coming of an envoy among us. Such honor is enough to—to—" The sweet voice choked suddenly on a sob, as if the answer to her prayer was too much for her to endure unmoved.

Dixon bent and took her chin in his hand, lifting her face to his. The steel-bright eyes were dazzling with diffused tears. The red mouth trembled. She was looking up at him with awe and worship upon her face, and suddenly he knew that he wanted no worship from her. He resented that look of respect and awe. He wanted—well, he wanted her to see a man, not a divine messenger. He wanted to—

Then the queerest madness came over him, deliciously—and he acted. He stooped swiftly and set his lips over the trembling red lips of the girl, and for an instant the whole strange world reeled and swam in a heady pleasure like nothing he had ever known before.

When he straightened and stood looking down upon her, she met his eyes with purest bewilderment in hers, one hand hovering at her lips and incomprehension radiant in every line of her. Her blue gaze was traveling over him from head to foot in swift, puzzled glances.

And then realization swept back upon him tremendously. To her he wore the writhing shape that was hers in reality. That troubled blue gaze was the gaze of a single pale eye which traveled over the crawling limbs of a monster. He was not even sure that, to her, kneeling denoted homage and wondered in what alien way she was actually expressing her awe.

It was an uncanny feeling which was to haunt him through all his hours here—the knowledge that what he looked upon was unreal, the wonder as to what was actually taking place behind the mask of humanity which only he could see. That kiss—how had it seemed to her? What nameless gesture had he seemed to perform before her eyes—her eye? For he had kissed a monstrosity that had no mouth. Remembering the glimpse he had caught of a one-eyed, featureless face crawling with alive colors, he shuddered and turned back to the kneeling girl as if for reassurance.

Dixon was aware of a curious emptiness within him because of this beauty which was only an illusion—had never been, would never be. He was looking straight into her steel-blue eyes now, and she was smiling very tremulously and with that puzzled look still upon her face. He could see the little shimmering tumult her heart made under the dazzle of her robe. And she was not even female He narrowed his eyes and strove to pierce the mirage for a moment; to convince himself that here knelt a colored horror of sinuosity and sexlessness. And everything within him cried out protestingly. She was human—she was lovely—she was everything desirable and sweet. And she did not even exist save as a crawling horror upon whom in her normal guise he could never dare to look.

Then, as if to refute that, she flashed up at him a small, uncertain smile which made her so unmistakably human and sweet that he disbelieved everything but her own reality, and she said, "What—what was the meaning of that, O divine envoy?"

He frowned. "You are to call me Dixon," he said. "And that was—well, just a form of greeting."

"The way they greet one another in great IL's domain —in Paradise? Then . . ." She rose in one swift motion. Before he realized what was happening she had risen upon her sandaled toes and her warm mouth was brushing his. "Then I return your greeting, O Dixon."

Involuntarily his arms closed around her. Her body was firm and soft and warm in his clasp—the body of a living human girl, a mirage more real than reality. And again he wondered what nameless rites she was actually performing behind the illusory veil which masked her real, writhing self. And because she felt so pleasant in his arms he released her abruptly and stepped back, knowing the first quickening of uneasiness. Good heaven, could it be possible for a man to fall in love with a hallucination?

She looked up at him serenely, evidently feeling that she had mastered a difficult point of divine etiquette.

"How pleasant a thing is this new way of greeting!" she murmured, half to herself. "And now, O Dixon, you have but to command me in all things. What would you in IL's world-city?"

Dixon debated swiftly with himself. After all, lovely though she seemed, she was—and he must bear this in mind constantly, lest something dangerous befall—she was a sinuous, faceless thing, a creeping horror with the tints of an incredible spectrum. She was no more than this, and he must find his way, by her help, into the god IL's temple and let the light-being look through his eyes so that he might find IL's vulnerable spot. After that— well, he must do as he was commanded. IL would be overthrown, his own sponsor would usurp the godship, and that would be all. As for these beings which peopled the world, no doubt the change of gods would be a startling thing, but there was no help for it. He had but to perform his own part and then go.

"O Dixon!" the sweet, light voice of the girl broke in upon his thoughts. "O Dixon, would you see how IL's temple is kept by his worshipers? Would you see how devoutly his world adores him?"

"Yes," said Dixon thankfully. "You may lead me to IL's temple."

She genuflected again, a poem of grace in that steel gown along which the light slid in long lines as she moved, and the dark hair swung forward about her face. Then she turned and crossed the terrace toward a ramp which led down into the city. They went down the slope of it—what eye-tormenting angles of spanning actually led downward he could not even guess—and emerged upon a broad street lined with pillared buildings. There were throngs of steel-robed people here who parted in devout rows as the priestess came down the ramp.

She paused at the head of the street and lifted her arms, and Dixon heard her voice ringing clearly over the crowd. "Great IL has answered our prayers at last," she cried. "He has sent us an envoy from his own divinity. Here is the messenger from our god!"

A murmur went over the crowd—a murmur of awe and rejoicing. And then they knelt in long, sinuous rows as if a wind had blown across a field of sword blades. And with incredible swiftness the whisper ran back along the street, from mouth to mouth. He imagined it rippling out and out, down and down, from terrace to terrace, until it reached the ultimate limits of the whole tiered world.

They stepped down among the kneeling throngs, walking a lane of steel worshipers, and by the time they had reached the end of the street Dixon could see flecks of light far away below hurrying upward as the news spread. Up through the pillared streets and the green terraces they came swarming, men and women in robes of linked metal, with intent, awe-struck faces upturned. Dixon moved on with a long stride, a divine messenger from a god marching in triumph through a city without ends or boundaries, for as far as he could see the steel flecks that were people flashed up through the buildings below. And their multitudes were breathtaking. The whole vast city swarmed with living steel as wave after wave of armored people rolled upward toward the heights. His brain reeled with the numbers of them.

Over the bowed heads of the throngs as they advanced, Dixon glanced curiously at the buildings which lined the streets, casting about for some clue to the sort of life those people led. He found nothing. The marble pillars and walls rose as blankly as stage sets along the streets. A mask had been set for him over the realities of the place, but it was not a living mask. There were no shops, no markets, no residences. Rows of noncommittal pillars faced him blankly, betraying no secrets. Apparently the light-being had been unable to do more than mask the strangeness of this world. It could not infuse into it the spirit of a daily life so utterly alien as man's.

They went on through the dead-faced streets, down another ramp, and always the people dropped to their knees, perfectly the illusion of humanity. What, he wondered, were they actually doing? In what weird, incredible way were they really expressing their devotion? It was, of course, better not to know.

Dixon watched the girl before him walking proudly and lightly through the homage-stricken throngs, her dark head high, the steel robe rippling over the loveliness of her body as she moved. Presently she paused for him, smiling over her shoulder in a way that made his heart quicken, and turned in under the great arch of a doorway.

It was not a particularly imposing structure; no more than a marble-columned building with a huge dark portal. But, once inside, Dixon stopped in stunned astonishment at the vastness spread out before him.

It must have occupied the whole interior of all the terraces above—a mighty dome about which the buildings and streets overhead were the merest shell. In the dimness he could not descry the limits of it, but he saw that the whole vast temple was built in the shape of a great dome. For temple it must be. He knew that instinctively. There was the shadow of divinity in it, somehow—a vast calm. And for an instant, as he stared about the great place, he forgot even the presence of the girl at his side.

In the very center of the wide, dark floor lay a pool of pale radiance which somehow gave the impression that it seethed and boiled, though its surface lay untroubled under the lofty dome of the roof. And above the pool the ceiling was shaped like a burning lens to gather and concentrate the radiance arising from it. This centered at the apex of the roof in a dazzle of light at which he could not look directly. He realized that the center of this burning brilliance must be just under the pillar which crowned the topmost terrace—the pillar upon which burned the flame of IL.

Beyond the column of light rising from the pool, Dixon saw dimly in the gloom of the great temple the glimmer of steel robes. There was an arch in the far wall, so distant he could scarcely make it out, and in this doorway a small steel figure stood. As he watched, the sonorous boom of a gong rang through the dimness. The air trembled with sound, and through the shaking twilight the figure stepped out resolutely, crossing the floor with even, unhurried strides. He could not tell at the distance if it was man or woman, but it approached the radiant pool with, somehow, a sort of restrained eagerness that he was at a loss to understand. It reached the brink and did not pause. The haze of light rising from the pool swallowed it without a flicker. And the great dome was empty again save for themselves.

Dixon turned, awe-struck, to the girl, questions hovering on his mouth. Just in time he remembered his role and rephrased the query: "And how do you interpret this, priestess?"

She smiled up at him bewilderingly. It irritated him that his heart made that odd little leap whenever she smiled so, and he missed the first of her answer in watching the way her lips moved to frame the words she spoke.

". . . continually, at every beat of the signal," she was saying, "so that there is never an interval through all time when one of us has not completed his cycles and is ready to return into the flame." The gong sounded above her light voice. "See? Here comes another. And for countless ages it has been so, for our numbers are great enough so that the stream of voluntary sacrifices need never falter. So we nourish IL's flame and keep it burning."

Dixon said nothing. His eyes were upon her, but the bright illusion was swimming curiously in a mist that was closing down over him, and he was becoming aware of a strange pulsing of his own blood, as if—yes, as if familiar waves of knowledge were beginning their beat through his receptive brain. For a timeless interval he stood rigid, receiving that intelligence, feeling all he had seen and heard draining out of him into the vast reservoir of knowledge which was the light-being, feeling the voiceless commands of it flowing in. Ripple after ripple of the incoming tide rose in his brain. And gradually, in measured beats, he learned that this pool was the source of the pale flame burning upon the pillar, but that it was not essentially a part of it. The god IL drew his power from the dissolving lives of those people who sacrificed themselves—and this was the only way to destroy them, for they could not die otherwise—but IL was not present in the pool. IL was the flame on the column, no more, feeding upon the reflection from below. And if the rising light could be cut off temporarily IL's power would fail at its source. The invader could make an entrance and fight it out with him.

And now for an instant all the thought flow ceased; then in sharply clear ripples of intense emphasis came the syllables of a word. It was a word without meaning to Dixon, a word whose very sounds were unlike those of any language that man speaks. But he knew that he must speak it, and that the cadences of the sound would somehow open the way for the light-being to enter. With the impression of that word upon him the ripples ceased. A profound quiet reigned in his mind.

Out of that quiet the great domed temple slowly took form about him again. He heard the gong notes trembling through the air and saw another steel-robed figure pacing toward the pool. He turned his head and looked down into the high priestess' face at his shoulder. He had only to speak the word now and accomplish IL's overthrow—and then leave. Leave her—never see her again, except perhaps in dreams.

Her eyes met his with a little kindling under the blueness of them, and her mouth trembled into a smile as she met his gaze. She had the look of one eager and taut and waiting, and there was perfect faith in her eyes. And in that instant he knew he could not betray it.

"No," he murmured aloud. "No, my dear; I can't—I simply can't do it!"

Her brows drew together in exquisite bewilderment. "Do what?" she asked in a light whisper, to match his own lowered tone. "Do what?" But somehow the answer seemed not to interest her, for she did not pause for a reply. She had met his eyes and was staring up in a sort of dazed surprise, her blue gaze plunging into his with rigid intensity. And slowly she began to speak, in a tiny, breathless murmur. "I think . . . I think I see, O Dixon, the strangest things . . . in your eyes. Dreadful things and shapes without meaning . . . and something like a veil between us. . . . Dixon . . . nothing is clear . . . and yet—and yet, Dixon, my own face is looking back at me out of your eyes."

He caught his breath suddenly in a painful gasp, and in one involuntary motion he had her in his arms. She clung to him blindly. He could feel the trembling that shivered through her steel-sheathed body, and her heart's pounding shook them both.

"I am afraid, Dixon—I am afraid!" she wailed softly. "What is it that frightens me so, Dixon?"

He did not answer. There was no answer. But he hugged her close and felt the sweet firmness of her body against his and knew helplessly that he loved the illusion that was herself and would always love it.

Dixon was frightened, too; frightened at the depth of the emotion that shook him, for he was remembering the clinging of her soft mouth to his, and how beautifully her body curved under the embrace of her metal robe, and that the loveliness which filled his arms and his heart was no more than an illusion to mask something so grotesque that he could never bear to look upon it unmasked. Lovely body, lovely face, sweet, warm mouth upon his—was this all? Could love rise from no more than a scrap of beautifully shaped flesh? Could any man love more than that with such intensity as shook him now?

He loosed her from one arm and set his finger under her chin, lifting her face to his. Her eyes met his own, blue and puzzled and afraid, and shining with something very splendid which all but blotted out her bewilderment and her terror.

"I love you," he murmured. "I don't care—I love you."

"Love?" she echoed in her light whisper. "Love?" And he saw in her eyes that the word had no meaning for her.

The room reeled about him for an instant. Somehow he had never thought of that. Knowing as he did of the immense gulf between them and the strangeness of the emotions which swayed these creatures of such alien race, yet it had not occurred to him that anywhere throughout the cosmos where living beings dwelt there could be a species to which love had no meaning. Was she, then, incapable of feeling it? Good heaven, was he doomed to love an empty body, soulless, the mirage masking a sexless being who could not return any emotion he knew?

He looked down and saw the diffused radiance behind her eyes, shining and very tender, and the bewilderment upon her face, and he thought, somehow, that he was hovering on the very brink of something vaster than anything he had ever known before—an idea too splendid to be grasped. Yet when he looked down into her eyes he thought he understood—almost—

Suddenly all about him the world trembled. It was as if the whole vast place were the reflection in a pool, and a ripple had passed blurringly over the surface. Then everything righted itself. But he understood. He had been here too long. The veil between him and this alien world was wearing thin.

"No—I *can't* go!" he groaned and gripped the girl closer in his arms.

He must have spoken aloud, for he felt her stir against him and heard her anxious voice. "Go? O Dixon, Dixon—take me with you! Don't leave me, Dixon!"

Some fantastic hope flowered suddenly within him. "Why not?" he demanded. "Why not? Tell me!" And he shook her a little in his urgency.

"I don't know," she faltered. "I only know that—that —O Dixon, that I shall be so lonely when you have gone. Take me—please take me!"

"Why?" he demanded inexorably. For he thought now that he was hovering very near the understanding of the vast and splendid thing which had almost dawned upon him before the world shook.

"Because I . . . because . . . I don't understand it, Dixon, I can't tell you why—I haven't the words. But since you came I—is it that I have been waiting for you always? For I never knew until you came how lonely I had been. And I cannot let you go without me. O Dixon, is this what you call love?"

There was pain in her voice and in her veiled eyes. And the thought came to him that love was like an infectious germ, spreading pain wherever it rooted itself. Had he brought it to her—infected her, too, with the hopeless passion he knew? For it was wildly hopeless. In a moment or so he must leave this alien place forever, and no power existent could maintain very long the illusory veil through which they knew love.

Could his own new love for her endure the sight of her real self? And what would happen to this strange flowering of an emotion nameless and unknown to her —her love for him? Could it bear the look of his human shape, unmasked? And yet, he asked himself desperately, could a love as deep and sincere as the love he bore her be so transient a thing that he could not endure the sight of her in another guise? Could—

Again that queer flickering flashed over the world. Dixon felt the ground underfoot tilt dangerously, and for a moment insane colors stabbed at his eyes and the whole room reeled and staggered. Then it was still again. He had scarcely noticed. He swung her around to face him, gripping her shoulders and staring down compellingly into her eyes.

"Listen!" he said rapidly, for he knew his time was limited now, perhaps to seconds. "Listen! Have you any idea what you are asking?"

"Only to go with you," she said. "To be with you, wherever you are. And if you are indeed IL's messenger —perhaps a part of his godhead—then shall I enter the flame and give myself to IL? In that way can I join you and be one with you?"

He shook his head. "I am not from IL. I have been sent to destroy him. I'm a man from a world so different from yours that you could never bear to look upon me in my real form. You see me as an illusion, just as I see you. And I must go back to my own world now— alone."

Her eyes were dizzy with trying to understand.

"You are—not from IL? Not as you seem? Another world? Oh, but take me with you! I must go—I must!"

"But, my dearest, I can't. Don't you understand? You couldn't live an instant in my world—nor I much longer in yours."

"Then I will die," she said calmly. "I will enter the flame and wait for you in death. I will wait forever."

"My darling, not even that." He said it gently. "Not even in death can we be together. For when you die you go back to IL, and I go—I go—back to another god, perhaps. I don't know. But not to IL."

She stood, blank-eyed, in his grasp, trying to force her mind into the incredible belief. When she spoke, the words came slowly, as if her thoughts were speaking aloud.

"I don't understand," she said. "But I know . . . you speak the truth. If I die by the flame—in the only way there is for me to die—we are parted forever. I can't! I won't! I will not let you go! Listen to me—" and her voice dropped to a soft whisper—"you say you came to destroy IL? Why?"

"As the envoy of another god, who would take his place."

"I have given my whole life to the worship of IL," she murmured to herself, very gently. And then, in a stronger voice: "But destroy him, Dixon! There may be a chance that way—there is none now. Oh, I may be a traitor—worse than a traitor. There is no word to describe one who betrays his god into destruction, no word terrible enough. But I would do it—yes, gladly, now. Destroy him, and let me seek another death somewhere, somehow—let me die as you die. Perhaps your god can release me into your sort of death, and I can wait for you there until you come. Oh, Dixon, please!"

The idea was a staggering one, but for a wild moment Dixon knew hope again. Might it not be that—that—

Quite suddenly he understood. He looked down on the loveliness of her with unseeing eyes. In these past few moments of insanity, learning that she loved him, too, enough that she begged death of him if in that way they might be united, in these few moments he came to realize that the flesh meant nothing. It was not her body he loved. And a great relief flooded him, to be sure that—sure that it was not merely infatuation, or desire for the loveliness which did not exist save as a mirage before his eyes. No, it was love, truly and completely, despite the shape she wore, despite the nameless sex that was hers. Love for herself—the essential self, however deeply buried beneath whatever terrible guise. And though her very substance was alien to him, and though no creature in all her ancestry had ever known love before, she loved him. Nothing else mattered.

And then without warning the great dome before him wavered and contorted into impossible angles, like the reflections in a flawed mirror. And Dixon felt the firm curved body in his arms melting fluidly into a different form and texture. It squirmed . . .

He stood at the entrance to a mighty room that staggered with frantic color, reeling with eye-stunning angles and incredible planes. And in his arms— He looked down. He clasped a creature at which he could not bear to look directly, a thing whose wild-looped limbs and sinuous body rippled and crawled with the moving tints of madness. It was slippery and horrible to the touch, and from the midst of a shifting, featureless face a great lucid eye stared up at him with desperate horror, as if it was looking upon something so frightful that the very sight was enough to unseat its reason.

Dixon closed his eyes after that one revolting glimpse, but he had seen in the eye upturned to him enough of dawning comprehension to be sure it was she whom he held. And he thought that despite the utter strangeness of that one staring eye there was somewhere in the clarity of it, and the steadfastness, a glimmer of the innermost spark which was the being he loved—that spark which had looked from the blue gaze he had seen in its human shape. With that inner spark of life she was the same.

He tightened his grip upon her—or it—though his flesh crept at the contact and he knew that the feel was as revolting to it as to himself, and looked out over that shallow, color-stained head upon the vast room before him. His eyes throbbed savagely from those fierce colors never meant for human eyes to see. And though the creature in his arms hung acquiescent, he knew the effort it must cost to preserve that calm.

A lump rose in his throat as he realized the significance of that—such utter faith in him, though he wore a shape terrible enough to bring the fear of madness into that great lucid eye when it rested upon him. But he knew he could not stand there long and retain his own sanity. Already the colors were raving almost audibly through his brain, and the ground heaved underfoot, and he was sure that neither of them could endure much more of this. So he gripped the dreadful thing which housed the being he loved, and almost of itself he felt that incredibly alien word rip itself from his lips.

It was not a word to be set down in any written characters. Its sound to his ears was vague and indeterminate, like a whisper heard over too great distances to have any form. But the moment it left his lips he felt a vast, imponderable shifting in the substance of the temple. And, like a shutter's closing, the room went black. Dixon gave one involuntary sob of relief as the maniacal colors ceased their assault upon his brain, and he felt the dreadful thing in his arms go rigid in the utter blackness. For a moment everything was still as death.

And then through the dark around them a tiny shiver ran, the least little stir of motion, the thinnest thread of sound. It pierced Dixon's very eardrums and shuddered thrillingly along his nerves. And with incredible swiftness that tiny stirring and that infinitesimal sound grew and swelled and ballooned into a maelstrom of rushing tumult, louder and louder, shriller and shriller. Around them in the blackness swooped and stormed the sounds of a mightier conflict than any living man could ever have heard before—a battle of gods, invisible in the blackness of utter void.

That stunning uproar mounted and intensified until he thought his head would burst with the infinite sound of it, and forces beyond comprehension stormed through the air. The floor seemed to dissolve under him, and space whirled in the dark so that he was conscious of neither up nor down. The air raved and shrieked. Blind and deafened and stunned by the magnitude of the conflict, Dixon hugged his dreadful burden and waited.

How long it went on he never knew. He was trying to think as the turmoil raged around his head, trying to guess what would come next; if the light-being in its victory could unite them in any way, in life or in death. He could think of that quite calmly now, death and union. For life without her, he knew unquestioningly, would be a sort of living death, alone and waiting. Living was where she was, and if she were dead, then life lay only in death for him. His head reeled with the wild wonderings and with the noise of battle raving about them both. For eternities, it seemed to him, the whole universe was a maelstrom, insanity shrieked in his ears, and all the powers of darkness swooped and screamed through the void about him. But, after an endless while, very gradually he began to realize that the tumult was abating. The roaring in his ears faded slowly; the wild forces storming through the dark diminished. By infinite degree the uproar died away. Presently again the stillness of death descended through the blackness upon the two who waited.

There was a long interval of silence, nerve-racking, ear-tormenting. And then, at long last, out of that darkness and silence spoke a voice, vast and bodiless and serene. And it was not the voice of the light-being. It spoke audibly in Dixon's brain, not in words, but in some nameless speech which used instead of syllables some series of thought forms that were intelligible to him.

"My chosen priestess," said the voice passionlessly, "so you would have had me destroyed?"

Dixon felt the convulsive start of the creature in his arms and realized dimly that the same wordless speech, then, was intelligible to them both. He realized that only vaguely, with one corner of his mind, for he was stunned and overwhelmed with the realization that it must be the god IL speaking—that his own sponsor had been overcome.

"And you, Dixon," the voice went on evenly, "sent by my enemy to open the way. You are a very alien creature, Dixon. Only by the power I wrested from that being which assaulted me can I perceive you at all, and your mind is a chaos to me. What spell have you cast over my chosen priestess, so that she no longer obeys me?"

"Have you never heard of love?" demanded Dixon aloud.

The query faded into the thick darkness without an echo, and a profound stillness followed in its wake. He stood in the blind dark and utter silence, clutching his love, waiting. Out of that quiet the god-voice came at last:

"Love"—in a musing murmur. "Love—no! there is no such thing in all my universe. What is it?"

Dixon stood helpless, mutely trying to frame an answer. For who can define love? He groped for the thought forms, and very stumblingly he tried to explain, knowing as he did so that it was as much for the benefit of her he held in his arms as for the god, because, although she loved, she could not know the meaning of love, or what it meant to him. When he had ceased, the silence fell again heavily.

At last IL said, "So—the reigning principle of your own system and dimension. I understand that much. But there is no such thing here. Why should it concern you? Love is a thing between the two sexes of your own race. This priestess of mine is of another sex than those you understand. There can be no such thing as this love between you."

"Yet I saw her first in the form of a woman," said Dixon. "And I love her."

"You love the image."

"At first it may be that I did. But now—no; there's much more of it than that. We may be alien to the very atoms. Our minds may be alien, and all our thoughts, and even our souls. But, after all, alien though we are, that alienage is of superficial things. Stripped down to the barest elemental beginning, we have one kinship— we share life. We are individually alive, animate, free-willed. Somewhere at the very core of our beings is the one vital spark of life, which in the last analysis is *self*, and with that one spark we love each other."

The deepest silence fell again when he had ended—a silence of the innermost brain.

Out of it at last IL said, "And you, my priestess? What do you say? Do you love him?"

Dixon felt the shape in his arms shudder uncontrollably. She—he could not think of her as "it"—stood in the very presence of her god, heard him address her in the black blindness of his presence, and the awe and terror of it was almost enough to shake her brain. But after a moment she answered in a small, faltering murmur, the very ghost of a reply, and in some curious mode of speech which was neither vocal nor entirely thought transfer. "I—I do not know that word, O mighty IL. I know only that there is no living for me outside his presence. I would have betrayed your godhead to free me, so that I might die in his way of death, and meet him again beyond—if there can be any beyond for us. I would do all this again without any hesitation if the choice was given me. If this is what you call love—yes; I love him."

"He is," said IL, "a creature of another race and world and dimension. You have seen his real form, and you know."

"I do not understand that," said the priestess in a surer voice. "I know nothing except that I cannot—will not live with him. It is not his body I . . . love, nor do I know what it is which commands me so. I know only that I do love him."

"And I you," said Dixon. It was a very strange sensation to be addressing her thus, from brain to brain. "The sight of you was dreadful to me, and I know how I must have looked to you. But the shock of that sight has taught me something. I know now. The shape you wear and the shape you seemed to wear before I saw you in reality are both illusions, both no more than garments which clothe that . . . that living, vital entity which is yourself—the real you. And your body does not matter to me now, for I know that it is no more than a mirage."

"Yes," she murmured. "Yes, I understand. You are right. The bodies do not matter now. It goes so much deeper than that."

"And what," broke in the voice of IL, "is your solution of this problem?"

It was Dixon who broke the silence that fell in mute answer to the query. "There can be no such thing as union for us anywhere in life. In death, perhaps—but I do not know. Do you?"

"No," said IL surprisingly.

"You—you do not? You—a god?"

"No. I have taken these beings who worship me back into the flame. The energy which was theirs in life supports me—but something escapes. I do not know what. Something too intangible even for me to guess at. No—I am a god, and I do not know what comes after death."

Dixon pondered that for a long while. There was an implication in it somewhere which gave him hope, but his brain was so dazed he could not grasp it. At last the light broke, and he said joyfully, "Then—why, then you cannot keep us apart! We can die and be free."

"Yes. I have no hold over you. Even if I would wreak vengeance upon you for your part in my betrayal, I could not. For death will release you into—I do not know what. But it will be release."

Dixon swallowed hard. Half-doubts and hesitations crowded his mind, but he heard his own voice saying steadily, "Will you do that for us—release us?"

In the silence as he waited for an answer he was trying to realize that he stood on the threshold of death; trying to understand, his mind probing ahead eagerly for the answer which might lie beyond. And in the timeless moment he waited he was very sure, for whatever lay ahead could not be extinction and surely not separation. This was the beginning; surely it could not end so soon, unfulfilled, all the questions unanswered.

No; this love which linked them, two beings so alien, could not flicker out with their lives. It was too great—too splendid, far too strong. He was no longer uncertain, no longer afraid, and hope began to torment him exquisitely. What lay beyond? What vast existences? What starry adventures, together? Almost impatiently he poised on the brink of death.

Through this IL's voice spoke with a vast, passionless calm. "Die, then," said IL.

For an instant the darkness lay unbroken about them. Then a little flicker ran indescribably through it. The air shook for a breathless moment.

And IL was alone.

Black God's Kiss

THEY BROUGHT IN Joiry's tall commander, struggling between two men-at-arms who tightly gripped the ropes which bound their captive's mailed arms. They picked their way between mounds of dead as they crossed the great hall toward the dais where the conqueror sat, and twice they slipped a little in the blood that spattered the flags. When they came to a halt before the mailed figure on the dais, Joiry's commander was breathing hard, and the voice that echoed hollowly under the helmet's confines was hoarse with fury and despair.

Guillaume the conqueror leaned on his mighty sword, hands crossed on its hilt, grinning down from his height upon the furious captive before him. He was a big man, Guillaume, and he looked bigger still in his spattered armor. There was blood on his hard, scarred face, and he was grinning a white grin that split his short, curly beard glitteringly. Very splendid and very dangerous he looked, leaning on his great sword and smiling down upon fallen Joiry's lord, struggling between the stolid men-at-arms.

"Unshell me this lobster," said Guillaume in his deep, lazy voice. "We'll see what sort of face the fellow has who gave us such a battle. Off with his helmet, you."

But a third man had to come up and slash the straps which held the iron helmet on, for the struggles of Joiry's commander were too fierce, even with bound arms, for either of the guards to release their hold. There was a moment of sharp struggle; then the straps parted and the helmet rolled loudly across the flagstones.

Guillaume's white teeth clicked on a startled oath. He

stared. Joiry's lady glared back at him from between her captors, wild red hair tousled, wild lion-yellow eyes ablaze.

"God curse you!" snarled the lady of Joiry between clenched teeth. "God blast your black heart!"

Guillaume scarcely heard her. He was still staring, as most men stared when they first set eyes upon Jirel of Joiry. She was tall as most men, and as savage as the wildest of them, and the fall of Joiry was bitter enough to break her heart as she stood snarling curses up at her tall conqueror. The face above her mail might not have been fair in a woman's head-dress, but in the steel setting of her armor it had a biting, sword-edge beauty as keen as the flash of blades. The red hair was short upon her high, defiant head, and the yellow blaze of her eyes held fury as a crucible holds fire.

Guillaume's stare melted into a slow smile. A little light kindled behind his eyes as he swept the long, strong lines of her with a practised gaze. The smile broadened, and suddenly he burst into full-throated laughter, a deep bull bellow of amusement and delight.

"By the Nails!" he roared. "Here's welcome for the warrior! And what forfeit d'ye offer, pretty one, for your life?"

She blazed a curse at him.

"So? Naughty words for a mouth so fair, my lady. Well, we'll not deny you put up a gallant battle. No man could have done better, and many have done worse. But against Guillaume—" He inflated his splendid chest and grinned down at her from the depths of his jutting beard. "Come to me, pretty one," he commanded. "I'll wager your mouth is sweeter than your words."

Jirel drove a spurred heel into the shin of one guard and twisted from his grip as he howled, bringing up an iron knee into the abdomen of the other. She had writhed from their grip and made three long strides toward the door before Guillaume caught her. She felt his arms closing about her from behind, and lashed out with both spiked heels in a futile assault upon his leg armor, twisting like a maniac, fighting with her knees and spurs, straining hopelessly at the ropes which bound her arms. Guillaume laughed and whirled her round, grinning

down into the blaze of her yellow eyes. Then deliberately he set a fist under her chin and tilted her mouth up to
his. There was a cessation of her hoarse curses.

"By Heaven, that's like kissing a sword-blade," said
Guillaume, lifting his lips at last.

Jirel choked something that was mercifully muffled as
she darted her head sidewise, like a serpent striking, and
sank her teeth into his neck. She missed the jugular by a
fraction of an inch.

Guillaume said nothing, then. He sought her head
with a steady hand, found it despite her wild writhing,
sank iron fingers deep into the hinges of her jaw, forcing
her teeth relentlessly apart. When he had her free he
glared down into the yellow hell of her eyes for an instant. The blaze of them was hot enough to scorch his
scarred face. He grinned and lifted his ungauntleted
hand, and with one heavy blow in the face he knocked
her halfway across the room. She lay still upon the flags.

Jirel opened her yellow eyes upon darkness. She lay
quiet for a while, collecting her scattered thoughts. By
degrees it came back to her, and she muffled upon her
arm a sound that was half curse and half sob. Joiry had
fallen. For a time she lay rigid in the dark, forcing herself to the realization.

The sound of feet shifting on stone near by brought
her out of that particular misery. She sat up cautiously,
feeling about her to determine in what part of Joiry its
liege lady was imprisoned. She knew that the sound she
had heard must be a sentry, and by the dank smell of
the darkness that she was underground. In one of the little dungeon cells, of course. With careful quietness she
got to her feet, muttering a curse as her head reeled for
an instant and then began to throb. In the utter dark she
felt around the cell. Presently she came to a little wood-
en stool in a corner, and was satisfied. She gripped one
leg of it with firm fingers and made her soundless way
around the wall until she had located the door.

The sentry remembered, afterward, that he had heard
the wildest shriek for help which had ever rung in his
ears, and he remembered unbolting the door. Afterward,

until they found him lying inside the locked cell with a cracked skull, he remembered nothing.

Jirel crept up the dark stairs of the north turret, murder in her heart. Many little hatreds she had known in her life, but no such blaze as this. Before her eyes in the night she could see Guillaume's scornful, scarred face laughing, the little jutting beard split with the whiteness of his mirth. Upon her mouth she felt the remembered weight of his, about her the strength of his arms. And such a blast of hot fury came over her that she reeled a little and clutched at the wall for support. She went on in a haze of red anger, and something like madness burning in her brain as a resolve slowly took shape out of the chaos of her hate. When that thought came to her she paused again, mid-step upon the stairs, and was conscious of a little coldness blowing over her. Then it was gone, and she shivered a little, shook her shoulders and grinned wolfishly, and went on.

By the stars she could see through the arrow-slits in the wall it must be near to midnight. She went softly on the stairs, and she encountered no one. Her little tower room at the top was empty. Even the straw pallet where the serving-wench slept had not been used that night. Jirel got herself out of her armor alone, somehow, after much striving and twisting. Her doeskin shirt was stiff with sweat and stained with blood. She tossed it disdainfully into a corner. The fury in her eyes had cooled now to a contained and secret flame. She smiled to herself as she slipped a fresh shirt of doeskin over her tousled red head and donned a brief tunic of link-mail. On her legs she buckled the greaves of some forgotten legionary, relic of the not long past days when Rome still ruled the world. She thrust a dagger through her belt and took her own long two-handed sword bare-bladed in her grip. Then she went down the stairs again.

She knew there must have been revelry and feasting in the great hall that night, and by the silence hanging so heavily now she was sure that most of her enemies lay still in drunken slumber, and she experienced a swift regret for the gallons of her good French wine so wasted. And the thought flashed through her head that a determined woman with a sharp sword might work some little damage among the drunken sleepers before she was overpowered. But she put that idea by, for Guillaume would have posted sentries to spare, and she must not give up her secret freedom so fruitlessly.

Down the dark stairs she went, and crossed one corner of the vast central hall whose darkness she was sure hid wine-deadened sleepers, and so into the lesser dimness of the rough little chapel that Joiry boasted. She had been sure she would find Father Gervase there, and she was not mistaken. He rose from his knees before the altar, dark in his robe, the starlight through the narrow window shining upon his tonsure.

"My daughter!" he whispered. "My daughter! How have you escaped? Shall I find you a mount? If you can pass the sentries you should be in your cousin's castle by daybreak."

She hushed him with a lifted hand.

"No," she said. "It is not outside I go this night. I have a more perilous journey even than that to make. Shrive me, father."

He stared at her.

"What is it?"

She dropped to her knees before him and gripped the rough cloth of his habit with urgent fingers.

"Shrive me, I say! I go down into hell tonight to pray the devil for a weapon, and it may be I shall not return."

Gervase bent and gripped her shoulders with hands that shook.

"Look at me!" he demanded. "Do you know what you're saying? You go—"

"Down!" She said it firmly. "Only you and I know that passage, father—and not even we can be sure of what lies beyond. But to gain a weapon against that man I would venture into perils even worse than that."

"If I thought you meant it," he whispered, "I would waken Guillaume now and give you into his arms. It would be a kinder fate, my daughter."

"It's that I would walk through hell to escape," she whispered back fiercely. "Can't you see? Oh, God knows I'm not innocent of the ways of light loving—but to be any man's fancy, for a night or two, before he snaps my neck or sells me into slavery—and above all, if that man were Guillaume! Can't you understand?"

"That would be shame enough," nodded Gervase. "But think, Jirel! For that shame there is atonement and absolution, and for that death the gates of heaven open wide. But this other—Jirel, Jirel, never through all eternity may you come out, body or soul, if you venture —down!"

She shrugged.

"To wreak my vengeance upon Guillaume I would go if I knew I should burn in hell forever."

"But Jirel, I do not think you understand. This is a worse fate than the deepest depths of hell-fire. This is —this is beyond all the bounds of the hells we know. And I think Satan's hottest flames were, the breath of paradise, compared to what may befall there."

"I know. Do you think I'd venture down if I could not be sure? Where else would I find such a weapon as I need, save outside God's dominion?"

"Jirel, you shall not!"

"Gervase, I go! Will you shrive me?" The hot yellow eyes blazed into his, lambent in the starlight.

After a moment he dropped his head. "You are my lady. I will give you God's blessing, but it will not avail you—there."

She went down into the dungeons again. She went down a long way through utter dark, over stones that were oozy and odorous with moisture, through blackness that had never known the light of day. She might have been a little afraid at other times, but that steady flame of hatred burning behind her eyes was a torch to light the way, and she could not wipe from her memory the feel of Guillaume's arms about her, the scornful press of his lips on her mouth. She whimpered a little, low in her throat, and a hot gust of hate went over her.

In the solid blackness she came at length to a wall, and she set herself to pulling the loose stones from this with her free hand, for she would not lay down the sword. They had never been laid in mortar, and they came out easily. When the way was clear she stepped through and found her feet upon a downward-sloping ramp of smooth stone. She cleared the rubble away from the hole in the wall, and enlarged it enough for a quick passage; for when she came back this way—if she did —it might well be that she would come very fast.

At the bottom of the slope she dropped to her knees on the cold floor and felt about. Her fingers traced the outline of a circle, the veriest crack in the stone. She felt until she found the ring in its center. That ring was of the coldest metal she had ever known, and the smoothest. She could put no name to it. The daylight had never shone upon such metal.

She tugged. The stone was reluctant, and at last she took her sword in her teeth and put both hands to the lifting. Even then it taxed the limit of her strength, and she was strong as many men. But at last it rose, with the strangest sighing sound, and a little prickle of goose-flesh rippled over her.

Now she took the sword back into her hand and knelt on the rim of the invisible blackness below. She had gone this path once before and once only, and never thought to find any necessity in life strong enough to drive her down again. The way was the strangest she had ever known. There was, she thought, no such passage in all the world save here. It had not been built for human feet to travel. It had not been built for feet at all. It was a narrow, polished shaft that cork-screwed round and round. A snake might have slipped in it and gone shooting down, round and round in dizzy circles—but no snake on earth was big enough to fill that shaft. No human travelers had worn the sides of the spiral so smooth, and she did not care to speculate on what creatures had polished it so, through what ages of passage.

She might never have made that first trip down, nor anyone after her, had not some unknown human hacked the notches which made it possible to descend slowly; that is, she thought it must have been a human. At any rate, the notches were roughly shaped for hands and feet, and spaced not too far apart; but who and when and how she could not even guess. As to the beings who made the shaft, in long-forgotten ages—well, there were devils on earth before man, and the world was very old.

She turned on her face and slid feet-first into the curving tunnel. That first time she and Gervase had gone down in sweating terror of what lay below, and with devils tugging at their heels. Now she slid easily, not bothering to find toeholds, but slipping swiftly round and round the long spirals with only her hands to break the speed when she went too fast. Round and round she went, round and round.

It was a long way down. Before she had gone very far the curious dizziness she had known before came over her again, a dizziness not entirely induced by the spirals she whirled around, but a deeper, atomic unsteadiness as if not only she but also the substances around her were shifting. There was something queer about the angles of those curves. She was no scholar in geometry or aught else, but she felt intuitively that the bend and slant of the way she went were somehow outside any other angles or bends she had ever known. They led into the unknown and the dark, but it seemed to her obscurely that they led into deeper darkness and mystery than the merely physical, as if, though she could not put it clearly even into thoughts, the peculiar and exact lines of the tunnel had been carefully angled to lead through poly-dimensional space as well as through the underground—perhaps through time, too. She did not know she was thinking such things; but all about her was a blurred dizziness as she shot down and round, and she knew that the way she went took her on a stranger journey than any other way she had ever traveled.

Down, and down. She was sliding fast, but she knew how long it would be. On that first trip they had taken alarm as the passage spiraled so endlessly and with thoughts of the long climb back had tried to stop before it was too late. They had found it impossible. Once embarked, there was no halting. She had tried, and such waves of sick blurring had come over her that she came near to unconsciousness. It was as if she had tried to halt some inexorable process of nature, half finished. They could only go on. The very atoms of their bodies shrieked in rebellion against a reversal of the change.

And the way up, when they returned, had not been difficult. They had had visions of a back-breaking climb up interminable curves, but again the uncanny difference of those angles from those they knew was manifested. In a queer way they seemed to defy gravity, or perhaps led through some way outside the power of it. They had been sick and dizzy on the return, as on the way down, but through the clouds of that confusion it had seemed to them that they slipped as easily up the shaft as they had gone down; or perhaps that, once in the tunnel, there was neither up nor down.

The passage leveled gradually. This was the worst part for a human to travel, though it must have eased the speed of whatever beings the shaft was made for. It was too narrow for her to turn in, and she had to lever herself face down and feet first, along the horizontal smoothness of the floor, pushing with her hands. She was glad when her questing heels met open space and she slid from the mouth of the shaft and stood upright in the dark.

Here she paused to collect herself. Yes, this was the beginning of the long passage she and Father Gervase had traveled on that long-ago journey of exploration. By the veriest accident they had found the place, and only the veriest bravado had brought them thus far. He had gone on a greater distance than she—she was younger then, and more amenable to authority—and had come back white-faced in the torchlight and hurried her up the shaft again.

She went on carefully, feeling her way, remembering what she herself had seen in the darkness a little farther on, wondering in spite of herself, and with a tiny catch at her heart, what it was that had sent Father Gervase so hastily back. She had never been entirely satisfied with his explanations. It had been about here—or was it a little farther on? The stillness was like a roaring in her ears.

Then ahead of her the darkness moved. It was just that—a vast, imponderable shifting of the solid dark. Jesu! This was new! She gripped the cross at her throat with one hand and her sword-hilt with the other. Then it was upon her, striking like a hurricane, whirling her against the walls and shrieking in her ears like a thousand wind-devils—a wild cyclone of the dark that buffeted her mercilessly and tore at her flying hair and raved in her ears with the myriad voices of all lost things crying in the night. The voices were piteous in their terror and loneliness. Tears came to her eyes even as she shivered with nameless dread, for the whirlwind was alive with a dreadful instinct, an animate thing sweeping through the dark of the underground; an unholy thing that made her flesh crawl even though it touched her to the heart with its pitiful little lost voices wailing in the wind where no wind could possibly be.

And then it was gone. In that one flash of an instant it vanished, leaving no whisper to commemorate its passage. Only in the heart of it could one hear the sad little voices wailing or the wild shriek of the wind. She found herself standing stunned, her sword yet gripped futilely in one hand and the tears running down her face. Poor little lost voices, wailing. She wiped the tears away with a shaking hand and set her teeth hard against the weakness of reaction that flooded her. Yet it was a good five minutes before she could force herself on. After a few steps her knees ceased to tremble.

The floor was dry and smooth underfoot. It sloped a little downward, and she wondered into what unplumbed deeps she had descended by now. The silence had fallen heavily again, and she found herself straining for some other sound than the soft padding of her own boots. Then her foot slipped in sudden wetness. She bent, exploring fingers outstretched, feeling without reason that the wetness would be red if she could see it. But her fingers traced the immense outline of a footprint—splayed and three-toed like a frog's, but of monster size. It was a fresh footprint. She had a vivid flash of memory —that thing she had glimpsed in the torchlight on the other trip down. But she had had light then, and now she was blind in the dark, the creature's natural habitat. . . .

For a moment she was not Jirel of Joiry, vengeful fury on the trail of a devilish weapon, but a frightened

woman alone in the unholy dark. That memory had
been so vivid. . . . Then she saw Guillaume's scornful,
laughing face again, the little beard dark along the line
of his jaw, the strong teeth white with his laughter; and
something hot and sustaining swept over her like a thin
flame, and she was Joiry again, vengeful and resolute.
She went on more slowly, her sword swinging in a semi-
circle before every third step, that she might not be surprised too suddenly by some nightmare monster clasping
her in smothering arms. But the flesh crept upon her un-
protected back.

The smooth passage went on and on. She could feel
the cold walls on either hand, and her upswung sword
grazed the roof. It was like crawling through some
worm's tunnel, blindly under the weight of countless
tons of earth. She felt the pressure of it above and about
her, overwhelming, and found herself praying that the
end of this tunnel-crawling might come soon, whatever
the end might bring.

But when it came it was a stranger thing than she had
ever dreamed. Abruptly she felt the immense, imponderable oppression cease. No longer was she conscious
of the tons of earth pressing about her. The walls had
fallen away and her feet struck a sudden rubble instead
of the smooth floor. But the darkness that had bandaged
her eyes was changed too, indescribably. It was no longer darkness, but void; not an absence of light, but simple
nothingness. Abysses opened around her, yet she could
see nothing. She only knew that she stood at the threshold of some immense space, and sensed nameless things
about her, and battled vainly against that nothingness
which was all her straining eyes could see. And at her
throat something constricted painfully.

She lifted her hand and found the chain of her crucifix taut and vibrant around her neck. At that she smiled
a little grimly, for she began to understand. The crucifix.
She found her hand shaking despite herself, but she unfastened the chain and dropped the cross to the ground.
Then she gasped.

All about her, as suddenly as the awakening from a

dream, the nothingness had opened out into un-dreamed-of distances. She stood high on a hilltop under a sky spangled with strange stars. Below she caught glimpses of misty plains and valleys with mountain peaks rising far away. And at her feet a ravening circle of small, slavering, blind things leaped with clashing teeth.

They were obscene and hard to distinguish against the darkness of the hillside, and the noise they made was re-volting. Her sword swung up of itself, almost, and slashed furiously at the little dark horrors leaping up around her legs. They died squashily, splattering her bare thighs with unpleasantness, and after a few had gone silent un-der the blade the rest fled into the dark with quick, frightened pantings, their feet making a queer splashing noise on the stones.

Jirel gathered a handful of the coarse grass which grew there and wiped her legs of the obscene splatters, looking about with quickened breath upon this land so unholy that one who bore a cross might not even see it. Here, if anywhere, one might find a weapon such as she sought. Behind her in the hillside was the low tunnel opening from which she had emerged. Overhead the strange stars shone. She did not recognize a single con-stellation, and if the brighter sparks were planets they were strange ones, tinged with violet and green and yel-low. One was vividly crimson, like a point of fire. Far out over the rolling land below she could discern a mighty column of light. It did not blaze, nor illuminate the dark about. It cast no shadows. It simply was a great pillar of luminance towering high in the night. It seemed artificial—perhaps man-made, though she scarcely dared hope for men here.

She had half expected, despite her brave words, to come out upon the storied and familiar red-hot pave of hell, and this pleasant, starlit land surprised her and made her more wary. The things that built the tunnel could not have been human. She had no right to expect men here. She was a little stunned by finding open sky so far underground, though she was intelligent enough to realize that however she had come, she was not under-ground now. No cavity in the earth could contain this

starry sky. She came of a credulous age, and she accepted her surroundings without too much questioning,
though she was a little disappointed, if the truth were
known, in the pleasantness of the mistily starlit place.
The fiery streets of hell would have been a likelier local-
ity in which to find a weapon against Guillaume.

When she had cleansed her sword on the grass and
wiped her legs clean, she turned slowly down the hill.
The distant column beckoned her, and after a moment
of indecision she turned toward it. She had no time to
waste, and this was the likeliest place to find what she
sought.

The coarse grass brushed her legs and whispered
round her feet. She stumbled now and then on the rubble, for the hill was steep, but she reached the bottom
without mishap, and struck out across the meadows toward that blaze of faraway brilliance. It seemed to her
that she walked more lightly, somehow. The grass
scarcely bent underfoot, and she found she could take
long sailing strides like one who runs with wings on his
heels. It felt like a dream. The gravity pull of the place
must have been less than she was accustomed to, but she
only knew that she was skimming over the ground with
amazing speed.

Traveling so, she passed through the meadows over
the strange, coarse grass, over a brook or two that spoke
endlessly to itself in a curious language that was almost
speech, certainly not the usual gurgle of earth's running
water. Once she ran into a blotch of darkness, like some
pocket of void in the air, and struggled through gasping
and blinking outraged eyes. She was beginning to realize
that the land was not so innocently normal as it looked.

On and on she went, at that surprising speed, while
the meadows skimmed past beneath her flying feet and
gradually the light drew nearer. She saw now that it was
a round tower of sheeted luminance, as if walls of solid
flame rose up from the ground. Yet it seemed to be
steady, nor did it cast any illumination upon the sky.

Before much time had elapsed, with her dreamlike
speed she had almost reached her goal. The ground was

becoming marshy underfoot, and presently the smell of swamps rose in her nostrils and she saw that between her and the light stretched a belt of unstable ground tufted with black reedy grass. Here and there she could see dim white blotches moving. They might be beasts, or only wisps of mist. The starlight was not very illuminating.

She began to pick her way carefully across the black, quaking morasses. Where the tufts of grass rose she found firmer ground, and she leaped from clump to clump with that amazing lightness, so that her feet barely touched the black ooze. Here and there slow bubbles rose through the mud and broke thickly. She did not like the place.

Halfway across, she saw one of the white blotches approaching her with slow, erratic movements. It bumped along unevenly, and at first she thought it might be inanimate, its approach was so indirect and purposeless. Then it blundered nearer, with that queer bumpy gait, making sucking noses in the ooze and splashing as it came. In the starlight she saw suddenly what it was, and for an instant her heart paused and sickness rose overwhelmingly in her throat. It was a woman—a beautiful woman whose white bare body had the curves and loveliness of some marble statue. She was crouching like a frog, and as Jirel watched in stupefaction she straightened her legs abruptly and leaped as a frog leaps, only more clumsily, falling forward into the ooze a little distance beyond the watching woman. She did not seem to see Jirel. The mud-spattered face was blank. She blundered on through the mud in awkward leaps. Jirel watched until the woman was no more than a white wandering blur in the dark, and above the shock of that sight pity was rising, and uncomprehending resentment against whatever had brought so lovely a creature into this—into blundering in frog leaps aimlessly through the mud, with empty mind and blind, staring eyes. For the second time that night she knew the sting of unaccustomed tears as she went on.

The sight, though, had given her reassurance. The human form was not unknown here. There might be leathery devils with hoofs and horns, such as she still half expected, but she would not be alone in her humanity; though if all the rest were as piteously mindless as the one she had seen—she did not follow that thought. It was too unpleasant. She was glad when the marsh was past and she need not see any longer the awkward white shapes bumping along through the dark.

She struck out across the narrow space which lay between her and the tower. She saw now that it was a building, and that the light composed it. She could not understand that, but she saw it. Walls and columns outlined the tower, solid sheets of light with definite boundaries, not radiant. As she came nearer she saw that it was in motion, apparently spurting up from some source underground as if the light illuminated sheets of water rushing upward under great pressure. Yet she felt intuitively that it was not water, but incarnate light.

She came forward hesitantly, gripping her sword. The area around the tremendous pillar was paved with something black and smooth that did not reflect the light. Out of it sprang the uprushing walls of brilliance with their sharply defined edges. The magnitude of the thing dwarfed her to infinitesimal size. She stared upward with undazzled eyes, trying to understand. If there could be such a thing as solid, non-radiating light, this was it.

She was very near under the mighty tower before she could see the details of the building clearly. They were strange to her—great pillars and arches around the base, and one stupendous portal, all molded out of the rushing, prisoned light. She turned toward the opening after a moment, for the light had a tangible look. She did not believe she could have walked through it even had she dared.

When that tremendous portal arched over her she peered in, affrighted by the very size of the place. She thought she could hear the hiss and spurt of the light surging upward. She was looking into a mighty globe inside, a hall shaped like the interior of a bubble, though the curve was so vast she was scarcely aware of it. And in the very center of the globe floated a light. Jirel blinked. A light, dwelling in a bubble of light. It glowed

there in midair with a pale, steady flame that was somehow alive and animate, and brighter than the serene illumination of the building, for it hurt her eyes to look at it
directly.

She stood on the threshold and stared, not quite daring to venture in. And as she hesitated a change came
over the light. A flash of rose tinged its pallor. The rose
deepened and darkened until it took on the color of
blood. And the shape underwent strange changes. It
lengthened, drew itself out narrowly, split at the bottom
into two branches, put out two tendrils from the top.
The blood-red paled again, and the light somehow lost
its brilliance, receded into the depths of the thing that
was forming. Jirel clutched her sword and forgot to
breathe, watching. The light was taking on the shape of
a human being—of a woman—of a tall woman in mail,
her red hair tousled and her eyes staring straight into the
duplicate eyes at the portal. . . .

"Welcome," said the Jirel suspended in the center of
the globe, her voice deep and resonant and clear in spite
of the distance between them. Jirel at the door held her
breath, wondering and afraid. This was herself, in every
detail, a mirrored Jirel—that was it, a Jirel mirrored
upon a surface which blazed and smoldered with barely
repressed light, so that the eyes gleamed with it and the
whole figure seemed to hold its shape by an effort, only
by that effort restraining itself from resolving into pure,
formless light again. But the voice was not her own. It
shook and resounded with a knowledge as alien as the
light-built walls. It mocked her. It said,

"Welcome! Enter into the portals, woman!"

She looked up warily at the rushing walls about her.
Instinctively she drew back.

"Enter, enter!" urged that mocking voice from her
own mirrored lips. And there was a note in it she did
not like.

"Enter!" cried the voice again, this time a command.

Jirel's eyes narrowed. Something intuitive warned her
back, and yet—she drew the dagger she had thrust in
her belt and with a quick motion she tossed it into the
great globe-shaped hall. It struck the floor without a
sound, and a brilliant light flared up around it, so bril-

liant she could not look upon what was happening; but it seemed to her that the knife expanded, grew large and nebulous and ringed with dazzling light. In less time than it takes to tell, it had faded out of sight as if the very atoms which composed it had flown apart and dispersed in the golden glow of that mighty bubble. The dazzle faded with the knife, leaving Jirel staring dazedly at a bare floor.

That other Jirel laughed, a rich, resonant laugh of scorn and malice.

"Stay out, then," said the voice. "You've more intelligence than I thought. Well, what would you here?"

Jirel found her voice with an effort.

"I seek a weapon," she said, "a weapon against a man I so hate that upon earth there is none terrible enough for my need."

"You so hate him, eh?" mused the voice.

"With all my heart!"

"With all your heart!" echoed the voice, and there was an undernote of laughter in it that she did not understand. The echoes of that mirth ran round and round the great globe. Jirel felt her cheeks burn with resentment against some implication in the derision which she could not put a name to. When the echoes of the laugh had faded the voice said indifferently,

"Give the man what you find at the black temple in the lake. I make you a gift of it."

The lips that were Jirel's twisted into a laugh of purest mockery; then all about that figure so perfectly her own the light flared out. She saw the outlines melting fluidly as she turned her dazzled eyes away. Before the echoes of that derision had died, a blinding, formless light burned once more in the midst of the bubble.

Jirel turned and stumbled away under the mighty column of the tower, a hand to her dazzled eyes. Not until she had reached the edge of the black, unreflecting circle that paved the ground around the pillar did she realize that she knew no way of finding the lake where her weapon lay. And not until then did she remember how fatal it is said to be to accept a gift from a demon. Buy it, or earn it, but never accept the gift. Well—she shrugged and stepped out upon the grass. She must surely be damned by now, for having ventured down of her own will into this curious place for such a purpose as hers. The soul can be lost but once.

She turned her face up to the strange stars and wondered in what direction her course lay. The sky looked blankly down upon her with its myriad meaningless eyes. A star fell as she watched, and in her superstitious soul she took it for an omen, and set off boldly over the dark meadows in the direction where the bright streak had faded. No swamps guarded the way here, and she was soon skimming along over the grass with that strange, dancing gait that the lightness of the place allowed her. And as she went she was remembering, as from long ago in some other far world, a man's arrogant mirth and the press of his mouth on hers. Hatred bubbled up hotly within her and broke from her lips in a little savage laugh of anticipation. What dreadful thing awaited her in the temple in the lake, what punishment from hell to be loosed by her own hands upon Guillaume? And though her soul was the price it cost her, she would count it a fair bargain if she could drive the laughter from his mouth and bring terror into the eyes that mocked her.

Thoughts like these kept her company for a long way upon her journey. She did not think to be lonely or afraid in the uncanny darkness across which no shadows fell from that mighty column behind her. The unchanging meadows flew past underfoot, lightly as meadows in a dream. It might almost have been that the earth moved instead of herself, so effortlessly did she go. She was sure now that she was heading in the right direction, for two more stars had fallen in the same arc across the sky.

The meadows were not untenanted. Sometimes, she felt presences near her in the dark, and once she ran full-tilt into a nest of little yapping horrors like those on the hilltop. They lunged up about her with clicking teeth, mad with a blind ferocity, and she swung her sword in frantic circles, sickened by the noise of them lunging splashily through the grass and splattering her sword with their deaths. She beat them off and went on, fighting her own sickness, for she had never known anything quite so nauseating as these little monstrosities.

She crossed a·brook that talked to itself in the darkness with that queer murmuring which came so near to speech, and a few strides beyond it she paused suddenly, feeling the ground tremble with the rolling thunder of hoofbeats approaching. She stood still, searching the dark anxiously, and presently the earth-shaking beat grew louder and she saw a white blur flung wide across the dimness to her left, and the sound of hoofs deepened and grew. Then out of the night swept a herd of snow-white horses. Magnificently they ran, manes tossing, tails streaming, feet pounding a rhythmic, heart-stirring roll along the ground. She caught her breath at the beauty of their motion. They swept by a little distance away, tossing their heads, spurning the ground with scornful feet.

But as they came abreast of her she saw one blunder a little and stumble against the next, and that one shook his head bewilderedly; and suddenly she realized that they were blind—all running so splendidly in a deeper dark than even she groped through. And she saw, too, their coats were roughened with sweat, and foam dripped from their lips, and their nostrils were flaring pools of scarlet. Now and again one stumbled from pure exhaustion. Yet they ran, frantically, blindly through the dark, driven by something outside their comprehension.

As the last one of all swept by her, sweat-crusted and staggering, she saw him toss his head high, spattering foam, and whinny shrilly to the stars. And it seemed to her that the sound was strangely articulate. Almost she heard the echoes of a name—"Julienne Julienne!"—in that high, despairing sound. And the incongruity of it, the bitter despair, clutched at her heart so sharply that for the third time that night she knew the sting of tears.

The dreadful humanity of that cry echoed in her ears as the thunder died away. She went on, blinking back the tears for that beautiful blind creature, staggering with exhaustion, calling a girl's name hopelessly from a beast's throat into the blank darkness wherein it was forever lost.

Then another star fell across the sky, and she hurried ahead, closing her mind to the strange, incomprehensible pathos that made an undernote of tears to the starry dark of this land. And the thought was growing in her mind that, though she had come into no brimstone pit where horned devils pranced over flames, yet perhaps it was after all a sort of hell through which she ran.

Presently in the distance she caught a glimmer of something bright. The ground dipped after that and she lost it, and skimmed through a hollow where pale things wavered away from her into the deeper dark. She never knew what they were, and was glad. When she came up onto higher ground again she saw it more clearly, an expanse of dim brilliance ahead. She hoped it was a lake, and ran more swiftly.

It *was* a lake—a lake that could never have existed outside some obscure hell like this. She stood on the brink doubtfully, wondering if this could be the place the light-devil had meant. Black, shining water stretched out before her, heaving gently with a motion unlike that of any water she had ever seen before. And in the depths of it, like fireflies caught in ice, gleamed myriad small lights. They were fixed there immovably, not stirring with the motion of the water. As she watched, something hissed above her and a streak of light split the dark air. She looked up in time to see something bright curving across the sky to fall without a splash into the water, and small ripples of phosphorescence spread sluggishly toward the shore, where they broke at her feet with the queerest whispering sound, as if each succeeding ripple spoke the syllable of a word.

She looked up, trying to locate the origin of the falling lights, but the strange stars looked down upon her blankly. She bent and stared down into the center of the spreading ripples, and where the thing had fallen she thought a new light twinkled through the water. She could not determine what it was, and after a curious moment she gave the question up and began to cast about for the temple the light-devil had spoken of.

After a moment she thought she saw something dark

in the center of the lake, and when she had stared for a few minutes it gradually became clearer, an arch of darkness against the starry background of the water. It might be a temple. She strolled slowly along the brim of the lake, trying to get a closer view of it, for the thing was no more than a darkness against the spangles of light, like some void in the sky where no stars shine. And presently she stumbled over something in the grass.

She looked down with startled yellow eyes, and saw a strange, indistinguishable darkness. It had solidity to the feel but scarcely to the eye, for she could not quite focus upon it. It was like trying to see something that did not exist save as a void, a darkness in the grass. It had the shape of a step, and when she followed with her eyes she saw that it was the beginning of a dim bridge stretching out over the lake, narrow and curved and made out of nothingness. It seemed to have no surface, and its edges were difficult to distinguish from the lesser gloom surrounding it. But the thing was tangible—an arch carved out of the solid dark—and it led out in the direction she wished to go. For she was naïvely sure now that the dim blot in the center of the lake was the temple she was searching for. The falling stars had guided her, and she could not have gone astray.

So she set her teeth and gripped her sword and put her foot upon the bridge. It was rock-firm under her, but scarcely more than a foot or so wide, and without rails. When she had gone a step or two she began to feel dizzy; for under her the water heaved with a motion that made her head swim, and the stars twinkled eerily in its depths. She dared not look away for fear of missing her footing on the narrow arch of darkness. It was like walking a bridge flung across the void, with stars underfoot and nothing but an unstable strip of nothingness to bear her up. Halfway across, the heaving of the water and the illusion of vast, constellated spaces beneath and the look her bridge had of being no more than empty space ahead, combined to send her head reeling; and as she stumbled on, the bridge seemed to be wavering with her, swinging in gigantic arcs across the starry void below.

Now she could see the temple more closely, though

scarcely more clearly than from the shore. It looked to be no more than an outlined emptiness against the star-crowded brilliance behind it, etching its arches and columns of blankness upon the twinkling waters. The bridge came down in a long dim swoop to its doorway. Jirel took the last few yards at a reckless run and stopped breathless under the arch that made the temple's vague doorway. She stood there panting and staring about narrow-eyed, sword poised in her hand. For though the place was empty and very still she felt a presence even as she set her foot upon the floor of it.

She was staring about a little space of blankness in the starry lake. It seemed to be no more than that. She could see the walls and columns where they were outlined against the water and where they made darknesses in the star-flecked sky, but where there was only dark behind them she could see nothing. It was a tiny place, no more than a few square yards of emptiness upon the face of the twinkling waters. And in its center an image stood.

She stared at it in silence, feeling a curious compulsion growing within her, like a vague command from something outside herself. The image was of some substance of nameless black, unlike the material which composed the building, for even in the dark she could see it clearly. It was a semi-human figure, crouching forward with out-thrust head, sexless and strange. Its one central eye was closed as if in rapture, and its mouth was pursed for a kiss. And though it was but an image and without even the semblance of life, she felt unmistakably the presence of something alive in the temple, something so alien and innominate that instinctively she drew away.

She stood there for a full minute, reluctant to enter the place where so alien a being dwelt, half-conscious of that voiceless compulsion growing up within her. And slowly she became aware that all the lines and angles of the half-seen building were curved to make the image their center and focus. The very bridge swooped its long arc to complete the centering. As she watched, it seemed to her that through the arches of the columns even the stars in lake and sky were grouped in patterns which took the image for their focus. Every line and curve in the dim world seemed to sweep round toward the squatting thing before her with its closed eye and expectant mouth.

Gradually the universal focusing of lines began to exert its influence upon her. She took a hesitant step forward without realizing the motion. But that step was all the dormant urge within her needed. With her one motion forward the compulsion closed down upon her with whirlwind impetuosity. Helplessly she felt herself advancing, helplessly with one small, sane portion of her mind she realized the madness that was gripping her, the blind, irresistible urge to do what every visible line in the temple's construction was made to compel. With stars swirling around her she advanced across the floor and laid her hands upon the rounded shoulders of the image—the sword, forgotten, making a sort of accolade against its hunched neck—and lifted her red head and laid her mouth blindly against the pursed lips of the image.

In a dream she took that kiss. In a dream of dizziness and confusion she seemed to feel the iron-cold lips stirring under hers. And through the union of that kiss— warm-blooded woman with image of nameless stone— through the meeting of their mouths something entered into her very soul; something cold and stunning; something alien beyond any words. It lay upon her shuddering soul like some frigid weight from the void, a bubble holding something unthinkably alien and dreadful. She could feel the heaviness of it upon some intangible part of her that shrank from the torch. It was like the weight of remorse or despair, only far colder and stranger and —somehow—more ominous, as if this weight were but the egg from which things might hatch too dreadful to put even into thoughts.

The moment of the kiss could have been no longer than a breath's space, but to her it was timeless. In a dream she felt the compulsion falling from her at last. In a dim dream she dropped her hands from its shoulders, finding the sword heavy in her grasp and staring dully at it for a while before clarity began its return to her cloudy mind. When she became completely aware of herself once more she was standing with slack body and dragging head before the blind, rapturous image, that dead weight upon her heart as dreary as an old sorrow, and more coldly ominous than anything she could find words for.

And with returning clarity the most staggering terror came over her, swiftly and suddenly—terror of the image and the temple of darkness, and the coldly spangled lake and of the whole, wide, dim, dreadful world about her. Desperately she longed for home again, even the red fury of hatred and the press of Guillaume's mouth and the hot arrogance of his eyes again. Anything but this. She found herself running without knowing why. Her feet skimmed over the narrow bridge lightly as a gull's wings dipping the water. In a brief instant the starry void of the lake flashed by beneath her and the solid earth was underfoot. She saw the great column of light far away across the dark meadows and beyond it a hilltop rising against the stars. And she ran.

She ran with terror at her heels and devils howling in the wind her own speed made. She ran from her own curiously alien body, heavy with its weight of inexplicable doom. She passed through the hollow where pale things wavered away, she fled over the uneven meadows in a frenzy of terror. She ran and ran, in those long light bounds the lesser gravity allowed her, fleeter than a deer, and her own panic choked in her throat and that weight upon her soul dragged at her too drearily for tears. She fled to escape it, and could not; and the ominous certainty that she carried something too dreadful to think of grew and grew.

For a long while she skimmed over the grass, tirelessly, wing-heeled, her red hair flying. The panic died after a while, but that sense of heavy disaster did not die. She felt somehow that tears would ease her, but something in the frigid darkness of her soul froze her tears in the ice of that gray and alien chill.

And gradually, through the inner dark, a fierce anticipation took form in her mind. Revenge upon Guillaume! She had taken from the temple only a kiss, so it was that which she must deliver to him. And savagely she exulted in the thought of what that kiss would release upon him, unsuspecting. She did not know, but it filled her with fierce joy to guess.

She had passed the column and skirted the morass where the white, blundering forms still bumped along awkwardly through the ooze, and was crossing the coarse grass toward the nearing hill when the sky began to pale along the horizon. And with that pallor a fresh terror took hold upon her, a wild horror of daylight in this unholy land. She was not sure if it was the light itself she so dreaded, or what that light would reveal in the dark stretches she had traversed so blindly—what unknown horrors she had skirted in the night. But she knew instinctively that if she valued her sanity she must be gone before the light had risen over the land. And she redoubled her efforts, spurring her wearying limbs to yet more skimming speed. But it would be a close race, for already the stars were blurring out, and a flush of curious green was broadening along the sky, and around her the air was turning to a vague, unpleasant gray.

She toiled up the steep hillside breathlessly. When she was halfway up, her own shadow began to take form upon the rocks, and it was unfamiliar and dreadfully significant of something just outside her range of understanding. She averted her eyes from it, afraid that at any moment the meaning might break upon her outraged brain.

She could see the top of the hill above her, dark against the paling sky, and she toiled up in frantic haste, clutching her sword and feeling that if she had to look in the full light upon the dreadful little abominations that had snapped around her feet when she first emerged she would collapse into screaming hysteria.

The cave-mouth yawned before her, invitingly black, a refuge from the dawning light behind her. She knew an almost irresistible desire to turn and look back from this vantage-point across the land she had traversed, and gripped her sword hard to conquer the perverse longing. There was a scuffling in the rocks at her feet, and she set her teeth in her underlip and swung viciously in brief arcs, without looking down. She heard small squeakings and the splashy sound of feet upon the stones, and felt her blade shear thrice through semi-solidity, to the click of little vicious teeth. Then they broke and ran off over the hillside, and she stumbled on, choking back the scream that wanted so fiercely to break from her lips.

She fought that growing desire all the way up to the cave-mouth, for she knew that if she gave way she would never cease shrieking until her throat went raw.

Blood was trickling from her bitten lip with the effort at silence when she reached the cave. And there, twinkling upon the stones, lay something small and bright and dearly familiar. With a sob of relief she bent and snatched up the crucifix she had torn from her throat when she came out into this land. And as her fingers shut upon it a vast, protecting darkness swooped around her. Gasping with relief, she groped her way the step or two that separated her from the cave.

Dark lay like a blanket over her eyes, and she welcomed it gladly, remembering how her shadow had lain so awfully upon the hillside as she climbed, remembering the first rays of savage sunlight beating upon her shoulders. She stumbled through the blackness, slowly getting control again over her shaking body and laboring lungs, slowly stilling the panic that the dawning day had roused so inexplicably within her. And as that terror died, the dull weight upon her spirit became strong again. She had all but forgotten it in her panic, but now the impending and unknown dreadfulness grew heavier and more oppressive in the darkness of the underground, and she groped along in a dull stupor of her own depression, slow with the weight of the strange doom she carried.

Nothing barred her way. In the dullness of her stupor she scarcely realized it, or expected any of the vague horrors that peopled the place to leap out upon her. Empty and unmenacing, the way stretched before her blindly stumbling feet. Only once did she hear the sound of another presence—the rasp of hoarse breathing and the scrape of a scaly hide against the stone—but it must have been outside the range of her own passage, for she encountered nothing.

When she had come to the end and a cold wall rose up before her, it was scarcely more than automatic habit that made her search along it with groping hand until she came to the mouth of the shaft. It sloped gently up into the dark. She crawled in, trailing her sword, until the rising incline and lowering roof forced her down upon her face. Then with toes and fingers she began to force herself up the spiral, slippery way.

Before she had gone very far she was advancing without effort, scarcely realizing that it was against gravity she moved. The curious dizziness of the shaft had come over her, the strange feeling of change in the very substance of her body, and through the cloudy numbness of it she felt herself sliding round and round the spirals, without effort. Again, obscurely, she had the feeling that in the peculiar angles of this shaft was neither up nor down. And for a long while the dizzy circling went on.

When the end came at last, and she felt her fingers gripping the edge of that upper opening which lay beneath the floor of Joiry's lowest dungeons, she heaved herself up warily and lay for a while on the cold floor in the dark, while slowly the clouds of dizziness passed from her mind, leaving only that ominous weight within. When the darkness had ceased to circle about her, and the floor steadied, she got up dully and swung the cover back over the opening, her hands shuddering from the feel of the cold, smooth ring which had never seen daylight.

When she turned from this task she was aware of the reason for the lessening in the gloom around her. A guttering light outlined the hole in the wall from which she had pulled the stones—was it a century ago? The brilliance all but blinded her after her long sojourn through blackness, and she stood there awhile, swaying a little, one hand to her eyes, before she went out into the familiar torchlight she knew waited her beyond. Father Gervase, she was sure, anxiously waiting her return. But even he had not dared to follow her through the hole in the wall, down to the brink of the shaft.

Somehow she felt that she should be giddy with relief at this safe homecoming, back to humanity again. But as she stumbled over the upward slope toward light and safety she was conscious of no more than the dullness of whatever unreleased horror it was which still lay so ominously upon her stunned soul.

She came through the gaping hole in the masonry into the full glare of torches awaiting her, remembering with a wry inward smile how wide she had made the opening in anticipation of flight from something dreadful when she came back that way. Well, there was no flight from the horror she bore within her. It seemed to her that her heart was slowing, too, missing a beat now and then and staggering like a weary runner.

She came out into the torchlight, stumbling with exhaustion, her mouth scarlet from the blood of her bitten lip and her bare greaved legs and bare sword-blade foul with the deaths of those little horrors that swarmed around the cave-mouth. From the tangle of red hair her eyes stared out with a bleak, frozen, inward look, as of one who has seen nameless things. That keen, steel-bright beauty which had been hers was as dull and fouled as her sword-blade, and at the look in her eyes Father Gervase shuddered and crossed himself.

They were waiting for her in an uneasy group—the priest anxious and dark, Guillaume splendid in the torchlight, tall and arrogant, a handful of men-at-arms holding the guttering lights and shifting uneasily from one foot to the other. When she saw Guillaume the light that flared up in her eyes blotted out for a moment the bleak dreadfulness behind them, and her slowing heart leaped like a spurred horse, sending the blood riotously through her veins. Guillaume, magnificent in his armor, leaning upon his sword and staring down at her from his scornful height, the little black beard jutting. Guillaume, to whom Joiry had fallen. Guillaume.

That which she carried at the core of her being was

heavier than anything else in the world, so heavy she could scarcely keep her knees from bending, so heavy her heart labored under its weight. Almost irresistibly she wanted to give way beneath it, to sink down and down under the crushing load, to lie prone and vanquished in the ice-gray, bleak place she was so dimly aware of through the clouds that were rising about her. But there was Guillaume, grim and grinning, and she hated him so very bitterly—she must make the effort. She must, at whatever cost, for she was coming to know that death lay in wait for her if she bore this burden long, that it was a two-edged weapon which could strike at its wielder if the blow were delayed too long. She knew this through the dim mists that were thickening in her brain, and she put all her strength into the immense effort it cost to cross the floor toward him. She stumbled a little, and made one faltering step and then another, and dropped her sword with a clang as she lifted her arms to him.

He caught her strongly, in a hard, warm clasp, and she heard his laugh triumphant and hateful as he bent his head to take the kiss she was raising her mouth to offer. He must have seen, in that last moment before their lips met, the savage glare of victory in her eyes, and been startled. But he did not hesitate. His mouth was heavy upon hers.

It was a long kiss. She felt him stiffen in her arms. She felt a coldness in the lips upon hers, and slowly the dark weight of what she bore lightened, lifted, cleared away from her cloudy mind. Strength flowed back through her richly. The whole world came alive to her once more. Presently she loosed his slack arms and stepped away, looking up into his face with a keen and dreadful triumph upon her own.

She saw the ruddiness of him draining away, and the rigidity of stone coming over his scarred features. Only his eyes remained alive, and there was torment in them, and understanding. She was glad—she had wanted him to understand what it cost to take Joiry's kiss unbidden. She smiled thinly into his tortured eyes, watching. And she saw something cold and alien seeping through him,

permeating him slowly with some unnameable emotion
which no man could ever have experienced before. She
could not name it, but she saw it in his eyes—some
dreadful emotion never made for flesh and blood to
know, some iron despair such as only an unguessable
being from the gray, formless void could ever have felt
before—too hideously alien for any human creature to
endure. Even she shuddered from the dreadful, cold
bleakness looking out of his eyes, and knew as she
watched that there must be many emotions and many
fears and joys too far outside man's comprehension for
any being of flesh to undergo, and live. Grayly she saw
it spreading through him, and the very substance of his
body shuddered under that iron weight.

And now came a visible, physical change. Watching,
she was aghast to think that in her own body and upon
her own soul she had borne the seed of this dreadful
flowering, and did not wonder that her heart had slowed
under the unbearable weight of it. He was standing rig-
idly with arms half bent, just as he stood when she slid
from his embrace. And now great shudders began to go
over him, as if he were wavering in the torchlight, some
gray-faced wraith in armor with torment in his eyes. She
saw the sweat beading his forehead. She saw a trickle of
blood from his mouth, as if he had bitten through his lip
in the agony of this new, incomprehensible emotion.
Then a last shiver went over him violently, and he flung
up his head, the little curling beard jutting ceilingward
and the muscles of his strong throat corded, and from
his lips broke a long, low cry of such utter, inhuman
strangeness that Jirel felt coldness rippling through her
veins and she put up her hands to her ears to shut it out.
It meant something—it expressed some dreadful emotion that was neither sorrow nor despair nor anger, but
infinitely alien and infinitely sad. Then his long legs buckled at the knees and he dropped with a clatter of mail
and lay still on the stone floor.

They knew he was dead. That was unmistakable in
the way he lay. Jirel stood very still, looking down upon
him, and strangely it seemed to her that all the lights in
the world had gone out. A moment before he had been

so big and vital, so magnificent in the torchlight—she could still feel his kiss upon her mouth, and the hard warmth of his arms. . . .

Suddenly and blindingly it came upon her what she had done. She knew now why such heady violence had flooded her whenever she thought of him—knew why the light-devil in her own form had laughed so derisively —knew the price she must pay for taking a gift from a demon. She knew that there was no light anywhere in the world, now that Guillaume was gone.

Father Gervase took her arm gently. She shook him off with an impatient shrug and dropped to one knee beside Guillaume's body, bending her head so that the red hair fell forward to hide her tears.

Tryst in Time

ERIC ROSNER AT twenty had worked his way round the world on cattle boats, killed his first man in a street brawl in Shanghai, escaped a firing squad by a hair-breadth, stowed away on a pole-bound exploring ship.

At twenty-five he had lost himself in Siberian wilderness, led a troup of Tatar bandits, commanded a Chinese regiment, fought in a hundred battles, impartially on either side.

At thirty there was not a continent nor a capital that had not known him, not a jungle nor a desert nor a mountain range that had not left scars upon his great Viking body. Tiger claws and the Russian knout, Chinese bullets and the knives of savage black warriors in African forests had written their tales of a full and perilous life upon him. At thirty he looked backward upon such a gorgeous, brawling, color-splashed career as few men of sixty can boast. But at thirty he was not content.

Life had been full for him, and yet as the years passed he was becoming increasingly aware of a need for something which those years were empty of. What it was he did not know. He was not even consciously aware of missing anything, but as time went on he turned more and more to a search for something new—anything new. Perhaps it was his subconscious hunting blindly for what life had lacked.

There was so very little that Eric Rosner had not done in his thirty riotous years that the search for newness rapidly became almost feverish, and almost in vain. Riches he had known, and poverty, much pleasure and much pain, and the extremes of human experience were old tales to him. Ennui replaced the zest for living that had sent him so gayly through the exultant years of his youth. And for a man like Eric Rosner ennui was like a little death.

Perhaps, in part, all this was because he had missed love. No girl of all the girls that had kissed him and adored him and wept when he left them had mattered a snap of the fingers to Eric Rosner. He searched on restlessly.

In this mood of feverish hunting for new things, he met the scientist, Walter Dow. It happened casually, and they might never have met a second time had not Eric said something offhand about the lack of adventure which life had to offer a man. And Dow laughed.

"What do you know about adventure?" he demanded. He was a little man with a shock of prematurely white hair and a face that crinkled into lines of derision as he laughed. "You've spent your life among dangers and gunfire—sure! But that's not real adventure. Science is the only field where true adventure exists. I mean it! The things that are waiting to be discovered offer fields of excitement like nothing you ever heard of. One man in a lifetime couldn't begin to touch the edges of what there is to know. I tell you I——"

"Oh, sure," interrupted Eric lazily. "I see what you mean. But all that's not for me. I'm a man of action; I haven't any brains. Hunching over a microscope isn't my idea of fun."

The argument that began then developed into a queer sort of antagonistic friendship which brought the two men together very often in the weeks that passed. But they were to know one another much more intimately than that before the true urgency of what lay in the minds of each became clear to the other.

Walter Dow had spent a lifetime in the worship of one god—inertia. "There is a bedrock," he used to say reverently, "over which the tides of time ebb and flow, over which all things material and immaterial, as the layman sees them, change and fade and form again. But the bedrock remains. Complete inertia! What couldn't we do if we attained it!"

"And what," asked Eric, "is inertia?"

Dow shot him a despairing glance.

"Everybody knows what inertia is. Newton's first law of motion is the law of inertia, stating that every body remains in a state of rest or of uniform motion in a straight line unless impressed forces change it. That's what makes people in a moving car swerve to one side when the car goes round a bend. It's what makes it so difficult for a horse to start a heavy load moving, though once it's in motion the strain eases. There's nothing that doesn't obey the law—nothing!

"But Newton didn't dream what measureless abysses of force lay behind his simple statement. Or what an understatement it was. Describing inertia by stating Newton's law is like describing the sea by saying there's foam on the waves. The inertia force is inherent in everything, just as there's moisture in everything. But behind that inertia, manifest so obscurely in matter, is a vastness of power much greater comparatively than the vastnesses of the seas which are the storehouses for the relatively tiny amounts of moisture in everything you see.

"I can't make you understand; you don't speak the language. And I sometimes wonder if I could explain even to another physicist all that I've discovered in the past ten years. But I do very firmly believe that it would be possible to anchor to that bedrock of essential, underlying inertia which is the base upon which matter builds and—and allow time itself to whirl by!"

"Yeah, and find yourself floating in space when you let go." Eric grinned. "Even I've heard that the universe is in motion through space. I don't know about time, but I'm pretty sure space would block your little scheme."

"I didn't mean you'd have to—to dig your anchor right into the rock," explained Dow with dignity. "It'd be a sort of a drag to slow you down, not a jerk that would snatch you right off the Earth. And it'd involve —immensities—even then. But it could be done. It will be done. By Heaven, I'll do it!"

Eric's sunburned face sobered.

"You're not kidding?" he asked. "A man could—

could drag his anchor and let time go by, and 'up-anchor' in another age? Say! Make me an anchor, and I'll be your guinea pig!"

Dow did not smile.

"That's the worst of it," he said. "All this is pure theory and will have to remain that, in spite of all I've bragged. It would be absolutely blind experimenting, and the very nature of the element I'm experimenting with precludes any proof of success or failure. I could —to be frank with you I *have*—sent objects out through time——"

"You have!" Eric leaned forward with a jerk and laid an urgent hand on Dow's arm. "You really have?"

"Well, I've made them vanish. I think it proves I've succeeded, but I have no way of knowing. The chances are countless millions to one against my landing an experiment in my own immediate future, with all the measureless vastness of time lying open. And, of course, I can't guide it."

"Suppose you landed in your own past?" queried Eric.

Dow smiled.

"The eternal question," he said. "The inevitable objection to the very idea of time travel. Well, you never did, did you? You know it never happened! I think there must be some inflexible law which forbids the same arrangement of matter, the pattern which is one's self, from occupying the same space time more than once. As if any given section of space time were a design in which any arrangement of atoms is possible, except that no pattern may appear exactly twice.

"You see, we know of time only enough to be sure that it's far beyond any human understanding. Though I think the past and the future may be visited, which on the face of it seems to predicate an absolutely preordained future, a fixed and unchangeable past—yet I do not believe that time is arbitrary. There must be many possible futures. The one we enter upon is not the only way. Have you ever heard that theory explained? It's not a new one—the idea that at every point of our progress we confront crossroads, with a free choice as to which we take. And a different future lies down each.

"I can transport you into the past, and you can create events there which never took place in the past we know —but the events are not new. They were ordained from the beginning, *if* you took that particular path. You are simply embarking upon a different path into a different future, a fixed and preordained future, yet one which will be strange to you because it lies outside your own layer of experience. So you have infinite freedom in all your actions, yet everything you can possibly do is already fixed in time."

"Why, then—then there's no limit to the excitement a man could find in navigating time," said Eric almost reverently. And then in sudden urgency, "Dow, you've got to fix it up for me! This is what I've been hunting!"

"Are you crazy, boy? This is nothing that can ever be proved safe except by the actual experiment, and the experiment could never return. You know that, don't you? From what blind groping I've done, it seems to me that time is not a constant flow, but an ebb and flux that can't be measured. It would be hard to explain to you. But you couldn't return—couldn't guide yourself. You wouldn't dare try it!"

"I'm fed up with certainty and safety! And as for returning, what have I here to return to? No, you can't scare me. I've got to try it!"

"Absolutely no," said Dow firmly.

But three months later he was standing under the great skylight of his laboratory, watching Eric buckle a flat metal pack on his heavy young shoulders. Though reluctance still lined the scientist's face, under its shock of white hair he was alight almost as hotly as the younger man, with the tremendous adventure of what was about to happen. It had taken weeks of persuasion and argument, and he was not wholly at ease even yet about the experiment, but the fever that burned in Eric Rosner was not to be denied.

Now that the way was open, it seemed to Eric that all his life he had lived toward this moment in the laboratory. The need for this launching upon time's broad river was what had driven him restless and feverish through the petty adventures which life had shown him. Peace was upon him now for the first time in months. There was something rather awe-inspiring about it.

"Look here," broke in Walter Dow upon the raptness of his mood. "Are you sure you understand?"

"I don't understand anything about the works, and I don't much care," said Eric. "All I know is I'm to snap these switches here"—he laid big sunburned hands on the two rods at his belt—"when I want to move along. That will throw out the anchor. Right?"

"As far as it goes, yes. That will increase your inertia sufficiently to make you immune to time and space and matter. You will be inert mentally and physically. You'll sink down, so to speak, to the bedrock, while time flows past you. I have in this pack on your back, connecting with the switches in the belt, the means to increase your inertia until no outside force can interrupt it. And a mechanism there will permit the switches to remain thrown until one small part, insulated from the inertia in a tiny time space of its own, trips the switches again and up-anchors. And if my calculations are correct—and I *think* they are—there you'll be in some other age than ours. You can escape from it by throwing the switches again and returning to inertia, to be released after an interval by the automatic insulated mechanism in your pack. Got it?"

"Got it!" Eric grinned all over his good-looking, sunburned face. "Everything ready now?"

"Yes—yes, except that—are you sure you want to risk it? This may be plain murder, boy! I don't know what will happen!"

"That's the beauty of it—not knowing. Don't worry, Walter. Call it suicide, not murder, if that helps you any. I'm going now. Good-by."

Dow choked a little as he gripped the younger man's hand hard, but Eric's face was shining with the fever to be gone, and at the last the scientist was almost reconciled by the sight of that rapt face. Almost he saw in the last instant before the switches closed a purpose vaster than his own, sweeping the work of his hands and the exultant young man before him into a whole that fulfilled some greater need than he could guess.

Then Eric's hands dropped to his belt. One last instant he stood there, tall under the clear radiance of the skylight, blond and sunburned, the tale of his riotous, brawling life clear upon his scarred, young face, but upon it, too, a raptness and an eagerness that sent a quick stab of unreasoning hope through the scientist's mind. Surely success would crown this experiment. Surely all the vital, throbbing aliveness, the strength and seasoned toughness of this brawny young man before him could not snuff into nothing as the switches closed. Danger awaited him—yes, danger against which the gun at his belt might not avail at all. But splendor, too. Splendor—— Envy clouded Dow's eyes for a moment, as the switches closed.

Past Eric's eyes eternity ebbed blindingly. Rushing blankness closed over him, but he was conscious of infinite motion, infinite change passing over him, by him, through him, as events beyond imagination streamed past that anchorage in inertia's eternal bedrock. For a timeless eternity it lasted. And then—and then——

A confusion of noises from very far away began to sound in his ears. That rushing blurriness abated and slowed and by degrees took on a nebulous shape. He was looking down from a height of about thirty feet upon a street scene which he identified roughly as Elizabethan by the costumes of those who moved through the crowd below him.

Something was wrong. The machine could not have worked perfectly somehow, for he did not feel that he was actually present. The scene was uncertain and wavery, like a faulty film reflecting upon an uneven screen. There must have been an obstruction somewhere in that particular time section, though what it was he never knew.

He leaned forward for a few minutes, looking down eagerly through the hazy uncertainty that shrouded the place. He did not seem to himself to be resting on anything; yet he was conscious of that forward bending as he looked down. It was inexplicable.

The noises rose up to him now loudly, now softly,

from the shifting, pushing throng. Shopkeepers bawled their wares from both sides of the street. Apprentice boys darted to and fro through the crowd, waylaying passers-by.

A girl in a scarlet cloak flung open a window and leaned out to wave a message to someone below, her bright hair falling about her face. In the room behind her, dimly seen, another girl moved forward and flung both arms about her waist, laughing, dragging her back. Their merriment rose clearly to Eric's ears.

But all this was not real. That cloudiness hazed it over time and again, until his eyes ached from trying to follow what was happening. Regretfully, he reached for the switches at his belt, and in a breath the whole place shimmered and vanished. Oblivion in a torrent poured over him as the centuries plunged by over the bedrock inertia to which he was anchored.

The automatic workings of the time machine on his shoulders clicked on. Then the switches threw themselves and the blankness cleared from Eric's mind again. He found himself staring through a screen of leaves upon a grassy meadow through which trickled a small brook. He was tangibly, actually here this time, standing on soft turf and feeling stir of a breeze through the leaves.

Over the slope of the meadow before him dingy white sheep moved slowly. A little curly-haired boy in a brief leather garment leaned on the grass drowsily, watching them. Sun lay yellow over the whole scene. It was peaceful and dreamy as an idyl, but for some obscure reason Eric's hands moved to his belt almost of their own accord, a feeling of disappointment stirring vaguely in his mind. This was not what he sought. Sought? Was he seeking? Almost one might think so, he told himself.

The thought troubled him as he clicked the switches at his belt. What was it that by its absence here made him dismiss the idyllic scene with a glance? He was hunting something, restlessly searching through the ages for—something. Then the tidal rush of the centuries over his anchorage blotted out wonder and all else in its oblivion.

Sunlight like a physical blow crashed down about him —blazing hot sun that beat violently upon marble pavement and struck blindingly up again into his eyes. For a few seconds he was aware of nothing more than this intolerable glare. Gradually out of the blazing heat the lines of marble walls became clear about him. He stood upon the floor of a dazzling white marble pit about twenty feet square. Against the opposite wall lay a man whose naked, blood-spattered body was so still under the down-blazing heat that Eric could not be sure that he was alive.

He had seen this much before the rising babble of excited voices above him mounted loud enough to pierce his dazed surprise. He looked up. Leaning over the pit's rim were faces—faces and arms and here and there a trail of velvet robe, a bright scarf's fringe. They were the faces of aristocrats, fine and dissipated and cruel. But all expression was wiped from every one now.

In that first glance he had of them he thought they must be Romans. He had little to judge by save their hair dressing, and only a momentary glimpse of that; for, as he raised his head, his eyes met the strange, smoke-blue eyes of a woman who leaned upon the marble rim just in front of him, and above. A little space separated her from those on each side. He had the swift impression that she was of higher rank than the rest— some fleeting touch of arrogance and pride in the face looking down on him. And it was a familiar face. Why he could not guess, but in that glimpse of her he was sure that he had seen those features somewhere before, and recently.

Then she lifted one bare arm upon whose whiteness the sun struck dazzlingly, and pointed downward. From behind her came the sound of metal upon stone, and in the blinding light he saw a man's arm move swiftly. The sun struck upon a long shaft of steel. The spear was hurtling straight for his breast as his hands flew to his belt. The switches clicked, and in one great sweeping blur the whole scene vanished.

After that came a blurry interval of unthinkable inertness. The centuries poured past. Then reality burst upon him again as the switches clicked off. He choked suddenly and gasped as an air thicker and moister than the air of a tropical swamp smothered his lungs. He stood there for a moment struggling with it, forcing himself to evener breathing, as his bewildered gaze swept the scene before him.

He stood in a square of ruined walls that must once have been a small building, though roof and sides had vanished now and little was left but a crumbling square outlining the long-fallen house. To one side a higher heap of stone, which was all that was left of the western wall, obstructed his view of what lay beyond. Over the fallen blocks before him he could see a vast paved square dotted with other buildings fallen into ruin. And beyond these, under a heavily clouded sky through which the obscured sun poured in a queer, grayly radiant light, buildings of barbaric colors and utterly alien architecture lifted their Cyclopean heights, massive as the walls of Karnak, but too strangely constructed to awake any memories.

Even at this distance he recognized those darker blotches upon the tremendous walls as the sign of a coming dissolution. It was a city more awfully impressive than any he had ever dreamed of, standing gigantic under the low, gray sky of this swamplike world—but its glory was past. Here and there gaps in the colossal walls spoke of fallen blocks and ruined buildings. By the thick, primordial air and the swamp smell and the unrecognizable architecture he knew that he gazed upon a scene of immortal antiquity, and his breath came quicker as he stared, wondering where the people were whose Cyclopean city this was, what name they bore and if history had ever recorded it.

A medley of curious sounds coming nearer awoke him from the awed trance into which he had sunk. Feet shuffling over pavement, the clang of metal shivering against metal, hoarse breathing, and a strange, intermittent hissing he could not account for. It came from that part of the great square which the crumbling wall beside him hid.

That queer hissing sounded loud. Someone yelled in a growling guttural, and he heard the beat of running feet, staggering and uncertain, coming nearer. Then a figure that was a dazzle of white and scarlet flashed through the aperture in the crumbling wall where a door must once have been. It was a girl. Her choked breath beat loud in the narrow place, and the scarlet that stained and streaked her was bright blood that gushed in ominous spurts from a deep gash in her side. She was incredibly white in the sunless day of this primordial city. Afterward he could never remember much more than that—her dazzling whiteness and the blood pumping in measured spurts from severed arteries—and the smoke blueness of her eyes.

He did not know what she had worn, or anything else about her, for his eyes met the smoky darkness of hers, and for a timeless moment they stared at one another, neither moving. He knew her. She was that royal Roman who had condemned him to death in the sun-hot pit; she was the laughing, red-cloaked girl who had leaned from the Elizabethan window. Incredibly, unquestionably, they three were the same blue-eyed girl.

A yell and a scrambling sound outside roused her from her tranced stare. He wondered wildly if he had not seen puzzled recognition in her filming eyes in that one long instant before she swung staggering toward the door. He knew she was dying as she turned, but some inner compulsion held him back, so that he did not offer to support her, only stood watching. After all, there was no help for her now. The smoke-blue eyes were glazing and life gushed scarlet out of her riven side.

He saw her reel back against the broken wall, and again he heard that strange hissing as her right hand rose and from a shining cylinder grasped in it a long stream of blue heat flared. There was a yell from outside. A throbbing silence broken only by the spatter of the girl's blood on the pavement. And then something very strange happened.

She turned and glanced over her shoulder and her eyes met his. Something choked in his throat. He was very near understanding a great many things in that instant while her filming blue gaze held his—why he had felt so urgently all his life long the need of something he had never neared, until now—— Words rushed to his lips, but he never spoke them. The instant passed in a flash.

The girl in that illuminating moment must have realized something yet hidden from him, for her lips trembled and an infinite tenderness softened her glazing eyes. And at the same instant her hand rose again, and for the last time he heard that searing hiss. She had turned her nameless weapon upon herself.

In a flare of blue brilliance he saw her literally melt before his eyes. The stones glowed hot, and the smell of burned flesh filled the inclosure. And Eric went sick with a sensation of devastating loss. She was dead— gone—out of all reach now, and the universe was so empty that—— He had no time to waste on his own emotion, for through the broken wall was pouring a mob of shambling things that were not yet men.

Big, hairy, apish brutes brandishing clubs and heavy stones, they surged in a disordered mob through the ruined stones. One or two of them carried curiously shaped rusty swords of no recognizable pattern. And Eric understood.

Dying, the girl would not leave even her untenanted body to their defilement. Pride had turned her hand to lay the consuming beam upon herself—an inbred pride that could have come only from generations of proud ancestry. It was a gesture as aristocratic and as intensely civilized as the weapon that destroyed her. He would have known by that gesture alone, without her flame-thrower or the unmistakable fineness of her body and her face, that she was eons in advance of the beasts she fled.

In the brief second while the brute-men stood awed in the broken wall, staring at the charred heap upon the pavement and at the tall golden man who stood over it, Eric's mind was busy, turning over quick wonderings, and speculations even as his hands reached for the switches at his belt.

Her race must have reared that immense, unearthly city, long ago. A forgotten race, wise in forgotten arts. Perhaps not born of earth. And the hordes of brutish things which would one day become men must have assailed them as time beat down their Cyclopean city and thinned their inbred ranks.

This girl, this unknown, unimaginably far-distant girl, perhaps star-born, certainly very alien—had died as all her race must be doomed to die, until the last flicker of that stupendous civilization was stamped out and earth forgot the very existence of the slim, long-legged human race which had once dwelt upon her surface when her own primordial man was still an apish beast.

But—they had not wholly died. He had seen her in other ages. Her smoky eyes had looked down upon him in the Roman pit; her own gay voice had called across the Elizabethan street. He was very sure of that. And the queer, stunning sense of loss which had swept over him as he saw her die lightened. She had died, but she was not gone. Her daughters lived through countless ages. He would find her again, somewhere, somehow, in some other age and land. He would comb the centuries until he found her. And he would ask her then what her last long stare had meant, so meltingly tender, so surely recognizing, as she turned the blue-hot blaze upon herself. He would——

A deep-throated bellow from the doorway in the wall startled him out of his thoughts even as he realized their absurdity. The foremost of the brute-men had overcome his awe. He lifted a rusty sword, forged by what strange hands for what unknown and forever forgotten purpose there was no way of knowing, and plunged forward.

Barely in time, Eric's hands closed on the switches and the stupendous, time-forgotten city swirled sidewise and melted forever into the abysses of the past.

In the mental and physical inertia that drowned him with its oblivion as the current closed he waited moveless, and once more the centuries rushed by. The inexorable machinery clicked on. After a timeless interval light broke again. He awoke into more than tropical sultriness, the stench of mud and musk and welter of prehistoric swamps. There was nothing here save great splashing monsters and the wriggling life of hot seas. He flicked the switches again.

The next time a broad plain surrounded him, feature-less to the horizon, unrecognizable, and the next a horde of hairy, yelling men charged up a rocky hill upon whose height he had materialized. After that he visited and left in rapid succession a ruined temple in the midst of a jungle, a camp of ragged nomads with slant eyes and crooked legs, and an inexplicable foggy place through which reverberated the roar of staccato guns which sounded like no guns he had ever heard. Nowhere appeared the girl with the smoke-blue eyes.

He was beginning to despair, when, after so many flashing scenes that he had lost count of them, the dark-ness of rushing centuries faded into a dawning scene of noise and confusion. He stood upon the trampled earth of a courtyard, hot under the rays of a broiling, noon-high sun.

He heard shouts in an unknown tongue, the trample of horses' feet and the impatient jingle of harness, the creak of wheels. Through the shining dust that eddied, cloudlike, under the feet of the crowd that bustled about the inclosure, he made out a train of heavy wagons about which strange, short, bearded men swarmed in busy confusion, heaving crates and bales into the vehi-cles and calling in odd gutturals. Men on horseback gal-loped to and fro recklessly through the crowd, and the heavy-headed oxen stood in patient twos at each wagon.

Eric found himself in a corner of the low wall that circled the yard, and, in the tumult, quite unnoticed so far. He stood there quietly, hand resting lightly on the butt of his revolver, watching the scene. He could not guess where he was, in what land or time, in the pres-ence of what alien race. The men were all little and dark and hairy, and somehow crooked, like gnomes. He had never heard a tongue like the gutturals they mouthed.

Then at the far side of the courtyard a lane opened in the crowd, and through it a column of the crooked brown men with curly-pronged pikes across their shoul-ders came marching. They had a captive with them—a girl. A tall girl, slim and straight, high-headed. Eric leaned forward eagerly. Yes, it was she. No mistaking the poise of that high, dark head, the swing of her body as she walked. As she came nearer he saw her eyes, but he did not need the smoky blue darkness of them to convince him.

She wore manacles on her wrists, and chains clanked between her ankles as she walked. A leather tunic hung from one shoulder in tatters, belted at the waist by a twisted thong from which an empty scabbard swung. She walked very proudly among the gnarled soldiers, looking out over their heads in studied disdain. At a glance the highbred aristocracy of her was clear, and he could not mistake the fact that her own people must be centuries in advance of the squat, dark race which held her captive.

The clamor had quieted now in the courtyard. Dust was settling over the long wagon train, the low-headed oxen, the horsemen stationed at intervals along the line. In silence, the crowd fell back as the soldiers and their aloof captive paced slowly across the courtyard. Tension was in the air.

Eric had the vague feeling that he should know what was to come. A haunting familiarity about this scene teased him. He racked a reluctant memory as he watched the procession near the center of the great yard. A stone block stood there, worn and stained. Not until the tall girl had actually reached that block, and the soldiers were forcing her to her knees, did Eric remember. Sacrifice—always before a caravan set forth in the very old days, when the gods were greedy and had to be bribed with human lives.

His gun was in his hand and he was plunging forward through the startled crowd before he quite realized what he was doing. They gave way before him in sheer amazement, falling back and staring with bulging eyes at this sudden apparition in their midst of a tall, yellow-headed Juggernaut yelling like a madman as he surged forward.

Not until he had reached the line of soldiers did he meet any resistance. They turned on him in gutturally shouting fury, and he shot them down as fast as his revolver would pump bullets. At that range he could not miss, and six of the squat gnomes crumpled to the dust in a haze of blue gun smoke.

They must have thought him a god dealing death in a crash of thunder and the hot blaze of lightning. They shrieked in panic terror, and the courtyard emptied like magic. Horses plunged and reared, squealing. Pandemonium streamed out of the inclosure, leaving behind only a haze of churned dust, slowly settling. Through the shimmer of it, across the huddle of bodies, Eric looked again into the smoky eyes of that girl he had last seen under the stupendous walls of the time-buried city. And again he thought he saw a puzzled and uncomprehending recognition on her face, shining even through her terror. She fronted him resolutely, standing up proudly in her chains and staring with frightened eyes that would not admit their fear.

"Don't be afraid," he said in as gentle a voice as he could command, for he knew the tone would convey a message, though the words did not. "We'd better get out of here before they come back."

He was reloading his gun as he spoke. She still did nothing but stare, wide-eyed, rigid in sternly suppressed terror. There was no time to waste now trying to quiet her fears. Already he saw dark, bearded faces peering around corners at him. He skirted the heap of fallen soldiers and swung the girl off her feet. She gasped as his arms closed, but no other sound escaped her as he hoisted her over one shoulder, holding her there with a clasp around her knees so that he might have his gun hand free. With long, unhurried strides he left the courtyard.

A mud-walled village ringed the big inclosure. Serenely, he went down the dusty street, wary eyes scanning the building, gun ready in one hand and the chained girl slung across his heavy shoulder. From behind shelter they watched him go, tall and golden under the noonday sun, a god out of nowhere. Legends were to grow up about that noon's events—a god come down to earth to claim his sacrifice in person.

When he reached the outskirts of the village he paused and set the girl on her feet, turning his attention to the shackles that bound her. The chains were apparently for ceremonial use rather than utilitarian, for in his powerful hands they snapped easily, and after a brief struggle with the metal links he had her free of chains, though the anklets and cuffs still gripped her limbs. These he could not loosen, but they were not heavy and she could, he thought, wear them without discomfort. He rose as the last chain gave in his hands, and stared round the wide circle of rolling hills that hemmed them in.

"What now?" he asked, looking down at her.

The uncertainty of his attitude and the query in his voice must have reassured her that he was at least human, for the look of terror faded a little from her eyes and she glanced back down the street as if searching for pursuers, and spoke to him—for the first time he heard her voice—in a low, lilting tongue that startled him by the hint of familiarity he caught in its cadences. He had a smattering of many languages, and he was sure that this was akin to one he knew, but for the moment he could not place it.

When he did not answer she laid an impatient hand on his arm and pulled him along a few steps, then paused and looked up inquiringly. Clearly she was anxious to leave the village. He shrugged and gestured helplessly. She nodded, as if in understanding, and set off at a rapid pace toward the hills. He followed her.

It was a tireless pace she set. The metal circles on wrists and ankles seemed not to hinder her, and she led the way over hill after hill, through clumps of woodland and past a swamp or two, without slackening her pace. For hours they traveled. The sun slid down the sky; the shadows lengthened across the hills. Not until darkness came did she pause. They had reached a little hollow ringed with trees. On one side of it a rocky outcropping formed a shelter, and a spring bubbled up among the stones. It was an ideal spot for a camp.

She turned and spoke for the second time, and he knew then why her language was familiar. Definitely it was akin to the Basque tongue. He had once had opportunity to pick up a little of that queer, ancient language, perhaps the oldest spoken in the world. It is thought to be the last remnant of the pre-Aryan tongues, and linked with vanished races and forgotten times. And the supposition must have been true, for this girl's speeched echoed it in bafflingly familiar phrases. Or—he paused here—was he in the future or the past from his own time? Well, no matter—she was saying something all but incomprehensible about fire, and looking about among the underbrush. Eric shrugged off his speculations on the subject of tongues and helped her gather firewood.

His matches caused her a few minutes of awe-struck terror when the fire was kindled under the overhanging rocks of the hillside. She quieted after a bit, though, and presently pressed him to a seat by the fire and vanished into the dark. He waited uneasily until she returned, stepping softly into the light with a kicking rabbit in her hands. He never understood, then or later, how it was that she could vanish into the hills and return with some small animal unhurt in her arms. He could scarcely believe her swift enough to run them down, and she had nothing with which to make snares. It was one of the many mysteries about her that he never fathomed.

They skinned and cleaned the little beast with his hunting knife, and she broiled it over the smoldering coals. It was larger and stronger than the rabbits of his own day, and its meat was tough and sharply tangy.

Afterward they sat by the carefully banked fire and tried to talk. Her name was Maia. Her people lived in a direction vaguely eastward and about one day's journey away, in a white-walled city. All his attempts to learn in what age he found himself were fruitless. He thought from her almost incomprehensible speech that she was telling him how ancient her race was, and how it had descended through countless generations from a race of gods who dwelt in a sky-high city in the world's beginning. It was all so vague and broken that he could not be sure.

She looked at him a great deal out of grave blue eyes as she talked, and there was in their depths a haunted remembrance. He was to recall that look of hers more clearly than anything else about her, afterward. So many times he caught the puzzled, brooding gaze searching his face in troubled incomprehension.

He sat there silently, scarcely heeding the occasional low cadences of her voice. He was learning the grave, sweet lines of her young face, the way her eyes tilted ever so faintly at the corners, the smooth plane of her cheek, the curved line on which her lips closed. And sometimes the wonder of their meeting, through so many ages, came down upon him breathlessly, the realization of something too vast and strange and wonderful to put into words, and he stared into the sweet, familiar face almost with awe, thinking of those other grave, dark eyes and serene faces, so like hers, that ranged through time. There was a tremendous purpose behind that patterning of faces through the centuries, too great for him to grasp.

He watched her talk, the firelight turning that dearly familiar face ruddy, and shining in the deep, troubled blueness of her eyes, and a strange and sudden tenderness came over him. He bent forward, a catch in his throat, laying his hands over hers, looking into the memory-haunted depths of her eyes.

He said not a word, but he stared deep and long, and he could have sworn that sudden answer lighted in her gaze, for one swift instant blotting out that puzzled straining after remembrance and turning her whole face serene and lovely with understanding. The moment held them enchanted, warm in the deeps of something so breathlessly lovely that he felt the sting of sudden hotness behind his eyes. In that instant all puzzlement and incomprehension was swept aside and the answer to the great purpose behind their meetings hovered almost within grasp.

Then, without warning, the girl's face crumpled into tears and she snatched her hands away, leaping to her feet with the long, startled bound of a wild thing and facing him in the firelight with clenched fists and swimming eyes. It was not rebellion against his clasp of her hands—surely she could see that he meant no violence

—but a revolt against some inner enemy that dwelt behind the tear-bright blue eyes. She stood irresolutely there for a moment, then made a helpless little gesture and dropped to the ground once more, sitting there with bowed shoulders and bent head, staring into the embers.

Presently her voice began softly, speaking in little disconnected phrases that fell monotonously into the silence. He made out enough to understand her sudden revulsion against that strange and lovely oneness of understanding that had gripped them both. She was betrothed. She made him realize that it was more than the simple plighting of vows between lovers. He caught vague references to religious ceremonies, marriage of high priest and chosen virgin, temple rites and the anger of a jealous god. That much he understood.

She must fulfill the requisites of the priest god's bride. No man must touch her until she came into the holy embrace of the church. She must not even know love for another man. And that, perhaps, was why she had pulled away from him in the firelight and struggled through tears with an inner enemy that reached traitorously out to the golden stranger who held her hands.

She was unshakable in her devotion to that concept. Eric had known, from the moment he first looked into her smoke-filled eyes, that she would be faithful to any ideal that stirred her. A girl like this had destroyed the body from which her soul was slipping, that barbarians might not defile it. A girl like this, imperiously royal and inflexibly cruel, had watched torture in a sun-hot pit, refusing to doubt her civilization's concept of the divine right of emperors over their subjects' lives. She was stubborn, this girl. Stubborn in her beliefs whether they were kind or cruel. She was of the stuff from which martyrs are made.

They stood watch in turn over the fire that night, she insisting on her share of it with a grave certainty that brooked no opposition. What the dangers were which made it impossible for both to sleep at once he did not know. On those times when he dropped off into slumber the last thing his closing eyes saw was the girl Maia's figure, slim and round in her torn leather tunic, warm in the firelight, serene in her determination upon her life's ordered plan. Nothing could swerve her. She was so fine —— An ache came up in his throat as he closed his eyes.

When he awoke in the morning she had brought in a brace of small, fat birds like quail and was preparing them at the edge of the spring. She smiled gravely as he sat up, but she said nothing, and she did not look at him any more than she could help. She was taking no chances with that traitor within.

In silence, they shared the birds she cooked over the embers. Afterward he tried to make her understand that he would take her as far as the gates of her city. At first she demurred. She knew this country well. She was strong and young, wise in the lore of the hills. She needed no escort. But Eric could not bring himself to leave her until he must. That moment of crystal understanding, the warm, sweet unity they had shared even for so short a breath had forged a bond between them that he could not bear to break.

And at last she consented. They spoke very little after that. They put out the fire and set off again over the rolling hills toward the bright patch on the sky where the sun was rising. All day they traveled. In her mysterious, secret way she found another rabbit when hunger came on them around noontide, and they paused to eat. In the afternoon the pack on his back that held that time machine began to irk Eric's Viking strength. She eyed it curiously as he hitched his load forward to ease its burden, but she said nothing.

Twilight was darkening over the hills when Maia paused on the crest of a little rise and pointed ahead. Eric saw a pattern of white houses ringed by a broken wall a little way distant upon the crown of a higher hill than the rest. And here she made it clear that she must leave him. He was not to accompany her within sight of the city walls.

He stood on the hilltop, watching her go. She did not look back. She walked lightly, surely, the long grass breaking like green surf about her knees, her head high and resolute. He watched her until she passed, a little far-off figure, under the broken wall, and its gateway swallowed her up out of his sight forever. And in his heart was a mingling of pain and loss and high anticipation. For he was growing increasingly sure now that there was much more than chance behind these brief and seemingly so futile meetings with the one deathless, blue-eyed girl.

He laid his hands on the switches at his belt confidently as that proudly moving young figure vanished under the gate. He had lost her—but not for long. Somewhere in the veiled, remote future, somewhere in the unexplored past she waited him. His fingers closed over the switch.

Darkly the rush of centuries swept over him, blotting away the hills and the green meadows between, and the nameless white city that was crumbling into decay. He would never see Maia again, but there were other Maias, waiting. Oblivion swallowed him up and his impatience and his dawning conviction of a vast purpose behind his journeyings, in the great grayness of its peace.

Out of that blankness a blue day dawned, bright over a moated castle's battlements. From a hilltop perhaps a quarter of a mile away he saw the surge of armored men under the walls, heard shouts and the clang of metal on metal drifting to him on the gentleness of a little breeze. And it occurred to him how often it was upon scenes of strife and sudden death that he chanced in his haphazard journeying. He wondered if they had been so thick in the past that the odds were against his coming into peaceful places, or if his own life of danger and adventuring had any influence upon the points in time which he visited so briefly.

But it mattered little. He looked around searchingly, wondering if another blue-eyed Maia dwelt near him in this medieval world. But there was nothing here. Green forest closed in at the hill's foot. Save for the castle there was no sign of civilization, no sign of men but for the shouting besiegers. Perhaps she lived somewhere in this blue, primitive world, but he could not risk a search for her. She was elsewhere, too.

Suddenly he was awed by the certainty of that—the incomprehensible vastness of his certainty and of her presence. She was everywhere. From time's beginning to time's close—she was. No era had not known her; no spot on the world's surface had not felt the press of her feet. And though the infinite future and the infinite past held her, and the earth's farthest corners, yet in reality every incarnation of her was here and now, available to him with no greater interval between her countless daughters than the instant flash of the centuries that poured over him when the switches closed. She was omnipresent, eternal. He knew her presences in the oblivion that swallowed him as his hands gripped the switches again and the beleaguered castle melted into the past.

Two children were playing by a shallow river. Eric walked slowly toward them through the warm sand. A little girl, a little boy in brief tunics of soiled white. Perhaps ten years old they were, and absorbed in their play at the water's edge. Not until his shadow fell across their castle of rocks and sand did they look up. And the girl child's eyes were blue as smoke in her small, tanned face.

Those familiar eyes met his. For a long moment she stared. Then she smiled hesitantly, very sweetly, and rose to her bare feet, shaking the sand from her tunic and looking up at him still with that grave, sweet smile illuminating her small face and a queer hesitation checking her speech.

At last she said, *"Ou e'voo?"* in the softest, gentlest voice imaginable. It was remotely recognizable as a tongue that might one day be—or once had been—French. "Who are you?"

"Je suis Eric," he told her gravely.

She shook her head a little. *"Zh n'compren——"* she began doubtfully, in that strange, garbled tongue so like French. But she broke off in her denial, for though the name was strange to her yet he was sure he saw recognition begin to dawn in the smoke-blue eyes he knew so well. *"Zh voo z'ai vu?"*

"Have you?" he asked her very gently, trying to distort his French into the queer sounds of hers. "Have you really seen me before?"

"I thought so," she murmured shyly, bewilderment muting her speech until it sounded scarcely above a childish whisper. "I have seen your face before—somewhere, once—long ago. Have I? Have I—Eric? I do not know your name. I never heard it before. But your face —you——— O, Eric dear—I do love you!"

Halfway through that speech she had changed her *"voo"* to the *"tu"* of intimacy, and the last of it came out on a little rush of childish affection, *"Eric, cher—zh t'aime!"*

Somewhere back among the willows that lined the shallow stream a woman's voice called sharply. The sound of feet among dead leaves approached. The little boy jumped to his feet, but the girl seemed not to hear. She was looking up at Eric with wide blue eyes, her small face rapt with a child's swift adoration. Ten years older and she might have questioned the possibility of that instant recognition, perhaps unconsciously checked the instant warmth that rose within her, but the child's mind accepted it without question.

The woman was very near now. He knew he must not frighten her. He stooped and kissed the little girl's cheek gently. Then he took her by the shoulders and turned her toward the woods into which the boy had already vanished.

"Go to your mother," he told her softly. And he laid his hands again on the switches. She was beginning to know him, he thought, as the river bank swirled sidewise into nothingness. Each time they met the recognition grew stronger. And though there was no continuity in their meetings, so that he seemed to be jumping back and forth through time and this child might be the remote ancestress or the far descendant of his resolute Maia, yet somehow—by no racial memory surely, for it was not down a direct line of women that he progressed, but haphazardly to and fro through their ranks—somehow they were beginning to know him. Oblivion blotted out his puzzling.

Out of the rushing dark a steel-walled city blazed into sudden, harsh life. He stood on one tower of its many heights, looking out and down over a dizzy vista of distances that swam with the reflections of sunlight on steel. He stood still for a moment, shading his eyes and staring. But he was impatient. Something instinctive in him, growing stronger now and surer of itself as this strange chain of circumstance and meeting drew on to its conclusion, told him that what he sought lay nowhere in this section out of time. Without a glance around the stupendous steel marvel of the city he gripped the switches once more, and in a shimmer and a dazzle the shining metropolis melted into oblivion.

A burst of wild yelling like the voices of wolves baying from savage human throats smote through the darkness at him even before the sight of what was coming. Then a plank flooring was under his feet and he looked out over a tossing surface of tousled heads and brandished fists and weapons, toward another platform, this of stone, the height of his across the thunderous sea of the mob. The crackle of flames was mounting even above that roaring. On the other platform, bound to a tall, charred stake, ringed with fagots and rising flames, the blue-eyed girl stood proudly. She was very straight against the pillar, chin high, looking out in disdain over the tumult below.

For the breath of a second Eric glanced round him, snatching at straws in a frantic effort to find some way of saving her. On the platform behind him speechless amazement had stricken dumb a little party of men and women in brightly colored garments of 16th Century cut. They must have been nobles, viewing the burning from this favored seat. Eric wasted only one glance at their stupefied surprise. He swung round again, his desperate eyes raking the mob. No hope there. It clamored for the tall girl's life in one tremendous, wolf-savage baying that ripped from every throat there in a single blending roar.

"Witch!" they yelled. "Death to the witch!" in an archaic English that he understood without too much difficulty, a blood-hungry baying that brooked no denial. They had not seen him yet. But the girl had.

Over their heads, through the little shimmering heat waves that were rising about her already in veils of scorching breath, her smoke-blue eyes met his. It was a meeting as tangible almost as the meeting of hands. And like the grip of hands so that gaze held, steady and unswerving for a long moment—burning witch of old England and tall young adventurer of modern America gazing with sure recognition in the eyes of each. Eric's heart jumped into a quickened beating as he saw the sureness in those smoke-blue eyes he had gazed into so often. She knew him—without any question or doubt she recognized him.

Over the wolf-baying of the mob he heard her voice in one high, clear scream.

"You've come! I knew you'd come!"

At the sound of it silence dropped over the crowd. Almost in one motion they swung round to follow her ecstatic stare. And in the instant of their stricken surprise at the man they saw there, tall and golden against the sky, a figure out of no experience they had ever had before—the witch's voice rang clear.

"You've come! O, I knew you would, in the end. *They* always said you would. *They* knew! And I must die for the knowledge I got from *Them*—but by that knowledge I know this is not the end. Somewhere, some day, we will meet again. Good-by—good-by, my dearest!"

Her voice had not faltered, though the flames were licking up about her, and now, in a great burst of crimson, they caught in the fagots and blazed up in a gush that enveloped her in raving inferno. Choked with horror, Eric swung up his gun hand. The bark of the report sent half the crowd to its knees in terror, and he saw through the flames the girl's tall figure slump suddenly against her bonds. This much at least he could do.

Then, in the midst of a silence so deep that the creak of the planks under his feet was loud as he moved, he sheathed the gun and closed his hands over the switches. Impatience boiled up in him as the prostrate crowd and the flame-wrapped witch and the whole ugly scene before him reeled into nothingness.

He was coming near the goal now. Each successive

step found recognition surer in her eyes. She knew him in this incarnation, and he was full of confidence now that the end and the solution was near. For though in all their meetings there had been barriers, so that they two could never wholly know one another or come into the unity of love and comprehension which each meeting promised, yet he knew very surely that in the end they must. All this had not been in vain.

In the oblivion that washed over him was so sure a consciousness of her omnipresence—in all the centuries that were sweeping past, in all the lands those centuries washed over, throughout time and space and life itself, her ever-present loveliness—that he welcomed the darkness as if he embraced the girl herself. It was full of her, one with her. He could not lose her or be far from her or even miss her now. She was everywhere, always. And the end was coming. Very soon—very soon he would know——

He woke out of the oblivion, blindly into darkness. Like the fold of wings it engulfed him. If he was standing on solid earth, he did not know it. He was straining every faculty to pierce that blinding dark, and he could not. It was a living darkness, pulsing with anticipation. He waited in silence.

Presently she spoke.

"I have waited so long," she said out of the blackness in her sweet, clear voice that he knew so well he did not need the evidence of his eyes to tell him who spoke.

"Is this the end?" he asked her breathlessly. "Is this the goal we've been traveling toward so long?"

"The end?" she murmured with a little catch of mirth in her voice. "Or the beginning, perhaps. Where in a circle is end or beginning? It is enough that we are together at last."

"But what—why——"

"Something went wrong, somewhere," she told him softly. "It doesn't matter now. We have expiated the forgotten sins that kept us apart to the very end. Our troubled reflections upon the river of time sought each other and never wholly met. And we, who should have been time's masters, struggled in the changing currents and knew only that everything was wrong with us, who did not know each other.

"But all that is ended now. Our lives are lived out and we can escape time and space into our own place at last. Our love has been so great a thing that though it never fulfilled itself, yet it brimmed time and the void to overflowing, so that everywhere you adventured the knowledge of my present tormented you—and I waited for you in vain. Forget it now. It's over. We have found ourselves at last."

"If I could only see you," he said fretfully, reaching out into the blackness. "It's so dark here. Where are we?"

"Dark?" the gentle voice laughed softly. "Dark? My dearest—this is not darkness! Wait a moment—here!"

Out of the night a hand clasped his. "Come with me." Together they stepped forward.

Greater Than Gods

THE DESK WAS glass-clear steel, the mirror above it a window that opened upon distance and sight and sound whenever the televisor buzzer rang. The two crystal cubes on the desk were three-dimensional photographs of a sort undreamed of before the Twenty-third Century dawned. But between them on the desk lay a letter whose message was older than the history of writing itself.

"My darling—" it began in a man's strongly slanting handwriting. But there Bill Cory had laid down his pen and run despairing fingers through his hair, looking from one crystal-cubed photograph to the other and swearing a little under his breath. It was fine stuff, he told himself savagely, when a man couldn't even make up his mind which of two girls he wanted to marry. Biology House of Science City, that trusted so faithfully the keenness and clarity of Dr. William Cory's decisions, would have shuddered to see him now.

For the hundredth time that afternoon he looked from one girl's face to the other, smiling at him from the crystal cubes, and chewed his lip unhappily. On his left, in the translucent block that had captured an immortal moment when dark Marta Mayhew smiled, the three-dimensional picture looked out at him with a flash of violet eyes. Dr. Marta Mayhew of Chemistry House, ivory whiteness and satin blackness. Not at all the sort of picture the mind conjures up of a leading chemist in Science City which houses the greatest scientists in the world.

Bill Cory wrinkled his forehead and looked at the other girl. Sallie Carlisle dimpled at him out of the crystal, as real as life itself to the last flying tendril of fair curls that seemed to float on a breeze frozen eternally into glass. Bill reached out to turn the cube a little, bringing the delicate line of her profile into view, and it was as if time stood still in the crystalline deeps and pretty Sallie in the breathing flesh paused for an eternal moment with her profile turned away.

After a long moment Bill Cory sighed and picked up his pen. After the "*darling*" of the letter he wrote firmly, "*Sallie.*"

"Dr. Cory," hesitated a voice at the door. Bill looked up, frowning. Miss Brown blinked at him nervously behind her glasses. "Dr. Ashley's—"

"Don't announce me, Brownie," interrupted a languid voice behind her. "I want to catch him loafing. Ah, Bill, writing love letters? May I come in?"

"Could I stop you?" Bill's grin erased the frown from his forehead. The tall and tousled young man in the doorway was Charles Ashley, head of Telepathy House, and though their acquaintance had long been on terms of good-natured insult, behind it lay Bill's deep recognition of a quality of genius in Ashley that few men ever attain. No one could have risen to the leadership of Telepathy House whose mind did not encompass many more levels of infinite understanding than the ordinary mind even recognizes.

"I've worked myself into a stupor," announced the head of Telepathy House, yawning. "Come on up to the Gardens for a swim, huh?"

"Can't." Bill laid down his pen. "I've got to see the pups—"

"Damn the pups! You think Science City quivers every time those little mutts yap! Let Miss Brown look after 'em. She knows more than you do about genetics, anyhow. Some day the Council's going to find it out and you'll go back to working for a living."

"Shut up," requested Bill with a grin. "How are the pups, Miss Brown?"

"Perfectly normal, doctor. I just gave them their three o'clock feeding and they're asleep now."

"Do they seem happy?" inquired Ashley solicitously.

"That's right, scoff," sighed Bill. "Those pups and I

will go ringing down the corridors of time, you mark my words."

Ashley nodded, half seriously. He knew it might well be true. The pups were the living proof of Bill's success in prenatal sex determination—six litters of squirming maleness with no female among them. They represented the fruit of long, painstaking experiments in the X-ray bombardment of chromosomes to separate and identify the genes carrying the factors of sex determination, of countless failures and immeasurable patience. If the pups grew into normal dogs—well, it would be one long sure stride nearer the day when, through Bill's own handiwork, the world would be perfectly balanced between male and female in exact proportion to the changing need.

Miss Brown vanished with a shy, self-effacing smile. As the door closed behind her, Ashley, who had been regarding the two photograph cubes on Bill's desk with a lifted eyebrow, arranged his long length on the couch against the wall and was heard to murmur: "Eenie-mee-nie-minie-mo. Which is it going to be, Will-yum?"

They were on terms too intimate for Bill to misunderstand, or pretend to.

"I don't know," he admitted miserably, glancing down in some hesitation at the letter beginning, "*My darling Sallie—*"

Ashley yawned again and fumbled for a cigarette. "You know," he murmured comfortably, "it's interesting to speculate on your possible futures. With Marta or Sallie, I mean. Maybe some day somebody will find a way to look ahead down the branching paths of the future and deliberately select the turning points that will carry him toward the goal he chooses. Now if you could know beforehand where life with Sallie would lead, or life with Marta, you might alter the whole course of human history. That is, if you're half as important as you think you are."

"Huh-uh," grunted Bill. "If you predicate a fixed future, then it's fixed already isn't it? And you'd have no real choice."

Ashley scratched a match deliberately and set his cigarette aglow before he said: "I think of the future as an infinite reservoir of an infinite number of futures, each of them fixed, yet malleable as clay. Do you see what I mean? At every point along our way we confront crossroads at which we make choices among the many possible things we may do the next moment. Each crossroad leads to a different future, all of them possible, all of them fixed, waiting for our choice to give them reality. Perhaps there's a—call it a Plane of Probability —where all these possible results of our possible choices exist simultaneously. Blueprints of things to come. When the physical time of matter catches up with, and fills in, any one particular plan, it becomes fixed in the present.

"But before time has caught up with it, while our choice at the crossroads is still unmade, an infinite number of possible futures must exist as it were in suspension, waiting for us in some unimaginable, dimensionless infinity. Can you imagine what it would be like to open a window upon that Probability Plane, look out into the infinities of the future, trace the consequences of future actions *before* we make them? We could mold the destiny of mankind! We could do what the gods must do, Bill! We'd be greater than gods We could look into the Cosmic Mind—the very brain that planned us—and of our own will choose among those plans!"

"Wake up, Ash," said Bill softly.

"You think I'm dreaming? It's not a new idea, really. The old philosopher, Berkeley, had a glimpse of it when he taught his theories of subjective idealism, that we're aware of the cosmos only through a greater awareness all around us, an infinite mind—

"Listen, Bill. If you vision these . . . these blueprints of possible futures, you've got to picture countless generations, finite as ourselves, existing simultaneously and completely in all the circumstances of their entire lives—yet all of them still unborn, still even uncertain of birth if the course of the present is diverted from their particular path. To themselves, they must seem as real as we to each other.

"Somewhere on the Plane of Probability, Bill, there

may be two diverging lines of your descendants, unborn
generations whose very existence hinges on your choice
here at the crossroads. Projections of yourself, really,
their lives and deaths trembling in the balance. Think
well before you choose!"

Bill grinned. "Suppose you go back to the Slum and
dope out a way for me to look into the Cosmic Plan," he
suggested.

Ashley shook his head.

"Wish I could. Boy, would you eat that word 'Slum'
then! Telepathy House wouldn't be the orphan child
around the City any longer if I could really open a window onto the Probability Plane. But I wouldn't bother
with you and your pint-sized problems. I'd look ahead
into the future of the City. It's the heart of the world,
now. Someday it may rule the world. And we're biased,
you know. We can't help being. With all the sciences
housed here under one city-wide roof, wielding powers
that kings never dreamed of— No, it may go to our
heads. We may overbalance into . . . into . . . well,
I'd like to look ahead and prevent it. And if this be
treason—" He shrugged and got up. "Sure you won't join
me?"

"Go on—get out. I'm a busy man."

"So I see." Ashley twitched an eyebrow at the two
crystal cubes. "Maybe it's good you can't look ahead.
The responsibility of choosing might be heavier than
you could bear. After all, we aren't gods and it must be
dangerous to usurp a god's prerogative. Well, see you
later.

Bill leaned in the doorway watching the lounging figure down the hall toward the landing platform where
crystal cars waited to go flashing along the great tubes
which artery Science City. Beyond, at the platform's
edge, the great central plaza of the City dropped away
in a breath-taking void a hundred stories deep. He stood
looking out blind-eyed, wondering if Sallie or Marta
would walk this hall in years to come.

Life would be more truly companionship with Marta,
perhaps. But did a family need two scientists? A man

wanted relaxation at home, and who could make life gayer than pretty Sallie with her genius for entertainment, her bubbling laughter? Yes, let it be Sallie. If there were indeed a Probability Plane where other possible futures hung suspended, halfway between walking and oblivion, let them wink out into nothingness.

He shut the door with a little slam to wake himself out of the dream, greeting the crystal-shrined girl on his desk with a smile. She was so real—the breeze blowing those curls was a breeze in motion. The lashes should flutter against the soft fullness of her lids—

Bill squeezed his eyes shut and shook his head to clear it. There was something wrong—the crystal was clouding—

A ringing in his ears grew louder in company with that curious blurring of vision. From infinitely far away, yet strangely in his own ears, a tiny voice came crying. A child's voice calling, "Daddy. . . . daddy!" A girl's voice, coming nearer, "Father—" A woman's voice saying over and over in a smooth sweet monotone, "Dr. Cory. . . . Dr. William Cory—"

Upon the darkness behind his closed lids a streaked and shifting light moved blurrily. He thought he saw towers in the sun, forests, robed people walking leisurely —and it all seemed to rush away from his closed eyes so bewilderingly—he lifted his lids to stare at—

To stare at the cube where Sallie smiled. Only this was not Sallie. He gaped with the blankness of a man confronting impossibilities. It was not wholly Sallie now, but there was a look of Sallie upon the lovely, suntouched features in the cube. All of her sweetness and softness, but it—something more. Something familiar. What upon this living, lovely face, with its level brown eyes and courageous mouth, reminded Bill of—himself?

His hands began to shake a little. He thrust them into his pockets and sat down without once taking his eyes from the living stare in the cube. There was amazement in that other stare, too, and a half-incredulous delight that brightened as he gazed.

Then the sweet curved lips moved—lips with the softness of Sallie's closing on the firm, strong line of Bill's. They said distinctly, in a sound that might have come from the cube itself or from somewhere deep within his own brain: "Dr. Cory . . . Dr. Cory, do you hear me?"

"I hear you," he heard himself saying hoarsely, like a man talking in a dream. "But—"

The face that was Sallie's and his blended blazed into joyful recognition, dimples denting the smooth cheeks with delicious mirth. "Oh, thank Heaven it *is* you! I've reached through at last. I've tried so hard, so long—"

"But who . . . what—" Bill choked a little on his own amazement and fell silent, marveling at the strange warm tenderness that was flooding up in him as he watched this familiar face he had never seen before. A tenderness more melting and protective and passionately selfless than he had ever imagined a man could feel. Dizzy with complete bewilderment, too confused to wonder if he dreamed, he tried again. "Who are you? What are you doing here? How did—"

"But I'm not there—not really." The sweet face smiled again, and Bill's heart swelled until his throat almost closed with a warmth of pride and tenderness he was too dizzy to analyze now. "I'm here—here at home in Eden, talking to you across the millennium! Look—"

Somehow, until then he had not seen beyond her. Sallie's face had smiled out of a mist of tulle, beyond which the cube had been crystal-clear. But behind the face which was no longer wholly Sallie's, a green hillside filled the cube. And, very strangely, it had no look of smallness. Though the cube's dimensions confined it, here was no miniature scene he gazed upon. He looked through the cube as through a window, out into a forest glade where upon a bank of green myrtle at the foot of a white garden wall a little group of tanned men and women reclined in a circle with closed eyes, lying almost like corpses on the dark, glossy leaves. But there was no relaxation in them. Tensity more of the spirit than the body knit the group into a whole, focused somehow upon the woman in the circle's center—this fair-haired woman who leaned forward with her elbows on her knees, chin in hand, staring brown-eyed and tensely into space—into Bill Cory's eyes. Dimly he realized that his perception had expanded as he stared. Awareness now of a whole countryside beyond her, just over the garden wall, made this cube that had housed Sallie's careless smile a window indeed, opening upon distance in space and time far outside his imagining.

He knew he was dreaming. He was sure of it, though the memory of what Ashley had been saying hovered uneasily in the back of his mind, too elusive now to be brought consciously into view. But in this impossible dream he clenched his hands hard in his pockets, taking a firm hold upon reality.

"Just who are you, and what do you want? And how did you—"

She chose to answer the last question first, breaking into it as if she could read his thoughts as she knelt staring on the myrtle leaves.

"I speak to you along an unbroken cord between us —father. Thousands of times removed, but—father. A cord that runs back through the lives that have parted us, yet which unite us. With the help of these people around me, their full mental strength supplementing mine, we've established contact at last, after so many failures, so much groping in mysteries which even I understand only partly, though my family for generations has been trained in the secrets of heredity and telepathy."

"But why—"

"Isn't the fact of achievement an end in itself? Success in establishing a two-way contact with the past, in talking to one's own ancestors—do I need more reason for attempting that than the pure joy of achieving it? You wonder why you were chosen. Is that it? Because you are the last man in a direct line of males to be born into my family before the blessed accident that saved the world from itself.

"Don't look so bewildered!" Laughter bubbled from the cube—or was it a sound in his own brain? "You aren't dreaming! Is it so incredible that along the unbroken cord of memories which links your mind to mine the current might run backward against the time flow?"

"But who are you? Your face—it's like—"

"My face is the face of the daughter that Sallie Cory bore you, thousands of years ago. That resemblance is a miracle and a mystery beyond all understanding—the mystery of heredity which is a stranger thing than the fact of our communication. We have wondered among ourselves if immortality itself—but no, I'll have mercy on you!"

This bewilderingly beloved face that had darkened with mystical brooding, flashed suddenly alive again with swift laughter, and hearing it, catching a lift of the brows that was his and a quirk of the soft lips that was Sallie's own, Bill made no effort to stem the tide of warm affection rising higher and higher in him. It was himself looking out of this cube through Sallie's brown eyes—himself exultant in achievement for the simple sake of achieving. She had called him father. Was this a father's love, selfless, unfathomable, for a lovely and beloved daughter?

"Don't wonder any more," laughed the voice in his ears. "Look—here's the past that lies between us. I want you to understand what parts your world from mine."

Softly the myrtle glade and the lovely smiling face that blended Sallie and Bill melted into the depths of a cloud forming inside the three dimensions of the cube. For a moment—nothing. Then motion was lifting behind the mist, shouldering the veils aside. Three-dimensional space seemed to open up all around him—

He saw a wedding procession coming down a church aisle toward him, Sallie smiling mistily through a cloud of silver tulle. And he knew at the sight of her that though it was only chance which had chosen her instead of dark Marta Mayhew, he could come to love Sallie Carlisle Cory with an intensity almost frightening.

He saw time go by with a swiftness like thought itself, events telescoping together with no sense of confusion, moving like memories through his mind, clear, yet condensed into split seconds. He was watching his own future, seeing a life that revolved around Sallie as the center of existence. He saw her flashing in and out of his laboratory as he worked, and whenever she entered, the whole room seemed to light up; whenever she left, he could scarcely work for the longing to follow.

He saw their first quarrel. Sallie, spinning in a shimmer of bright glass-silk as soft as gossamer, dimpled at the self which in this waking dream was more vividly Bill Cory than the Bill who watched. "See, darling, aren't I heavenly?" And he heard himself answering, "Edible, darling! But isn't that stuff expensive?"

Sallie's laughter was light. "Only fifteen hundred credits. That's dirt-cheap for a Skiparelle model."

He gasped. "Why Sallie, that's more than we're allowed for living expenses! I can't—"

"Oh, daddy'll pay for it if you're going to be stingy. I only wanted—"

"I'll buy my wife's clothes." Bill was grim. "But I can't afford Paris fashions, darling."

Sallie's pretty underlip pouted alarmingly. Tears sparkled in the soft brown eyes she lifted to his, and his heart melted almost painfully in one hopeless rush.

"Don't cry, sweetheart! You can keep it, just this once. But we'll have to make it up next month. Never again, Sallie, understand?"

Her nod was bright and oblivious as a child's.

But they didn't make it up. Sallie loved partying, and Bill loved Sallie, and nowadays there was much more hilarity than work going on behind the door in Biology House marked "Dr. William Vincent Cory." The television's panels were tuned to orchestras playing strong rhythm now, not to lectures and laboratory demonstrations as of old.

No man can do two jobs well. The work on sex determination began to strike snags in the path that had seemed almost clear to success, and Bill had so little time any more to smooth them out. Always Sallie was in the back of his mind, sweet, smiling, adorable.

Sallie wanted the baby to be born in her father's home. It was a lovely place, white-walled on low green hills above the Pacific. Sallie loved it. Even when little Sue was big enough to travel she hated to think of leaving. And the climate was so wonderful for the baby there—

Anyhow, by then the Council had begun to frown

over Bill Cory's work. After all, perhaps he wasn't really cut out to be a scientist—Sallie's happiness was more important than any man's job, and Sallie could never be really happy in Science City.

The second baby was a girl, too. There were a lot of girls being born nowadays. The telenews broadcasters joked about it. A good sign, they said. When a preponderance of boys was born, it had always meant war. Girls should bring peace and plenty for the new generation.

Peace and plenty—that was what mattered most to Bill and Sallie Cory now. That and their two exquisite daughters and their home on the green Pacific hills. Young Susan was growing up into a girlhood so enchanting that Bill suffused with pride and tenderness every time he thought of her. She had Sallie's beauty and blondeness, but there was a resolution in her that had been Bill's once, long ago. He liked to think of her, in daydreams, carrying on the work that he would never finish now.

Time ran on, years telescoping pleasantly into uneventful years. Presently the Cory girls were growing up . . . were married . . . were mothers. The grandchildren were girls, too. When Grandfather Cory joined his wife in the little graveyard on the sea-turned hill beyond the house, the Cory name died with him, though there was in his daughter's level eyes and in her daughter's look of serene resolution something more intrinsically Bill Cory than his name. The name might die, but something of the man who had borne it lived on in his descendants.

Girls continued to outnumber boys in the birth records as the generations passed. It was happening all over the world, for no reason that anyone could understand. It didn't matter much, really. Women in public offices were proving very efficient; certainly they governed more peacefully than men. The first woman president won her office on a platform that promised no war so long as a woman dwelt in the White House.

Of course, some things suffered under the matriarchy.

Women as a sex are not scientists, not inventors, not mechanics or engineers or architects. There were men enough to keep these essentially masculine arts alive—that is, as much of them as the new world needed. There were many changes. Science City, for instance. Important, of course, but not to the extent of draining the country dry to maintain it. Life went on very nicely without too much machinery.

The tendency was away from centralized living in these new days. Cities spread out instead of up. Skyscrapers were hopelessly old-fashioned. Now parklands and gardens stretched between low-roofed houses where the children played all day. And war was a barbarous memory from those nightmare years when men still ruled the world.

Old Dr. Phillips, head of the dwindling and outmoded Science City, provoked President Wiliston into a really inspiring fury when he criticized the modern tendency toward a non-mechanized rural civilization. It happened on the telenews, so that half the world heard it.

"But Madam President," he said, "don't you realize where we're heading? The world's going backward! It's no longer worth-while for our best minds to attempt bettering living conditions. We're throwing genius away! Do you realize that your cabinet yesterday flatly rejected the brilliant work of one of our most promising young men?"

"I do!" Alice Wiliston's voice rang with sudden violence over half the world. "That 'brilliant work,' as you call it, was a device that might have led to war! Do you think we want that? Remember the promise that the first woman president made the world, Dr. Phillips! So long as we sit in the White House there will be no need for war!"

And Elizabeth of England nodded in London; Julianna VII smiled into her Amsterdam telenews screen. While women ruled, war was outlawed. Peace and ease and plenty would dominate civilization, leisure for cultivation of the arts, humankind coming into its own at last, after so many ages of pain and blood and heartbreak.

Years telescoped into centuries of peace and plenty in

a garden world. Science had turned its genius to the sta-
bilization of the climate so that nowhere was shelter necessary from cold or storms; food was freely abundant
for all. The Garden that Adam and Eve forfeited in the
world's beginning had returned again to their remotest
descendants, and the whole earth was Eden.

And in this world that no longer demanded the slight-
est physical effort, mankind was turning to the cultivation of the mind. In these white, low-roofed houses set
among garden parks, men and women increasingly adventured into the realms beyond the flesh, exploring the
mysteries of the mind.

Bill Cory, leaning forward in his chair, had lost all
identity with himself. He was simply a consciousness
watching time unfold before him. The gravestone that
bore his name on the California hillside had long since
sunk into the sod, but if there is immortality at all, Bill
Cory watched himself move forward through the centuries, down the long, expanding line of his descendants.
Now and again, startlingly, his own face looked briefly
at him from some faraway child of his remote grandchildren. His face, and Sallie's.

He saw pretty Sue come and go like reflections in a
mirror. Not always Sue unmistakably and completely—
sometimes only her brown eyes lighted the face of a
many-times-great-granddaughter; sometimes the lift of
her smile or the tilt of her pretty nose alone was familiar
to him in a strange face. But sometimes Sue herself, perfect to the last detail, moved through the remote future.
And every time he saw those familiar features, his heart
contracted with an ache of tenderness for the daughter
he yet might never have.

It was for these beloved Susans that he was becoming
uneasy as he watched time go by in this lazy paradise
world. People were slowing mentally and physically.
What need any more for haste or trouble? Why worry
because certain unimportant knowledge was being lost
as time went on? The weather machines, the food machines were eternal; what else really mattered? Let the
birth rate decline, let the dwindling race of the inventive
and the ambitions fade like the anachronism it was. The
body had taken mankind as far as it could; the mind was

the vehicle for the future. In the vast reaches of infinity were fields aplenty for the adventurous spirit. Or one could simply drowse the days away—

Clouds thickened softly across the dreamy vistas of Eden. Bill Cory leaned back in his chair and rubbed his eyes with both hands. The hands were shaking, and he stared at them a little stupidly, still half lost in the wonder of what he had seen, in the strange welter of emotions that still warred in him—the memory of Sallie and his strong love for her, the memory of Sue's sweetness, the memory of pride in them both. And in the queer feeling that it had been himself in those many daughters of his through the ages, striving so hard for world peace to the ultimate end that mankind might achieve—*ruin*.

For it was wrong—it was bad. The whole world. The race of man was too splendid, too capable of working miracles, to end on a myrtle bank dreaming about abstractions. He had just seen a decadent, indolent civilization going down the last incline into oblivion as a result—yes, as a direct result—of his own action. He'd seen himself sinking into a fat, idle old age, without honor of achievement.

Suddenly and desperately he hoped that Ashley had been right—that this was not the inevitable and changeless future. If he tore up the letter lying on his desk now, if he never married Sallie, would not his work be finished successfully some day, and the castastrophe of unbalanced births avoided? Or could a man change his ordained future?

Almost fearfully he reached for the letter lying beside that clouded cube in which the years had mirrored themselves. Would he be able to take the letter up and rip it across—like this? The sound of tearing paper reassured him. So far, at least, he was still a free agent.

And knowing that, suddenly he was sorry. Not to marry Sallie, with her bubbling laugh. Never to see young Sue growing into beauty and courage and sweetness. Old age without achievement, had he said to himself a moment ago? Sue herself was achievement enough for any man. Sue and those other Susans down the long line of his descendants, incarnating again and again all that was finest in him, eternal as life itself through millenniums.

He did not want to meet again the brown eyes of this latest Susan who had come to him in the depths of the cube. While he looked, his reason was lost in his love for her, and not even against reason could he believe the world which had produced her to be anything but perfect, simply because this beloved daughter moved and breathed in it.

But the letter was torn. He would never marry Sallie if he could help himself. The cost was too high, even for such a reward as Sue. And an almost tremulous awe broke over him in a sudden tide as he realized what he was doing. This was what Ashley had dreamed of—opening a window into the Plane of Probability and learning enough to force the Cosmic Mind out of its course. Changing the shape of his own future and that of all mankind. Greater than gods—but he was no god. And Ashley had warned him that it might be dangerous to usurp a god's prerogative. Suddenly he was afraid.

He looked away from that cube which held his future, and across from it on his desk the violet eyes of Marta Mayhew caught his, fixed in their changeless smile. She was a girl, he thought, he remembered from half a lifetime ago, so much had happened since he glanced last into her face. Dark and lovely she was, her eyes meeting his almost as if there were vision behind their deep, long stare. Almost as if—

Light flared out in one white, blinding sheet that blotted out the cube and the violet-eyed face and the room around him. Involuntarily Bill clapped his hands to his eyes, seeing behind the darkness of his lids a dazzle of blurring colors. It had happened too quickly for wonder—he was not even thinking as he opened his eyes and looked into the cube where Marta's gaze had met him a moment before.

And then a great tide of awe and wonder came washing up into his consciousness, and he knew that Ashley had been right. There was an alternative future. There comes a point beyond which bewilderment and shock no longer affect the human brain, and Bill was outside wondering now, or groping for logical explanations. He only knew that he stood here staring into the cube from which Marta's eyes had smiled at him so short an instant ago—

They were still Marta's eyes, deep-colored in a boy face almost Bill's own, feature for feature, under a cap of blue steel. Somehow that other future had come to him, too. He was aware of a sudden urgent wonder *why* they had come so nearly together, though neither could be conscious of the other— But things were moving in the depths of the cube.

Behind the boy's face, three-dimensional perspective had started vividly back from the crystal surfaces, as if the cube were a wide window flung suddenly open upon a new world. In that world, a place of glass and shining chromium, faces crowded as if indeed at an open window, peering into his room. Steel-helmed faces with staring eyes. And foremost among them, leaning almost through the opened window into his own past, the steel-capped boy whose features were Bill's looked eagerly out, the sound of quickened breath through his lips a soft, clear sound in the room. There were Bill's lips, Bill's features—but Marta's gentle courage had somehow grown masculine in the lines of the boy's face, and her eyes met Bill's in his.

In the instant before those parted lips spoke, Bill knew him, and his throat closed on an unuttered cry of recognition—recognition of this face he had never seen before, yet could not mistake. The deep welling of love and pride in his heart would have told him the boy's identity, he thought, had he not known at sight who he was—would be—might one day be—

He heard his own voice saying doubtfully, "Son—?"

But if the boy heard he must not have understood. He was handicapped by no such emotion as stirred Bill. His clipped, metallic voice spoke as clearly as if indeed through an opened window: "Greetings from the United World, William Vincent Cory! Greetings from the Fifteenth Leader in the Fifth New Century, A. G."

Behind the disciplined, stern-featured young face others crowded, men with steel-hard features under steel caps. As the boy's voice paused, a dozen right arms slanted high, a dozen open palms turned forward in a salute that was old when Caesar took it in ancient Rome. A dozen voices rolled out in clipped accents, "Greetings, William Vincent Cory!"

Bill's bewildered stammer was incoherent, and the boy's face relaxed a little into a smile. He said: "We must explain, of course. For generations our scientists have been groping in the past, Dr. Cory. This is our first successful two-way contact, and for its demonstration to our Council, connection with you was selected as the most appropriate and fitting contact possible. Because your name is holy among us; we know all there is to know of your life and work, but we have wished to look upon your face and speak to you of our gratitude for molding mankind into the patterns of the United World.

"As a matter of record, I have been instructed to ask first at what point we have intersected the past. What date is it in your calendar?"

"Why, it's July 7, 2240," Bill heard his own voice stammer a little as he answered, and he was conscious of a broad and rather foolish grin overspreading his face. He couldn't help it. This was his boy—the child who wouldn't be born for years yet, who might, really, never be born. Yet he knew him, and he couldn't help smiling with pride, and warm, delighted amusement. So stern-faced, so conscious of his own responsibility! Marta's son and his—only of course it couldn't be, exactly. This scene he looked into must be far ahead in time—

"Twenty-two forty!" exclaimed the boy who was not his son. "Why, the Great Work isn't even finished yet then! We're earlier than we knew!"

"Who are you, son?" Bill couldn't keep the question back any longer.

"I'm John Williams Cory IV, sir," said the boy proudly. "Your direct descendant through the Williams line, and—First in the Candidates Class." He said it proudly, a look of almost worshiping awe lighting his resolute young face. "That means, of course, that I shall be the Sixteenth Leader when the great Dunn retires, and the sixth Cory—the sixth, sir!—to be called to that highest of all human stations, the Leadership!" The violet eyes so incongruous in that disciplined young face blazed with almost fanatic exaltation.

Behind him, a heavy-faced man moved forward, lifting the Roman salute, smiling wintrily beneath his steel helmet.

"I am Dunn, sir," he said in a voice as heavy as his features. "We've let Candidate Cory contact you because of the relationship, but it's my turn now to extend greetings from the System you made possible. I want to show it to you, but first let me thank you for founding the greatest family the United World has ever known. No other name has appeared more than twice on the great role of Leaders, but we have had five Corys—and the finest of them all is yet to come!"

Bill saw a wave of clear red mount his boy's proud, exalted face, and his own heart quickened with love and pride. For this was his son, by whatever name he went here. The memory of his lovely daughter had been drowned out momentarily in the deep uprushing of pride in this tall, blue-eyed boy with his disciplined face and his look of leashed eagerness. There was drive and strength and power of will in that young face now.

He scarcely heard Dunn's heavy voice from the room beyond the cube, so eagerly was he scanning the face of this son he yet might never have, learning almost hungrily the already familiar features, at once hard and eager and exultant. That mouth was his, tight and straight, and the cheeks that creased with deep hollows when he smiled, but the violet eyes were his mother's eyes, and the gentle inflexibility of Marta's courage at once strengthened and softened the features that were Bill's own. The best of them both was here, shining now with something more than either had ever known—an almost fanatic devotion to some stern purpose as exalting as worship, as inflexible as duty—

"Your own future, sir," Dunn was saying. "But our past, of course. Would you like to see it, Dr. Cory, so that you may understand just how directly we owe to you all that our world is today?"

"Yes—v-very much." Bill grinned at his own stammer, suddenly light-hearted and incredulous. All this

was a dream. He knew that, of course. Why, the very
coincidences in it proved that. Or—were they coincidences? Desperately he tried to clarify the thought taking form in his mind, a terrifying vast thought, terrifying form in his mind, a terrifyingly vast thought, terrify-
— If it were real, then there was more than chance here.
It could be no accident that these two children of his,
groping blindly in the dark for contact with him, had
succeeded at so nearly the same moment. There would
be reason behind it, reason too vast for comprehension.
He parted his lips to speak, but Dunn was already
speaking.

"Look then, William Vincent Cory! Watch your own
greatness unfolding in the years that lie ahead."

Hazily the scene in the cube blurred. The beloved,
blue-eyed face of the boy he might never have, faded as
a dream fades—a dream fading in a dream, he thought
dimly—

This time it was Marta coming down the church aisle
toward him, looking like a violet-eyed madonna coifed
and veiled in white lace. He knew that he did not love
her, now. His heart was still sore with the memory of
Sallie. But love would come; with a woman like this it
could not but come. There was tenderness and humor
and passion on that raptly lifted face, and a strength that
would call out the strength in him, not a weakness such
as dimpled in Sallie's face to evoke an underlying weakness in himself. For weakness was in him. He knew it. It
would depend upon the woman who shared his life
which quality overcame the other.

Life would be good with Marta. He saw it unfolding
before him in a long succession of days, work and play
and companionship that brought out the best in both.
And the memory of the strange vision in which he
thought he loved Sallie faded. This was the woman he
loved. Her courage and humor, her violet eyes bright
with pride of him—

Life went by—clear, condensed, swift. He saw his
own work moving steadily toward success, Marta's eager
encouragement tiding him over the low ebbs when diffi-

culties threatened. She was so full of pride in her brilliant young husband that her enthusiasm almost ran away with her. It was she who insisted upon making the discovery public.

"I want to flaunt you before the world!" she urged. "Let's report to the Council now, darling. Aw, please, Bill!"

"We're not ready yet," he protested feebly. "Let's wait—"

"What for? Look." She shook a record sheet under his nose. "A hundred per cent success in the last dozen experiments! What more do you want? It's time to make an official report—announce what you're doing to the world! You've been all the way from fruit flies to monkeys. You'll have to make a report to the Council anyhow before you can take the next step. And remember, darling, when you come to that, I'm first in line as a candidate."

He seized her shoulders in a heavy grip, frowning down into the eagerness of her lifted face. "There'll be no guinea pigs in this family! When Junior Cory comes into the world he—or she—will do it without benefit of X-rays. Understand?"

"But darling, I thought the whole idea was to give parents their choice of boys or girls in the family."

"The thing's not perfected yet to the point where I'd want to risk my own wife. And anyhow . . . anyhow, I've got a funny notion I'd rather just take what comes. Don't know why, exactly, but—"

"Bill, I do believe you're superstitious! Well, we'll fight that out later. But right now, you're going to make a full report of your success to the Council, and I'm going to be the proudest wife in the City. And that's final!"

So the report was made public. It created a tremendous furor: the world clamored for the magical stuff that would put the molding of the future into their hands. Bill Cory blushed and grinned for a delighted public in the telenews screens, promising the great gift soon, and Marta glowed with vicarious pride.

By the time he had made his first experiment with a

human subject, the puppies which were the result of his first successful mammalian experiment were beginning to worry him a little. Miss Brown was the first to notice it. She came in from the kennels one day with a frown behind her steel-rimmed spectacles.

"Dr. Cory, has someone been training those dogs?"

"Training them?" Bill looked up, puzzled. "Of course not. Why?"

"Well, they've got the makings of the finest trained dogs on Earth. Either the whole lot of them is exceptionally intelligent or . . . or . . . something. They just fall over each other obeying every command you can make clear to them."

Bill straightened from his microscope. "Um-m-m . . . funny. Usually one or two dogs in a litter are more intelligent and obedient than the rest. But to have every one in six litters a canine genius is something pretty queer. What do you make of it?"

"I wouldn't call it genius, exactly. As I say, I'm not sure if it's unusual intelligence or . . . well, maybe a strong strain of obedience, or lack of initiative, or . . . it's too soon to say. But they're not normal dogs, Dr. Cory."

It was too soon to say. Tests simply showed the pups to be extraordinarily amenable to training, but what quality in them made this so was difficult to determine. Bill was not sure just what it implied, but an uneasiness in him woke and would not be quieted.

The first "X-ray" babies began to be born. Without exception they were fine, strong, healthy infants, and without exception of the predetermined sex. The Council was delighted; the parents were delighted; everyone was delighted except Bill. The memory of those oddly obedient pups haunted him—

Within three years the Cory System was available to the public. The experimental babies had made such an excellent showing that, in the end, Bill gave in to the insistent world, though something in the recesses of his mind urged delay. Yet he couldn't explain it. The babies were all healthy, normal, intelligent children. Unusually amenable to authority, yes, but that was an asset, not a liability.

Presently all over the world the first crops of Cory System babies began to appear, and gradually Bill's misgivings faded. By then Bill Junior had arrived to take his mind off other people's children, but even now he was obscurely glad that little Bill was a boy on his own initiative, not because his prents had forced masculinity upon him. There was no rhyme or reason to Bill's queer obsession that his own child should not be a product of the X-ray system, but he had been firm about it.

And in later years he had reason to be glad. Bill Jr. grew up fast. He had Marta's violet eyes and his father's darkly blond hair, and a laughing resolution all his own. He was going to be an architect, and neither his mother's shocked protest at this treason to the family profession, nor Bill's not wholly concealed disappointment could swerve him. But he was a good lad. Between school terms he and his father had entirely marvelous vacations together, and for Bill the world revolved about this beloved, talented, headstrong youngster whose presence upon Earth seemed reason enough for Bill's whole existence.

He was glad, even, that the boy *was* stubborn. For there could be no question now about a weakness in the children of the Cory System births. In all ways but one they were quite normal, it was true, but initiative seemed to have been left out of them. It was as if the act of predetermining their sex had robbed them of all ability to make any decisions of their own. Excellent followers they were—but no leaders sprang up among them.

And it was dangerous to fill with unquestioning followers of the strongest man a world in which General George Hamilton controlled the United States. He was in his fourth term as president as the first great group of Cory System children came to maturity. Fiercely and sincerely he believed in the subjugation of the many to the State, and this new generation found in him an almost divinely inspired leader.

General George dreamed of a United World in which all races lived in blind obedience and willing sacrifice

for the common good. And he was a man to make his
dreams come true. Of course, he admitted, there would
be opposition at first. There might be bloody wars, but
in his magnificent dreams he believed sincerely that no
price could be too high, that the end justified any means
necessary to achieve it. And it seemed like the
coöperation of Heaven itself to find almost an entire
generation coming into adulthood ready to accept his
leadership implicitly.

He understood why. It was no secret now what effect
the Cory System had upon the children it produced.
They would follow the strongest leader with blind faith.
But upon this one generation of followers General
George knew he could build a future that would live after him in the magnificent fulfillment of his most magnificent dreams. For a war lord needs a nation of soldiers, a
great crop of boy babies to grow into armies, and surprisingly few saw the real motive behind General
George's constant cry for boys, boys, boys—huge families of them. Fathers of many sons were feted and re-
warded. Everybody knew there was the certainty of war
behind this constant appeal for families of sons, but
comparatively few realized that since the best way to be
sure of boys was the use of the Cory System, the whole
new generation would be blind followers of the strongest
leader, just as their fathers were. Perhaps the Cory System might have died of its own great weakness, its one
flaw, had not General George so purposefully demanded
sons of his followers.

General George died before the first great war was
over. His last words, gasped in the bursting tumult of a
bomb raid over Washington were, "Carry on—unite the
world!" And his vice-president and second in command, Phillip Spaulding, was ready to snatch up the falling torch and light the world to union.

Half the United States lay in smoking ruins before the
Great War ended. But General George had builded well
upon that most enduring of all foundations—the faith of
men. "Be fruitful and multiply," was a command his followers had obeyed implicitly, and Spaulding had mighty

resources of human brawn and human obedience to draw upon.

The great general had died gladly for his dream, and he had not died in vain. Half the world was united under his starry banners within a decade after his death; the United World of his vision came into being less than fifty years later.

With peace and blind faith and prosperity, Science City indeed came into its own. And because a taste of power had made the Leaders hungry, the eyes of the City turned upward toward starry space. During the command of the Fourth Leader after the immortal General George, the first successful space voyage was achieved. The first living man stood knee-deep in the dead pumice dust of the moon and a mighty forward stride for mankind was recorded.

It was only a step. Mars came next, three generations later. After a brief and bloody war, its decadent inhabitants surrendered and the Seventh Leader began to have giddily intoxicating dreams of a United Solar System—

Time telescoped by. Generation melted into generation in changing tides over a world population that seemed unaltering in its by now age-old uniforms of George Blue. And in a sense they were unaltering. Mankind was fixed in a mold—a good enough mold for the military life of the U. W.—the United World. The Cory System had long ago become compulsory, and men and women were produced exactly in the ratio that the Leaders decreed. But it was significant that the Leader class came into the world in the old haphazard fashion of the days before the legendary Dr. Cory's discovery.

The name of Cory was a proud one. It had long been a tradition in that famous family that the founder's great System should not be used among themselves. They were high among the Leader class. Several of the Leaders had borne the surname of Cory, though the office of course was not hereditary, but passed after rigid training and strict examination to the most eligible of the Candidates Class when an old Leader passed his prime.

And among the mighty Corys, family resemblance was strong. Generations saw the inevitable dilution of the original strain, but stubbornly through the years the

Cory features came and went. Sometimes only the darkly blond hair of the first great Bill, sometimes the violent eyes which his pretty Marta had bequeathed her son, sometimes the very face of young Bill Jr. himself, that had roused an ache of pride and love in his father's heart whenever he saw those beloved features.

The Cory eyes looked now upon two worlds, triumphantly regimented to the last tiny detail. Mankind was proving his supremacy over himself—over his weaknesses and his sentimental, selfish desires for personal happiness as opposed to the great common good. Few succumbed to such shameful yearnings, but when they did, every man was a spy against his neighbor, as stern as the Leader himself in crushing these threats to the U. W.'s strength. It should be the individual's holiest and most mystically passionate dream to sacrifice his happiness for the Leader and the U. W., and the Leader and the United World lived for the sole purpose of seeing that he did.

Marvelous was the progress of mankind. The elements had long since been conquered; the atom had yielded up its incalculable power in the harness of the machines, space itself was a highway for the vehicles of the U. W.

Under the blue-black skies of Mars, mankind's checkerboard cities patterned the hot red soil; under the soft gray clouds of Venus, those roofed and checkered cities spread from a common center through jungles steaming in more than tropic heat. Many-mooned Jupiter was drawing the covetous eyes of the Leaders in their skyhigh cities of glass and steel.

And moving through these patterned cities upon three worlds, the followers of the Leader went about their ways, resolute, unfaltering, their faces set in one pattern of determination.

It was not a happy pattern. There was little laughter here; the only emotion upon the serious faces, aside from the shadow of that same exaltation that blazed in the Leader's eyes, was a subtle furtiveness, a sidelong quality that by intuition seemed to distrust its neighbors. Bill recognized it. Every man's duty was to sacrifice for the Cause not only his personal desires and happiness, but his personal honor as well; he must keep relentlessly alert for traitorous weakness in his friends, his associates, his own family.

Mistily the panorama of the centuries began to melt into itself, to fade, while behind it a blue-eyed face, helmed in blue steel, took form to smile straight into Bill's eyes. A tense, expectant smile, supremely confident.

Bill sat back and breathed deeply, avoiding for a moment the proudly smiling face of his son. "I'm—there!" he was thinking. "That was me being born again and again, working with all my heart to crush out human happiness— But there was Sue, too, generations of her —yes, and of me—working just as sincerely toward an opposite goal, a world without war. Either way they've got me. If I don't finish my work, the world unbalances toward matriarchy; if I do, mankind turns into a machine. It's bad. Either way it's bad—"

"The doctor is almost overwhelmed at the realization of his own greatness," Dunn's voice murmured from the window into the future. Bill recognized it for a sort of apology, and sat up with an effort to meet the pride-bright eyes of the boy who one day might be his son. There was nothing but happy expectancy of praise on the boy's face, but Dunn must have read a little doubt in Bill's, for he said heavily, as if to overwhelm that doubt:

"We build toward one common end, all of us—we have no thought for any smaller purpose than the conquest of the Solar System for the mighty race of man! And this great purpose is yours no less than ours, Dr. Cory."

"Manpower is what counts, you know, sir." Young Billy's voice took up the tale as Dunn's died. "We've got tremendous reserves, and we're piling up still more. Lots of room yet on Mars to fill up, and Venus is almost untouched yet. And after that, we'll breed men and women adapted to Jupiter's gravity, perhaps . . . oh, there'll be no end to our power, sir! We'll go on and on— Who knows? There may come a day when we're a United Universe!"

For an instant, hearing the young voice shake with eagerness, Bill doubted his own doubtfulness. The mighty race of many! And he was part of it, living in this far-off future no less than he lived now in the flesh, in the burning ardor of this iron-faced boy. For a moment he forgot to be amazed and incredulous that he stood in the Twenty-third Century and looked as if through a window into the Thirtieth, talking with the unborn descendant of his yet unconceived son. For this moment it was all accomplished reality, a very magnificent and blood-stirring present achieved directly through his own efforts.

"Father . . . father!" The voice was sweet and high in the core of his brain. And memory came back in an overwhelming rush that for an instant drowned out everything but a father's awareness of special love for a favorite daughter.

"Yes, Susan . . . yes, dear." He murmured it aloud, swinging around toward the cube that housed his other future. Sue leaned forward upon her knees among the myrtle leaves, her brown eyes wide and a little frightened upon his. There was a crease between her winged brows that dented Bill's own forehead as he faced her. For a moment it was almost as if each of them looked into a mirror which reflected the features of the other, identical in nearly every detail. Then Sallie's smile dimpled the cheeks of her far-descended daughter, and Sue laughed a small, uneasy laugh.

"What is it, father? Is something wrong?"

He opened his lips to speak—but what could he say? What could he possibly say to her, who did not even dream that her own time was anything but inevitable? How could he explain to a living, warmly breathing woman that she did not exist, might never exist?

He stared at her unhappily, groping for words he could not find. But before he spoke—

"Dr. Cory, sir— Is anything wrong?" He turned back to Billy with a harried crease between his brows and then stared wildly from one face to the other. How could they help hearing one another? But obviously Billy, from his window into the present, saw simply the cube that held Sallie's immortal smile, while Sue, from

hers, looked upon Marta's changeless face. It seemed to
Bill that the boy and the girl had spoken in voices almost identical, using words nearly the same, though neither was aware of the other. How could they be? They
could not even exist simultaneously in the same world.
He might have one of these beloved children or the other; not both. Equally beloved children, between whom
he must choose—and how could he choose?

"Father—" said Sue on a rising inflection of alarm.
"There *is* something wrong. I . . . feel it in your mind
— Oh, what is it, father?"

Bill sat speechless, staring from one face to the other
of these mutually exclusive children. Here they stood,
with their worlds behind them, looking anxiously at him
with the same little crease between the brows of each.
And he could not even speak to either without convinc-
ing the other he was a madman talking to empty air. He
wanted insanely to laugh. It was a deadlock beyond all
solution. Yet he must answer them—he must make his
choice—

As he sat there groping in vain for words, a curious
awareness began to take shape in his mind. How strange
it was that these two should have been the ones to reach
him, out of all the generations behind each that had
been searching the past. And why had they established
contact at so nearly the same time, when they had all his
life span to grope through, hunting him for such different reasons, in such different ways? There was more
than accident here, if all this were not a dream—

Billy and Sue—so similar despite the wide divergence
of their words, a wider divergence than the mind can
well grasp, for how can one measure the distance between mutually incompatible things? Billy who was all
of Bill Cory that was strong and resolute and proud;
Sue, who incarnated his gentler qualities, the tenderness,
the deep desire for peace. They were such poles apart
—why, *they were the poles!* The positive and negative
qualities that, together, made up all that was best in Bill
Cory. Even their worlds were like two halves of a whole;
one all that was strong and ruthless, the other the epito-

me of gentle, abstract idealism. And both were bad, as all extremes must be.

And if he could understand the purpose behind the fact that these two poles of human destiny had reached back in their own pasts to find him at the same moment —if he could understand why the two halves of his soul, split into positive and negative entities, stood here clothed almost in his own flesh to torture him with indecision, perhaps—

He could not choose between them, for there was no choice, but there was a deeper question here than the simple question of conduct. He groped for it blindly, wondering if the answer to everything might not lie in the answer to that question. For there was purpose here vaster than anything man has words for—something loomed behind it to shadowy heights that made his mind reel a little as he tried to understand.

He said inadequately to both his staring children: "But why . . . how did you . . . at this very moment out of all time—"

To Billy it was mere gibberish, but Sue must have understood the question in his mind, for after a moment, in a puzzled murmur, she said:

"I—don't know, exactly. There *is* something here beyond the simple fact of success. I . . . I feel it— I can sense something behind my own actions that . . . that frightens me. Something guiding and controlling my own mind— Oh, father, father, I'm afraid!"

Every protective instinct in him leaped ahead of reaquestions. "Your . . . your sister— Oh, Sue, honey, I won't let anything happen to you!"

"*Dr. Cory!*" Young Billy's voice cracked a little in horror at what must have sounded to him like raving madness. Behind him, staring faces went tense with bewilderment. Above their rising murmurs Sue wailed, "Father!" in a frightened echo to Billy's, "Dr. Cory, are you ill, sir?"

"Oh, wait a minute, both of you!" said Bill wildly. And then in a stammer, to stop Billy's almost hysterical questions. "Your . . . your sister— Oh, Sue, honey, I hear you! I'll take care of you! Wait a minute!"

In the depths of the cube the boy's face seemed to

freeze, the eyes that were Marta's going blank beneath the steel cap, Bill's very mouth moving stiffly with the stiffness of his lips.

"But you never had a daughter—"

"No, but I might have, if—I mean, if I'd married Sallie of course you'd never even— Oh, God!" Bill gave it up and pressed both hands over his eyes to shut out the sight of the boy's amazed incredulity, knowing he'd said too much, yet too numbed and confused now for diplomacy. The only clear idea in his head was that he must somehow be fair to both of them, the boy and the girl. Each must understand why he—

"Is the doctor ill, Candidate Cory?" Dunn's voice was heavy from the cube.

Bill heard the boy's voice stammering: "No—that is, I don't—" And then, faltering, more softly: "Leader, was the great doctor ever—mad?"

"Good God, boy!"

"But—speak to him, Leader!"

Bill looked up haggardly as Dunn's voice rolled out with the sternness of a general addressing armies. "Pull yourself together, sir! You never had a daughter! Don't you remember?"

Bill laughed wildly. "Remember? I've never even had a son yet! I'm not married—not even engaged! How can I remember what hasn't happened?"

"But you *will* marry Marta Mayhew! You did marry her! You founded the great line of Corys and gave the world your—"

"Father . . . father! What's wrong?" Sue's sweet wail was in his ears. He glanced toward her window momentarily, seeing the terror in the soft brown eyes that stared at him, but he could only murmur: "Hush, darling—wait, please!" before he faced the Leader and said with a strong effort at calmness, "None of all that has happened—yet."

"But it will—it must—it *did!*"

"Even if I never married Marta, never had a son?"

Dunn's dark face convulsed with a grimace of exasperated anger.

"But good Lord, man, look here!" He seized Billy's blue-uniformed shoulders with both hands, thrusting him forward. "You did have a son! This is his descendant, the living likeness of young Cory Junior! This world . . . I myself . . . all of us . . . we're the result of that marriage of yours! And you never had a daughter! Are you trying to tell us we don't exist? Is this a . . . a dream I'm showing you?" And he shook the boy's broad young shoulders between his hands. "You're looking at us, hearing us, talking to us! Can't you see that you must have married Marta Mayhew?"

"Father, I want you! Come back!" Sue's wail was insistent.

Bill groaned. "Wait a minute, Dunn." And then, turning, "Yes, honey, what is it?"

On her knees among the myrtle leaves Sue leaned forward among the sun-flecked shadows of her cool green glade, crying: "Father, you won't . . . you can't believe them? I heard . . . through your ears I heard them, and I can understand a little through your mind linked with mine. I can understand what you're thinking . . . but it can't be true! You're telling yourself that we're still on the Probability Plane . . . but that's just a theory! That's nothing but speculation about the future! How could I be anything but real? Why, it's silly! Look at me! Listen to me! Here I am! Oh, don't let me go on thinking that maybe . . . maybe you're right, after all. But it *was* Sallie Carlisle you married, wasn't it, father? Please say it was!"

Bill gulped. "Wait, honey. Let me explain to them first." He knew he shouldn't have started the whole incredible argument. You can't convince a living human that he doesn't exist. They'd only think him mad. Well —Sue might understand. Her training in metaphysics and telepathy might make it possible. But Billy—

He turned with a deep breath and a mental squaring of shoulders, determined to try, anyhow. For he must be fair. He began: "Dunn, did you ever hear of the Plane of Probability?"

At the man's incredulous stare he knew a dizzy moment of wonder whether he, too, lived in an illusion as vivid as theirs, and in that instant the foundations of time itself rocked beneath his feet. But he had no time now for speculation. Young Billy must understand, no matter how mad Dunn believed him, and Sue must know why he did what he must do—though he didn't understand himself, yet, what that would be. His head was ringing with bewilderment.

"The . . . the Plane of Probability?" In Dunn's eyes upon his he saw a momentary conviction flare that, reality or not, and history be damned, this man was mad. And then, doubtfully, the Leader went on, "Hm-m-m . . . yes, somewhere I *have* heard— Oh, I remember. Some clap-trap jargon the old Telepathy House fakers used to use before we cleared them out of Science City. But what's that nonsense got to—"

"It's not nonsense." Bill closed his eyes in a sudden, almost intolerable longing for peace, for time to think what he must do. But no, the thing must be settled now, without time for thinking. And perhaps that was the best way, after all. A man's brain would crack if he paused to think out this madness. Only he must say something to young Billy— And what could he say? How could he face either of these beloved children and, to their uncomprehending, pleading faces, refuse them life? If he could only break the connection that riveted them all into a sort of triple time balance— But he couldn't. He must make it clear to Billy—

"It's not nonsense," he heard his own voice repeating wildly. "The future—you and your world—is a probability only. I'm a free agent. If I never marry Marta, never perfect the sex-determination idea, the probable future shifts to . . . to another pattern. *And that as bad as yours, or worse!*" he finished to himself.

"Is he mad?" Billy's voice was a whisper in the screen.

The Leader said as if to himself, in an awed and stumbling voice, "I don't . . . I can't . . . the thing's preposterous! And yet he *is* unmarried, the Great Work's still unfinished. Suppose he never— But we're real! We're flesh and blood, aren't we? He stamped a booted foot on the floor as if to test the foundations of his world. "We're descended in an unbroken line from this . . . this madman. Lord in heaven, are we all mad?"

"Father! Come back!" Sue's voice shrilled in Bill's ears. He turned desperately, glad of an excuse to escape the haunted stares from that other window even though he must face hers. She had risen to her feet among the myrtle leaves. The glade was cool and still about her in this lazy, sunlit world of her own future. She was crying desperately, "Don't listen, father! I can feel the confusion in your mind. I know what they're saying! But they aren't real, father—they can't be! You never had a son, don't you remember? All this you're saying is just . . . just talk, isn't it? That silly stuff about the Probability Plane—it's nothing but speculation! Oh, say it is, father! We've got such a lovely world, we love living so . . . I want to live, father! I *am* real! We've fought so hard, for so many centuries, for peace and happiness and our beautiful garden world. Don't let it snuff out into nothingness! But"—she laughed uncertainly—"how could you, when it's all around us, and has been for thousands of years? I . . . oh, father!" Her voice broke on a little quivering gulp that made Bill's heart quiver with it, and he ached intolerably with the rising of her tears. She was his to protect and cherish, forever. How could he—

"Dr. Cory—do you hear me? Oh, please listen!" Young Billy's familiar voice reached out to him from that other future. He glanced toward him once, and then put his hands to his ears and whirled from them both, the two voices mingling in an insane chaos of pleading.

Sue on her myrtle bank in a future immeasurably far ahead, child of a decadent world slipping easily down the slope of oblivion.

Billy's world might be as glorious as he believed, but the price was too high to pay for it. Bill remembered the set, unsmiling faces he had seen in the streets of that world. These were men his own work had robbed of the initiative that was their birthright. Happiness was their birthright, too, and the power to make the decisions that determined their own futures.

No, not even for such achievements as theirs must mankind be robbed of the inalienable right to choose for himself. If it lay in Bill Cory's power to outlaw a system which destroyed men's freedom and honor and joy, even for such an end as mankind's immortal progress, he had no choice to make. The price was too high. Confusedly he remembered something out of the dim past: "What shall it profit a man if he gain the whole world and lose his own soul. . . .?"

But—the alternative. Bill groaned. Happiness, peace, freedom, honor—yes, Sue's world had all that Billy's lacked. And to what end? Indolence and decadence and extinction for the great race that Billy's civilization would spread gloriously among the stars.

"But I'm thinking of *choice*," groaned Bill to himself. "And I haven't got any choice! If I marry Sallie and don't finish my work—one future follows. If I marry Marta and do finish it, the other comes. And both are bad—but what can I do? Man or mankind; which has the stronger claim? Happiness and extinction—or unhappiness and splendid immortality; which is better?"

"Cory—Dr. Cory!" It was Dunn's voice, heavy enough to break through the daze of bewilderment that shrouded Bill's brain. He turned. The Leader's iron-hard face under the steel helmet was settling into lines of fixed resolution. Bill saw that he had reached some decision, and knew a sudden, dazed admiration for the man. After all, he had not been chosen Leader for nothing.

"You're a fool to tell us all this, Cory. Mad, or a fool, or both. Don't you know what it means? Don't think we established this connection unprepared for trouble! The same force that carries the sight and sound of us from our age to yours can carry destruction, too! Nowhere in our past is there a record that William Cory was killed by a blast of atom-gun fire as he sat at his desk—but, by God, sir, if you can change that past, so can we!"

"It would mean wiping yourself out, you know," Bill reminded him as steadily as he could, searching the angry eyes of this man who must never have faced resolute opposition before, and wondering if the man had yet accepted a truth that must seem insanely impossible to him. He wanted overwhelmingly to laugh, and yet somewhere inside him a chilly conviction was growing that it might be possible for the children of his unborn son, in a future that would never exist, to blast him out of being. He said: "You and your whole world would vanish if I died."

"But not unavenged!" The Leader said it savagely, and then hesitated. "But what am I saying? You've driven me almost as mad as you! Look, man, try to be sensible! Can you imagine yourself dissolving into nothingness that never existed? Neither can I!"

"But if you could kill me, then how could your world ever have been born?"

"To hell with all that!" exploded Dunn. "I'm no metaphysician! I'm a fighting man! I'll take the chance!"

"Please, Dr. Cory—" Billy pressed forward against the very surface of the cube, as if he could thrust himself back into his own past and lay urgent hands upon this man so like him, staring white-faced and stubborn into the future. Perhaps it was more than the desire for peace that spoke in his shaken voice. If Bill Cory, looking into that young face so like his own, had felt affection and recognition for it, then must not the boy know a feeling akin to it as he saw himself in Cory's features? Perhaps it was that subtle, strange identification between the two that made the boy's voice tremble a little as if with the first weakening of belief. When he spoke he seemed to be acknowledging the possibility of doubt, almost without realizing it. He said in that shaken, ardent voice:

"Please, try to understand! It's not death we're afraid of. All of us would die now, willingly, if our deaths could further the common good. What we can't endure to face is the death of our civilization, this marvelous thing that makes mankind immortal. Think of that, sir! This is the only right thing possible for you to do! Would we feel so strongly if we weren't *sure?* Can you condemn your own race to eternity on one small planet, when you could give them the universe to expand in and every good thing science can offer?"

"Father . . . father!" It was Sue again, frantic and far away.

But before Bill could turn to her, Dunn's voice broke in heavily over both the others. "Wait—I've made up my mind!" Billy fell back a little, turning to his Leader with a blaze of sudden hope. Bill stared. "As I see it," went on Dunn, "the whole preposterous question hinges on the marriage you make. Naturally I can't concede even to myself that you could possibly marry anyone but the woman you *did* marry—but if you honestly feel that there's any question in your mind about it, I'll settle it for you."

He turned to nod toward a corner of the room in which he stood that was outside Bill's range, and in a moment the blue-uniformed, staring crowd about him parted and a low, rakish barrel of blue-gleaming steel glided noiselessly forward toward that surface of the cube which was a window into the past-future that parted Bill and themselves. Bill had never seen anything like it before, but he recognized its lethal quality. It crouched streamlined down upon its base as if for a lunge, and its mouth facing him was a dark doorway for death itself. Dunn bent behind it and laid his hand upon a half-visible lever in its base.

"Now," he said heavily. "William Cory, there seems to be a question in your mind as to whether we could reach you with our weapons. Let me assure you that the force-beam which connects us can carry more than sight and sound into your world! I hope I shan't have to demonstrate that. I hope you'll be sensible enough to turn to that televisor screen in the wall behind you and call Marta Mayhew."

"M—Marta?" Bill heard the quiver in his voice. "Why—"

"You will call her, and in our sight and hearing you are going to ask her to marry you. That much choice is yours, marriage or death. Do you hear me?"

Bill wanted insanely to laugh. Shotgun wedding from a mythical future—"You can't threaten me with that popgun forever," he said with a quaver of mirth he could not control. "How do you know I'll marry her once you're away?"

"You'll keep your word," said Dunn serenely. "Don't forget, Cory, we know you much better than you know yourself. We know your future far more completely than you saw it. We know how your character will develop with age. Yes, you're an honorable man. Once you've asked her to marry you, and heard her say yes—and she will—you won't try to back out. No, the promise given and received between you constitutes a marriage as surely as if we'd seen the ceremony performed. You see, we trust your honor, William Cory."

"But—" Bill got no further than that, for explosively in his brain a sweet, high voice was sobbing:

"Father, father, what are you doing? What's happened? Why don't you speak to me?"

In the tension Bill had nearly forgotten Sue, but the sound of that familiar voice tore at him with sudden, almost intolerable poignancy. Sue—the promise to protect her had risen to his lips involuntarily at the very mention of danger. It was answer to an urgency rooted race-deep, the instinct to protect the helpless and the loved. For a moment he forgot the gun trained on him from the other window; he forgot Billy and the world behind him. He was conscious only of his daughter crying in terror for help—for help from him and for protection against him at once, in a dizzy confusion that made his head swim.

"Sue—" he began uncertainly.

"Cory, we're waiting!" Dunn's voice had an ominous undernote.

But there was a solution. He never knew just when he first became aware of it. A long while ago, perhaps, subconsciously, the promise of it had begun to take shape in his mind. He did not know when he first realized that—but he thought he knew whence it came. There was a sureness and a vastness about it that did not originate in himself. It was the Cosmic Mind indeed in which his own small soul was floundering, and out of that unthinkably limitless Plan, along with the problem came at last the solution. (*There must be balance . . . the force that swings the worlds in their orbits can permit of no question without an answer—*)

There was no confusion here; there had never been.

This was not chance. Purpose was behind it, and sudden confidence came flooding into him from outside. He turned with resolution so calm upon his face that Billy sighed and smiled, and Dunn's tense face relaxed.

"Thank God, sir," breathed Billy, "I knew you'd come to your senses. Believe me, sir, you won't be sorry."

"Wait," said Bill to them both, and laid his hand on the button beneath his desk that rang a bell in his laboratory. "Wait and see."

In three worlds and times, three people very nearly identical in more than the flesh alone—perhaps three facets of the same personality, who can say?—stood silent and tense and waiting. It seemed like a very long time before the door opened and Miss Brown came into the room, hesitating on the threshold with her calm, pleasant face questioning.

"You want me, Dr. Cory?"

Bill did not answer for a moment. He was pouring his whole soul into this last long stare that said good-by to the young son he would never know. For understanding from some vast and nameless source was flooding his mind now, and he knew what was coming and why it would be so. He looked across the desk and gazed his last upon Sue's familiar face so like his own, the fruit of a love he would never share with pretty Sallie. And then, drawing a deep breath, he gulped and said distinctly:

"Miss Brown, will you marry me?"

Dunn had given him the key—a promise given and received between this woman and himself would be irrevocable, would swing the path of the future into a channel that led to no world that either Billy or Sue could know.

Bill got his first glimmer of hope for that future from the way the quiet woman in the doorway accepted his question. She did not stare or giggle or stammer. After one long, deep look into his eyes—he saw for the first time that hers were gray and cool behind the lenses—she answered calmly.

"Thank you, Dr. Cory. I shall be very happy to marry you."

And then—it came. In the very core of his brain, heartbreak and despair exploded in a long, wailing scream of faith betrayed as pretty Sue, his beloved, his darling, winked out into the oblivion from which she would never now emerge. The lazy green Eden was gone forever; the sweet fair girl on her knees among the myrtle leaves had never been—would never be.

Upon that other window surface, in one last flash of unbearable clearness, young Billy's incredulous features stared at him. Behind that beloved, betrayed face he saw the face of the Leader twisting with fury. In the last flashing instant while the vanishing, never-to-exist future still lingered in the cube, Bill saw an explosion of white-hot violence glare blindingly from the gun mouth, a heat and violence that seared the very brain. Would it have reached him—could it have harmed him? He never knew, for it lasted scarcely a heartbeat before eternity closed over the vanishing world in a soundless, fathomless, all-swallowing tide.

Where that world had stretched so vividly a moment ago, now Marta's violet gaze looked out into the room through crystal. Across the desk Sallie's lovely, careless smile glowed changelessly. They had been gateways to the future—but the gates were closed. There would never be such futures now; there never had been. In the Cosmic Mind, the great Plan of Things, two half-formed ideas went out like blown candle flames.

And Bill turned to the gray-eyed woman in the doorway with a long, deep, shaken sigh. In his own mind as he faced her, thoughts too vast for formulation moved cloudily.

"I know now something no man was ever sure of before—our oneness with the Plan. There are many, many futures. I couldn't face the knowledge of another, but I think—yes, I believe, ours will be the best. She won't let me neglect the work we're doing, but neither will she force me to give it to the world unperfected. Maybe, between us, we can work out that kink that robs the embryo of determination, and then—who knows?

"Who knows why all this had to happen? There was

Purpose behind it—all of it—but I'll never understand just why. I only know that the futures are infinite—and that I haven't lost Billy or Sue. I couldn't have done what I did without being sure of that. I couldn't lose them, because they're me—the best of me, going on forever. Perhaps I'll never die, really—not the real me—until these incarnations of the best that's in me, whatever form and face and name they wear, work out mankind's ultimate destiny in some future I'll never see. There was reason behind all this. Maybe, after all, I'll understand—some day."

He said nothing aloud, but he held out his hand to the woman in the door and smiled down confidently into her cool, gray eyes.

Fruit of Knowledge

IT WAS THE first Sabbath. Down the open glades of
Eden a breeze stirred softly. Nothing else in sight moved
except a small winged head that fluttered, yawning,
across the glade and vanished among leaves that drew
back to receive it. The air quivered behind it like a wake
left in water of incomparable clarity. From far away and
far above a faint drift of singing echoed, "Hosannah . . .
hosannah . . . hosannah—" The seraphim were singing
about the Throne.

A pool at the edge of the glade gave back light and
color like a great, dim jewel. It gave back reflections,
too. The woman who bent over it had just discovered
that. She was leaning above the water until her cloudy
dark hair almost dipped into the surface. There was a
curious shadow all about her, like a thin garment which
did not quite conceal how lovely she was, and though no
breeze stirred just now, that shadow garment moved uneasily upon her and her hair lifted a little as if upon a
breeze that did not blow.

She was so quiet that a passing cherub-head paused
above the water to look, too, hanging like a humming-
bird motionless over its own reflection in the pool.

"Pretty!" approved the cherub in a small, piping
voice. "New here, aren't you?"

The woman looked up with a slow smile, putting back
the veil of her hair.

"Yes, I am," she answered softly. Her voice did not
sound quite sure of itself. She had never spoken aloud
before until this moment.

"You'll like the Garden," said the cherub in a slightly

patronizing tone, giving his rainbow wings a shake. "Anything I can do for you? I'm not busy just now. Be glad to show you around."

"Thank you," smiled the woman, her voice sounding a little more confident. "I'll find my way."

The cherub shrugged his colored wings. "Just as you say. By the way, I suppose they warned you about the Tree?"

The woman glanced up at him rather quickly, her shadowy eyes narrowing.

"The Tree? Is there danger?"

"Oh, no. You mustn't touch it, that's all. It's the one in the middle of the Garden, the Tree of the Knowledge of Good and Evil—you can't miss it. I saw the Man looking at it yesterday for quite a while. That reminds me, have you met the Man?"

The woman bent her head so that the hair swung forward to veil her face. From behind it, in a voice that sounded as if she might be smiling, she said:

"He's waiting for me now."

"Oh?" said the cherub, impressed. "Well, you'll find him over by the orange grove east of the Tree. He's resting. It's the Day of Rest, you know." The cherub tilted an intimate eyebrow heavenward and added: "He's resting, too. Hear the singing? He made the Man only yesterday, right out of this very earth you're standing on. We were all watching. It was wonderful— Afterward, He called the man Adam, and then Adam named the animals— By the way, what's your name?"

The woman smiled down at her own veiled reflection in the water. After a moment—

"Lilith," she said.

The cherub stared, his eyes widening into two blue circles of surprise. He was speechless for an instant. Then he pursed his pink mouth to whistle softly.

"Why," he stammered, "you . . . you're the Queen of Air and Darkness!"

Smiling up at him from the corners of her eyes, the woman nodded. The cherub stared at her big-eyed for a moment longer, too overcome for speech. Then, suddenly, he beat his rainbow pinions together and darted off through the trees without another word, the translucent air rippling in a lazy, half-visible wake behind him. Lilith looked after him with a shadowy smile on her face. He was going to warn Adam. The smile deepened. Let him.

Lilith turned for one last glance into the mirror of the pool at the strange new shape she had just put on. It was the newest thing in creation—not even God knew about it. And rather surprisingly, she thought she was going to like it. She did not feel nearly as stifled and heavy as she had expected to feel, and there was something distinctly pleasant in the softness of the breeze pouring caressingly about her body, the fragrance of springtime sweet in her nostrils, the grass under her bare feet. The Garden was beautiful with a beauty she had not realized until she saw it through human eyes. Everything she saw through them, indeed, was curiously different now. Here in this flesh all her faculties seemed refocused, as if she, who had always seen with such crystal clarity, now looked through rainbows at everything she saw. But it was a pleasant refocusing. She wished she had longer to enjoy her tenancy in this five-sensed flesh she shared with Adam.

But she had very little time. She glanced up toward the bright, unchanging glory above the trees as if she could pierce the floor of heaven and see God resting on the unimaginable splendor of the Throne while the seraphim chanted in long, shining rows about him. At any moment he might stir and lean forward over Eden, looking down. Lilith instinctively shrugged her shadowy garment closer about her. If he did not look too closely, he might not pierce that shadow. But if he did— A little thrill of excitement, like forked lightning, went through the strange new flesh she wore. She liked danger.

She bent over the pool for one last look at herself, and the pool was a great, dim eye looking back at her, almost sentient, almost aware of her. This was a living Garden. The translucent air quivered with a rhythmic pulsing through the trees; the ground was resilient under her feet; vines drew back to let her pass beneath them. Lilith, turning away through the swimming air after the

cherub, puzzled a little as she walked through the parting trees. The relation was very close between flesh and
earth—perhaps her body was so responsive to the beauty of the Garden because it aped so closely flesh that
had been a part of the Garden yesterday. And if even
she felt that kinship, what must Adam feel, who was
himself earth only yesterday?

The Garden was like a vast, half-sentient entity all
around her, pulsing subtly with the pulse of the lucent
air. Had God drawn from this immense and throbbing
fecundity all the life which peopled Eden? Was Adam
merely an extension of it, a focus and intensification of
the same life which pulsed through the Garden? Creation was too new; she could only guess.

She thought, too, of the Tree of Knowledge as she
walked smoothly through the trees. That Tree, tempting
and forbidden. Why? Was God testing Man somehow?
Was Man then, not quite finished, after all? Was there
any flaw in Eden? Suddenly she knew that there must
be. Her very presence here was proof of it, for she,
above all others, had no right to intrude into this magical closed sphere which was God's greatest work. Yet
here she walked through the heart of it, and not even
God knew, yet—

Lilith slanted a smile up through the leaves toward
the choruses of the seraphim whose singing swelled and
sank and swelled again, unutterably sweet high above
the trees. The animals watched her pass with wide, bewildered eyes, somehow not quite at ease, although no
such thing as fear had yet stirred through the Garden.
Lilith glanced at them curiously as she passed. They
were pretty things. She liked Eden.

Presently a swooning fragrance came drifting to her
through the trees, almost too sweet to enjoy, and she
heard a small voice piping excitedly: "Lilith . . . Air
and Darkness— He won't like it! Michael ought to
know—"

Lilith smiled and stepped clear of the trees into the
full, soft glow of Eden's sun. It did not touch the shadow that dimly veiled the pale contours of this newest

shape in Eden. Once or twice that intangible breeze lifted her hair in a great, dim cloud about her, though no
leaves moved. She stood quiet, staring across the glade,
and as she stared she felt the first small tremor of distrust in this new flesh she wore.

For on a grassy bank in the sunlight, under the blos-
soming orange trees, lay Adam. And the trees and the
flowers of Eden had seemed beautiful to the eyes of this
body Lilith wore, and the breezes and the perfumes had
delighted it—but here was flawless perfection newly
shaped out of the warm red earth of Eden into the image of its Maker, and the sight of him frightened Lilith
because it pleased her so. She did not trust a beauty that
brought her to a standstill under the trees, not quite certain why she had stopped.

He sprawled in long-limbed magnificence on the
grass, laughing up at the cherub with his curly yellow
head thrown back. Every line of him and every motion
had a splendid male beauty as perfect as Omnipotence
could make it. Though he wore no clothing he was no
more naked than she, for there was a curious glow all
about him, a garment of subtle glory that clothed him as
if with an all-enveloping halo.

The cherub danced excitedly up and down in the air
above him, shrilling:

"She shouldn't be here! You know she shouldn't!
She's evil, that's what she is! God won't like it! She—"
Then above Adam's head he caught Lilith's eye, gulped
a time or two, piped one last admonishing, "Better
watch out!" and fluttered away among the leaves, looking back over one wing as he flew.

Adam's gaze followed the cherub's. The laughter faded from his face and he got up slowly, the long, smooth
muscles sliding beautifully under his garment of subtle
glory as he moved. He was utter perfection in everything
he did, flawless, new-made at the hands of God. He
came toward her slowly, a shining wonder on his face.

Lilith stared at him distrustfully. The other glories of
the Garden had pleased her abstractly, in a way that left
her mistress of herself. But here was something she did
not understand at all. The eternal Lilith looked out, bewildered, through the eyes of a body that found some-

thing strange and wonderful in Adam. She laid a hand on the upper part of that body which rose and fell with her breathing, and felt something beating strongly beneath the smooth, curved surface of the stuff called flesh.

Adam came toward her slowly. They met in the middle of the glade, and for a long moment neither spoke. Then Adam said in a marveling voice, resonant and deep:

"You . . . you're just as I knew you'd be— I knew you'd be somewhere, if I could only find you. Where were you hiding?"

With an effort Lilith mastered this odd, swimming warmth in her which she did not understand. After all, he was nothing but a certain limited awareness housed in newly shaped flesh, and it made no real difference at all what shape that flesh wore. Her business was too dangerous for her to linger here admiring him because by some accident he was pleasing to the eyes of her newly acquired body. She made her voice like honey in her throat and looked up at him under her lashes, crooning:

"I wasn't here at all, until you thought of me."

"Until I—" Adam's golden brows met.

"God made you in His image," said Lilith, fluttering the lashes. "There's so much of God in you still—didn't you know you could create, too, if you desired strongly enough?"

She remembered that deep need of his pulsing out and out in great, demanding waves from the Garden, and how it had seemed a call addressed to her alone. She had delighted as she yielded to it, deliberately subordinating her will to the will of the unseen caller in the Garden. She had let it draw her down out of the swimming void, let it mold flesh around her in the shape it chose, until all her being was incased in the strange, soft, yielding substance which was proving so treacherously responsive to the things she was encountering in Eden.

Adam shook his curly head uncomprehendingly. "You weren't here. I couldn't find you," he repeated, as if he had not heard her. "I watched all day among the animals, and they were all in twos but Man. I knew you must be somewhere. I knew just how you'd look. I thought I'd call you Eve when I found you—Eve, the Mother of All Living. Do you like it?"

"It's a good name," murmured Lilith, coming nearer to him, "but not for me. I'm Lilith, who came out of the dark because you needed me." She smiled a heady smile at him, and the shadowy garment drew thin across her shoulders as she lifted her arms. Adam seemed a little uncertain about what to do with his own arms as she clasped her hands behind his neck and tiptoed a little, lifting her face.

"Lilith?" he echoed in a bemused voice. "I like the sound. What does it mean?"

"Never mind," she crooned in her sweetest voice. "I came because you wanted me." And then, in a murmur: "Bend your head, Adam. I want to show you something—"

It was the first kiss in Eden. When it was over, Lilith opened her eyes and looked up at Adam aghast, so deeply moved by the pleasantness of that kiss that she could scarcely remember the purpose that had prompted it. Adam blinked dizzily down at her. He had found what to do with his arms. He stammered, still in that bemused voice:

"Thank God, you did come! I wish He could have sent you sooner. We—"

Lilith recovered herself enough to murmur gently: "Don't you understand, dear? God didn't send me. It was you, yourself, waiting and wanting me, that let me take shape out of . . . never mind . . . and come to you in the body you pictured for me, because I knew what wonderful things we could accomplish here in Eden, together. You're God's own image, and you have greater powers than you know, Adam." The tremendous idea that had come to her in the ether when she first heard his soundless call glowed in her voice. "There's no limit to what we could do here, together! Greater things than even God ever dreamed—"

"You're so pretty," interrupted Adam, smiling down

at her with his disarming, empty smile. "I'm so glad you came—"

Lilith let the rest of her eagerness run out in a long sigh. It was no use trying to talk to him now. He was too new. Powerful with a godlike power, yes, but unaware of it—unaware even of himself as an individual being. He had not tasted the Fruit of Knowledge and his innocence was as flawless as his beauty. Nothing was in his mind, or could be, that God had not put there at his shaping from the warm earth of Eden.

And perhaps it was best, after all. Adam was too close to godhood to see eye to eye with her in all she might want to do. If he never tasted knowledge, then he would ask no questions—and so he must never touch the Tree.

The Tree— It reminded her that Eden was still a testing ground, not a finished creation. She thought she knew now what the flaw in man had been which made it possible for Lilith, of all the creatures of ether, to stand here at the very focus of all the power and beauty and innocence in Eden. Lilith, who was evil incarnate and knew it very well. God had made Adam incomplete, and not, perhaps, realized the flaw. And out of Adam's need Adam himself had created woman—who was not complete either. Lilith realized it suddenly, and began to understand the depth of her reaction to this magnificent creature who still held her in his arms.

There was an idea somewhere back of all this which was immensely important, but her mind would not pursue it. Her mind kept sliding off the question to dwell cloudily on the Man upon whose shoulder she was leaning. What curious stuff this flesh was! While she wore it, not even the absorbing question of God's purpose, not even her own peril here, could quite obliterate the knowledge of Adam's presence, his arm about her. Values had changed in a frightening way, and the most frightening thing of all was that she did not care. She laid her head back on his shoulder and inhaled the honeyed perfume of the orange blossoms, futilely reminding herself that she was dangerously wasting time. At any moment God might look down and see her, and there was so much to be done before that happened. She must

master this delicious fogging of the senses whenever
Adam's arm tightened about her. The Garden must be
fortified, and she must begin now.

Sighing, she laced her fingers through Adam's and
crooned in the softest voice:

"I want to see the Garden. Won't you show it to me?"

His voice was warm as he answered:

"I want to! I hoped you'd ask me that. It's such a
wonderful place."

A cherub fluttered across the valley as they strolled
eastward, and paused on beating wings to frown down at
them.

"Wait till *He* looks down," he piped. "Just wait, that's
all!" Adam laughed, and the cherub clucked disapprov-
ingly and fluttered off, shaking his head.

Lilith, leaning on Adam's shoulder, laughed, too. She
was glad that he could not understand the cherub's
warnings, deaf in the perfection of his innocence. So
long as she could prevent it he would never taste that
Fruit. The knowledge of evil was not in him and it must
never be. For she was herself, as she realized well, the
essence of abstract evil as opposed to abstract good—
balancing it, making it possible. Her part was as necessary as God's in the scheme of creation, for light cannot
exist without dark, nor positive without negative, nor
good without evil.

Yet she did not feel in the least evil just now. There
was no antagonism at all between her negation and the
strong positive innocence of the man beside her.

"Look," said Adam, sweeping a long-armed gesture.
A low hillside lay before them, starry with flowers except
for a scar in its side where the raw, bare earth of Eden
showed through. The scar was already healing over with
a faint mist of green. "That's where I was made," said
Adam softly. "Right out of that hillside. Does it seem
rather . . . rather wonderful to you, Lilith?"

"If it does to you," she crooned, and meant it.
"Why?"

"The animals don't seem to understand. I hoped you
would. It's as if the . . . the whole Garden were part
of me. If there are other men, do you suppose they'll
love the earth like this, Lilith, for its own sake? Do you

think they'll have this same feeling about the place where they were born? Will one certain hill or valley be almost one flesh with theirs, so that they'd sicken away from it and fight and die if they had to, to keep it—as I think I would? Do you feel it, too?"

The air went pulsing past them, sweet with the music of the seraphim, while Lilith looked out over the valley that had brought Adam to birth. She was trying hard, but she could not quite grasp that passionate identification with the earth of Eden which beat like blood through Adam's veins.

"Eden *is* you," she murmured. "I can understand that. You mustn't ever leave it."

"Leave it?" laughed Adam. "Where else is there? Eden belongs to us forever—and you belong to me."

Lilith let herself relax delightfully against his shoulder, knowing suddenly that she loved this irresponsible, dangerous flesh even while she distrusted it. And—

Something was wrong. The sudden awareness of it chilled her and she glanced uneasily about, but it was several minutes before her fleshbound senses located the wrongness. Then she put her head back and stared up through the trees with puckered brows.

"What is it?" Adam smiled down at her. "Angels? They go over quite often, you know."

Lilith did not answer. She was listening hard. Until now all Eden had echoed faintly and sweetly with the chanting of seraphim about the Throne. But now the sounds that sifted down through the bright, translucent air were not carols of praise. There was trouble in heaven. She could hear faraway shouts in great, ringing, golden voices from infinitely high above, the clash and hiss of flaming swords, and now and again a crash as if part of the very walls of heaven had crumbled inward under some unimaginable onslaught.

It was hard to believe—but there was war in heaven.

A wave of relief went delightfully through Lilith. Good—let them fight. She smiled to herself and snuggled closer to Adam's side. The trouble, whatever it might be, would keep God's attention distracted a while longer from what went on in Eden, and she was devoutly grateful for that. She needed this respite. She had awhile longer, than, to accustom herself to the vagaries of this strange body, and to the strange reaction Adam was causing, before the war was over in heaven and war began in Eden between Lilith and God.

A shudder of terror and anticipation went over her again as she thought of that. She was not sure God could destroy her if He would, for she was a creature of the darkness beyond His light and her existence was necessary to the structure he was rearing in heaven and upon earth. Without the existence of such as Lilith, the balance of creation might tip over. No, God would not —perhaps could not—destroy her, but He could punish very terribly.

This flesh, for instance. It was so soft, so perishable. She was aware of a definite cleavage between the mind and the body that housed it. Perhaps God had been wise in choosing this fragile container instead of some imperishable substance into which to pour all the innocence, the power that was Adam. It was dangerous to trust such power in an independent body—as Lilith meant to prove to God if her plan went well. But it was no part of that plan—now—to have an angered God destroy His fleshly image.

She must think of some way to prevent it. Presently she would waken out of this warm, delightful fog that persisted so long as Adam's arm was about her, but there was no hurry yet. Not while war raged in heaven. She had never known a mood like this before, when cloudy emotions moved like smoke through her mind and nothing in creation had real significance except this magnificent male upon whose shoulder she leaned.

Then Adam looked down at her and smiled, and all the noises of war above blanked out as if they had never been. The Garden, half sentient, stirred uneasily from grass roots to treetops in response to those ringing battle shouts from above; but the Man and the woman did not even hear.

Time was nothing. Imperceptibly it passed, and presently a soft green twilight deepened over Eden. Adam and Lilith paused after a while on a mossy bank above a stream that tinkled over stones. Sitting with her head on Adam's shoulder and listening to the sound of the water, Lilith remembered how lightly life was rooted in this flesh of theirs.

"Adam," she murmured, "awhile ago you mentioned dying. Do you know about death?"

"Death?" said Adam comfortably. "I don't remember. I think I never heard of it."

"I hope," she said, "that you never will. It would mean leaving Eden, you know."

His arm went rigid around her. "I couldn't! I wouldn't!"

"You're not immortal, dear. It could happen, unless—"

"Unless what? Tell me!"

"If there were a Tree of Life," she said slowly, measuring her words, "a Tree whose fruit would give you immortality as the fruit of that other Tree would give you knowledge, then I think not even God could drive you out of Eden."

"A Tree of Life—" he echoed softly. "What would it be like?"

Lilith closed her eyes. "A dark Tree, I think," she answered, almost in a whisper. "Dark limbs, dark leaves —pale, shining fruit hanging among them like lanterns. Can't you see it?"

Adam was silent. She glanced up at him. His eyes were shut and a look of intense longing was on his face in the twilight. There was silence about them for a long while. Presently she felt the tenseness of his body slacken beside her. He breathed out in a long sigh.

"I think there is a Tree of Life," he said. "I think it's in the center of the Garden near the other Tree. I'm sure it's there. The fruit are pale, just as you thought. They send out a light like moonlight in the dark. Tomorrow we'll taste them."

And Lilith relaxed against his shoulder with a sigh of her own. Tomorrow he would be immortal, like herself. She listened anxiously, and still heard the faraway battle cries of the seraphim echoing through the sky. War in heaven and peace on earth—

Through the deepening twilight of Eden no sound came except the music of the water and, somewhere off through the trees, a crooning lullaby in a tiny, piping voice as some cherub sang himself to sleep. Somewhere nearer other small voices squabbled drowsily a while, then fell silent. The most delightful lassitude was stealing over Lilith's body. She turned her cheek against Adam's shoulder and felt that cloudy fogging of the senses which she was coming to know so well—close like water above her head.

And the evening and the morning were the eighth day.

Lilith woke first. Birds were singing gloriously, and as she lay there on Adam's shoulder a cherub flashed across the stream on dazzling wings, caroling at the top of his piping voice. He did not see them. The pleasant delirium of a spring morning filled the whole wakening Garden, and Lilith sat up with a smile. Adam scarcely stirred. Lilith looked down at him with a glow of tenderness that alarmed her. She was coming to identify herself with Adam, as Adam was one with the Garden—this flesh was a treacherous thing.

Suddenly, blindingly, she knew that. Terror of what it was doing to the entity which was Lilith rolled over her in a great wave, and without thinking, almost without realizing what she did, she sprang up and out of the flesh that was betraying her. Up, up through the crystal morning she sprang, impalpable as the air around her. Up and up until the Adam that flesh had valued too highly was invisible, and the very treetops that hid him were a feathery green blur and she could see the walls that closed the Garden in, the rivers running out of it like four great blades of silver in the morning sun.

Beside the sleeping Adam nothing was left but the faintest blur of a woman shape, wrapped in shadow that made it almost invisible against the moss. The eye could scarcely have made it out there under the trees.

Lilith swam delightfully through the bright, still emptiness of the early morning. From here she could hear quite clearly the strong hosannahs of the seraphim pouring out in mighty golden choruses over the jasper walls. Whatever trouble had raged in heaven yesterday, today it was resolved. She scarcely troubled her mind about it.

She was free—free of the flesh and the terrifying weakness that had gone with it. She could see clearly now, no longer deluded by the distortions of value that had made life in that flesh so confusing. Her thoughts were not colored by it any more. Adam was nothing but a superb vessel now, brimmed with the power of God. Her perspective had been too warped down there in Eden to realize how little that magnificent body of his mattered in comparison to the power inherent in it.

She let the cold, clear ether bathe her of illusions while the timeless time of the void swam motionless around her. She had been in greater danger than she knew; it had taken this morning dip in the luminous heights to cleanse her mind of Adam. Refreshed, fortified against that perilous weakness, she could return now and take up her mission again. And she must do it quickly, before God noticed her. *Or was he watching already?*

She swooped luxuriantly in a long, airy curve and plummeted toward Eden.

Adam still slept timelessly upon the moss. Lilith dropped closer, shrugging herself together in anticipation of entering and filling out into life the body she had thrown off. And then—then a shock like the shock of lightning jolted her in midair until the Garden reeled beneath her. For where she had left only the faint, ephemeral husk of a woman beside Adam, a woman of firm, pale flesh lay now, asleep on the Man's shoulder. Golden hair spilled in a long skein across the moss, and the woman's head moved a little to the rhythm of Adam's breathing.

Lilith recovered herself and hovered nearer, incandescent with such jealousy and rage as she had never dreamed could touch her. The woman was clothed in a softly glowing halo as Adam was clothed. But it was Lilith's own shape she wore beneath that halo.

A sick dismay shook Lilith bodilessly in the air. God *had* been watching, then—waiting, perhaps, to strike. He had been here—it might have been no longer than a moment ago. She knew it by the very silence of the place. Everything was still hushed and awed by the recent Presence. God had passed by, and God had seen that tenantless garment of flesh she had cast off to swim in the ether, and God had known her whole scheme in one flash of His all-seeing eye.

He had taken the flesh she had worn, then, and used it for His own purposes—her precious, responsive flesh that had glowed at the touch of Adam's hand belonged now to another woman, slept in her place on Adam's shoulder. Lilith shook with intolerable emotion at the thought of it. She would not—

Adam was waking. Lilith hovered closer, watching jealously as he yawned, blinked, smiled, turned his curly head to look down at the woman beside him. Then he sat up so abruptly that the golden creature at his side cried out in a sweet, high voice and opened eyes bluer than a cherub's to stare at him reproachfully. Lilith, hating her, still saw that she had beauty of a sort comparable to Adam's, exquisite, brimming with the glorious emptiness of utter innocence. There was a roundness and an appealing softness to her that was new in Eden, but the shape she wore was Lilith's and none other.

Adam stared down at her in amazement.

"L-Lilith—" he stammered. "Who are you? Where's Lilith? I—"

"Who is Lilith?" demanded the golden girl in a soft, hurt voice, sitting up and pushing the glowing hair back with both hands in a lovely, smooth gesture. "I don't know. I can't remember—" She let the words die and stared about the Garden with a blue gaze luminous with wonder. Then the eyes came back to Adam and she smiled very sweetly.

Adam had put a hand to his side, a pucker of the first pain in Eden drawing his golden brows together. For no reason at all he was remembering the scarred bank from which the earth that shaped him had been taken. He opened his mouth to speak.

And then out of the glow of the morning a vast, bodiless Voice spoke quietly.

"I have taken a rib from your side, Man," said the Voice. The whole glade trembled at the sound; the brook ceased its tinkling, the leaves stood still upon the trees. Not a bird sang. Filling the whole morning, the whole Garden, the Voice went on: "Out of the flesh of your flesh I have made a helpmate and a wife for you. Forsaking all others, cleave unto her. *Forsaking all others*—"

The Voice ceased not suddenly, but by echoing degrees that made the leaves shiver upon the trees in rhythm to Its fading syllables, "Forsaking all others . . . all others . . . all others—"

And then it was as if a light ceased to glow in the Garden which, until it went out, no one had perceived. The air dimmed a little, and thickened and dulled, so that one blinked in the aftermath when the presence of God was withdrawn.

The woman drew closer to Adam's side, putting out uncertain hands to him, frightened by the quiet, tremendous Voice and the silence of the Garden. Adam dropped an arm automatically about her, stilling her fright against his shoulder. He bent his head as the Voice ceased to echo through the shaken air.

"Yes, Lord," he said obediently. There was an instant more of silence everywhere. Then timidly the brook sent a tentative ripple of sound into the air, a bird piped once, a breeze began to flow. God had withdrawn.

Bodiless, trembling with emotions she had no name for, Lilith watched the Man and the woman alone on the moss bank she had shared last night with Adam. He looked down at the frightened girl huddling against him.

"I suppose you're Eve," he said, a certain gentleness in his voice that made Lilith writhe.

"If you say so," murmured the girl, glancing up at him under a flutter of lashes. Lilith hated him. Over her fair head Adam looked out across the quiet glade.

"Lilith?" he said. "Lilith—"

A warm rush of answer focused all Lilith's being into one responding cry.

"Yes, Adam. . . yes! I'm here!"

He might have heard her bodiless reply, it was so passionate an answer to his call, but at that instant Eve said with childish petulance:

"Who is this Lilith, Adam? Why do you keep calling her? Won't I do?"

Adam looked down uncertainly. While he hesitated, Eve deliberately snuggled against him with a warm little wriggle that was Lilith's alone. By that, if by no other sign, Lilith knew it was her very flesh God had taken to mold this pale girl from Adam's rib, using the same pattern which Adam had designed for Lilith. Eve wore it now, and in that shape knew, without learning them, all the subtle tricks that Lilith's age-old wisdom had evolved during the brief while she dwelt in the body. Lilith's lost flesh, Lilith's delightful use of it, Lilith's Adam—all were Eve's now.

Fury and wild despair and an intolerable ache that made the world turn black around her blinded Lilith to the two beneath the tree. She could not bear to watch them any longer. With a soundless wail of despair she turned and flung herself up again into the limitless heights above Eden.

But this time the ether was no anodyne for her grief. It had been no true anodyne before, she knew now. For a disease was upon her that had its seed, perhaps, in the flesh she wore briefly—but too long. God had made Adam incomplete, and Adam to assuage his need had flung out a net to trap some unwary creature for his own. Shame burned in her. The Queen of Air and Darkness, like some mindless elemental, had fallen into his trap; he had used her as she had meant to use him. She was a part of him, trapped in the flesh that was incomplete without him, and her need for him was so deep that she could not escape, even though that body was no longer hers. The roots of her disease had been in the flesh, but the virulence had spread into the very essence of the being which was Lilith and no bath in the deeps of space could cleanse her now. In the flesh or out of it, on earth or in ether, an insatiable need was upon her that could never be slaked.

And a dreadful suspicion was taking shape in her mind. Adam in his innocence could never have planned this. Had God known, all along? Had it been no error, after all, that Adam was created incomplete? And was this a punishment designed by God for tampering with his plan? Suddenly she thought that it must be. There would be no awe-inspiring struggle between light and dark such as she had half expected when God recognized her presence. There would be no struggle at all. She was vanquished, judged and punished all at a blow. No glory was in it, only this unbearable longing, a spiritual hunger more insatiable than any hunger the flesh could feel for the man she would never have again. She clove the airy heights above Eden for what might have been a thousand years, or a moment, had time existed in the void, knowing only that Adam was lost to her forever.

Forever? She writhed around in mid-ether, checking the wild, aimless upward flight. Forever? Adam still looked out across the Garden and called her name, even while he held that pale usurper in his arms. Perhaps God had not realized the strength of the strange unity between the man and the first woman in Eden. Perhaps God had not thought that she would fight. Perhaps there was a chance left, after all—

Downward through the luminous gulf she plunged, down and down until Eden expanded like a bubble beneath her and the strong choruses of the seraphim were sweet again above the Garden. Adam and Eve were still beside the brook where she had left them. Eve on a rock was splashing her small feet and flashing blue-eyed glances over her shoulder that made Adam smile when he met them. Lilith hated her.

"Adam!" squealed Eve as the plunging Lilith came into hearing. "Look out—I'm slipping! Catch me! Quick!" It was the same croon Lilith had put into the throat of the body she had lost. Remembering how roundly and softly it had come swelling up in her throat, she writhed with a vitriolic helplessness that made the Garden dance in waves like heat around her.

"Catch me!" cried Eve again in the most appealing voice in the world. Adam sprang to clasp her as she slid. She threw both pale arms about his neck and crowed with laughter so infectious that two passing cherubs paused in midair to rock with answering mirth and beat each other over the shoulders with their wings.

"*Adam . . . Adam . . . Adam*—" wailed Lilith voicelessly. It was a silent wail, but all her heartbreak and despair and intolerable longing went into it, and above Eve's golden head Adam looked up, the laughter dying on his face. "*Adam!*" cried Lilith again. And this time he heard.

But he did not answer directly. Association with women was beginning to teach him tact. Instead he beckoned to the reeling cherubs. Rosy with mirth, they fluttered nearer. Eve looked up in big-eyed surprise as the plump little heads balanced on rainbow wings swooped laughing toward her and poised to await Adam's pleasure.

"These are a couple of our cherubs," said Adam. "Dan and Bethuel, from over toward the Tree. They have a nest there. Tell her about the Tree, will you, boys? Eve dear, I'll be getting you some fruit for breakfast. Wait for me here."

She obeyed with only a wistful glance after him as the cherubs burst into eager chatter, squabbling a little as they spoke.

"Well, there's this Tree in the middle of the Garden—"

"Tell her about the Fruit, Dan. You mustn't—"

"Yes, you mustn't touch—"

"No, that's not right, Dan. Michael says you can touch it, you just can't eat—"

"Don't interrupt me! Now it's like this. You see, there's a Tree—"

Adam went slowly off down to the brook. A lie had never yet been spoken in Eden. He was hunting fruit. But Lilith saw him searching the dappled spaces between the trees, too, a certain wistfulness on his face, and she came down with a rustle of invisibility through the leaves.

"Adam . . . Adam!"

"Lilith! Where are you?"

With a tremendous effort Lilith focused her whole being into an intensity so strong that although she re-

mained bodiless, voiceless, intangible, yet the strength of
her desire was enough to make Adam hear her dimly,
see her remotely in a wavering outline against the
leaves, in the shape he had created for her. She held it
with difficulty, shimmering before his eyes.

"Lilith!" he cried, and reached her in two long
strides, putting out his arms. She leaned into them. But
the muscular, light-sheathed arms closed about her and
through her and met in empty air.

She called his name miserably, quivering against him
through all her bodiless body. But she could feel him no
more than he could touch her, and the old ache she had
known in mid-ether came back with a rush. Even here
in his arms, then, she was forbidden to touch the Man.
She could never be more than a wraith of the air to him,
while Eve—while Eve, in her stolen body—

"Adam!" cried Lilith again. "You were mine first!
Can you hear me? Adam, you could bring me back if
you tried! You did it once—you could again. Try, try!"

He stared down at her dim face, the flowers on the
hillside beyond visible through it.

"What's wrong, Lilith? I can hardly see you!"

"You wanted me once badly enough to bring me out
of nowhere into the flesh," she cried desperately.
"Adam, Adam—want me again!"

He stared down at her. "I do," he said, his voice unexpectedly shaken. And then, more strongly, "Come
back, Lilith! What's happened to you? Come back!"

Lilith closed her eyes, feeling reality pour marvelously along her bodiless limbs. Faintly now she could feel
grass underfoot, Adam's chest against her anxious
hands; his arms were around her and in his embrace she
was taking shape out of nothingness, summoned into
flesh again by the godhood in this image of God. And
then—

"Adam . . . Adam!" Eve's sweet, clear voice rang
lightly among the leaves. "Adam, where are you? I want
to go look at the Tree, Adam. Where are you, dear?"

"Hurry!" urged Lilith desperately, beating her half-
tangible hands against his chest.

Adam's arms loosed a little about her. He glanced

across his shoulder, his handsome, empty face clouded. He was remembering.

"Forsaking all others—" he murmured, in a voice not entirely his own. Lilith shuddered a little against him, recognizing the timbre of that Voice which had spoken in the silence. *"Forsaking all others—"* God had said that. "Forsaking all others but Eve—"

His arms dropped from about Lilith. "I . . . I'll . . . will you wait for me?" he said hesitantly, stepping back from her half-real shape, lovely and shadow-veiled under the shadow of the trees. "I'll be back—"

"Adam!" called Eve again, nearer and very sweetly. "Adam, I'm lost! Adam! Adam, where are you?"

"Coming," said Adam. He looked once more at Lilith, a long look. Then he turned and ran lightly off through trees that parted to receive him, the glow of his half-divinity shining upon the leaves as he passed. Lilith watched the beautiful, light-glowing figure as far as she could see it.

Then she put her half-real hands to her face and her knees loosened beneath her and she doubled down in a heap upon the grass, her shadowy hair billowing out around her on a breeze that blew from nowhere, not touching the leaves. She was half-flesh now. She had tears. She found a certain relief in the discovery that she could weep.

The next sound she heard—it seemed a long while after—was a faint hiss. Cloaked in the tented shadow of her hair, she considered it a while, hiccupping now and then with receding sobs. Presently she looked up. Then she gasped and got to her feet with the effortless ease of the half-material.

The serpent looked at her sidewise out of slanted eyes, grinning. In the green gloom under the trees he was so handsome that even she, who had seen Adam, was aware of a little thrill of admiration. In those days the serpent went upright like a man, nor was he exactly non-human in shape, but his beauty was as different from man's as day is from night. He was lithe and gorgeously scaled and by any standards a supremely hand-some, supremely male creature.

All about him in shadowy outline a radiance stood out that was vaguely an angel shape, winged, tremendous. It invested the serpent body with a glow that was not its own. Out of that celestial radiance the serpent said in a cool voice:

"The Queen of Air and Darkness! I didn't expect you here. What are you doing in that body?"

Lilith collected herself, hiccupped once more and stood up, the cloudy hair moving uneasily about her. She said with a grim composure:

"The same thing I suspect you're doing in that one, only you'll have to do better if you want to deceive any-body. What brings you to Eden—Lucifer?"

The serpent glanced down at himself and sent one or two long, sliding ripples gliding along his iridescent body. The angel shape that hung in the air about him gradually faded, and the beauty deepened as it focused it-self more strongly in the flesh he wore. After a moment he glanced up.

"How's that—better? Oh, I came down for a purpose. I have—business with Adam." His cool voice took on a note of grimness. "You may have heard a little trouble in heaven yesterday. That was me."

"Trouble?" echoed Lilith. She had almost forgotten the sounds of combat and the great battle cries of the seraphim in the depths of her own grief.

"It was a fine fight while it lasted," Lucifer grinned. "Blood running like water down the golden streets! I tell you, it was a relief to hear something beside 'hosan-nah' in heaven for a change! Well"—he shrugged—"they won. Too many of them were fools and stood by Jehovah. But we gave them a good fight, and we took part of the jasper walls with us when they hurled us over." He gave her a satisfied nod. "God won, but he'll think twice before He insults me again."

"Insults you?" echoed Lilith. "How?"

Lucifer drew himself up to a magnificent height. Radiance glowed along his scaled and gleaming body. "God made me of fire! Shall I bow down before this . . . this lump of clay they call Adam? He may be good enough for the other angels to worship when God points a finger, but he isn't good enough for me!"

"Is that why you're here?"

"Isn't it reason enough? I have a quarrel with this Adam!"

"You couldn't touch him," said Lilith desperately. "He's God's image, and remember, you were no match for God."

Lucifer stretched his magnificent, gleaming height and glared down at her.

"The creature's made of clay. He must have a flaw somewhere. What is it? You know him."

Lilith looked up at him speechless, a great excitement beginning to swell so tremendously in her that her half-formed body could hardly contain it. There was a chance! God himself had put a weapon straight into her hands!

"Yes, there is a flaw," she said. "I'll tell you . . . if you'll give me a promise."

"All right, I give it," said Lucifer carelessly. "Tell me."

She hesitated, choosing her words. "Your feud isn't with Adam. He never asked you to worship him. God did that. Your quarrel is with God, not Adam. The Man himself you can't touch, but God had given him a . . . a wife," she choked when she said it. "I think there's a weakness in her, and through her you could spoil God's plan. But you must spare the Man—for me."

Lucifer whistled soundlessly, lifting his brows. "Oh—?"

"I saw him first," said Lilith defensively. "I want him."

The serpent looked at her narrowly. "Why? No . . . never mind. I won't quarrel with you. I may have an idea to suggest to you later, if a plan of mine works out. You and I together could make quite a thing of hell."

Lilith winced a little. She and Adam together had had great prospects, once, too. Perhaps they still had—if God were not listening.

"You promise not to touch him, then?"

"Yes, I won't hurt your precious clod. You're right

—my quarrel's with God, not that animated lump of clay named Adam. What's the secret?"

"Eden," said Lilith slowly, "is testing ground. There are flaws in it, there must be, or neither of us would be here. God planted a Tree in the middle of the Garden and forbade anyone to touch it. That's the test . . . I think I see it now. It's a test of obedience. God doesn't trust man—he made him too strong. The Tree is the knowledge of Good and Evil, and God doesn't dare let that knowledge exist in the Garden, because he controls Man only by Man's ignorance of his own power. If either of them eats, then God will have to destroy that one quickly. You tempt the woman to eat, Lucifer, and leave Adam and Eden to me!"

The serpent eyed her sidelong. He laughed.

"If either of them fails in this test you're talking about, then God will know neither can be trusted, won't he? He'll know their present form's imperfect, and he'll destroy them both and work out some other plan for the world."

Lilith drew a deep breath. Excitement was rising like a tide in her, and the wind from nowhere swirled the dark hair in a cloud about her shoulders.

"Let him try!" she cried exultantly. "I can save Adam. God made a mistake when he put such power in the Garden. He shouldn't have left it living, half-conscious of itself. He shouldn't have let Adam know how close he is to the earth he was taken from. Adam and the Garden are one flesh, and the power of God is in them both. God can't destroy one without the other, and together they are very strong— If they defied God together, and I helped them—"

Lucifer looked at her, a trace of compassion on his handsome, reptilian face.

"God defeated *me*," he reminded her. "Do you think He couldn't you?"

She gave him a proud glance. "I am the Queen of Air and Darkness. I have secrets of my own, and powers not even God can control. If I join them with Adam's, and the Garden's. . . . God made the Garden alive and powerful, and Adam is one flesh with it, each incomplete without the other as Man is without woman. Adam has Eve now—but when Eve's gone he'll remember Lilith. I'll see that he remembers! And I'll see that he understands his danger. With my help, perhaps he can avert it."

"If God destroys Eve," said Lucifer, "he'll destroy Adam, too. They're one pattern."

"But he may not destroy them at the same time. I'll gamble on that. I'd kill her myself if I could, but I can't touch anything in the Garden without its own consent. . . . No, I'll have to wait until Eve proves to God her unfitness to wear flesh, and while he punishes her I must seize that moment to rouse the Garden. It's almost aware of itself already. I think I could awaken it —through Adam, perhaps. Adam and Eden are almost one, as Adam and I will be again if we can get rid of Eve. None of us separately has the power to defy God, but Eden and Adam and I together might do it!" She tossed back her head and the wild dark hair swirled like a fog about her. "Eden is an entity of its own—I think I could close a shell of space around us, and there are places in my Darkness where we could hide even from God!"

Lucifer narrowed his eyes at her. "It might work," he nodded slowly. "You're mad—but it might work, with my help. The woman is beautiful, in her way—" He laughed. "And what a revenge on God!"

"The woman," mused Lilith, "is in my body, and I am evil. . . . I think enough evil remains there that Eve will find you—interesting. Good luck, Lucifer!"

In a hollow, velvety cup in the Garden's very center the two Trees stood. One at the edge of the clearing was a dark Tree, the leaves folded like a cloak about a pale glow from within where the Fruit of Life hung hidden. But in the center of the hollow the Tree of Knowledge flaunted its scarlet fruit that burned with a flame almost of their own among the green and glossy leaves. Here was the heart of the Garden. Out of the Tree of the Knowledge of Good and Evil the beat went pulsing that shook the air of Eden.

Eve set one small, bare foot upon the downward slope

and looked back timidly over her shoulder. The serpent flicked a forked red tongue at her. His voice was cool and clear, and sweet as honey.

"*Eva*," he said softly. "*Eva—*"

She smiled and went on, he rippling after her with an unearthly beauty to his gait that is lost forever now. No one knows today how the serpent walked before the Fall. Of all human creatures only Eve knows that, and there were things Eve never told Adam.

They paused under the shadow of the Tree. In long, slow rhythms the air went pulsing past them. Eve's fair hair stirred a little, so strong was the rhythm here. All the Fruit of the Tree pushed out among the leaves to see her, and the nearer branches bent caressingly toward this woman who was of the flesh of Adam.

The nearest branch stooped down enticingly. Eve reached for a scarlet apple that dipped into her hand. Almost of itself it snapped free of the twig that held it. Eve stared at the apple in her palm, and her hand began to shake. She drew back against the serpent, a little whimper of terror rising in her throat.

The serpent dropped a coiled embrace about the lovely, light-clothed pallor of her body and bent his handsome, slanted head to hers, whispering at her ear in a voice so cool and sweet that the terror faded from her face. She smiled a little, and her hand steadied.

She lifted the Fruit of Knowledge to her lips. There was a hush all through the Garden as she hesitated for a long moment, the red fruit at her red mouth, her teeth denting the scarlet cheek of Knowledge. The last few timeless moments stood still while innocence yet reigned over Eden.

Then the serpent whispered again, urgently: "*Eva—*" he said.

Lilith stood shivering in Adam's arms.

"You were mine first," she was whispering fiercely. "You and I and the Garden—don't you remember? I was your wife before her, and you belong to me!"

Adam could see his own arms through the ephemeral stuff of Lilith's body. He was shaken by the violence in her voice, but his mind was too fogged with the un-thinking blank of innocence to understand very clearly. He tried hard.

The rhythm that pulsed through Eden was curiously uneven now. Lilith knew what it meant, and excitement choked her. She cried more desperately:

"Adam . . . Adam! Don't let anything separate us, you and the Garden and I! You can hold us together if you try! I know you can! You—"

One great, annihilating throb shook through the air like thunder. The whole Garden reeled with it and every tree in Eden bowed as if before a tremendous wind. Adam looked up, aghast. But Lilith laughed a wild, excited laugh and cried, "This is it! Oh, hurry, Adam, hurry!"

She slipped through his arms that were still clasped about her and went fluttering effortlessly off through branches that did not impede her passage, Adam following half stunned with the stunned Garden. All Eden was still reeling from the violence of what had just happened beneath the Tree.

Lilith watched the sky as she ran. Would a great bolt of lightning come ravening down out of heaven to blast the woman out of being before they reached the Tree? "Wait, wait!" she panted voicelessly to God. "Give me a moment longer—" Would a bolt strike Adam, too, as he slipped through the parting trees beside her? "Hurry!" she gasped again.

Breathless, they paused at the edge of the hollow where the Tree stood. Looking down, they could see Eve just clear of the shadow of it, the fruit in her hand with one white bite flawing its scarlet cheek. She was staring about the Garden as if she had never seen it before. *Where was God? Why had He not blasted her as she stood there?*

Lilith in her first wild glance could not see the serpent except for a glitter of iridescence back in the shadow of the Tree. Even in her terrible excitement she smiled wryly. Lucifer was taking no chances with God.

But she had no time to waste now on Lucifer or on Eve. For some inexplicable reason God was staying His hand, and she must make the most of the respite. For when God was finished with Eve He would turn to Adam, and before that much had to be done. Adam was her business now, and the living Eden, and all eternity waited on what the next few moments held.

She stood out on the lip of the hollow and a great dark wind from nowhere swelled monstrously about her, tossing out her hair until it was a cloud that shut her from sight. Out of the cloud her voice came rolling in tremendous rhythms paced to the rhythm at which Eden breathed—and Adam.

"Garden!" she called. "Eden—hear me! I am Lilith, the wife of Adam—"

She could feel a vast, dim awareness stirring around her. All through Eden the wakening motion ran, drawing closer, welling up deeply from the earth underfoot, monstrously, wonderfully, a world coming alive at her call.

"Adam!" she cried. "Adam, do you hear me? You and Eden are one flesh, and Eve has destroyed you both. She has just brought knowledge into Eden, where God dares not let it exist. God will destroy you all, because of Eve . . . unless you listen to me—"

She felt Adam's attention torn away from Eve and focusing upon herself in fear and wonder. She felt the Garden's wakening awareness draw around him with growing intensity, until it was as if the earth of Eden and the flesh of Man quickened into one, married by the same need for one another as the thought of parting and destruction shuddered through each.

Was this what God had planned as an ending for His divine scheme, as it was the beginning of Lilith's? She had no time to wonder, but the thought crossed her mind awesomely even as she wooed the Garden in a voice as sweet and coaxing as the voice she used to Adam.

And the whole great Garden shuddered ponderously around her, awareness thrilling down every tendril and branch and blade, pulsing up out of the very hill on which she stood. And all of it was Adam. The Garden heard and hung upon her words, and Adam heard, and they three together were all that existed. Success was in her hands. She could feel it. And then—

"Adam . . . Adam!" screamed Eve beneath the Tree.

Lilith's sonorous voice paused in its invocation; the Garden hesitated around her.

"Adam!" cried Eve again, terror flattening all the sweetness out of her voice.

And behind Lilith, in a drugged voice, Adam said: "Eve—?"

"God . . . God, destroy her now!" prayed Lilith soundlessly. And aloud, "Eve has no part in Eden! Don't listen to her, Adam! She'll destroy you and the Garden together!"

"Adam, Adam! Where are you?"

"Coming—" said Adam, still in that thick, drugged voice.

Lilith whirled in the mist of her cloudy hair. Where was God! Why had He stayed His hand? Now was the time to strike, if her hope were not to fail. Now, now! Surely the lightning would come ravening down from heaven if she could hold Adam a moment longer—

"Adam, wait!" she cried desperately. "Adam, you know you love me! If you leave—"

Her voice faltered as he peered at her as blindly as if he had never seen her before. The haloed light was like fire all around him, and her words had been a drug to him as they had been to the Garden, until the earth that loved and listened to her had been one with his own earth-formed flesh; a moment ago there had been nothing in creation for Adam or for Eden but this one woman speaking out of the dark. But now—

"Adam!" screamed Eve again in that flat, frightened voice.

"Don't listen!" cried Lilith frantically. "She doesn't belong here! You can't save her now! God will destroy her, and He'll destroy you, too, if you leave me! Stay here and let her die! You and I will be alone again, in the Garden . . . Adam, don't listen!"

"I . . . I have to listen," he stammered almost stupidly. "Get out of my way, Lilith. Don't you understand? She's my own flesh—I have to go."

Lilith stared at him dumbly. His own flesh! She had forgotten that. She had leaned too heavily on his oneness with the Garden—she had forgotten he was one with Eve, too. The prospect of defeat was suddenly like lead in her. If God would only strike now— She swayed forward in one last desperate effort to hold him back from Eve while the Garden stirred uneasily around them, frightened with Lilith's terror, torn with Adam's distress. She wavered between Adam and the valley as if her ephemeral body could hold him, but he went through her as if through a cloud and stumbled blindly downhill toward the terrified Eve beneath the Tree with the fruit in her hand and a dreadful knowledge on her face.

From here Lilith could see what Adam had not yet. She laughed suddenly, wildly, and cried:

"Look at her, Adam! Look!" And Adam blinked and looked.

Eve stood naked beneath the Tree. That burning beauty which had clothed her like a garment was gone with her divine innocence and she was no longer the flawless goddess who had wakened on Adam's shoulder that morning. She stood shivering a little, looking forlorn and somehow pinched and thin, almost a caricature of the perfect beauty that had gone down the hill with the serpent an hour ago. But she did not know that. She looked up at Adam as he hesitated above her, and smiled uncertainly with a sort of leer in her smile.

"Oh, there you are," she said, and even her voice was harsher now. "Everything looked so . . . so queer, for a minute. Look." She held up the fruit. "It's good. Better than anything *you* ever gave me. Try it."

Lilith stared at her from the hilltop with a horror that for a moment blanked out her growing terror because of God's delay. Was knowledge, then, as ugly as this? Why had it destroyed Eve's beauty as if it were some evil thing? Perfect knowledge should have increased her strength and loveliness in the instant before God struck her down, if— Suddenly Lilith understood. Perfect knowledge! But Eve had only tasted the fruit, and she had only a warped half-knowledge from that single taste. The beauty of her innocence was lost, but she had not yet gained the beauty of perfect knowledge. Was this why God delayed? So long as her knowledge was imperfect perhaps she was no menace to God's power in Eden. And yet she had disobeyed, she had proved herself unworthy of the trust of God— Then why did He hesitate? Why had He not blasted her as she stood there with the apple at her lips? A panic was rising in Lilith's throat. *Could it be that He was laughing, even now?* Was He giving her the respite she had prayed for, and watching her fail in spite of it?

"Taste the apple," said Eve again, holding it out.

"Adam!" cried Lilith despairingly from the edge of the hill. "Adam, look at me! You loved me first—don't you remember? Look at me, Adam!"

And Adam turned to look. The wind, which had clouded her from sight in the darkness of her hair, had calmed. She stood now, luminous on the hilltop, the darkness parted like a river by the whiteness of her shoulders. And she was beautiful with a beauty that no mortal woman will ever wear again.

"I was first!" cried Lilith. "You loved me before her —come back to me now, before God strikes you both! Come back, Adam!"

He stared up at her miserably. He looked back at the flawed, shivering creature at his side, knowledge curiously horrible in her eyes. He stared at Eve, too, a long stare. And then he reached for the apple.

"Adam—no!" shrieked Lilith. "See what knowledge did to Eve! You'll be ugly and naked, like her! Don't taste it, Adam! You don't know what you're doing!"

Over the poised red fruit he looked up at her. The light quivered gloriously all around him. He stood like a god beneath the Tree, radiant, perfect.

"Yes, I know," he said, in a clearer voice than she had ever heard him use before.

"God will destroy you!" wailed Lilith, and rolled her eyes up to look for the falling thunderbolt that might be hurtling downward even now.

"I know," said Adam again. And then, after a pause, "You don't understand, Lilith. Eve is my own flesh, closer than Eden—closer than you. Don't you remember what God said? *Forsaking all others—*"

"Eve!" screamed Lilith hopelessly. "Stop him! Your

punishment's certain—are you going to drag him down, too?"

Eve looked up, knowledge dark in her blue eyes. She laughed a thin laugh and the last vestige of her beauty went with it.

"Leave him to you?" she sneered. "Oh no! He and I are one flesh—we'll go together. Taste the apple, Adam!"

He turned it obediently in his hand; his teeth crunched through scarlet skin into the sweet white flesh inside. There was a tremendous silence all through the Garden; nothing stirred in Eden while Adam chewed and swallowed the Fruit of Knowledge. And then turned to stare down into Eve's lifted eyes while awareness of himself as an individual, free-willed being dawned gradually across his awakening mind.

And then the burning glory that clothed him paled, shimmered, went out along his limbs. He, too, was naked. The queer, pinched look of humanity shivered over that magnificent body, and he was no longer magnificent, no longer Adam.

Lilith had forgotten to look for God. Sickness of the heart was swelling terribly in her, and for a moment she no longer cared about God, or Eden, or the future. This was not Adam any more— It would never be Adam again—

"Listen," said Eve in a small, intimate voice to Adam. "How quiet it is! Why, it's the music. The seraphim aren't singing any more around the Throne!"

Lilith glanced up apathetically. That meant, then, that God was coming— But even as she looked up a great golden chorus resounded serenely from high over Eden. Adam tipped his tarnished head to listen.

"You're right," he agreed. "They've stopped their song."

Lilith did not hear him. That dreadful sickness in her was swelling and changing, and she knew now what it was—hatred. Hatred of Adam and Eve and the thing they had done to her. Hatred of these naked caricatures, who had been the magnificent half-god she had loved and the shape she had put on to delight him. True, they might finish the eating of knowledge and grow perfect again, but it would be a perfection that shut her out. They were one flesh together, and even God had failed her now. Looking down, she loathed them both. Eve's very existence was an insult to the unflawed perfection which Lilith still wore, and Adam—Adam shivering beneath the Tree with a warped, imperfect knowledge leering in his eyes—

A sob swelled in her throat. He had been flawless once—she would never forget that. Almost she loved the memory still as it lingered about this shivering human creature beneath the Tree. So long as he was alive she knew now she would never be free of it; this weakness would torment her still for the flesh that had once been Adam. The prospect of an eternity of longing for him, who would never exist again, was suddenly unbearable to her.

She tipped her head back and looked up through the glory above Eden where golden voices chanted that neither Adam nor Eve would ever hear again.

"Jehovah!" she sobbed. "Jehovah! Come down and destroy us all! You were right—they are both too flawed to bring anything but misery to all who know them. God, come down and give us peace!"

Eve squealed in terror at Adam's side. "Listen!" she cried. "Adam, listen to her!"

Answering human terror dawned across the pinched features that had once been Adam's handsome, immortal face. "The Tree of Life!" he shouted. "No one can touch us if we eat that fruit!"

He whirled to scramble up the slope toward the dark Tree, and Lilith's heart ached to watch how heavily he moved. Yesterday's wonderful, easy litheness was gone with his beauty, and his body was a burden to him now.

But he was not to reach the Tree of Life. For suddenly glory brightened unbearably over the Garden. A silence was in the sky, and the breeze ceased to blow through Eden.

"Adam," said a Voice in the great silence of the Garden, *"hast thou eaten of the Tree?"*

Adam glanced up the slope at Lilith, standing despairingly against the sky. He looked at Eve beside him, a clumsy caricature of the loveliness he had dreamed of. There was bitterness in his voice.

"The woman thou gavest me—" he began reproachfully, and then hesitated, meeting Eve's eyes. The old godlike goodness was lost to him now, but he had not fallen low enough yet to let Eve know what he was thinking. He could not say, "The woman Thou gavest me has ruined us both—but I had a woman of my own before her and she never did me any harm." No, he could not hurt this flesh of his flesh so deeply, but he was human now and he could not let her go unrebuked. He went on sulkily, "—she gave me the apple, and I ate."

The Voice said awfully, "Eve—?"

Perhaps Eve was remembering that other voice, cool and sweet, murmuring, "Eva—" in the cool, green dimness of the Garden, the voice that had whispered secrets she would never share with Adam. Perhaps if he had been beside her now—but he was not, and her resentment bubbled to her lips in speech.

"The serpent beguiled me," she told God sullenly, "and I ate."

There was silence for a moment in the Garden. Then the Voice said, "Lucifer—" with a sorrow in the sound that had not stirred for the man's plight, or the woman's. "Lucifer, my enemy, come forth from the Tree." There was a divine compassion in the Voice even as It pronounced sentence. "Upon thy belly shalt thou go, and dust shalt thou eat all the days of thy life—"

Out from beneath the shadow of the Tree a flat and shining length came pouring through the grass. This was the hour for the shedding of beauty: the serpent had lost the fire-bright splendor that had been his while Lucifer dwelt in his flesh, but traces lingered yet in the unearthly fluidness of his motion, in his shining iridescence. He lifted a wedged head toward Eve, flickered his tongue at her once and then dropped back into the grass. Its ripple above him marked his course away. Eve drew one long, sobbing breath for that green twilight hour in the Garden, that Adam would never guess, as she watched him ripple away.

"Adam, Eve," went on the Voice quietly, "the Garden is not for you." There was a passionless pity in It as the Garden stood still to listen. "I made your flesh too weak, because your godhood was too strong to trust. You are not to blame for that—the fault was Mine. But Adam . . . Eve . . . what power did I put in you, that the very elements of fire and darkness find kinship with you? What flaw is in you, that though you are the only two human things alive, yet you cannot keep faith with one another?"

Adam glanced miserably up toward Lilith standing motionless on the hill's edge, clothed in the flawless beauty he had dreamed for her and would never see again. Eve's eyes followed the serpent through the grass that was blurred for her because of the first tears of Eden. Neither of them answered.

"You are not fit yet to put forth your hand to the Tree of Life, and eat, and live forever," went on the Voice after a moment.

"Man . . . woman . . . you are not yet fit for perfect knowledge or immortality. You are not yet fit for trust. But for Lilith the tale would have spun itself out here in the walls of Eden, but now you must go beyond temptation and work your own salvation out in the sweat of your brow, in the lands beyond the Garden. Adam, I dare not trust you any longer in your kinship with the earth I shaped you from. Cursed is the ground for your sake, Adam—it shall be one with you no longer. But I promise this . . . in the end you shall return to it—" The Voice fell silent, and there was from far above the flash of a flaming sword over the gate of Eden.

In the silence Lilith laughed. It was a clear, ringing sound from the hill's edge: "Deal with me now," she said in an empty voice. "I have no desire to exist any longer in a world that has no Adam—destroy me, Jehovah."

The Voice said emotionlessly, "You are punished already, by the fruit of what you did."

"Punished enough!" wailed Lilith in sudden despair. "Make an end of it, Jehovah!"

"With man's end," said God quietly. "No, sooner. You four among you have shattered a plan in Eden that

you must shape anew before your travail ends. Let the
four of you build a new plan with the elements of your
being—Adam is Earth, Lucifer is Fire, Lilith is Air and
Darkness, Eve the Mother of All Living, the fertile seas
from which all living springs. Earth, Air, Fire and Water
—you thought your plan was better than Mine. Work it
out for yourselves!"

"What is our part to be, Lord?" asked Adam in a
small, humbled voice.

"Earth and water," said the Voice. "The kingdom of
earth for you and the woman and your children after
you."

"I was Adam's wife before her," wailed Lilith jealously. "What of me . . . and mine?"

The Voice fell silent for a while. Then it said quietly:
"Make your own choice, Queen of Air and Darkness."

"Let my children and Adam's haunt hers to their
graves, then!" decided Lilith instantly. "Mine are the
disinherited—let them take vengeance! Let her and hers
beware of my children who wail in the night, and know
she deserves their wrath. Let them remind her always
that Adam was mine before her!"

"So be it," said the Voice. And for an instant there
was silence in Eden while the shadow of times to come
brooded inscrutably in the mind of God. Lilith caught
flashes of it in the glory so bright over Eden that every
grass blade had a splendor which hurt the eyes. She saw
man loving his birthplace upon earth with a deep-rooted
love that made it as dear as his very flesh to him, so that
dimly he might remember the hour when all earth was
as close to him as his newly created body. She saw man
cleaving to one woman as dear as the flesh of his flesh,
yet remembering the unattainable and the lost—Lilith,
perfect in Eden. She looked down from the hilltop and
met Adam's eyes, and voicelessly between them a long
farewell went flashing.

No one was watching Eve. She was blinking through
tears, remembering a twilight hour and a fire-bright
beauty that the dust had quenched a moment ago at
God's command. And then . . . then there was the faintest rustling in the air around her, and a cool, clear voice
was murmuring:

"Eva—" against her cheek.

She stared. There was nothing. But—

"Eva," said the voice again. "Give me my vengeance too—upon the Man. Pretty Eva, do you hear me? Call your first child Kayn . . . Eva, will you do as I say? Call him Kayn the Spear of my vengeance, for he shall set murder loose among Adam's sons. Remember, Eva—"

And Eve echoed in a small, obedient whisper, "Cain . . . Cain."

No Woman Born

SHE HAD BEEN the loveliest creature whose image ever moved along the airways. John Harris, who was once her manager, remembered doggedly how beautiful she had been as he rose in the silent elevator toward the room where Deirdre sat waiting for him.

Since the theater fire that had destroyed her a year ago, he had never been quite able to let himself remember her beauty clearly, except when some old poster, half in tatters, flaunted her face at him, or a maudlin memorial program flashed her image unexpectedly across the television screen. But now he had to remember.

The elevator came to a sighing stop and the door slid open. John Harris hesitated. He knew in his mind that he had to go on, but his reluctant muscles almost refused him. He was thinking helplessly, as he had not allowed himself to think until this moment, of the fabulous grace that had poured through her wonderful dancer's body, remembering her soft and husky voice with the little burr in it that had fascinated the audiences of the whole world.

There had never been anyone so beautiful.

In times before her, other actresses had been lovely and adulated, but never before Deirdre's day had the entire world been able to take one woman so wholly to its heart. So few outside the capitals had ever seen Bernhardt or the fabulous Jersey Lily. And the beauties of the movie screen had had to limit their audiences to those who could reach the theaters. But Deirdre's image had once moved glowingly across the television screens of every home in the civilized world. And in many outside the bounds of civilization. Her soft, husky songs had sounded in the depths of jungles, her lovely, languorous body had woven its patterns of rhythm in desert tents and polar huts. The whole world knew every smooth motion of her body and ever cadence of her voice, and the way a subtle radiance had seemed to go on behind her features when she smiled.

And the whole world had mourned her when she died in the theater fire.

Harris could not quite think of her as other than dead, though he knew what sat waiting him in the room ahead. He kept remembering the old words James Stephens wrote long ago for another Deirdre, also lovely and beloved and unforgotten after two thousand years.

The time comes when our hearts sink utterly,
When we remember Deirdre and her tale,
And that her lips are dust. . . .
There has been again no woman born
Who was so beautiful; not one so beautiful
Of all the women born—

That wasn't quite true, of course—there had been one. Or maybe, after all, this Deirdre who died only a year ago had been beautiful in the sense of perfection. He thought the other one might not have been either, for there are always women with perfection of feature in the world, and they are not the ones that legend remembers. It was the light within, shining through her charming, imperfect features, that had made this Deirdre's face so lovely. No one else he had ever seen had anything like the magic of the lost Deirdre.

Let all men go apart and mourn together—
No man can ever love her. Not a man
Can dream to be her lover. . . . No man say—
What could one say to her? There are no words
That one could say to her.

No, no words at all. And it was going to be impossible to go through with this. Harris knew it overwhelmingly just as his finger touched the buzzer. But the door opened almost instantly, and then it was too late.

Maltzer stood just inside, peering out through his heavy spectacles. You could see how tensely he had been waiting. Harris was a little shocked to see that the man was trembling. It was hard to think of the confident and imperturbable Maltzer, whom he had known briefly a year ago, as shaken like this. He wondered if Deirdre herself were as tremulous with sheer nerves—but it was not time yet to let himself think of that.

"Come in, come in," Maltzer said irritably. There was no reason for irritation. The year's work, so much of it in secrecy and solitude, must have tried him physically and mentally to the very breaking point.

"She all right?" Harris asked inanely, stepping inside.

"Oh yes . . . yes, *she's* all right." Maltzer bit his thumbnail and glanced over his shoulder at an inner door, where Harris guessed she would be waiting.

"No," Maltzer said, as he took an involuntary step toward it. "We'd better have a talk first. Come over and sit down. Drink?"

Harris nodded, and watched Maltzer's hands tremble as he tilted the decanter. The man was clearly on the very verge of collapse, and Harris felt a sudden cold uncertainty open up in him in the one place where until now he had been oddly confident.

"She *is* all right?" he demanded, taking the glass.

"Oh yes, she's perfect. She's so confident it scares me." Maltzer gulped his drink and poured another before he sat down.

"What's wrong, then?"

"Nothing, I guess. Or . . . well, I don't know. I'm not sure any more. I've worked toward this meeting for nearly a year, but now—well, I'm not sure it's time yet. I'm just not sure."

He stared at Harris, his eyes large and indistinguishable behind the lenses. He was a thin, wire-taut man with all the bone and sinew showing plainly beneath the dark skin of his face. Thinner, now, than he had been a year ago when Harris saw him last.

"I've been too close to her," he said now. "I have no perspective any more. All I can see is my own work. And I'm just not sure that's ready yet for you or anyone to see."

"She thinks so?"

"I never saw a woman so confident." Maltzer drank, the glass clicking on his teeth. He looked up suddenly through the distorting lenses. "Of course a failure now would mean—well, absolute collapse," he said.

Harris nodded. He was thinking of the year of incredibly painstaking work that lay behind this meeting, the immense fund of knowledge, of infinite patience, the secret collaboration of artists, sculptors, designers, scientists, and the genius of Maltzer governing them all as an orchestra conductor governs his players.

He was thinking too, with a certain unreasoning jealousy, of the strange, cold, passionless intimacy between Maltzer and Deirdre in that year, a closer intimacy than any two humans can ever have shared before. In a sense the Deirdre whom he saw in a few minutes would *be* Maltzer, just as he thought he detected in Maltzer now and then small mannerisms of inflection and motion that had been Deirdre's own. There had been between them a sort of unimaginable marriage stranger than anything that could ever have taken place before.

"—so many complications," Maltzer was saying in his worried voice with its faintest possible echo of Deirdre's lovely, cadenced rhythm. (The sweet, soft huskiness he would never hear again.) "There was shock, of course. Terrible shock. And a great fear of fire. We had to conquer that before we could take the first steps. But we did it. When you go in you'll probably find her sitting before the fire." He caught the startled question in Harris' eyes and smiled. "No, she can't feel the warmth now, of course. But she likes to watch the flames. She's mastered any abnormal fear of them quite beautifully."

"She can—" Harris hesitated. "Her eyesight's normal now?"

"Perfect," Maltzer said. "Perfect vision was fairly simple to provide. After all, that sort of thing has already been worked out, in other connections. I might even say her vision's a little better than perfect, from our own standpoint." He shook his head irritably. "I'm not worried about the mechanics of the thing. Luckily they got to her before the brain was touched at all. Shock was the only danger to her sensory centers, and we took care of all that first of all, as soon as communication could be established. Even so, it needed great courage on her part. Great courage." He was silent for a moment, staring into his empty glass.

"Harris," he said suddenly, without looking up, "have I made a mistake? Should we have let her die?"

Harris shook his head helplessly. It was an unanswerable question. It had tormented the whole world for a year now. There had been hundreds of answers and thousands of words written on the subject. Has anyone the right to preserve a brain alive when its body is destroyed? Even if a new body can be provided, necessarily so very unlike the old?

"It's not that she's—ugly—now," Maltzer went on hurriedly, as if afraid of an answer. "Metal isn't ugly. And Deirdre . . . . well, you'll see. I tell you, I can't see myself. I know the whole mechanism so well—it's just mechanics to me. Maybe she's—grotesque. I don't know. Often I've wished I hadn't been on the spot, with all my ideas, just when the fire broke out. Or that it could have been anyone but Deirdre. She was so beautiful— Still, if it had been someone else I think the whole thing might have failed completely. It takes more than just an uninjured brain. It takes strength and courage beyond common, and—well, something more. Something—unquenchable. Deirdre has it. She's still Deirdre. In a way she's still beautiful. But I'm not sure anybody but myself could see that. And you know what she plans?"

"No—what?"

"She's going back on the air-screen."

Harris looked at him in stunned disbelief.

"She *is* still beautiful," Maltzer told him fiercely. "She's got courage, and a serenity that amazes me. And she isn't in the least worried or resentful about what's happened. Or afraid what the verdict of the public will be. But I am, Harris. I'm terrified."

They looked at each other for a moment more, neither speaking. Then Maltzer shrugged and stood up.

"She's in there," he said, gesturing with his glass.

Harris turned without a word, not giving himself time to hesitate. He crossed toward the inner door.

The room was full of a soft, clear, indirect light that climaxed in the fire crackling on a white tiled hearth. Harris paused inside the door, his heart beating thickly. He did not see her for a moment. It was a perfectly commonplace room, bright, light, with pleasant furniture, and flowers on the tables. Their perfume was sweet on the clear air. He did not see Deirdre.

Then a chair by the fire creaked as she shifted her weight in it. The high back hid her, but she spoke. And for one dreadful moment it was the voice of an automaton that sounded in the room, metallic, without inflection.

"Hel-lo—" said the voice. Then she laughed and tried again. And it was the old, familiar, sweet huskiness he had not hoped to hear again as long as he lived.

In spite of himself he said, "Deirdre!" and her image rose before him as if she herself had risen unchanged from the chair, tall, golden, swaying a little with her wonderful dancer's poise, the lovely, imperfect features lighted by the glow that made them beautiful. It was the cruelest thing his memory could have done to him. And yet the voice—after that one lapse, the voice was perfect.

"Come and look at me, John," she said.

He crossed the floor slowly, forcing himself to move. That instant's flash of vivid recollection had nearly wrecked his hard-won poise. He tried to keep his mind perfectly blank as he came at last to the verge of seeing what no one but Maltzer had so far seen or known about in its entirety. No one at all had known what shape would be forged to clothe the most beautiful woman on Earth, now that her beauty was gone.

He had envisioned many shapes. Great, lurching robot forms, cylindrical, with hinged arms and legs. A glass case with the brain floating in it and appendages to serve its needs. Grotesque visions, like nightmares come nearly true. And each more inadequate than the last, for what metal shape could possibly do more than house ungraciously the mind and brain that had once enchanted a whole world?

Then he came around the wing of the chair, and saw her.

The human brain is often too complicated a mechanism to function perfectly. Harris' brain was called upon now to perform a very elaborate series of shifting impressions. First, incongruously, he remembered a curious inhuman figure he had once glimpsed leaning over the fence rail outside a farmhouse. For an instant the shape had stood up integrated, ungainly, impossibly human, before the glancing eye resolved it into an arrangement of brooms and buckets. What the eye had found only roughly humanoid, the suggestible brain had accepted fully formed. It was thus now, with Deirdre.

The first impression that his eyes and mind took from sight of her was shocked and incredulous, for his brain said to him unbelievingly, *"This is Deirdre! She hasn't changed at all!"*

Then the shift of perspective took over, and even more shockingly, eye and brain said, "No, not Deirdre —not human. Nothing but metal coils. Not Deirdre at all—" And that was the worst. It was like walking from a dream of someone beloved and lost, and facing anew, after that heartbreaking reassurance of sleep, the inflexible fact that nothing can bring the lost to life again. Deirdre was gone, and this was only machinery heaped in a flowered chair.

Then the machinery moved, exquisitely, smoothly, with a grace as familiar as the swaying poise he remembered. The sweet, husky voice of Deirdre said,

"It's me, John darling. It really is, you know."

And it was.

That was the third metamorphosis, and the final one. Illusion steadied and became factual, real. It was Deirdre.

He sat down bonelessly. He had no muscles. He looked at her speechless and unthinking, letting his senses take in the sight of her without trying to rationalize what he saw.

She was golden still. They had kept that much of her,

the first impression of warmth and color which had once belonged to her sleek hair and the apricot tints of her skin. But they had had the good sense to go no farther. They had not tried to make a wax image of the lost Deirdre. (*No woman born who was so beautiful—Not one so beautiful, of all the women born—*)

And so she had no face. She had only a smooth, delicately modeled ovoid for her head, with a . . . a sort of crescent-shaped mask across the frontal area where her eyes would have been if she had needed eyes. A narrow, curved quarter-moon, with the horns turned upward. It was filled in with something translucent, like cloudy crystal, and tinted the aquamarine of the eyes Deirdre used to have. Through that, then, she saw the world. Through that she looked without eyes, and behind it, as behind the eyes of a human—she was.

Except for that, she had no features. And it had been wise of those who designed her, he realized now. Subconsciously he had been dreading some clumsy attempt at human features that might creak like a marionette's in parodies of animation. The eyes, perhaps, had had to open in the same place upon her head, and at the same distance apart, to make easy for her an adjustment to the stereoscopic vision she used to have. But he was glad they had not given her two eye-shaped openings with glass marbles inside them. The mask was better.

(Oddly enough, he did not once think of the naked brain that must lie inside the metal. The mask was symbol enough for the woman within. It was enigmatic; you did not know if her gaze was on you searchingly, or wholly withdrawn. And it had no variations of brilliance such as once had played across the incomparable mobility of Deirdre's face. But eyes, even human eyes, are as a matter of fact enigmatic enough. They have no expression except what the lids impart; they take all animation from the features. We automatically watch the eyes of the friend we speak with, but if he happens to be lying down so that he speaks across his shoulder and his face is upside-down to us, quite as automatically we watch the mouth. The gaze keeps shifting nervously between mouth and eyes in their reversed order, for it is the position in the face, not the feature itself, which we are ac-

customed to accept as the seat of the soul. Deirdre's
mask was in that proper place; it was easy to accept it as
a mask over eyes.)

She had, Harris realized as the first shock quieted, a
very beautifully shaped head—a bare, golden skull. She
turned it a little, gracefully upon her neck of metal, and
he saw that the artist who shaped it had given her the
most delicate suggestion of cheekbones, narrowing in
the blankness below the mask to the hint of a human
face. Not too much. Just enough so that when the head
turned you saw by its modeling that it had moved, lend-
ing perspective and foreshortening to the expressionless
golden helmet. Light did not slip uninterrupted as if
over the surface of a golden egg. Brancusi himself had
never made anything more simple or more subtle than
the modeling of Deirdre's head.

But all expression, of course, was gone. All expression had gone up in the smoke of the theater fire, with
the lovely, mobile, radiant features which had meant
Deirdre.

As for her body, he could not see its shape. A garment
hid her. But they had made no incongruous attempt to
give her back the clothing that once had made her famous. Even the softness of cloth would have called the
mind too sharply to the remembrance that no human
body lay beneath the folds, nor does metal need the incongruity of cloth for its protection. Yet without garments, he realized, she would have looked oddly naked,
since her new body was humanoid, not angular machinery.

The designer had solved his paradox by giving her a
robe of very fine metal mesh. It hung from the gentle
slope of her shoulders in straight, pliant folds like a
longer Grecian chlamys, flexible, yet with weight enough
of its own not to cling too revealingly to whatever metal
shape lay beneath.

The arms they had given her were left bare, and the
feet and ankles. And Maltzer had performed his greatest
miracle in the limbs of the new Deirdre. It was a mechanical miracle basically, but the eye appreciated first
that he had also showed supreme artistry and understanding.

Her arms were pale shining gold, tapered smoothly, without modeling, and flexible their whole length in diminishing metal bracelets fitting one inside the other clear down to the slim, round wrists. The hands were more nearly human than any other feature about her, though they, too, were fitted together in delicate, small sections that slid upon one another with the flexibility almost of flesh. The fingers' bases were solider than human, and the fingers themselves tapered to longer tips.

Her feet, too, beneath the tapering broader rings of the metal ankles, had been constructed upon the model of human feet. Their finely tooled sliding segments gave her an arch and a heel and a flexible forward section formed almost like the *sollerets* of medieval armor.

She looked, indeed, very much like a creature in armor, with her delicately plated limbs and her featureless head like a helmet with a visor of glass, and her robe of chain-mail. But no knight in armor ever moved as Deirdre moved, or wore his armor upon a body of such inhumanly fine proportions. Only a knight from another world, or a knight of Oberon's court, might have shared that delicate likeness.

Briefly he had been surprised at the smallness and exquisite proportions of her. He had been expecting the ponderous mass of such robots as he had seen, wholly automatons. And then he realized that for them, much of the space had to be devoted to the inadequate mechanical brains that guided them about their duties. Deirdre's brain still preserved and proved the craftsmanship of an artisan far defter than man. Only the body was of metal, and it did not seem complex, though he had not yet been told how it was motivated.

Harris had no idea how long he sat staring at the figure in the cushioned chair. She was still lovely—indeed, she was still Deirdre—and as he looked he let the careful schooling of his face relax. There was no need to hide his thoughts from her.

She stirred upon the cushions, the long, flexible arms moving with a litheness that was not quite human. The motion disturbed him as the body itself had not, and in spite of himself his face froze a little. He had the feeling that from behind the crescent mask she was watching him very closely.

Slowly she rose.

The motion was very smooth. Also it was serpentine, as if the body beneath the coat of mail were made in the same interlocking sections as her limbs. He had expected and feared mechanical rigidity; nothing had prepared him for this more than human suppleness.

She stood quietly, letting the heavy mailed folds of her garment settle about her. They fell together with a faint ringing sound, like small bells far off, and hung beautifully in pale golden, sculptured folds. He had risen automatically as she did. Now he faced her, staring. He had never seen her stand perfectly still, and she was not doing it now. She swayed just a bit, vitality burning inextinguishably in her brain as once it had burned in her body, and stolid immobility was as impossible to her as it had always been. The golden garment caught points of light from the fire and glimmered at him with tiny reflections as she moved.

Then she put her featureless helmeted head a little to one side, and he heard her laughter as familiar in its small, throaty, intimate sound as he had ever heard it from her living throat. And every gesture, every attitude, every flowing of motion into motion was so utterly Deirdre that the overwhelming illusion swept his mind again and this was the flesh-and-blood woman as clearly as if he saw her standing there whole once more, like Phoenix from the fire.

"Well, John," she said in the soft, husky, amused voice he remembered perfectly. "Well, John, is it I?" She knew it was. Perfect assurance sounded in the voice. "The shock will wear off, you know. It'll be easier and easier as time goes on. I'm quite used to myself now. See?"

She turned away from him and crossed the room smoothly, with the old, poised, dancer's glide, to the mirror that paneled one side of the room. And before it, as he had so often seen her preen before, he watched her preening now, running flexible metallic hands down the folds of her metal garment, turning to admire herself over one metal shoulder, making the mailed folds tinkle and sway as she struck an arabesque position before the glass.

His knees let him down into the chair she had vacated. Mingled shock and relief loosened all his muscles in him, and she was more poised and confident than he.

"It's a miracle," he said with conviction. "It's *you*. But I don't see how——" He had meant, "——how, without face or body——" but clearly he could not finish that sentence.

She finished it for him in her own mind, and answered without self-consciousness. "It's motion, mostly," she said, still admiring her own suppleness in the mirror. "See?" And very lightly on her springy, armored feet she flashed through an enchaînement of brilliant steps, swinging round with a pirouette to face him. "That was what Maltzer and I worked out between us, after I began to get myself under control again." Her voice was somber for a moment, remembering a dark time in the past. Then she went on, "It wasn't easy, of course, but it was fascinating. You'll never guess how fascinating, John! We knew we couldn't work out anything like a facsimile of the way I used to look, so we had to find some other basis to build on. And motion is the other basis of recognition, after actual physical likeness."

She moved lightly across the carpet toward the window and stood looking down, her featureless face averted a little and the light shining across the delicately hinted curves of the cheekbones.

"Luckily," she said, her voice amused, "I never was beautiful. It was all—well, vivacity, I suppose, and muscular co-ordination. Years and years of training, and all of it engraved here"—she struck her golden helmet a light, ringing blow with golden knuckles—"in the habit patterns grooved into my brain. So this body . . . did he tell you? . . . works entirely through the brain. Electromagnetic currents flowing along from ring to ring, like this." She rippled a boneless arm at him with a motion like flowing water. "Nothing holds me together—nothing!—except muscles of magnetic currents. And if I'd been somebody else—somebody who moved differently, why the flexible rings would have moved differently too, guided by the impulse from another brain. I'm not conscious of doing anything I haven't always done. The same impulses that used to go out to my muscles go out now to—this." And she made a shuddering, serpentine motion of both arms at him, like a Cambodian dancer, and then laughed wholeheartedly, the sound of it ringing through the room with such full-throated merriment that he could not help seeing again the familiar face crinkled with pleasure, the white teeth shining. "It's all perfectly subconscious now," she told him. "It took lots of practice at first, of course, but now even my signature looks just as it always did—the co-ordination is duplicated that delicately." She rippled her arms at him again and chuckled.

"But the voice, too," Harris protested inadequately. "It's *your* voice, Deirdre."

"The voice isn't only a matter of throat construction and breath control, my darling Johnnie! At least, so Professor Maltzer assured me a year ago, and I certainly haven't any reason to doubt him!" She laughed again. She was laughing a little too much, with a touch of the bright, hysteric over-excitement he remembered so well. But if any woman ever had reason for mild hysteria, surely Deirdre had it now.

The laughter rippled and ended, and she went on, her voice eager. "He says voice control is almost wholly a matter of hearing what you produce, once you've got adequate mechanism, of course. That's why deaf people, with the same vocal cords as ever, let their voices change completely and lose all inflection when they've been deaf long enough. And luckily, you see, I'm not deaf!"

She swung around to him, the folds of her robe twinkling and ringing, and rippled up and up a clear, true scale to a lovely high note, and then cascaded down again like water over a falls. But she left him no time for applause. "Perfectly simple, you see. All it took was a little matter of genius from the professor to get it worked out for me! He started with a new variation of the old Vodor you must remember hearing about, years ago. Originally, of course, the thing was ponderous. You know how it worked—speech broken down to a few basic sounds and built up again in combinations produced from a keyboard. I think originally the sounds were a sort of *ktch* and a *shooshing* noise, but we've got it all worked to a flexibility and range quite as good as human now. All I do is—well, mentally play on the keyboard of my . . . my sound-unit, I suppose it's called. It's much more complicated than that, of course, but I've learned to do it unconsciously. And I regulate it by ear, quite automatically now. If you were—*here*—instead of me, and you'd had the same practice. your own voice would be coming out of the same keyboard and diaphragm instead of mine. It's all a matter of the brain patterns that operated the body and now operate the machinery. They send out very strong impulses that are stepped up as much as necessary somewhere or other in here—" Her hands waved vaguely over the mesh-robed body.

She was silent a moment, looking out the window. Then she turned away and crossed the floor to the fire, sinking again into the flowered chair. Her helmet-skull turned its mask to face him and he could feel a quiet scrutiny behind the aquamarine of its gaze.

"It's—odd," she said, "being here in this . . . this . . . instead of a body. But not as odd or as alien as you might think. I've thought about it a lot—I've had plenty of time to think—and I've begun to realize what a tremendous force the human ego really is. I'm not sure I want to suggest it has any mystical power it can impress on mechanical things, but it does seem to have a power of some sort. It does instill its own force into inanimate objects, and they take on a personality of their own. People do impress their personalities on the houses they live in, you know. I've noticed that often. Even empty rooms. And it happens with other things too, especially, I think, with inanimate things that men depend on for their lives. Ships, for instance—they always have personalities of their own.

"And planes—in wars you always hear of planes crippled too badly to fly, but struggling back anyhow with their crews. Even guns acquire a sort of ego. Ships and guns and planes are 'she' to the men who operate them and depend on them for their lives. It's as if machinery with complicated moving parts almost simulates life, and does acquire from the men who used it—well, not exactly life, of course—but a personality. I don't know what. Maybe it absorbs some of the actual electrical impulses their brains throw off, especially in times of stress.

"Well, after awhile I began to accept the idea that this new body of mine could behave at least as responsively as a ship or a plane. Quite apart from the fact that my own brain controls its 'muscles.' I believe there's an affinity between men and the machines they make. They make them out of their own brains, really, a sort of mental conception and gestation, and the result responds to the minds that created them, and to all human minds that understand and manipulate them."

She stirred uneasily and smoothed a flexible hand along her mesh-robed metal thigh. "So this is myself," she said. "Metal—but me. And it grows more and more myself the longer I live in it. It's my house and the machine my life depends on, but much more intimately in each case than any real house or machine ever was before to any other human. And you know, I wonder if in time I'll forget what flesh felt like—my own flesh, when I touched it like this—and the metal against the metal will be so much the same I'll never even notice?"

Harris did not try to answer her. He sat without moving, watching her expressionless face. In a moment she went on,

"I'll tell you the best thing, John," she said, her voice softening to the old intimacy he remembered so well that he could see superimposed upon the blank skull the warm, intent look that belonged with the voice. "I'm not going to live forever. It may not sound like a—best thing—but it is, John. You know, for awhile that was the worst of all, after I knew I was—after I woke up again. The thought of living on and on in a body that wasn't mine, seeing everyone I knew grow old and die, and not being able to stop—

"But Maltzer says my brain will probably wear out quite normally—except, of couse, that I won't have to worry about looking old!—and when it gets tired and stops, the body I'm in won't be any longer. The magnetic muscles that hold it into my own shape and motions will let go when the brain lets go, and there'll be nothing but a . . . a pile of disconnected rings. If they ever assemble it again, it won't be me." She hesitated. "I like that, John," she said, and he felt from behind the mask a searching of his face.

He knew and understood that somber satisfaction. He could not put it into words; neither of them wanted to do that. But he understood. It was the conviction of mortality, in spite of her immortal body. She was not cut off from the rest of her race in the essence of their humanity, for though she wore a body of steel and they perishable flesh, yet she must perish too, and the same fears and faiths still united her to mortals and humans, though she wore the body of Oberon's inhuman knight. Even in her death she must be unique—dissolution in a shower of tinkling and clashing rings, he thought, and almost envied her the finality and beauty of that particular death—but afterward, oneness with humanity in however much or little awaited them all. So she could feel that this exile in metal was only temporary, in spite of everything.

(And providing, of course, that the mind inside the metal did not veer from its inherited humanity as the years went by. A dweller in a house may impress his personality upon the walls, but subtly the walls too, may impress their own shape upon the ego of the man. Neither of them thought of that, at that time.)

Deirdre sat a moment longer in silence. Then the mood vanished and she rose again, spinning so that the robe belled out ringing about her ankles. She rippled another scale up and down, faultlessly and with the same familiar sweetness of tone that had made her famous.

"So I'm going right back on the stage, John," she said serenely. "I can still sing. I can still dance. I'm still myself in everything that matters, and I can't imagine doing anything else for the rest of my life."

He could not answer without stammering a little. "Do you think . . . will they accept you, Deirdre? After all—"

"They'll accept me," she said in that confident voice. "Oh, they'll come to see a freak at first, of course, but they'll stay to watch—Deirdre. And come back again and again just as they always did. You'll see, my dear."

But hearing her sureness, suddenly Harris himself was unsure. Maltzer had not been, either. She was so regally confident, and disappointment would be so deadly a blow at all that remained of her—

She was so delicate a being now, really. Nothing but a glowing and radiant mind poised in metal, dominating it, bending the steel to the illusion of her lost loveliness with a sheer self-confidence that gleamed through the metal body. But the brain sat delicately on its poise of reason. She had been through intolerable stresses already, perhaps more terrible depths of despair and self-knowledge than any human brain had yet endured before her, for—since Lazarus himself—who had come back from the dead?

But if the world did not accept her as beautiful, what then? If they laughed, or pitied her, or came only to watch a jointed freak performing as if on strings where the loveliness of Deirdre had once enchanted them, what then? And he could not be perfectly sure they would not. He had known her too well in the flesh to see her objectively even now, in metal. Every inflection of her voice called up the vivid memory of the face that had flashed its evanescent beauty in some look to match the tone. She was Deirdre to Harris simply because she had been so intimately familiar in every poise and attitude, through so many years. But people who knew her only slightly, or saw her for the first time in metal—what would they see?

A marionette? Or the real grace and loveliness shining through?

He had no possible way of knowing. He saw her too clearly as she had been to see her now at all, except so linked with the past that she was not wholly metal. And he knew what Maltzer feared, for Maltzer's psychic blindness toward her lay at the other extreme. He had never known Deirdre except as a machine, and he could not see her objectively any more than Harris could. To Maltzer she was pure metal, a robot his own hands and brain had devised, mysteriously animated by the mind of Deirdre, to be sure, but to all outward seeming a thing of metal solely. He had worked so long over each intricate part of her body, he knew so well how every jointure in it was put together, that he could not see the whole. He had studied many film records of her, of course, as she used to be. in order to gauge the accuracy of his facsimile, but this thing he had made was a copy only. He was too close to Deirdre to see her. And Harris, in a way, was too far. The indomitable Deirdre herself shone so vividly through the metal that his mind kept superimposing one upon the other.

How would an audience react to her? Where in the scale between these two extremes would their verdict fall?

For Deirdre, there was only one possible answer.

"I'm not worried," Deirdre said serenely, and spread her golden hands to the fire to watch lights dancing in reflection upon their shining surfaces. "I'm still myself. I've always had . . . well, power over my audiences. Any good performer knows when he's got it. Mine isn't gone. I can still give them what I always gave, only now with greater variations and more depths than I'd ever have done before. Why, look—" She gave a little wriggle of excitement.

"You know the arabesque principle—getting the longest possible distance from fingertip to toetip with a long, slow curve through the whole length? And the brace of the other leg and arm giving contrast? Well, look at me. I don't work on hinges now. I can make every motion a long curve if I want to. My body's different enough now to work out a whole new school of dancing. Of course there'll be things I used to do that I won't attempt now —no more dancing *sur les pointes*, for instance—but the new things will more than balance the loss. I've been practicing. Do you know I can turn a hundred *fouettés* now without a flaw? And I think I could go right on and turn a thousand, if I wanted."

She made the firelight flash on her hands, and her robe rang musically as she moved her shoulders a little. "I've already worked out one new dance for myself," she said. "God knows I'm no choreographer, but I did want to experiment first. Later, you know, really creative men like Massanchine or Fokhileff may want to do something entirely new for me—a whole new sequence

of movements based on a new technique. And music—
that could be quite different, too. Oh, there's no end to
the possibilities! Even my voice has more range and
power. Luckily I'm not an actress—it would be silly to
try to play Camille or Juliet with a cast of ordinary people. Not that I couldn't, you know." She turned her head
to stare at Harris through the mask of glass. "I honestly
think I could. But it isn't necessary. There's too much
else. Oh, I'm not worried!"

"Maltzer's worried," Harris reminded her.

She swung away from the fire, her metal robe ringing,
and into her voice came the old note of distress that
went with a furrowing of her forehead and a sidewise tilt
of the head. The head went sidewise as it had always
done, and he could see the furrowed brow almost as
clearly as if flesh still clothed her.

"I know. And I'm worried about him, John. He's
worked so awfully hard over me. This is the doldrums
now, the let-down period, I suppose. I know what's on
his mind. He's afraid I'll look just the same to the world
as I look to him. Tooled metal. He's in a position no one
ever quite achieved before, isn't he? Rather like God."
Her voice rippled a little with amusement. "I suppose to
God we must look like a collection of cells and corpus-
cles ourselves. But Maltzer lacks a god's detached viewpoint."

"He can't see you as I do, anyhow." Harris was
choosing his words with difficulty. "I wonder, though—
would it help him any if you postponed your debut
awhile? You've been with him too closely, I think. You
don't quite realize how near a breakdown he is. I was
shocked when I saw him just now."

The golden head shook. "No. He's close to a breaking
point, maybe, but I think the only cure's action. He
wants me to retire and stay out of sight, John. Always.
He's afraid for anyone to see me except a few old
friends who remember me as I was. People he can trust
to be—kind." She laughed. It was very strange to hear
that ripple of mirth from the blank, unfeatured skull.
Harris was seized with sudden panic at the thought of
what reaction it might evoke in an audience of strangers.
As if he had spoken the fear aloud, her voice denied it.

"I don't need kindness. And it's no kindness to Maltzer to hide me under a bushel. He *has* worked too hard, I know. He's driven himself to a breaking point. But it'll be a complete negation of all he's worked for if I hide myself now. You don't know what a tremendous lot of geniuses and artistry went into me, John. The whole idea from the start was to recreate what I'd lost so that it could be proved that beauty and talent need not be sacrificed by the destruction of parts or all the body.

"It wasn't only for me that we meant to prove that. There'll be others who suffer injuries that once might have ruined them. This was to end all suffering like that forever. It was Maltzer's gift to the whole race as well as to me. He's really a humanitarian, John, like most great men. He'd never have given up a year of his life to this work if it had been for any one individual alone. He was seeing thousands of others beyond me as he worked. And I won't let him ruin all he's achieved because he's afraid to prove it now he's got it. The whole wonderful achievement will be worthless if I don't take the final step. I think his breakdown, in the end, would be worse and more final if I never tried than if I tried and failed."

Harris sat in silence. There was no answer he could make to that. He hoped the little twinge of shamefaced jealousy he suddenly felt did not show, as he was reminded anew of the intimacy closer than marriage which had of necessity bound these two together. And he knew that any reaction of his would in its way be almost as prejudiced as Maltzer's, for a reason at once the same and entirely opposite. Except that he himself came fresh to the problem, while Maltzer's viewpoint was colored by a year of overwork and physical and mental exhaustion.

"What are you going to do?" he asked.

She was standing before the fire when he spoke, swaying just a little so that highlights danced all along her golden body. Now she turned with a serpentine grace and sank into the cushioned chair beside her. It came to him suddenly that she was much more than humanly graceful—quite as much as he had once feared she would be less than human.

"I've already arranged for a performance," she told

him, her voice a little shaken with a familiar mixture of excitement and defiance.

Harris sat up with a start. "How? Where? There hasn't been any publicity at all yet, has there? I didn't know—"

"Now, now, Johnnie," her amused voice soothed him. "You'll be handling everything just as usual once I get started back to work—that is, if you still want to. But this I've arranged for myself. It's going to be a surprise. I . . . I felt it had to be a surprise." She wriggled a little among the cushions. "Audience psychology is something I've always felt rather than known, and I do feel this is the way it ought to be done. There's no precedent. Nothing like this ever happened before. I'll have to go by my own intuition."

"You mean it's to be a complete surprise?"

"I think it must be. I don't want the audience coming in with preconceived ideas. I want them to see me exactly as I am now *first*, before they know who or what they're seeing. They must realize I can still give as good a performance as ever before they remember and compare it with my past performances. I don't want them to come ready to pity my handicaps—I haven't got any! —or full of morbid curiosity. So I'm going on the air after the regular eight-o'clock telecast of the feature from Teleo City. I'm just going to do one specialty in the usual vaude program. It's all been arranged. They'll build up to it, of course, as the highlight of the evening, but they aren't to say who I am until the end of the performance—if the audience hasn't recognized me already, by then."

"Audience?"

"Of course. Surely you haven't forgotten they still play to a theater audience at Teleo City? That's why I want to make my debut there. I've always played better when there were people in the studio, so I could gauge reactions. I think most performers do. Anyhow, it's all arranged."

"Does Maltzer know?"

She wriggled uncomfortably. "Not yet."

"But he'll have to give his permission too, won't he? I mean—"

"Now look, John! That's another idea you and Maltzer will have to get out of your minds. I don't belong to him. In a way he's just been my doctor through a long illness, but I'm free to discharge him whenever I choose. If there were ever any legal disagreement, I suppose he'd be entitled to quite a lot of money for the work he's done on my new body—for the body itself, really, since it's his own machine, in one sense. But he doesn't own it, or me. I'm not sure just how the question would be decided by the courts—there again, we've got a problem without precedent. The body may be his work, but the brain that makes it something more than a collection of metal rings is *me,* and he couldn't restrain me against my will even if he wanted to. Not legally, and not—" She hesitated oddly and looked away. For the first time Harris was aware of something beneath the surface of her mind which was quite strange to him.

"Well, anyhow," she went on, "that question won't come up. Maltzer and I have been much too close in the past year to clash over anything as essential as this. He knows in his heart that I'm right, and he won't try to restrain me. His work won't be completed until I do what I was built to do. And I intend to do it."

That strange little quiver of something—something un-Deirdre—which had so briefly trembled beneath the surface of familiarity stuck in Harris' mind as something he must recall and examine later. Now he said only,

"All right. I suppose I agree with you. How soon are you going to do it?"

She turned her head so that even the glass mask through which she looked out at the world was foreshortened away from him, and the golden helmet with its hint of sculptured cheekbone was entirely enigmatic.

"Tonight," she said.

Maltzer's thin hand shook so badly that he could not turn the dial. He tried twice and then laughed nervously and shrugged at Harris.

"You get her," he said.

Harris glanced at his watch. "It isn't time yet. She won't be on for half an hour."

Maltzer made a gesture of violent impatience. "Get it, get it!"

Harris shrugged a little in turn and twisted the dial. On the tilted screen above them shadows and sound blurred together and then clarified into a somber medieval hall, vast, vaulted, people in bright costume moving like pygmies through its dimness. Since the play concerned Mary of Scotland, the actors were dressed in something approximating Elizabethan garb, but as every era tends to translate costume into terms of the current fashions, the women's hair was dressed in a style that would have startled Elizabeth, and their footgear was entirely anachronistic.

The hall dissolved and a face swam up into soft focus upon the screen. The dark, lush beauty of the actress who was playing the Stuart queen glowed at them in velvety perfection from the clouds of her pearl-strewn hair. Maltzer groaned.

"She's competing with *that*," he said hollowly.

"You think she can't?"

Maltzer slapped the chair arms with angry palms. Then the quivering of his fingers seemed suddenly to strike him, and he muttered to himself, "Look at 'em! I'm not even fit to handle a hammer and saw." But the mutter was an aside. "Of course she can't compete," he cried irritably. "She hasn't any sex. She isn't female any more. She doesn't know that yet, but she'll learn."

Harris stared at him, feeling a little stunned. Somehow the thought had not occurred to him before at all, so vividly had the illusion of the old Deirdre hung about the new one.

"She's an abstraction now," Maltzer went on, drumming his palms upon the chair in quick, nervous rhythms. "I don't know what it'll do to her, but there'll be change. Remember Abelard? She's lost everything that made her essentially what the public wanted, and she's going to find it out the hard way. After that—" He grimaced savagely and was silent.

"She hasn't lost everything," Harris defended. "She can dance and sing as well as ever, maybe better. She still has grace and charm and—"

"Yes, but where did the grace and charm come from?

Not out of the habit patterns in her brain. No, out of human contacts, out of all the things that stimulate sensitive minds to creativeness. And she's lost three of her five senses. Everything she can't see and hear is gone. One of the strongest stimuli to a woman of her type was the knowledge of sex competition. You know how she sparkled when a man came into the room? All that's gone, and it was an essential. You know how liquor stimulated her? She's lost that. She couldn't taste food or drink even if she needed it. Perfume, flowers, all the odors we respond to mean nothing to her now. She can't feel anything with tactual delicacy any more. She used to surround herself with luxuries—she drew her stimuli from them—and that's all gone too. She's withdrawn from all physical contacts."

He squinted at the screen, not seeing it, his face drawn into lines like the lines of a skull. All flesh seemed to have dissolved off his bones in the past year, and Harris thought almost jealously that even in that way he seemed to be drawing nearer Deirdre in her fleshlessness with every passing week.

"Sight," Maltzer said, "is the most highly civilized of the senses. It was the last to come. The other senses tie us in closely with the very roots of life; I think we perceive with them more keenly than we know. The things we realize through taste and smell and feeling stimulate directly, without a detour through the centers of conscious thought. You know how often a taste or odor will recall a memory to you so subtly you don't know exactly what caused it? We need those primitive senses to tie us in with nature and the race. Through those ties Deirdre drew her vitality without realizing it. Sight is a cold, intellectual thing compared with the other senses. But it's all she has to draw on now. She isn't a human being any more, and I think what humanity is left in her will drain out little by little and never be replaced. Abelard, in a way, was a prototype. But Deirdre's loss is complete."

"She isn't human," Harris agreed slowly. "But she isn't pure robot either. She's something somewhere between the two, and I think it's a mistake to try to guess just where, or what the outcome will be."

"I don't have to guess," Maltzer said in a grim voice.

"I know. I wish I'd let her die. I've done something to her a thousand times worse than the fire ever could. I should have let her die in it."

"Wait," said Harris. "Wait and see. I think you're wrong."

On the television screen Mary of Scotland climbed the scaffold to her doom, the gown of traditional scarlet clinging warmly to supple young curves as anachronistic in their way as the slippers beneath the gown, for—as everyone but playwrights knows—Mary was well into middle age before she died. Gracefully this latter-day Mary bent her head, sweeping the long hair aside, kneeling to the block.

Maltzer watched stonily, seeing another woman entirely.

"I shouldn't have let her," he was muttering. "I shouldn't have let her do it."

"Do you really think you'd have stopped her if you could?" Harris asked quietly. And the other man after a moment's pause shook his head jerkily.

"No, I suppose not. I keep thinking if I worked and waited a little longer maybe I could make it easier for her, but—no, I suppose not. She's got to face them sooner or later, being herself." He stood up abruptly, shoving back his chair. "If she only weren't so . . . so frail. She doesn't realize how delicately poised her very sanity is. We gave her what we could—the artists and the designers and I, all gave our very best—but she's so pitifully handicapped even with all we could do. She'll always be an abstraction and a . . . a freak, cut off from the world by handicaps worse in their way than anything any human being ever suffered before. Sooner or later she'll realize it. And then—" He began to pace up and down with quick, uneven steps, striking his hands together. His face was twitching with a little *tic* that drew up one eye to a squint and released it again at irregular intervals. Harris could see how very near collapse the man was.

"Can you imagine what it's like?" Maltzer demanded fiercely. "Penned into a mechanical body like that, shut out from all human contacts except what leaks in by way of sight and sound? To know you aren't human any longer? She's been through shocks enough already. When that shock fully hits her—"

"Shut up," said Harris roughly. "You won't do her any good if you break down yourself. Look—the vande's starting."

Great golden curtains had swept together over the unhappy Queen of Scotland and were parting again now, all sorrow and frustration wiped away once more as cleanly as the passing centuries had already expunged them. Now a line of tiny dancers under the tremendous arch of the stage kicked and pranced with the precision of little mechanical dolls too small and perfect to be real. Vision rushed down upon them and swept along the row, face after stiffly smiling face racketing by like fence pickets. Then the sight rose into the rafters and looked down upon them from a great height, the grotesquely foreshortened figures still prancing in perfect rhythm even from this inhuman angle.

There was applause from an invisible audience. Then someone came out and did a dance with lighted torches that streamed long, weaving ribbons of fire among clouds of what looked like cotton wool but was most probably asbestos. Then a company in gorgeous pseudo-period costumes postured its way through the new singing ballet form of dance, roughly following a plot which had been announced as *Les Sylphides,* but had little in common with it. Afterward the precision dancers came on again, solemn and charming as performing dolls.

Maltzer began to show signs of dangerous tension as act succeeded act. Deirdre's was to be the last, of course. It seemed very long indeed before a face in close-up blotted out the stage, and a master of ceremonies with features like an amiable marionette's announced a very special number as the finale. His voice was almost cracking with excitement—perhaps he, too, had not been told until a moment before what lay in store for the audience.

Neither of the listening men heard what it was he said, but both were conscious of a certain indefinable excitement rising among the audience, murmurs and rustlings and a mounting anticipation as if time had run backward here and knowledge of the great surprise had already broken upon them.

Then the golden curtains appeared again. They quivered and swept apart on long upward arcs, and between them the stage was full of a shimmering golden haze. It was, Harris realized in a moment, simply a series of gauze curtains, but the effect was one of strange and wonderful anticipation, as if something very splendid must be hidden in the haze. The world might have looked like this on the first morning of creation, before heaven and earth took form in the mind of God. It was a singularly fortunate choice of stage set in its symbolism, though Harris wondered how much necessity had figured in its selection, for there could not have been much time to prepare an elaborate set.

The audience sat perfectly silent, and the air was tense. This was no ordinary pause before an act. No one had been told, surely, and yet they seemed to guess—

The shimmering haze trembled and began to thin, veil by veil. Beyond was darkness, and what looked like a row of shining pillars set in a balustrade that began gradually to take shape as the haze drew back in shining folds. Now they could see that the balustrade curved up from left and right to the head of a sweep of stairs. Stage and stairs were carpeted in black velvet; black velvet draperies hung just ajar behind the balcony, with a glimpse of dark sky beyond them trembling with dim synthetic stars.

The last curtain of golden gauze withdrew. The stage was empty. Or it seemed empty. But even through the aerial distances between this screen and the place it mirrored, Harris thought that the audience was not waiting for the performer to come on from the wings. There was no rustling, no coughing, no sense of impatience. A presence upon the stage was in command from the first drawing of the curtains; it filled the theater with its calm domination. It gauged its timing, holding the audience as a conductor with lifted baton gathers and holds the eyes of his orchestra.

For a moment everything was motionless upon the

stage. Then, at the head of the stairs, where the two curves of the pillared balustrade swept together, a figure stirred.

Until that moment she had seemed another shining column in the row. Now she swayed deliberately, light catching and winking and running molten along her limbs and her robe of metal mesh. She swayed just enough to show that she was there. Then, with every eye upon her, she stood quietly to let them look their fill. The screen did not swoop to a close-up upon her. Her enigma remained inviolate and the television watchers saw her no more clearly than the audience in the theater.

Many must have thought her at first some wonderfully animate robot, hung perhaps from wires invisible against the velvet, for certainly she was no woman dressed in metal—her proportions were too thin and fine for that. And perhaps the impression of robotism was what she meant to convey at first. She stood quiet, swaying just a little, a masked and inscrutable figure, faceless, very slender in her robe that hung in folds as pure as a Grecian chlamys, though she did not look Grecian at all. In the visored golden helmet and the robe of mail that odd likeness to knighthood was there again, with its implications of medieval richness behind the simple lines. Except that in her exquisite slimness she called to mind no human figure in armor, not even the comparative delicacy of a St. Joan. It was the chivalry and delicacy of some other world implicit in her outlines.

A breath of surprise had rippled over the audience when she moved. Now they were tensely silent again, waiting. And the tension, the anticipation, was far deeper than the surface importance of the scene could ever have evoked. Even those who thought her a manikin seemed to feel the forerunning of greater revelations.

Now she swayed and came slowly down the steps, moving with a suppleness just a little better than human. The swaying strengthened. By the time she reached the stage floor she was dancing. But it was no dance that any human creature could ever have performed. The long, slow, languorous rhythms of her body would have been impossible to a figure hinged at its joints as human figures hinge. (Harris remembered incredulously that he had feared once to find her jointed like a mechanical robot. But it was humanity that seemed, by contrast, jointed and mechanical now.)

The languor and the rhythm of her patterns looked impromptu, as all good dances should, but Harris knew what hours of composition and rehearsal must lie behind it, what laborious graving into her brain of strange new pathways, the first to replace the old ones and govern the mastery of metal limbs.

To and fro over the velvet carpet, against the velvet background, she wove the intricacies of her serpentine dance, leisurely and yet with such hypnotic effect that the air seemed full of looping rhythms, as if her long, tapering limbs had left their own replicas hanging upon the air and fading only slowly as she moved away. In her mind, Harris knew, the stage was a whole, a background to be filled in completely with the measured patterns of her dance, and she seemed almost to project that completed pattern to her audience so that they saw her everywhere at once, her golden rhythms fading upon the air long after she had gone.

Now there was music, looping and hanging in echoes after her like the shining festoons she wove with her body. But it was no orchestral music. She was humming, deep and sweet and wordlessly, as she glided her easy, intricate path about the stage. And the volume of the music was amazing. It seemed to fill the theater, and it was not amplified by hidden loudspeakers. You could tell that. Somehow, until you heard the music she made, you had never realized before the subtle distortions that amplification puts into music. This was utterly pure and true as perhaps no ear in all her audience had ever heard music before.

While she danced the audience did not seem to breathe. Perhaps they were beginning already to suspect who and what it was that moved before them without any fanfare of the publicity they had been half-expecting for weeks now. And yet, without the publicity, it was not easy to believe the dancer they watched was not some cunningly motivated manikin swinging on unseen wires about the stage.

Nothing she had done yet had been human. The dance was no dance a human being could have performed. The music she hummed came from a throat without vocal cords. But now the long, slow rhythms were drawing to their close, the pattern tightening in to a finale. And she ended as inhumanly as she had danced, willing them not to interrupt her with applause, dominating them now as she had always done. For her implication here was that a machine might have performed the dance, and a machine expects no applause. If they thought unseen operators had put her through those wonderful paces, they would wait for the operators to appear for their bows. But the audience was obedient. It sat silently, waiting for what came next. But its silence was tense and breathless.

The dance ended as it had begun. Slowly, almost carelessly, she swung up the velvet stairs, moving with rhythms as perfect as her music. But when she reached the head of the stairs she turned to face her audience, and for a moment stood motionless, like a creature of metal, without volition, the hands of the operator slack upon its strings.

Then, startlingly, she laughed.

It was lovely laughter, low and sweet and full-throated. She threw her head back and let her body sway and her shoulders shake, and the laughter, like the music, filled the theater, gaining volume from the great hollow of the roof and sounding in the ears of every listener, not loud, but as intimately as if each sat alone with the woman who laughed.

And she was a woman now. Humanity had dropped over her like a tangible garment. No one who had ever heard that laughter before could mistake it here. But before the reality of who she was had quite time to dawn upon her listeners she let the laughter deepen into music, as no human voice could have done. She was humming a familiar refrain close in the ear of every hearer. And the humming in turn swung into words. She sang in her clear, light, lovely voice:

"The yellow rose of Eden, is blooming in my heart—"

It was Deirdre's song. She had sung it first upon the airways a month before the theater fire that had consumed her. It was a commonplace little melody, simple enough to take first place in the fancy of a nation that had always liked its songs simple. But it had a certain sincerity too, and no taint of the vulgarity of tune and rhythm that foredooms so many popular songs to oblivion after their novelty fades.

No one else was ever able to sing it quite as Deirdre did. It had been identified with her so closely that though for awhile after her accident singers tried to make it a memorial for her, they failed so conspicuously to give it her unmistakable flair that the song died from their sheer inability to sing it. No one ever hummed the tune without thinking of her and the pleasant, nostalgic sadness of something lovely and lost.

But it was not a sad song now. If anyone had doubted whose brain and ego motivated this shining metal suppleness, they could doubt no longer. For the voice was Deirdre, and the song. And the lovely, poised grace of her mannerisms that made up recognition as certainly as sight of a familiar face.

She had not finished the first line of her song before the audience knew her.

And they did not let her finish. The accolade of their interruption was a tribute more eloquent than polite waiting could ever have been. First a breath of incredulity rippled over the theater, and a long, sighing gasp that reminded Harris irrelevantly as he listened to the gasp which still goes up from matinee audiences at the first glimpse of the fabulous Valentino, so many generations dead. But this gasp did not sigh itself away and vanish. Tremendous tension lay behind it, and the rising tide of excitement rippled up in little murmurs and spatterings of applause that ran together into one overwhelming roar. It shook the theater. The television screen trembled and blurred a little to the volume of that transmitted applause.

Silenced before it, Deirdre stood gesturing on the

stage, bowing and bowing as the noise rolled up about her, shaking perceptibly with the triumph of her own emotion.

Harris had an intolerable feeling that she was smiling radiantly and that the tears were pouring down her cheeks. He even thought, just as Maltzer leaned forward to switch off the screen, that she was blowing kisses over the audience in the time-honored gesture of the grateful actress, her golden arms shining as she scattered kisses abroad from the featureless helmet, the face that had no mouth.

"Well?" Harris said, not without triumph.

Maltzer shook his head jerkily, the glasses unsteady on his nose so that the blurred eyes behind them seemed to shift.

"Of course they applauded, you fool," he said in a savage voice. "I might have known they would under this set-up. It doesn't prove anything. Oh, she was smart to surprise them—I admit that. But they were applauding themselves as much as her. Excitement, gratitude for letting them in on a historic performance, mass hysteria —*you* know. It's from now on the test will come, and this hasn't helped any to prepare her for it. Morbid curiosity when the news gets out—people laughing when she forgets she isn't human. And they will, you know. There are always those who will. And the novelty wearing off. The slow draining away of humanity for lack of contact with any human stimuli any more—"

Harris remembered suddenly and reluctantly the moment that afternoon which he had shunted aside mentally, to consider later. The sense of something unfamiliar beneath the surface of Deirdre's speech. Was Maltzer right? Was the drainage already at work? Or was there something deeper than this obvious answer to the question? Certainly she had been through experiences too terrible for ordinary people to comprehend. Scars might still remain. Or, with her body, had she put on a strange, metallic something of the mind, that spoke to no sense which human minds could answer?

For a few minutes neither of them spoke. Then

Maltzer rose abruptly and stood looking down at Harris with an abstract scowl.

"I wish you'd go now," he said.

Harris glanced up at him, startled. Maltzer began to pace again, his steps quick and uneven. Over his shoulder he said,

"I've made up my mind, Harris. I've got to put a stop to this."

Harris rose. "Listen," he said. "Tell me one thing. What makes you so certain you're right? Can you deny that most of it's speculation—hearsay evidence? Remember, I talked to Deirdre, and she was just as sure as you are in the opposite direction. Have you any real reason for what you think?"

Maltzer took his glasses off and rubbed his nose carefully, taking a long time about it. He seemed reluctant to answer. But when he did, at last, there was a confidence in his voice Harris had not expected.

"I have a reason," he said. "But you won't believe it. Nobody would."

"Try me."

Maltzer shook his head. "Nobody *could* believe it. No two people were ever in quite the same relationship before as Deirdre and I have been. I helped her come back out of complete—oblivion. I knew her before she had voice or hearing. She was only a frantic mind when I first made contact with her, half insane with all that had happened and fear of what would happen next. In a very literal sense she was reborn out of that condition, and I had to guide her through every step of the way. I came to know her thoughts before she thought them. And once you've been that close to another mind, you don't lose the contact easily." He put the glasses back on and looked blurrily at Harris through the heavy lenses. "Deirdre is worried," he said. "I know it. You won't believe me, but I can—well, sense it. I tell you, I've been too close to her very mind itself to make any mistake. You don't see it, maybe. Maybe even she doesn't know it yet. But the worry's there. When I'm with her, I feel it. And I don't want it to come any nearer the surface of her mind than it's come already. I'm going to put a stop to this before it's too late."

Harris had no comment for that. It was too entirely outside his own experience. He said nothing for a moment. Then he asked simply, "How?"

"I'm not sure yet. I've got to decide before she comes back. And I want to see her alone."

"I think you're wrong," Harris told him quietly. "I think you're imagining things. I don't think you *can* stop her."

Maltzer gave him a slanted glance. "I can stop her," he said, in a curious voice. He went on quickly, "She has enough already—she's nearly human. She can live normally as other people live, without going back on the screen. Maybe this taste of it will be enough. I've got to convince her it is. If she retires now, she'll never guess how cruel her own audiences could be, and maybe that deep sense of—distress, uneasiness, whatever it is— won't come to the surface. It mustn't. She's too fragile to stand that." He slapped his hands together sharply. "I've got to stop her. For her own sake I've got to do it!" He swung round again to face Harris. "Will you go now?"

Never in his life had Harris wanted less to leave a place. Briefly he thought of saying simply, "No I won't." But he had to admit in his own mind that Maltzer was at least partly right. This was a matter between Deirdre and her creator, the culmination, perhaps, of that year's long intimacy so like marriage that this final trial for supremacy was a need he recognized.

He would not, he thought, forbid the showdown if he could. Perhaps the whole year had been building up to this one moment between them in which one or the other must prove himself victor. Neither was very well stable just now, after the long strain of the year past. It might very well be that the mental salvation of one or both hinged upon the outcome of the clash. But because each was so strongly motivated not by selfish concern but by solicitude for the other in this strange combat, Harris knew he must leave them to settle the thing alone.

He was in the street and hailing a taxi before the full significance of something Maltzer had said came to him. *"I can stop her,"* he had declared, with an odd inflection in his voice.

Suddenly Harris felt cold. Maltzer had made her—of course he could stop her if he chose. Was there some key in that supple golden body that could immobilize it at its maker's will? Could she be imprisoned in the cage of her own body? No body before in all history, he thought, could have been designed more truly to be a prison for its mind than Deirdre's, if Maltzer chose to turn the key that locked her in. There must be many ways to do it. He could simply withhold whatever source of nourishment kept her brain alive, if that were the way he chose.

But Harris could not believe he would do it. The man wasn't insane. He would not defeat his own purpose. His determination rose from his solicitude for Deirdre; he would not even in the last extremity try to save her by imprisoning her in the jail of her own skull.

For a moment Harris hesitated on the curb, almost turning back. But what could he do? Even granting that Maltzer would resort to such tactics, self-defeating in their very nature, how could any man on earth prevent him if he did it subtly enough? But he never would. Harris knew he never would. He got into his cab slowly, frowning. He would see them both tomorrow.

He did not. Harris was swamped with excited calls about yesterday's performance, but the message he was awaiting did not come. The day went by very slowly. Toward evening he surrendered and called Maltzer's apartment.

It was Deirdre's face that answered, and for once he saw no remembered features superimposed upon the blankness of her helmet. Masked and faceless, she looked at him inscrutably.

"Is everything all right?" he asked, a little uncomfortable.

"Yes, of course," she said, and her voice was a bit metallic for the first time, as if she were thinking so deeply of some other matter that she did not trouble to pitch it properly. "I had a long talk with Maltzer last night, if that's what you mean. You know what he wants. But nothing's been decided yet."

Harris felt oddly rebuffed by the sudden realization of the metal of her. It was impossible to read anything from face or voice. Each had its mask.

"What are you going to do?" he asked.

"Exactly as I'd planned," she told him, without inflection.

Harris floundered a little. Then, with an effort at practicality, he said, "Do you want me to go to work on bookings, then?"

She shook the delicately modeled skull. "Not yet. You saw the reviews today, of course. They—*did* like me." It was an understatement, and for the first time a note of warmth sounded in her voice. But the preoccupation was still there, too. "I'd already planned to make them wait awhile after my first performance," she went on. "A couple of weeks, anyhow. You remember that little farm of mine in Jersey, John? I'm going over today. I won't see anyone except the servants there. Not even Maltzer. Not even you. I've got a lot to think about. Maltzer has agreed to let everything go until we've both thought things over. He's taking a rest, too. I'll see you the moment I get back, John. Is that all right?"

She blanked out almost before he had time to nod and while the beginning of a stammered argument was still on his lips. He sat there staring at the screen.

The two weeks that went by before Maltzer called him again were the longest Harris had ever spent. He thought of many things in the interval. He believed he could sense in that last talk with Deirdre something of the inner unrest that Maltzer had spoken of—more an abstraction than a distress, but some thought had occupied her mind which she would not—or was it that she could not?—share even with her closest confidants. He even wondered whether, if her mind was as delicately poised as Maltzer feared, one would ever know whether or not it had slipped. There was so little evidence one way or the other in the unchanging outward form of her.

Most of all he wondered what two weeks in a new environment would do to her untried body and newly patterned brain. If Maltzer were right, then there might be some perceptible—drainage—by the time they met again. He tried not to think of that.

Maltzer televised him on the morning set for her return. He looked very bad. The rest must have been no rest at all. His face was almost a skull now, and the blurred eyes behind their lenses burned. But he seemed curiously at peace, in spite of his appearance. Harris thought he had reached some decision, but whatever it was had not stopped his hands from shaking or the nervous *tic* that drew his face sidewise into a grimace at intervals.

"Come over," he said briefly, without preamble. "She'll be here in half an hour." And he blanked out without waiting for an answer.

When Harris arrived, he was standing by the window looking down and steadying his trembling hands on the sill.

"I can't stop her," he said in a monotone, and again without preamble. Harris had the impression that for the two weeks his thoughts must have run over and over the same track, until any spoken word was simply a vocal interlude in the circling of his mind. "I couldn't do it. I even tried threats, but she knew I didn't mean them. There's only one way out, Harris." He glanced up briefly, hollow-eyed behind the lenses. "Never mind. I'll tell you later."

"Did you explain everything to her that you did to me?"

"Nearly all. I even taxed her with that . . . that sense of distress I *know* she feels. She denied it. She was lying. We both knew. It was worse after the performance than before. When I saw her that night, I tell you I *knew*—she senses something wrong, but she won't admit it." He shrugged. "Well—"

Faintly in the silence they heard the humming of the elevator descending from the helicopter platform on the roof. Both men turned to the door.

She had not changed at all. Foolishly, Harris was a little surprised. Then he caught himself and remembered that she would never change—never, until she died. He himself might grow white-haired and senile; she would move before him then as she moved now, supple, golden, enigmatic.

Still, he thought she caught her breath a little when

she saw Maltzer and the depths of his swift degenera-
tion. She had no breath to catch, but her voice was
shaken as she greeted them.

"I'm glad you're both here," she said, a slight hesitation in her speech. "It's a wonderful day outside. Jersey
was glorious. I'd forgotten how lovely it is in summer.
Was the sanitarium any good, Maltzer?"

He jerked his head irritably and did not answer. She
went on talking in a light voice, skimming the surface,
saying nothing important.

This time Harris saw her as he supposed her audiences would, eventually, when the surprise had worn off
and the image of the living Deirdre faded from memory.
She was all metal now, the Deirdre they would know
from today on. And she was not less lovely. She was not
even less human—yet. Her motion was a miracle of flexible grace, a pouring of suppleness along every limb.
(From now on, Harris realized suddenly, it was her
body and not her face that would have mobility to express emotion; she must act with her limbs and her lithe,
robed torso.)

But there was something wrong. Harris sensed it almost tangibly in her inflections, her elusiveness, the way
she fenced with words. This was what Maltzer had
meant, this was what Harris himself had felt just before
she left for the country. Only now it was strong—certain. Between them and the old Deirdre whose voice still
spoke to them a veil of—detachment—had been drawn.
Behind it she was in distress. Somehow, somewhere, she
had made some discovery that affected her profoundly.
And Harris was terribly afraid that he knew what the
discovery must be. Maltzer was right.

He was still leaning against the window, staring out
unseeingly over the vast panorama of New York,
webbed with traffic bridges, winking with sunlit glass, its
vertiginous distances plunging downward into the blue
shadows of Earth-level. He said now, breaking into the
light-voiced chatter, "Are you all right, Deirdre?"

She laughed. It was lovely laughter. She moved lithely
across the room, sunlight glinting on her musical mailed
robe, and stooped to a cigarette box on a table. Her fingers were deft.

"Have one?" she said, and carried the box to Maltzer. He let her put the brown cylinder between his lips and hold a light to it, but he did not seem to be noticing what he did. She replaced the box and then crossed to a mirror on the far wall and began experimenting with a series of gliding ripples that wove patterns of pale gold in the glass. "Of course I'm all right," she said.

"You're lying."

Deirdre did not turn. She was watching him in the mirror, but the ripple of her motion went on slowly, languorously, undisturbed.

"No," she told them both.

Maltzer drew deeply on his cigarette. Then with a hard pull he unsealed the window and tossed the smoking stub far out over the gulfs below. He said,

"You can't deceive me, Deirdre." His voice, suddenly, was quite calm. "I created you, my dear. I know. I've sensed that uneasiness in you growing and growing for a long while now. It's much stronger today than it was two weeks ago. Something happened to you in the country. I don't know what it was, but you've changed. Will you admit to yourself what it is, Deirdre? Have you realized yet that you must not go back on the screen?"

"Why, no," said Deirdre, still not looking at him except obliquely, in the glass. Her gestures were slower now, weaving lazy patterns in the air. "No, I haven't changed my mind."

She was all metal—outwardly. She was taking unfair advantage of her own metal-hood. She had withdrawn far within, behind the mask of her voice and her facelessness. Even her body, whose involuntary motions might have betrayed what she was feeling, in the only way she could be subject to betrayal now, she was putting through ritual motions that disguised it completely. As long as these looping, weaving patterns occupied her, no one had any way of guessing even from her motion what went on in the hidden brain inside her helmet.

Harris was struck suddenly and for the first time with the completeness of her withdrawal. When he had seen her last in this apartment she had been wholly Deirdre, not masked at all, overflowing the metal with the warmth and ardor of the woman he had known so well.

Since then—since the performance on the stage—he had not seen the familiar Deirdre again. Passionately he wondered why. Had she begun to suspect even in her moment of triumph what a fickle master an audience could be? Had she caught, perhaps, the sound of whispers and laughter among some small portion of her watchers, though the great majority praised her?

Or was Maltzer right? Perhaps Harris' first interview with her had been the last bright burning of the lost Deirdre, animated by excitement and the pleasure of meeting after so long a time, animation summoned up in a last strong effort to convince him. Now she was gone, but whether in self-protection against the possible cruelties of human beings, or whether in withdrawal to metal-hood, he could not guess. Humanity might be draining out of her fast, and the brassy taint of metal permeating the brain it housed.

Maltzer laid his trembling hand on the edge of the opened window and looked out. He said in a deepened voice, the querulous note gone for the first time:

"I've made a terrible mistake, Deirdre. I've done you irreparable harm." He paused a moment, but Deirdre said nothing. Harris dared not speak. In a moment Maltzer went on. "I've made you vulnerable, and given you no weapons to fight your enemies with. And the human race is your enemy, my dear, whether you admit it now or later. I think you know that. I think it's why you're so silent. I think you must have suspected it on the stage two weeks ago, and verified it in Jersey while you were gone. They're going to hate you, after a while, because you are still beautiful, and they're going to persecute you because you are different—and helpless. Once the novelty wears off, my dear, your audience will be simply a mob."

He was not looking at her. He had bent forward a little, looking out the window and down. His hair stirred in the wind that blew very strongly up this high, and whined thinly around the open edge of the glass.

"I meant what I did for you," he said, "to be for everyone who meets with accidents that might have ruined them. I should have known my gift would mean worse ruin than any mutilation could be. I know now that there's only one legitimate way a human being can create life. When he tries another way, as I did, he has a lesson to learn. Remember the lesson of the student Frankenstein? He learned, too. In a way, he was lucky —the way he learned. He didn't have to watch what happened afterward. Maybe he wouldn't have had the courage—I know I haven't.'"

Harris found himself standing without remembering that he rose. He knew suddenly what was about to happen. He understood Maltzer's air of resolution, his new, unnatural calm. He knew, even, why Maltzer had asked him here today, so that Deirdre might not be left alone. For he remembered that Frankenstein, too, had paid with his life for the unlawful creation of life.

Maltzer was leaning head and shoulders from the window now, looking down with almost hypnotized fascination. His voice came back to them remotely in the breeze, as if a barrier already lay between them.

Deirdre had not moved. Her expressionless mask, in the mirror, watched him calmly. She *must* have understood. Yet she gave no sign, except that the weaving of her arms had almost stopped now, she moved so slowly. Like a dance seen in a nightmare, under water.

It was impossible, of course, for her to express any emotion. The fact that her face showed none now should not, in fairness, he held against her. But she watched so wholly without feeling— Neither of them moved toward the window. A false step, now, might send him over. They were quiet, listening to his voice.

"We who bring life into the world unlawfully," said Maltzer, almost thoughtfully, "must make room for it by withdrawing our own. That seems to be an inflexible rule. It works automatically. The thing we create makes living unbearable. No, it's nothing you can help, my dear. I've asked you to do something I created you incapable of doing. I made you to perform a function, and I've been asking you to forego the one thing you were made to do. I believe that if you do it, it will destroy you, but the whole guilt is mine, not yours. I'm not even asking you to give up the screen, any more. I know you can't, and live. But I can't live and watch you. I put all my skill and all my love in one final masterpiece, and I can't bear to watch it destroyed. I can't live and watch you do only what I made you to do, and ruin yourself because you must do it.

"But before I go, I have to make sure you understand." He leaned a little farther, looking down, and his voice grew more remote as the glass came between them. He was saying almost unbearable things now, but very distantly, in a cool, passionless tone filtered through wind and glass, and with the distant humming of the city mingled with it, so that the words were curiously robbed of poignancy. "I can be a coward," he said, "and escape the consequences of what I've done, but I can't go and leave you—not understanding. It would be even worse than the thought of your failure, to think of you bewildered and confused when the mob turns on you. What I'm telling you, my dear, won't be any real news—I think you sense it already, though you may not admit it to yourself. We've been too close to lie to each other, Deirdre—I know when you aren't telling the truth. I know the distress that's been growing in your mind. You are not wholly human, my dear. I think you know that. In so many ways, in spite of all I could do, you must always be less than human. You've lost the senses of perception that kept you in touch with humanity. Sight and hearing are all that remain, and sight, as I've said before, was the last and coldest of the senses to develop. And you're so delicately poised on a sort of thin edge of reason. You're only a clear, glowing mind animating a metal body, like a candle flame in a glass. And as precariously vulnerable to the wind."

He paused. "Try not to let them ruin you completely," he said after a while. "When they turn against you, when they find out you're more helpless than they—I wish I could have made you stronger, Deirdre. But I couldn't. I had too much skill for your good and mine, but not quite enough skill for that."

He was silent again, briefly, looking down. He was balanced precariously now, more than halfway over the sill and supported only by one hand on the glass. Harris watched with an agonized uncertainty, not sure whether a sudden leap might catch him in time or send him over. Deirdre was still weaving her golden patterns, slowly and unchangingly, watching the mirror and its reflection, her face and masked eyes enigmatic.

"I wish one thing, though," Maltzer said in his remote voice. "I wish—before I finish—that you'd tell me the truth, Deirdre. I'd be happier if I were sure I'd—reached you. Do you understand what I've said? Do you believe me? Because if you don't, then I know you're lost beyond all hope. If you'll admit your own doubt—and I know you do doubt—I can think there may be a chance for you after all. Were you lying to me, Deirdre? Do you know how . . . how wrong I've made you?"

There was silence. Then very softly, a breath of sound, Deirdre answered. The voice seemed to hang in midair, because she had no lips to move and localize it for the imagination.

"Will you listen, Maltzer?" she asked.

"I'll wait," he said. "Go on. Yes or no?"

Slowly she let her arms drop to her sides. Very smoothly and quietly she turned from the mirror and faced him. She swayed a little, making her metal robe ring.

"I'll answer you," she said. "But I don't think I'll answer that. Not with yes or no, anyhow. I'm going to walk a little, Maltzer. I have something to tell you, and I can't talk standing still. Will you let me move about without—going over?"

He nodded distantly. "You can't interfere from that distance," he said. "But keep the distance. What do you want to say?"

She began to pace a little way up and down her end of the room, moving with liquid ease. The table with the cigarette box was in her way, and she pushed it aside carefully, watching Maltzer and making no swift motions to startle him.

"I'm not—well, sub-human," she said, a faint note of indignation in her voice. "I'll prove it in a minute, but I want to say something else first. You must promise to wait and listen. There's a flaw in your argument, and I resent it. I'm not a Frankenstein monster made out of dead flesh. I'm myself—alive. You didn't create my life, you only preserved it. I'm not a robot, with compulsions built into me that I have to obey. I'm free-willed and independent, and, Maltzer—I'm human."

Harris had relaxed a little. She knew what she was doing. He had no idea what she planned, but he was willing to wait now. She was not the indifferent automaton he had thought. He watched her come to the table again in a lap of her pacing, and stoop over it, her eyeless mask turned to Maltzer to make sure a variation of her movement did not startle him.

"I'm human," she repeated, her voice humming faintly and very sweetly. "Do you think I'm not?" she asked, straightening and facing them both. And then suddenly, almost overwhelmingly, the warmth and the old ardent charm were radiant all around her. She was robot no longer, enigmatic no longer. Harris could see as clearly as in their first meeting the remembered flesh still gracious and beautiful as her voice evoked his memory. She stood swaying a little, as she had always swayed, her head on one side, and she was chuckling at them both. It was such a soft and lovely sound, so warmly familiar.

"Of course I'm myself," she told them, and as the words sounded in their ears neither of them could doubt it. There was hypnosis in her voice. She turned away and began to pace again, and so powerful was the human personality which she had called up about her that it beat out at them in deep pulses, as if her body were a furnace to send out those comforting waves of warmth. "I have handicaps, I know," she said. "But my audiences will never know. I won't let them know. I think you'll believe me, both of you, when I say I could play Juliet just as I am now, with a cast of ordinary people, and make the world accept it. Do you think I could, John? Maltzer, don't you believe I could?"

She paused at the far end of her pacing path and turned to face them, and they both stared at her without speaking. To Harris she was the Deirdre he had always known, pale gold, exquisitely graceful in remembered postures, the inner radiance of her shining through metal as brilliantly as it had ever shone through flesh. He did not wonder, now, if it were real. Later he would think again that it might be only a disguise, something like a garment she had put off with her lost body, to wear again only when she chose. Now the spell of her compelling charm was too strong for wonder. He watched, convinced for the moment that she was all she seemed to be. She could play Juliet if she said she could. She could sway a whole audience as easily as she swayed himself. Indeed, there was something about her just now more convincingly human than anything he had noticed before. He realized that in a split second of awareness before he saw what it was.

She was looking at Maltzer. He, too, watched, spellbound in spite of himself, not dissenting. She glanced from one to the other. Then she put back her head and laughter came welling and choking from her in a great, full-throated tide. She shook in the strength of it. Harris could almost see her round throat pulsing with the sweet low-pitched waves of laughter that were shaking her. Honest mirth, with a little derision in it.

Then she lifted one arm and tossed her cigarette into the empty fireplace.

Harris choked, and his mind went blank for one moment of blind denial. He had not sat here watching a robot smoke and accepting it as normal. He could not! And yet he had. That had been the final touch of conviction which swayed his hypnotized mind into accepting her humanity. And she had done it so deftly, so naturally, wearing her radiant humanity with such rightness, that his watching mind had not even questioned what she did.

He glanced at Maltzer. The man was still halfway over the window ledge, but through the opening of the window he, too, was staring in stupefied disbelief and Harris knew they had shared the same delusion.

Deirdre was still shaking a little with laughter. "Well," she demanded, the rich chuckling making her voice quiver, "am I all robot, after all?"

Harris opened his mouth to speak, but he did not utter a word. This was not his show. The byplay lay wholly between Deirdre and Maltzer; he must not interfere. He turned his head to the window and waited.

And Maltzer for a moment seemed shaken in his conviction.

"You . . . you *are* an actress," he admitted slowly. "But I . . . I'm not convinced I'm wrong. I think—" He paused. The querulous note was in his voice again, and he seemed racked once more by the old doubts and dismay. Then Harris saw him stiffen. He saw the resolution come back, and understood why it had come. Maltzer had gone too far already upon the cold and lonely path he had chosen to turn back, even for stronger evidence than this. He had reached his conclusions only after mental turmoil too terrible to face again. Safety and peace lay in the course he had steeled himself to follow. He was too tired, too exhausted by months of conflict, to retrace his path and begin all over. Harris could see him groping for a way out, and in a moment he saw him find it.

"That was a trick," he said hollowly. "Maybe you could play it on a larger audience, too. Maybe you have more tricks to use. I might be wrong. But Deirdre"—his voice grew urgent—"you haven't answered the one thing I've got to know. You can't answer it. You *do* feel—dismay. You've learned your own inadequacy, however well you can hide it from us—even from us. I *know*. Can you deny that, Deirdre?"

She was not laughing now. She let her arms fall, and the flexible golden body seemed to droop a little all over, as if the brain that a moment before had been sending out strong, sure waves of confidence had slackened its power, and the intangible muscles of her limbs slackened with it. Some of the glowing humanity began to fade. It receded within her and was gone, as if the fire in the furnace of her body were sinking and cooling.

"Maltzer," she said uncertainly, "I can't answer that—yet. I can't—"

And then, while they waited in anxiety for her to finish the sentence, she *blazed*. She ceased to be a figure in stasis—she *blazed*.

It was something no eyes could watch and translate into terms the brain could follow; her motion was too swift. Maltzer in the window was a whole long room-length away. He had thought himself safe at such a distance, knowing no normal being could reach him before he moved. But Deirdre was neither normal nor human.

In the same instant she stood drooping by the mirror she was simultaneously at Maltzer's side. Her motion negated time and destroyed space. And as a glowing cigarette tip in the dark describes closed circles before the eye when the holder moves it swiftly, so Deirdre blazed in one continuous flash of golden motion across the room.

But curiously, she was not blurred. Harris, watching, felt his mind go blank again, but less in surprise than because no normal eyes and brain could perceive what it was he looked at.

(In that moment of intolerable suspense his complex human brain paused suddenly, annihilating time in its own way, and withdrew to a cool corner of its own to analyze in a flashing second what it was he had just seen. The brain could do it timelessly; words are slow. But he knew he had watched a sort of tesseract of human motion, a parable of fourth-dimensional activity. A one-dimensional point, moved through space, creates a two-dimensional line, which in motion creates a three-dimensional cube. Theoretically the cube, in motion, would produce a fourth-dimensional figure. No human creature had ever seen a figure of three dimensions moved through space and time before—until this moment. She had not blurred; every motion she made was distinct, but not like moving figures on a strip of film. Not like anything that those who use our language had ever seen before, or created words to express. The mind saw, but without perceiving. Neither words nor thoughts could resolve what happened into terms for human brains. And perhaps she had not actually and literally moved through the fourth dimension. Perhaps—since Harris was able to see her—it had been almost and not quite that unimaginable thing. But it was close enough.)

While to the slow mind's eye she was still standing at the far end of the room, she was already at Maltzer's side, her long, flexible fingers gentle but very firm upon his arms. She waited—

The room shimmered. There was sudden violent heat beating upon Harris' face. Then the air steadied again and Deirdre was saying softly, in a mournful whisper:

"I'm sorry—I had to do it. I'm sorry—I didn't mean you to know—"

Time caught up with Harris. He saw it overtake Maltzer too, saw the man jerk convulsively away from the grasping hands, in a ludicrously futile effort to forestall what had already happened. Even thought was slow, compared with Deirdre's swiftness.

The sharp outward jerk was strong. It was strong enough to break the grasp of human hands and catapult Maltzer out and down into the swimming gulfs of New York. The mind leaped ahead to a logical conclusion and saw him twisting and turning and diminishing with dreadful rapidity to a tiny point of darkness that dropped away through sunlight toward the shadows near the earth. The mind even conjured up a shrill, thin cry that plummeted away with the falling body and hung behind it in the shaken air.

But the mind was reckoning on human factors.

Very gently and smoothly Deirdre lifted Maltzer from the window sill and with effortless ease carried him well back into the safety of the room. She set him down before a sofa and her golden fingers unwrapped themselves from his arms slowly, so that he could regain control of his own body before she released him.

He sank to the sofa without a word. Nobody spoke for an unmeasurable length of time. Harris could not. Deirdre waited patiently. It was Maltzer who regained speech first, and it came back on the old track, as if his mind had not yet relinquished the rut it had worn so deep.

"All right," he said breathlessly. "All right, you can stop me this time. But I know, you see. I know! You can't hide your feeling from me, Deirdre. I know the trouble you feel. And next time—next time I won't wait to talk!"

Deirdre made the sound of a sigh. She had no lungs to expel the breath she was imitating, but it was hard to realize that. It was hard to understand why she was not panting heavily from the terrible exertion of the past minutes; the mind knew why, but could not accept the reason. She was still too human.

"You still don't see," she said. "Think, Maltzer, think!"

There was a hassock beside the sofa. She sank upon it gracefully, clasping her robed knees. Her head tilted back to watch Maltzer's face. She saw only stunned stupidity on it now; he had passed through too much emotional storm to think at all.

"All right," she told him. "Listen—I'll admit it. You're right. I *am* unhappy. I do know what you said was true—but not for the reason you think. Humanity and I are far apart, and drawing farther. The gap will be hard to bridge. Do you hear me, Maltzer?"

Harris saw the tremendous effort that went into Maltzer's wakening. He saw the man pull his mind back into focus and sit up on the sofa with weary stiffness.

"You . . . you do admit it, then?" he asked in a bewildered voice.

Deirdre shook her head sharply.

"Do you still think of me as delicate?" she demanded. "Do you know I carried you here at arm's length halfway across the room? Do you realize you weigh *nothing* to me? I could"—she glanced around the room and gestured with sudden, rather appalling violence—"tear this building down," she said quietly. "I could tear my way through these walls, I think. I've found no limit yet to the strength I can put forth if I try." She held up her golden hands and looked at them. "The metal would break, perhaps," she said reflectively, "but then, I have no feeling—"

Maltzer gasped, "*Deirdre*—"

She looked up with what must have been a smile. It sounded clearly in her voice. "Oh, I won't. I wouldn't have to do it with my hands, if I wanted. Look—listen!"

She put her head back and a deep, vibrating hum gathered and grew in what one still thought of as her throat. It deepened swiftly and the ears began to ring. It was deeper, and the furniture vibrated. The walls began almost imperceptibly to shake. The room was full and bursting with a sound that shook every atom upon its neighbor with a terrible, disrupting force.

The sound ceased. The humming died. Then Deirdre

laughed and made another and quite differently pitched sound. It seemed to reach out like an arm in one straight direction—toward the window. The opened panel shook. Deirdre intensified her hum, and slowly, with imperceptible jolts that merged into smoothness, the window jarred itself shut.

"You see?" Deirdre said. "You see?"

But still Maltzer could only stare. Harris was staring too, his mind beginning slowly to accept what she implied. Both were too stunned to leap ahead to any conclusions yet.

Deirdre rose impatiently and began to pace again, in a ringing of metal robe and a twinkling of reflected lights. She was pantherlike in her suppleness. They could see the power behind that lithe motion now; they no longer thought of her as helpless, but they were far still from grasping the truth.

"You were wrong about me, Maltzer," she said with an effort at patience in her voice. "But you were right too, in a way you didn't guess. I'm not afraid of humanity. I haven't anything to fear from them. Why"—her voice took on a tinge of contempt—"already I've set a fashion in women's clothing. By next week you won't see a woman on the street without a mask like mine, and every dress that isn't cut like a chlamys will be out of style. I'm not afraid of humanity! I won't lose touch with them unless I want to. I've learned a lot—I've learned too much already."

Her voice faded for a moment, and Harris had a quick and appalling vision of her experimenting in the solitude of her farm, testing the range of her voice, testing her eyesight—could she see microscopically and telescopically?—and was her hearing as abnormally flexible as her voice?

"You were afraid I had lost feeling and scent and taste," she went on, still pacing with that powerful, tigerish tread. "Hearing and sight would not be enough, you think? But why do you think sight is the last of the senses? It may be the latest, Maltzer—Harris—*but why do you think it's the last?*"

She may not have whispered that. Perhaps it was only their hearing that made it seem thin and distant, as the brain contracted and would not let the thought come through in its stunning entirety.

"No," Deirdre said, "I haven't lost contact with the human race. I never will, unless I want to. It's too easy . . . too easy."

She was watching her shining feet as she paced, and her masked face was averted. Sorrow sounded in her soft voice now.

"I didn't mean to let you know," she said. "I never would have, if this hadn't happened. But I couldn't let you go believing you'd failed. You made a perfect machine, Maltzer. More perfect than you knew."

"But Deirdre—" breathed Maltzer, his eyes fascinated and still incredulous upon her, "but Deirdre, if we did succeed—what's wrong? I can feel it now—I've felt it all along. You're so unhappy—you still are. Why, Deirdre?"

She lifted her head and looked at him, eyelessly, but with a piercing stare.

"Why are you so sure of that?" she asked gently.

"You think I could be mistaken, knowing you as I do? But I'm not Frankenstein . . . you say my creation's flawless. Then what—"

"Could you ever duplicate this body?" she asked.

Maltzer glanced down at his shaking hands. "I don't know. I doubt it. I—"

"Could anyone else?"

He was silent. Deirdre answered for him. "I don't believe anyone could. I think I was an accident. A sort of mutation halfway between flesh and metal. Something accidental and . . . and unnatural, turning off on a wrong course of evolution that never reaches a dead end. Another brain in a body like this might die or go mad, as you thought I would. The synapses are too delicate. You were—call it lucky—with me. From what I know now, I don't think a . . . a baroque like me could happen again." She paused a moment. "What you did was kindle the fire for the Phoenix, in a way. And the Phoenix rises perfect and renewed from its own ashes. Do you remember why it had to reproduce itself that way?"

Maltzer shook his head.

"I'll tell you," she said. "It was because there was only one Phoenix. Only one in the whole world."

They looked at each other in silence. Then Deirdre shrugged a little.

"He always came out of the fire perfect, of course. I'm not weak, Maltzer. You needn't let that thought bother you any more. I'm not vulnerable and helpless. I'm not sub-human." She laughed dryly. "I suppose," she said, "that I'm—superhuman."

"But—not happy."

"I'm afraid. It isn't unhappiness, Maltzer—it's fear. I don't want to draw so far away from the human race. I wish I needn't. That's why I'm going back on the stage —to keep in touch with them while I can. But I wish there could be others like me. I'm . . . I'm lonely, Maltzer."

Silence again. Then Maltzer said, in a voice as distant as when he had spoken to them through glass, over gulfs as deep as oblivion:

"Then I am Frankenstein, after all."

"Perhaps you are," Deirdre said very softly. "I don't know. Perhaps you are."

She turned away and moved smoothly, powerfully, down the room to the window. Now that Harris knew, he could almost hear the sheer power purring along her limbs as she walked. She leaned the golden forehead against the glass—it clinked faintly, with a musical sound—and looked down into the depths Maltzer had hung above. Her voice was reflective as she looked into those dizzy spaces which had offered oblivion to her creator.

"There's one limit I can think of," she said, almost inaudibly. "Only one. My brain will wear out in another forty years or so. Between now and then I'll learn . . . I'll change . . . I'll know more than I can guess today. I'll change— That's frightening. I don't like to think about that." She laid a curved golden hand on the latch and pushed the window open a little, very easily. Wind whined around its edge. "I could put a stop to it now, if I wanted," she said. "If I wanted. But I can't, really. There's so much still untried. My brain's human, and no human brain could leave such possibilities untested. I wonder, though . . . I do wonder—"

Her voice was soft and familiar in Harris' ears, the voice Deirdre had spoken and sung with, sweetly enough to enchant a world. But as preoccupation came over her a certain flatness crept into the sound. When she was not listening to her own voice, it did not keep quite to the pitch of trueness. It sounded as if she spoke in a room of brass, and echoes from the walls resounded in the tones that spoke there.

"I wonder," she repeated, the distant taint of metal already in her voice.

Daemon

Padre, THE WORDS come slowly. It is a long time now since I have spoken in the Portuguese tongue. For more than a year, my companions here were those who do not speak with the tongues of men. And you must remember, *padre,* that in Rio, where I was born, I was named Luiz *o Bobo,* which is to say, Luiz the Simple. There was something wrong with my head, so that my hands were always clumsy and my feet stumbled over each other. I could not remember very much. But I could see things. Yes, *padre,* I could see things such as other men do not know.

I can see things now. Do you know who stands beside you, *padre,* listening while I talk? Never mind that. I am Luiz *o Bobo* still, though here on this island there were great powers of healing, and I can remember now the things that happened to me years ago. More easily than I remember what happened last week or the week before that. The year has been like a single day, for time on this island is not like time outside. When a man lives with *them,* there is no time.

The *ninfas,* I mean. And the others. . .

I am not lying. Why should I? I am going to die, quite soon now. You were right to tell me that, *padre.* But I knew. I knew already. Your crucifix is very pretty, *padre.* I like the way it shines in the sun. But that is not for me. You see, I have always known the things that walk beside men—other men. Not me. Perhaps they are souls, and I have no soul, being simple. Or perhaps they are daemons such as only clever men have. Or perhaps they are both these things. I do not know. But I know that I am dying. After the *ninfas* go away, I would not care to live.

Since you ask how I came to this place, I will tell you if the time remains to me. You will not believe. This is the one place on earth, I think, where they lingered still —those things you do not believe.

But before I speak of them, I must go back to an earlier day, when I was young beside the blue bay of Rio, under Sugar Loaf. I remember the docks of Rio, and the children who mocked me. I was big and strong, but I was *o Bobo* with a mind that knew no yesterday or tomorrow.

Minha avó, my grandmother, was kind to me. She was from Ceará, where the yearly droughts kill hope, and she was half blind, with pain in her back always. She worked so that we could eat, and she did not scold me too much. I know that she was good. It was something I could see; I have always had that power.

One morning my grandmother did not waken. She was cold when I touched her hand. That did not frighten me for the—good thing—about her lingered for a while. I closed her eyes and kissed her, and then I went away. I was hungry, and because I was *o Bobo,* I thought that someone might give me food, out of kindness. . . .

In the end, I foraged from the rubbish-heaps.

I did not starve. But I was lost and alone. Have you ever felt that, *padre?* It is like a bitter wind from the mountains and no sheepskin cloak can shut it out. One night I wandered into a sailors' saloon, and I remember that there were many dark shapes with eyes that shone, hovering beside the men who drank there. The men had red, windburned faces and tarry hands. They made me drink *'guardiente* until the room whirled around and went dark.

I woke in a dirty bunk. I heard planks groaning and the floor rocked under me.

Yes, *padre,* I had been shanghaied. I stumbled on deck, half blind in the dazzling sunlight, and there I found a man who had a strange and shining daemon. He was the captain of the ship, though I did not know it then. I scarcely saw the man at all. I was looking at the daemon.

Now, most men have shapes that walk behind them, *padre*. Perhaps you know that, too. Some of them are dark, like the shapes I saw in the saloon. Some of them are bright, like that which followed my grandmother. Some of them are colored, pale colors like ashes or rainbows. But this man had a scarlet daemon. And it was a scarlet beside which blood itself is ashen. The color blinded me. And yet it drew me, too. I could not take my eyes away, nor could I look at it long without pain. I never saw a color more beautiful, nor more frightening. It made my heart shrink within me, and quiver like a dog that fears the whip. If I have a soul, perhaps it was my soul that quivered. And I feared the beauty of the color as much as I feared the terror it awoke in me. It is not good to see beauty in that which is evil.

Other men upon the deck had daemons too. Dark shapes and pale shapes that followed them like their shadows. But I saw all the daemons waver away from the red, beautiful thing that hung above the captain of the ship.

The other daemons watched out of burning eyes. The red daemon had no eyes. Its beautiful, blind face was turned always toward the captain, as if it saw only through his vision. I could see the lines of its closed lids. And my terror of its beauty, and my terror of its evil, were nothing to my terror of the moment when the red daemon might lift those lids and look out upon the world.

The captain's name was Jonah Stryker. He was a cruel man, dangerous to be near. The men hated him. They were at his mercy while we were at sea, and the captain was at the mercy of his daemon. That was why I could not hate him as the others did. Perhaps it was pity I felt for Jonah Stryker. And you, who know men better than I, will understand that the pity I had for him made the captain hate me more bitterly than even his crew hated him.

When I came on deck that first morning, because I was blinded by the sun and by the redness of the scarlet daemon, and because I was ignorant and bewildered, I broke a shipboard rule. What it was, I do not know. There were so many, and I never could remember very clearly in those days. Perhaps I walked between him and the wind. Would that be wrong on a clipper ship, *padre?* I never understood.

The captain shouted at me, in the Yankee tongue, evil words whose meaning I did not know, but the daemon glowed redder when he spoke them. And he struck me with his fist, so that I fell. There was a look of secret bliss on the blind crimson face hovering above his, because of the anger that rose in him. I thought that through the captain's eyes the closed eyes of the daemon were watching me.

I wept. In that moment, for the first time, I knew how truly alone a man like me must be. For I had no daemon. It was not the simple loneliness for my grandmother or for human companionship that brought the tears to my eyes. That I could endure. But I saw the look of joy upon the blind daemon-face because of the captain's evil, and I remembered the look of joy that a bright shape sometimes wears who follows a good man. And I knew that no deed of mine would ever bring joy or sorrow to that which moves behind a man with a soul.

I lay upon the bright, hot deck and wept, not because of the blow, but because I knew suddenly, for the first time, that I was alone. No daemon for good or evil would ever follow me. Perhaps because I have no soul. *That* loneliness, father, is something not even you could understand.

The captain seized my arm and pulled me roughly to my feet. I did not understand, then, the words he spoke in his Yankee tongue, though later I picked up enough of that speech to know what men were saying around me. You may think it strange that *o Bobo* could learn a foreign tongue. It was easy for me. Easier, perhaps, than for a wiser man. Much I read upon the faces of their daemons, and there were many words whose real sounds I did not know, but whose meaning I found in the hum of thoughts about a man's head.

The captain shouted for a man named Barton, and the first mate hurried up, looking frightened. The captain pushed me back against the rail so that I staggered, seeing him and the deck and the watching daemons through the rainbows that tears cast before one's eyes.

There was loud talk, and many gestures toward me and the other two men who had been shanghaied from the port of Rio. The first mate tapped his head when he pointed to me, and the captain cursed again in the tongue of the foreigners, so that his daemon smiled very sweetly at his shoulder.

I think that was the first time I let the captain see pity on my face when I looked at him.

That was the one thing he could not bear. He snatched a belaying pin from the rail and struck me in the face with it, so that I felt the teeth break in my mouth. The blood I spat upon the deck was a beautiful color, but it looked paler than water beside the color of the captain's daemon. I remember all the daemons but the red one leaned a little forward when they saw blood running, snuffing up the smell and the brightness of it like incense. The red one did not even turn his blind face.

The captain struck me again because I had soiled his deck. My first task aboard the *Dancing Martha* was to scrub up my own blood from the planking.

Afterward they dragged me to the galley and threw me into the narrow alley at the cook's feet. I burned my hands on the stove. The captain laughed to see me jump back from it. It is a terrible thing that, though I heard his laughter many times a day, I never heard mirth in it. But there was mirth on his daemon's face.

Pain was with me for many days thereafter, because of the beating and the burns, but I was glad in a way. Pain kept my mind from the loneliness I had just discovered in myself. Those were bad days, *padre*. The worst days of my life. Afterward, when I was no longer lonely, I looked back upon them as a soul in paradise might look back on purgatory.

No, I am still alone. Nothing follows me as things follow other men. But here on the island I found the *ninfas*, and I was content.

I found them because of the Shaughnessy. I can understand him today in a way I could not do just then. He was a wise man and I am *o Bobo,* but I think I know some of his thoughts now, because today I, too, know I am going to die.

The Shaughnessy lived many days with death. I do not know how long. It was weeks and months in coming to him, though it lived in his lungs and his heart as a child lives within its mother, biding its time to be born. The Shaughnessy was a passenger. He had much money, so that he could do what he willed with his last days of living. Also he came of a great family in a foreign land called Ireland. The captain hated him for many reasons. He scorned him because of his weakness, and he feared him because he was ill. Perhaps he envied him too, because his people had once been kings and because the Shaughnessy was not afraid to die. The captain, I know, feared death. He feared it most terribly. He was right to fear it. He could not know that a daemon rode upon his shoulder, smiling its sweet, secret smile, but some instinct must have warned him that it was there, biding its time like the death in the Shaughnessy's lungs.

I saw the captain die. I know he was right to fear the hour of his daemon. . . .

Those were bad days on the ship. They were worse because of the great beauty all around us. I had never been at sea before, and the motion of the ship was a wonder to me, the clouds of straining sail above us and the sea all about, streaked with the colors of the currents and dazzling where the sun-track lay. White gulls followed us with their yellow feet tucked up as they soared over the deck, and porpoises followed too, playing in great arcs about the ship and dripping diamonds in the sun.

I worked hard, for no more wages than freedom from blows when I did well, and the scraps that were left from the table after the cook had eaten his fill. The cook was not a bad man like the captain, but he was not a good man, either. He did not care. His daemon was smoky, asleep, indifferent to the cook and the world.

It was the Shaughnessy who made my life worth the trouble of living. If it had not been for him, I might have surrendered life and gone into the breathing sea some night when no one was looking. It would not have been a sin for me, as it would be for a man with a soul.

But because of the Shaughnessy I did not. He had a strange sort of daemon himself, mother-of-pearl in the light, with gleams of darker colors when the shadows of night came on. He may have been a bad man in his day. I do not know. The presence of death in him opened his eyes, perhaps. I know only that to me he was very kind. His daemon grew brighter as the man himself grew weak with the oncoming of death.

He told me many tales. I have never seen the foreign country of Ireland, but I walked there often in my dreams because of the tales he told. The foreign isles called Greece grew clear to me too, because the Shaughnessy had dwelt there and loved them.

And he told me of things which he said were not really true, but I thought he said that with only half his mind, because I saw them so clearly while he talked. Great Odysseus was a man of flesh and blood to me, with a shining daemon on his shoulder, and the voyage that took so many enchanted years was a voyage I almost remembered, as if I myself had toiled among the crew.

He told me of burning Sappho, and I knew why the poet used that word for her, and I think the Shaughnessy knew too, though we did not speak of it. I knew how dazzling the thing must have been that followed her through the white streets of Lesbos and leaned upon her shoulder while she sang.

He told me of the nereids and the oceanids, and once I think I saw, far away in the sun-track that blinded my eyes, a mighty head rise dripping from the water, and heard the music of a wreathed horn as Triton called to his fish-tailed girls.

The *Dancing Martha* stopped at Jamaica for a cargo of sugar and rum. Then we struck out across the blue water toward a country called England. But our luck was bad. Nothing was right about the ship on that voyage. Our water-casks had not been cleaned as they should be, and the drinking water became foul. A man can pick the maggots out of his salt pork if he must, but bad water is a thing he cannot mend.

So the captain ordered our course changed for a little island he knew in these waters. It was too tiny to be inhabited, a rock rising out of the great blue deeps with a fresh spring bubbling high up in a cup of the forested crags.

I saw it rising in the dawn like a green cloud on the horizon. Then it was a jewel of green as we drew nearer, floating on the blue water. And my heart was a bubble in my chest, shining with rainbow colors, lighter than the air around me. Part of my mind thought that the island was an isle in Rio Bay, and somehow I felt that I had come home again and would find my grandmother waiting on the shore. I forgot so much in those days. I forgot that she was dead. I thought we would circle the island and come in across the dancing Bay to the foot of the Rua d'Oporto, with the lovely city rising on its hills above the water.

I felt so sure of all this that I ran to tell the Shaughnessy of my delight in homecoming. And because I was hurrying, and blind to all on deck with the vision of Rio in my eyes, I blundered into the captain himself. He staggered and caught my arm to save his footing, and we were so close together that for a moment the crimson daemon swayed above my own head, its eyeless face turned down to mine.

I looked up at that beautiful, smiling face, so near that I could touch it and yet, I knew, farther away than the farthest star. I looked at it and screamed in terror. I had never been so near a daemon before, and I could feel its breath on my face, sweet-smelling, burning my skin with its scorching cold.

The captain was white with his anger and his—his envy? Perhaps it was envy he felt even of me, o Bobo, for a man with a daemon like that one hanging on his shoulder may well envy the man without a soul. He hated me bitterly, because he knew I pitied him, and to receive the pity of o Bobo must be a very humbling thing. Also he knew that I could not look at him for more than a moment or two, because of the blinding color of his daemon. I think he did not know why I blinked and looked away, shuddering inside, whenever he crossed my path. But he knew it was not the angry fear which other men felt for him which made me avert my eyes. I think he sensed that because he was damned I could not gaze upon him long, and that too made him hate and fear and envy the lowliest man in his crew.

All the color went out of his face as he looked at me, and the daemon above him flushed a deeper and lovelier scarlet, and the captain reached for a belaying pin with a hand that trembled. That which looked out of his eyes was not a man at all, but a daemon, and a daemon that quivered with joy as I was quivering with terror.

I heard the bone crack when the club came down upon my skull. I saw lightning dazzle across my eyes and my head was filled with brightness. I remember almost nothing more of that bad time. A little night closed around me and I saw through it only when the lightning of the captain's blows illumined the dark. I heard his daemon laughing.

When the day came back to me, I was lying on the deck with the Shaughnessy kneeling beside me bathing my face with something that stung. His daemon watched me over his shoulder, bright mother-of-pearl colors, its face compassionate. I did not look at it. The loneliness in me was sharper than the pain of my body, because no daemon of my own hung shining over my hurts, and no daemon ever would.

The Shaughnessy spoke in the soft, hushing Portuguese of Lisboa, that always sounded so strange to me.

"Lie still, Luiz," he was saying. "Don't cry. I'll see that he never touches you again."

I did not know until then that I was weeping. It was not for pain. It was for the look on his daemon's face, and for loneliness.

The Shaughnessy said, "When he comes back from the island, I'll have it out with him." He said more than that, but I was not listening. I was struggling with a thought, and thoughts came hard through the sleepiness that always clouded my brain.

The Shaughnessy meant kindly, but I knew the captain was master upon the ship. And it still seemed to me that we were anchored in the bay of Rio and my grandmother awaited me on the shore.

I sat up. Beyond the rail the high green island was

bright, sunshine winking from the water all around it,
and from the leaves that clothed its slopes. I knew what
I was going to do.

When the Shaughnessy went away for more water, I
got to my feet. There was much pain in my head, and all
my body ached from the captain's blows, and the deck
was reeling underfoot with a motion the waves could not
give it. When I got to the rail, I fell across it before I
could jump, and slid into the sea very quietly.

I remember only flashes after that. Salt water burning
me, and great waves lifting and falling all around me,
and the breath hot in my lungs when the water did not
burn even hotter there. Then there was sand under my
knees, and I crawled up a little beach and I think I fell
asleep in the shelter of a clump of palms.

Then I dreamed that it was dark, with stars hanging
overhead almost near enough to touch, and so bright
they burned my eyes. I dreamed I heard men calling me
through the trees, and I did not answer. I dreamed I
heard voices quarreling, the captain's voice loud and angry, the Shaughnessy's tight and thin. I dreamed of oar-
locks creaking and water splashing from dipping blades,
and the sound of it receding into the warmth and darkness.

I put up a hand to touch a star cluster that hung
above my head, and the cluster was bright and tingling
to feel. Then I saw that it was the Shaughnessy's face.

I said, "Oh, *s'nhor*," in a whisper, because I remembered that the captain had spoken from very close by.

The Shaughnessy smiled at me in the starlight. "Don't
whisper, Luiz. We're alone now."

I was happy on the island. The Shaughnessy was kind
to me, and the days were long and bright, and the island
itself was friendly. One knows that of a place. And I
thought, in those days, that I would never see the captain again or his beautiful scarlet daemon smiling its
blind, secret smile above his shoulder. He had left us to
die upon the island, and one of us did die.

The Shaughnessy said that another man might have

perished of the blows the captain gave me. But I think because my brain is such a simple thing it mended easily, and perhaps the blow that made my skull crack let in a little more of wit than I had owned before. Or perhaps happiness did it, plenty of food to eat, and the Shaughnessy's tales of the things that—that you do not believe, *meu padre.*

The Shaughnessy grew weak as I grew strong. He lay all day in the shade of a broad tree by the shore, and as his strength failed him, his daemon grew brighter and more remote, as if it were already halfway through the veil of another world.

When I was well again, the Shaughnessy showed me how to build a thatched lean-to that would withstand the rain.

"There may be hurricanes, Luiz," he said to me. "This *barraca* will be blown down. Will you remember how to build another?"

"Sim," I said. "I shall remember. You will show me."

"No, Luiz. I shall not be here. You must remember."

He told me many things, over and over again, very patiently. How to find the shellfish on the rocks when the tide was out, how to trap fish in the stream, what fruit I might eat and what I must never touch. It was not easy for me. When I tried to remember too much it made my head hurt.

I explored the island, coming back to tell him all I had found. At first I was sure that when I had crossed the high hills and stood upon their peaks I would see the beautiful slopes of Rio shining across the water. My heart sank when I stood for the first time upon the heights and saw only more ocean, empty, heaving between me and the horizon.

But I soon forgot again, and Rio and the past faded from my mind. I found the pool cupped high in a hollow of the crags, where clear sweet water bubbled up in the shadow of the trees and the streamlet dropped away in a series of pools and falls toward the levels far below. I found groves of pale trees with leaves like streaming hair, rustling with the noise of the waterfall. I found no people here, and yet I felt always that there were watchers among the leaves, and it seemed to me that laughter sounded sometimes behind me, smothered when I turned my head.

When I told the Shaughnessy this he smiled at me.

"I've told you too many tales," he said. "But if anyone could see them, I think it would be you, Luiz."

"Sim, s'nhor," I said. "Tell me again of the forest-women. Could they be here, do you think, *s'nhor?"*

He let sand trickle through his fingers, watching it as if the fall of sand had some meaning to his mind that I could not fathom.

"Ah, well," he said, "they might be. They like the olive groves of Greece best, and the tall trees on Olympus. But every mountain has its oread. Here, too, perhaps. The Little People left Ireland years ago and for all I know the oreads have fled from civilization too, and found such places as this to put them in mind of home. . . .

"There was one who turned into a fountain once, long ago. I saw that fountain in Greece. I drank from it. There must have been a sort of magic in the waters, for I always went back to Greece after that. I'd leave, but I couldn't stay away long." He smiled at me. "Maybe now, because I can't go back again, the oreads have come to me here."

I looked hard at him to see if he meant what he said, but he shook his head and smiled again. "I think they haven't come for me. Maybe for you, Luiz. Belief is what they want. If you believe, perhaps you'll really see them. I'd be the last man to deny a thing like that. You'll need something like them to keep you company, my friend—afterward." And he trickled sand through his fingers again, watching it fall with a look upon his face I did not understand.

The night came swiftly on that island. It was a lovely place. The Shaughnessy said islands have a magic all their own, for they are the place where earth and ocean meet. We used to lie on the shore watching the fire that burned upon the edges of the waves lap up the beach and breathe away again, and the Shaughnessy told me many tales. His voice was growing weaker, and he did not trouble so much any more to test my memory for the lessons he had taught. But he spoke of ancient magic, and more and more in these last days, his mind turned back to the wonders of the country called Ireland.

He told me of the little green people with their lanterns low down among the ferns. He told me of the *unicórnio,* swift as the swiftest bird, a magical stag with one horn upon its forehead as long as the shaft of a spear and as sharp as whatever is sharpest. And he told me of Pan, goat-footed, moving through the woodland with laughter running brfore him and panic behind, the same panic terror which my language and the Shaughnessy's get from his name. *Pânico,* we Brazilians call it.

One evening he called to me and held up a wooden cross. "Luiz, look at this," he said. I saw that upon the arms of the cross he had made deep carvings with his knife. "This is my name," he told me. "If anyone ever comes here asking for me, you must show them this cross."

I looked at it closely. I knew what he meant about the name—it is that sort of enchantment in which markings can speak with a voice too tiny for the ears to hear. I am *o Bobo* and I never learned to read, so that I do not understand how this may be done.

"Some day," the Shaughnessy went on, "I think someone will come. My people at home may not be satisfied with whatever story Captain Stryker invents for them. Or a drunken sailor may talk. If they do find this island, Luiz, I want this cross above my grave to tell them who I was. And for another reason," he said thoughtfully. "For another reason too. But that need not worry you, *meu amigo.*"

He told me where to dig the bed for him. He did not tell me to put in the leaves and the flowers. I thought of that myself, three days later, when the time came. . . .

Because he had wished it, I put him in the earth. I did not like doing it. But in a way I feared not to carry out his commands, for the daemon of the Shaughnessy still hovered about him, very bright, very bright—so bright I could not look it in the face. I thought there was music coming from it, but I could not be sure.

I put the flowers over him and then the earth. There was more to go back in the grave than I had taken out, so I made a mound above him, as long as the Shaughnessy was long, and I drove in the stake of the wooden cross, above where his head was, as he had told me. Then for a moment I laid my ear to the markings to see if I could hear what they were saying, for it seemed to me that the sound of his name, whispered to me by the marks his hands had made, would lighten my loneliness a little. But I heard nothing.

When I looked up, I saw his daemon glow like the sun at noon, a light so bright I could not bear it upon my eyes. I put my hands before them. When I took them down again, there was no daemon.

You will not believe me when I tell you this, *padre,* but in that moment the—the feel of the island changed. All the leaves, I think, turned the other way on the trees, once, with a rustle like one vast syllable whispered for that time only, and never again.

I think I know what the syllable was. Perhaps I will tell you, later—if you let me.

And the island breathed. It was like a man who has held his breath for a long while, in fear or pain, and let it run out deeply when the fear or the pain departed.

I did not know, then, what it was. But I thought I would go up the steep rocks to the pool, because I wanted a place that would not remind me of the Shaughnessy. So I climbed the crags among the hanging trees. And it seemed to me that I heard laughter when the wind rustled among them. Once I saw what I thought must be a *ninfa,* brown and green in the forest. But she was too shy. I turned my head, and the brown and green stilled into the bark and foliage of the tree.

When I came to the pool, the unicorn was drinking. He was very beautiful, whiter than foam, whiter than a cloud, and his mane lay upon his great shoulders like spray upon the shoulder of a wave. The tip of his long, spiraled horn just touched the water as he drank, so that the ripples ran outward in circles all around it. He tossed his head when he scented me, and I saw the glittering diamonds of the water sparkling from his velvet muzzle. He had eyes as green as a pool with leaves reflecting in it, and a spot of bright gold in the center of each eye.

Very slowly, with the greatest stateliness, he turned from the water and moved away into the forest. I know I heard a singing where he disappeared.

I was still *o Bobo* then. I drank where he had drunk, thinking there was a strange, sweet taste to the water now, and then I went down to the *barraca* on the beach, for I had forgotten already and thought perhaps the Shaughnessy might be there. . . .

Night came, and I slept. Dawn came, and I woke again. I bathed in the ocean. I gathered shellfish and fruit, and drank of the little stream that fell from the mountain pool. And as I leaned to drink, two white dripping arms rose up to clasp my neck, and a mouth as wet and cold as the water pressed mine. It was the kiss of acceptance.

After that the *ninfas* of the island no longer hid their faces from me.

My hair and beard grew long. My garments tore upon the bushes and became the rags you see now. I did not care. It did not matter. It was not my face they saw. They saw my simpleness. And I was one with the *ninfas* and the others.

The oread of the mountain came out to me often, beside the pool where the unicorn came to drink. She was wise and strange, being immortal. The eyes slanted upward in her head, and her hair was a shower of green leaves blowing always backward in a wind that moved about her when no other breezes blew. She used to sit beside the pool in the hot, still afternoons, the unicorn lying beside her and her brown fingers combing out his silver mane. Her wise slanting eyes, the color of shadows in the forest, and his round green eyes the color of the pool, with the flecks of gold in each, used to watch me as we talked.

The oread told me many things. Many things I could never tell you, *padre*. But it was as the Shaughnessy had guessed. Because I believed, they were glad of my presence there. While the Shaughnessy lived, they could not come out into the plane of being, but they watched from the other side. . . . They had been afraid. But they were afraid no longer.

For many years they have been homeless now, blowing about the world in search of some spot of land where no disbelief dwells, and where one other thing has not taken footing. . . . They told me of the isles of Greece, with love and longing upon their tongues, and it seemed to me that I heard the Shaughnessy speak again in their words.

They told me of the One I had not yet seen, or more than glimpsed. That happened when I chanced to pass near the Shaughnessy's grave in the dimness of the evening, and I saw the cross that bore his name had fallen. I took it up and held it to my ear again, hoping the tiny voices of the markings would whisper. But that is a mystery which has never been given me.

I saw the—the One—loitering by that grave. But when I put up the cross, he went away, slowly, sauntering into the dark woods, and a thin piping floated back to me from the spot where he had vanished.

Perhaps the One did not care for my presence there. The others welcomed me. It was not often any more, they said, that men like me were free to move among them. Since the hour of their banishment, they told me, and wept when they spoke of that hour, there had been too few among mankind who really knew them.

I asked about the banishment, and they said that it had happened long ago, very long ago. A great star had stood still in the sky over a stable in a town whose name I do not know. Once I knew it. I do not remember now. It was a town with a beautiful name.

The skies opened and there was singing in the heavens, and after that the gods of Greece had to flee. They have been fleeing ever since.

They were glad I had come to join them. And I was doubly glad. For the first time since my grandmother died, I knew I was not alone. Even the Shaughnessy had not been as close to me as these *ninfas* were. For the Shaughnessy had a daemon. The *ninfas* are immortal, but they have no souls. That, I think, is why they welcomed me so warmly. We without souls are glad of companionship among others of our kind. There is a lone-

liness among our kind that can only be assuaged by
huddling together. The *ninfas* knew it, who must live
forever, and I shared it with them, who may die before
this night is over.

Well, it was good to live upon the island. The days
and the months went by beautifully, full of clear colors
and the smell of the sea and the stars at night as bright
as lanterns just above us. I even grew less *Bobo,* because
the *ninfas* spoke wisdom of a kind I never heard among
men. They were good months.

And then, one day, Jonah Stryker came back to the
island.

You know, *padre,* why he came. The Shaughnessy in
his wisdom had guessed that in Ireland men of the
Shaughnessy's family might ask questions of Captain
Stryker—questions the captain could not answer. But it
had not been guessed that the captain might return to
the island, swiftly, before the Shaughnessy's people
could discover the truth, with the thought in his evil
mind of wiping out all traces of the two he had left to
die.

I was sitting on the shore that day, listening to the
songs of two *ninfas* of the nereid kind as they lay in the
edge of the surf, with the waves breaking over them
when the water lapped up the slopes of sand. They were
swaying their beautiful rainbow colored fish-bodies as
they sang, and I heard the whisper of the surf in their
voices, and the long rhythms of the undersea.

But suddenly there came a break in their song, and I
saw upon one face before me, and then the other, a look
of terror come. The green blood in their veins sank back
with fear, and they looked at me, white with pallor and
strangely transparent, as if they had halfway ceased to
be. With one motion they turned their heads and stared
out to sea.

I stared too. I think the first thing I saw was that flash
of burning crimson, far out over the waves. And my
heart quivered within me like a dog that fears the whip.
I knew that beautiful, terrible color too well.

It was only then that I saw the *Dancing Martha,* lying

at anchor beyond a ridge of rock. Between the ship and
the shore a small boat rocked upon the waves, light
flashing from oar-blades as the one man in the boat bent
and rose and bent to his work. Above him, hanging like
a crimson cloud, the terrible scarlet glowed.

When I looked back, the *ninfas* had vanished. Whether they slid back into the sea, or whether they melted
away into nothingness before me I shall never know
now. I did not see them again.

I went back a little way into the forest, and watched
from among the trees. No dryads spoke to me, but I
could hear their quick breathing and the leaves trembled
all about me. I could not look at the scarlet daemon
coming nearer and nearer over the blue water, but I
could not look away long, either. It was so beautiful and
so evil.

The captain was alone in the boat. I was not quite so
Bobo then and I understood why. He beached the boat
and climbed up the slope of sand, the daemon swaying
behind him like a crimson shadow. I could see its blind
eyes and the beautiful, quiet face shut up with bliss because of the thing the captain had come to do. He was
carrying in his hand a long shining pistol, and he walked
carefully, looking to left and right. His face was anxious,
and his mouth had grown more cruel in the months
since I saw him last.

I was sorry for him, but I was very frightened, too. I
knew he meant to kill whomever he found alive upon
the island, so that no tongue could tell the Shaughnessy's
people of his wicked deed.

He found my thatched *barraca* at the edge of the
shore, and kicked it to pieces with his heavy boots. Then
he went on until he saw the long mound above the
Shaughnessy's bed, with the cross standing where his
head lay. He bent over the cross, and the markings upon
it spoke to him as they would never speak to me. I
heard nothing, but he heard and knew. He put out his
hand and pulled up the cross from the Shaughnessy's
grave.

Then he went to the ruins of my *barraca* and to the
embers of the fire I kept smouldering there. He broke
the cross upon his knee and fed the pieces into the hot

coals. The wood was dry. I saw it catch flame and burn. I saw, too, the faint stirring of wind that sprang up with the flames, and I heard the sighing that ran through the trees around me. Now there was nothing here to tell the searchers who might come afterward that the Shaughnessy lay in the island earth. Nothing—except myself.

He saw my footprints around the ruined *barraca*. He stooped to look. When he rose again and peered around the shore and forest, I could see his eyes shine, and it was the daemon who looked out of them, not the man.

Following my tracks, he began to move slowly toward the forest where I was hiding.

Then I was very frightened. I rose and fled through the trees, and I heard the dryads whimpering about me as I ran. They drew back their boughs to let me pass and swept them back after me to bar the way. I ran and ran, upward among the rocks, until I came to the pool of the unicorn, and the oread of the mountain stood there waiting for me, her arm across the unicorn's neck.

There was a rising wind upon the island. The leaves threshed and talked among themselves, and the oread's leafy hair blew backward from her face with its wise slanting eyes. The unicorn's silver mane tossed in that wind and the water ruffled in the pool.

"There is trouble coming, Luiz," the oread told me.

"The daemon. I know." I nodded to her, and then blinked, because it seemed to me that she and the unicorn, like the sea-*ninfas*, were growing so pale I could see the trees behind them through their bodies. But perhaps that was because the scarlet of the daemon had hurt my eyes.

"There is a man with a soul again upon our island," the oread said. "A man who does not believe. Perhaps we will have to go, Luiz."

"The Shaughnessy had a daemon too," I told her. "Yet you were here before his daemon left him to the earth. Why must you go now?"

"His was a good daemon. Even so, we were not fully here while he lived. You must remember, Luiz, that hour I told you of when a star stood above a stable where a child lay, and all our power went from us. where the souls of men dwell, we cannot stay. This new man has brought a very evil soul with him. It frightens us. Yet since he had burned the cross, perhaps the Master can fight. . . ."

"The Master?" I asked.

"The One we serve. The One you serve, Luiz. The One I think the Shaughnessy served, though he did not know it. The Lord of the opened eyes and the far places. He could not come until the Sign was taken down. Once you had a glimpse of him, when the Sign fell by accident from the grave, but perhaps you have forgotten that."

"I have not forgotten. I am not so *Bobo* now."

She smiled at me, and I could see the tree behind her through the smile.

"Then perhaps you can help the Master when the time comes. We cannot help. We are too weak already, because of the presence of the unbeliever, the man with the daemon. See?" She touched my hand, and I felt not the firm, soft brush of fingers but only a coolness like mist blowing across my skin.

"Perhaps the Master can fight him," the oread said, and her voice was very faint, like a voice from far away, though she spoke from so near to me. "I do not know about that. We must go, Luiz. We may not meet again. Good-by, *caro bobo*, while I can still say goodby. . . ." The last of it was faint as the hushing of the leaves, and the oread and the unicorn together looked like smoke blowing from a campfire across the glade.

The knowledge of my loneliness came over me then more painfully than I had felt it since that hour when I first looked upon the captain's daemon and knew at last what my own sorrow was. But I had no time to grieve, for there was a sudden frightened whispering among the leaves behind me, and then the crackle of feet in boots, and then a flicker of terrible crimson among the trees.

I ran. I did not know where I ran. I heard the dryads crying, so it must have been among trees. But at last I came out upon the shore again and I saw the Shaughnessy's long grave without a cross above it. And I stopped short, and a thrill of terror went through me. For there was a Something that crouched upon the grave.

The fear in me then was a new thing. A monstrous, dim fear that moves like a cloud about the Master. I knew he meant me no harm, but the fear was heavy upon me, making my head spin with panic. *Pânico. . . .*

The Master rose upon the grave, and he stamped his goat-hoofed foot twice and set the pipes to his bearded lips. I heard a thin, strange wailing music that made the blood chill inside me. And at the first sound of it there came again what I had heard once before upon the island.

The leaves upon all the trees turned over once, with a great single whispering of one syllable. The syllable was the Master's name. I fled from it in the *pânico* all men have felt who hear that name pronounced. I fled to the edge of the beach, and I could flee no farther. So I crouched behind a hillock of rock on the wet sand, and watched what came after me from the trees.

It was the captain, with his daemon swaying like smoke above his head. He carried the long pistol ready, and his eyes moved from left to right along the beach, seeking like a wild beast for his quarry.

He saw the Master, standing upon the Shaughnessy's grave.

I saw how he stopped, rigid, like a man of stone. The daemon swayed forward above his head, he stopped so suddenly. I saw how he stared. And such was his disbelief, that for an instant I thought even the outlines of the Master grew hazy. There is great power in the men with souls.

I stood up behind my rock. I cried above the noises of the surf, "Master—Great Pan—I believe!"

He heard me. He tossed his horned head and his bulk was solid again. He set the pipes to his lips.

Captain Stryker whirled when he heard me. The long pistol swung up and there was a flash and a roar, and something went by me with a whine of anger. It did not touch me.

Then the music of the pipes began. A terrible music, thin and high, like the ringing in the ears that has no source. It seized the captain as if with thin, strong fingers, making him turn back to the sound. He stood rigid again, staring, straining. The daemon above him turned uneasily from side to side, like a snake swaying.

Then Captain Stryker ran. I saw the sand fly up from under his boots as he fled southward along the shore. His daemon went after him, a red shadow with its eyes still closed, and after them both went Pan, moving delicately on the goathoofs, the pipes to his lips and his horns shining golden in the sun.

And that midday terror I think was greater than any terror that can stalk a man by dark.

I waited beside my rock. The sea was empty behind me except for the *Dancing Martha* waiting the captain's orders at its anchor. But no *ninfas* came in on the foam to keep me company; no heads rose wreathed with seaweed out of the water. The sea was empty and the island was empty too, except for a man and a daemon and the Piper who followed at their heels.

Myself I do not count. I have no soul.

It was nearly dark when they came back along the beach. I think the Piper had hunted them clear around the island, going slowly on his delicate hoofs, never hurrying, never faltering, and that dreadful thin music always in the captain's ears.

I saw the captain's face when he came back in the twilight. It was an old man's face, haggard, white, with deep lines in it and eyes as wild as Pan's. His clothing was torn to ribbons and his hands bled, but he still held the pistol and the red daemon still hung swaying above him.

I think the captain did not know that he had come back to his starting place. By that time, all places must have looked alike to him. He came wavering toward me blindly. I rose up behind my rock.

When he saw me he lifted the pistol again and gasped some Yankee words. He was a strong man, Captain Stryker. With all he had endured in that long chase, he still had the power to remember he must kill me. I did not think he had reloaded the pistol, and I stood up facing him across the sand.

Behind him Pan's pipes shrilled a warning, but the Master did not draw nearer to come between us. The red daemon swayed at the captain's back, and I knew why Pan did not come to my aid. Those who lost their power when the Child was born can never lay hands upon men who possess a soul. Even a soul as evil as the captain's stood like a rock between him and the touch of Pan. Only the pipes could reach a human's ears, but there was that in the sound of the pipes which did all Pan needed to do.

It could not save me. I heard the captain laugh, without breath, a strange, hoarse sound, and I saw the lightning dazzle from the pistol's mouth. The crash it made was like a blow that struck me here, in the chest. I almost fell. That blow was heavy, but I scarcely noticed it then. There was too much to do.

The captain was laughing, and I thought of the Shaughnessy, and I stumbled forward and took the pistol by its hot muzzle with my hand. I am strong. I tore it from the captain's fist and he stood there gaping at me, not believing anything he saw. He breathed in dreadful, deep gasps, and I found I was gasping too, but I did not know why just then.

The captain's eyes met mine, and I think he saw that even now I had no hate for him—only pity. For the man behind the eyes vanished and the crimson daemon of his rage looked out, because I dared to feel sorrow for him. I looked into the eyes that were not his, but the eyes behind the closed lids of the beautiful, blind face above him. It I hated, not him. And it was it I struck. I lifted the pistol and smashed it into the captain's face.

I was not very clear in my head just then. I struck the daemon with my blow, but it was the captain who reeled backward three steps and then fell. I am very strong. One blow was all I needed.

For a moment there was no sound in all the island. Even the waves kept their peace. The captain shuddered and gave one sigh, like that of a man who comes back to living reluctantly. He got his hands beneath him and rose upon them, peering at me through the hair that had fallen across his forehead. He was snarling like an animal.

I do not know what he intended then. I think he would have fought me until one of us was dead. But above him just then I saw the daemon stir. It was the first time I had ever seen it move except in answer to the captain's motion. All his life it had followed him, blind, silent, a shadow that echoed his gait and gestures. Now for the first time it did not obey him.

Now it rose up to a great, shining height above his head, and its color was suddenly very deep, very bright and deep, a blinding thing that hung above him too hot in color to look at. Over the beautiful blind face a look of triumph came. I saw ecstasy dawn over that face in all its glory and its evil.

I knew that this was the hour of the daemon.

Some knowledge deeper than any wisdom warned me to cover my eyes. For I saw its lids flicker, and I knew it would not be good to watch when that terrible gaze looked out at last upon a world it had never seen except through the captain's eyes.

I fell to my knees and covered my face. And the captain, seeing that, must have known at long last what it was I saw behind him. I think now that in the hour of a man's death, he knows. I think in that last moment he knows, and turns, and for the first time and the last, looks his daemon in the face.

I did not see him do it. I did not see anything. But I heard a great, resonant cry, like the mighty music that beats through paradise, a cry full of triumph and thanksgiving, and joy at the end of a long, long, weary road. There was mirth in it, and beauty, and all the evil the mind can compass.

Then fire glowed through my fingers and through my eyelids and into my brain. I could not shut it out. I did not even need to lift my head to see, for that sight would have blazed through my very bones.

I saw the daemon fall upon its master.

The captain sprang to his feet with a howl like a beast's howl, no mind or soul in it. He threw back his head and his arms went up to beat that swooping, beautiful, crimson thing away.

No flesh could oppose it. This was its hour. What sets that hour I do not know, but the daemon knew, and nothing could stop it now.

I saw the flaming thing descend upon the captain like a falling star. Through his defending arms it swept, and through his flesh and his bones and into the hollows where the soul dwells.

He stood for an instant transfixed, motionless, glowing with that bath of crimson light. Then I saw the crimson begin to shine *through* him, so that the shadows of his bones stood out upon the skin. And then fire shot up, wreathing from his eyes and mouth and nostrils. He was a lantern of flesh for that fire of the burning spirit. But he was a lantern that is consumed by the flame it carries. . . .

When the color became too bright for the eyes to bear it, I tried to turn away. I could not. The pain in my chest was too great. I thought of the Shaughnessy in that moment, who knew, too, what pain in the chest was like. I think that was the first moment when it came to me that, like the Shaughnessy, I too was going to die.

Before my eyes, the captain burned in the fire of his daemon, burned and burned, his living eyes looking out at me through the crimson glory, and the laughter of the daemon very sweet above the sound of the whining flame. I could not watch and I could not turn away.

But at last the whine began to die. Then the laughter roared out in one great peal of triumph, and the beautiful crimson color, so dreadfully more crimson than blood, flared in a great burst of light that turned to blackness against my eyeballs.

When I could see again, the captain's body lay flat upon the sand. I know death when I see it. He was not burned at all. He looked as any dead man looks, flat and silent. It was his soul I had watched burning, not his body.

The daemon had gone back again to its own place. I knew that, for I could feel my aloneness on the island.

The Others had gone too. The presence of that fiery daemon was more, in the end, than their power could endure. Perhaps they shun an evil soul more fearfully than a good one, knowing themselves nothing of good and evil, but fearing what they do not understand.

You know, *padre,* what came after. The men from the *Dancing Martha* took their captain away next morning.

They were frightened of the island. They looked for that which had killed him, but they did not look far, and I hid in the empty forest until they went away.

I do not remember their going. There was a burning in my chest, and this blood I breathe out ran from time to time, as it does now. I do not like the sight of it. Blood is a beautiful color, but it reminds me of too much that was beautiful also, and much redder. . . .

Then you came, *padre*. I do not know how long thereafter. I know the Shaughnessy's people brought you with their ship, to find him or his grave. You know now. And I am glad you came. It is good to have a man like you beside me at this time. I wish I had a daemon of my own, to grow very bright and vanish when I die, but that is not for *o Bobo* and I am used to that kind of loneliness.

I would not live, you see, now that the *ninfas* are gone. To be with them was good, and we comforted one another in our loneliness but, *padre,* I will tell you this much. It was a chilly comfort we gave each other, at the best. I am a man, though *bobo,* and I know. They are *ninfas,* and will never guess how warm and wonderful it must be to own a soul. I would not tell them if I could. I was sorry for the *ninfas, padre*. They are, you see, immortal.

As for me, I will forget loneliness in a little while. I will forget everything. I would not want to be a *ninfa* and live forever.

There is one behind you, *padre*. It is very bright. It watches me across your shoulder, and its eyes are wise and sad. No, daemon, this is no time for sadness. Be sorry for the *ninfas,* daemon, and for men like him who burned upon this beach. But not for me. I am well content.

I will go now.

Vintage Season

THREE PEOPLE CAME up the walk to the old mansion just at dawn on a perfect May morning. Oliver Wilson in his pajamas watched them from an upper window through a haze of conflicting emotions, resentment predominant. He didn't want them there.

They were foreigners. He knew only that much about them. They had the curious name of Sancisco, and their first names, scrawled in loops on the lease, appeared to be Omerie, Kleph and Klia, though it was impossible as he looked down upon them now to sort them out by signature. He hadn't even been sure whether they would be men or women, and he had expected something a little less cosmopolitan.

Oliver's heart sank a little as he watched them follow the taxi driver up the walk. He had hoped for less self-assurance in his unwelcome tenants, because he meant to force them out of the house if he could. It didn't look very promising from here.

The man went first. He was tall and dark, and he wore his clothes and carried his body with that peculiar arrogant assurance that comes from perfect confidence in every phase of one's being. The two women were laughing as they followed him. Their voices were light and sweet, and their faces were beautiful, each in its own exotic way, but the first thing Oliver thought of when he looked at them was, Expensive!

It was not only that patina of perfection that seemed to dwell in every line of their incredibly flawless garments. There are degrees of wealth beyond which wealth itself ceases to have significance. Oliver had seen before, on rare occasions, something like this assurance that the earth turning beneath their well-shod feet turned only to their whim.

It puzzled him a little in this case, because he had the feeling as the three came up the walk that the beautiful clothing they wore so confidently was not clothing they were accustomed to. There was a curious air of condescension in the way they moved. Like women in costume. They minced a little on their delicate high heels, held out an arm to stare at the cut of the sleeve, twisted now and then inside their garments as if the clothing sat strangely on them, as if they were accustomed to something entirely different.

And there was an elegance about the way the garments fitted them which even to Oliver looked strikingly unusual. Only an actress on the screen, who can stop time and the film to adjust every disarrayed fold so that she looks perpetually perfect, might appear thus elegantly clad. But let these women move as they liked, and each fold of their clothing followed perfectly with the movement and fell perfectly into place again. One might almost suspect the garments were not cut of ordinary cloth, or that they were cut according to some unknown, subtle scheme, with many artful hidden seams placed by a tailor incredibly skilled at his trade.

They seemed excited. They talked in high, clear, very sweet voices, looking up at the perfect blue and transparent sky in which dawn was still frankly pink. They looked at the trees on the lawn, the leaves translucently green with an under color of golden newness, the edges crimped from constriction in the recent bud.

Happily and with excitement in their voices they called to the man, and when he answered his own voice blended so perfectly in cadence with theirs that it sounded like three people singing together. Their voices, like their clothing, seemed to have an elegance far beyond the ordinary, to be under a control such as Oliver Wilson had never dreamed of before this morning.

The taxi driver brought up the luggage, which was of a beautiful pale stuff that did not look quite like leather, and had curves in it so subtle it seemed square until you saw how two or three pieces of it fitted together when carried, into a perfectly balanced block. It was scuffed, as if from much use. And though there was a great deal of it, the taxi man did not seem to find his burden heavy. Oliver saw him look down at it now and then and heft the weight incredulously.

One of the women had very black hair and skin like cream, and smoke-blue eyes heavy-lidded with the weight of her lashes. It was the other woman Oliver's gaze followed as she came up the walk. Her hair was a clear, pale red, and her face had a softness that he thought would be like velvet to touch. She was tanned to a warm amber darker than her hair.

Just as they reached the porch steps the fair woman lifted her head and looked up. She gazed straight into Oliver's eyes and he saw that hers were very blue, and just a little amused, as if she had known he was there all along. Also they were frankly admiring.

Feeling a bit dizzy, Oliver hurried back to his room to dress.

"We are here on a vacation," the dark man said, accepting the keys. "We will not wish to be disturbed, as I made clear in our correspondence. You have engaged a cook and housemaid for us, I understand? We will expect you to move your own belongings out of the house, then, and—"

"Wait," Oliver said uncomfortably. "Something's come up. I—" He hesitated, not sure just how to present it. These were such increasingly odd people. Even their speech was odd. They spoke so distinctly, not slurring any of the words into contractions. English seemed as familiar to them as a native tongue, but they all spoke as trained singers sing, with perfect breath control and voice placement.

And there was a coldness in the man's voice, as if some gulf lay between him and Oliver, so deep no feeling of human contact could bridge it.

"I wonder," Oliver said, "if I could find you better living quarters somewhere else in town. There's a place across the street that—"

The dark woman said, "Oh, no!" in a lightly horrified voice, and all three of them laughed. It was cool, distant laughter that did not include Oliver.

The dark man said, "We chose this house carefully, Mr. Wilson. We would not be interested in living anywhere else."

Oliver said desperately, "I don't see why. It isn't even a modern house. I have two others in much better condition. Even across the street you'd have a fine view of the city. Here there isn't anything. The other houses cut off the view, and—"

"We engaged rooms here, Mr. Wilson," the man said with finality. "We expect to use them. Now will you make arrangements to leave as soon as possible?"

Oliver said, "No," and looked stubborn. "That isn't in the lease. You can live here until next month, since you paid for it, but you can't put me out. I'm staying."

The man opened his mouth to say something. He looked coldly at Oliver and closed it again. The feeling of aloofness was chill between them. There was a moment's silence. Then the man said, "Very well. Be kind enough to stay out of our way."

It was a little odd that he didn't inquire into Oliver's motives. Oliver was not yet sure enough of the man to explain. He couldn't very well say, "Since the lease was signed, I've been offered three times what the house is worth if I'll sell it before the end of May." He couldn't say, "I want the money, and I'm going to use my own nuisance-value to annoy you until you're willing to move out." After all, there seemed no reason why they shouldn't. After seeing them, there seemed doubly no reason, for it was clear they must be accustomed to surroundings infinitely better than this timeworn old house.

It was very strange, the value this house had so suddenly acquired. There was no reason at all why two groups of semi-anonymous people should be so eager to possess it for the month of May.

In silence Oliver showed his tenants upstairs to the three big bedrooms across the front of the house. He was intensely conscious of the red-haired woman and the way she watched him with a sort of obviously covert interest, quite warmly, and with a curious undertone to her interest that he could not quite place. It was famil-

iar, but elusive. He thought how pleasant it would be to
talk to her alone, if only to try to capture that elusive attitude and put a name to it.

Afterward he went down to the telephone and called
his fiancée.

Sue's voice squeaked a little with excitement over the
wire.

"Oliver, so early? Why, it's hardly six yet. Did you
tell them what I said? Are they going to go?"

"Can't tell yet. I doubt it. After all, Sue, I did take
their money, you know."

"Oliver, they've got to go! You've got to do something!"

"I'm trying, Sue. But I don't like it."

"Well, there isn't any reason why they shouldn't stay
somewhere else. And we're going to need that money.
You'll just have to think of something, Oliver."

Oliver met his own worried eyes in the mirror above
the telephone and scowled at himself. His straw-colored
hair was tangled and there was a shining stubble on his
pleasant, tanned face. He was sorry the red-haired woman had first seen him in his untidy condition. Then his
conscience smote him at the sound of Sue's determined
voice and he said:

"I'll try, darling. I'll try. But I did take their money."

They had, in fact, paid a great deal of money, con-
siderably more than the rooms were worth even in that
year of high prices and high wages. The country was just
moving into one of those fabulous eras which are later
referred to as the Gay Forties or the Golden Sixties—a
pleasant period of national euphoria. It was a stimulat-
ing time to be alive—while it lasted.

"All right," Oliver said resignedly. "I'll do my best."

But he was conscious, as the next few days went by,
that he was not doing his best. There were several reasons for that. From the beginning the idea of making
himself a nuisance to his tenants had been Sue's, not
Oliver's. And if Oliver had been a little less determined
the whole project would never have got under way. Reason was on Sue's side, but—

For one thing, the tenants were so fascinating. All they said and did had a queer sort of inversion to it, as if a mirror had been held up to ordinary living and in the reflection showed strange variations from the norm. Their minds worked on a different basic premise, Oliver thought, from his own. They seemed to derive covert amusement from the most unamusing things; they patronized, they were aloof with a quality of cold detachment which did not prevent them from laughing inexplicably far too often for Oliver's comfort.

He saw them occasionally, on their way to and from their rooms. They were polite and distant, not, he suspected, from anger at his presence but from sheer indifference.

Most of the day they spent out of the house. The perfect May weather held unbroken and they seemed to give themselves up wholeheartedly to admiration of it, entirely confident that the warm, pale-gold sunshine and the scented air would not be interrupted by rain or cold. They were so sure of it that Oliver felt uneasy.

They took only one meal a day in the house, a late dinner. And their reactions to the meal were unpredictable. Laughter greeted some of the dishes, and a sort of delicate disgust others. No one would touch the salad, for instance. And the fish seemed to cause a wave of queer embarrassment around the table.

They dressed elaborately for each dinner. The man —his name was Omerie—looked extremely handsome in his dinner clothes, but he seemed a little sulky and Oliver twice heard the women laughing because he had to wear black. Oliver entertained a sudden vision, for no reason, of the man in garments as bright and as subtly cut as the women's, and it seemed somehow very right for him. He wore even the dark clothing with a certain flamboyance, as if cloth-of-gold would be more normal for him.

When they were in the house at other mealtimes, they ate in their rooms. They must have brought a great deal of food with them, from whatever mysterious place they had come. Oliver wondered with increasing curiosity where it might be. Delicious odors drifted into the hall sometimes, at odd hours, from their closed doors. Oliver could not identify them, but almost always they smelled irresistible. A few times the food smell was rather shockingly unpleasant, almost nauseating. It takes a connoisseur, Oliver reflected, to appreciate the decadent. And these people, most certainly, were connoisseurs.

Why they lived so contentedly in this huge ramshackle old house was a question that disturbed his dreams at night. Or why they refused to move. He caught some fascinating glimpses into their rooms, which appeared to have been changed almost completely by additions he could not have defined very clearly from the brief sights he had of them. The feeling of luxury which his first glance at them had evoked was confirmed by the richness of the hangings they had apparently brought with them, the half-glimpsed ornaments, the pictures on the walls, even the whiffs of exotic perfume that floated from half-open doors.

He saw the women go by him in the halls, moving softly through the brown dimness in their gowns so uncannily perfect in fit, so lushly rich, so glowingly colored they seemed unreal. That poise born of confidence in the subservience of the world gave them an imperious aloofness, but more than once Oliver, meeting the blue gaze of the woman with the red hair and the soft, tanned skin, thought he saw quickened interest there. She smiled at him in the dimness and went by in a haze of fragrance and a halo of incredible richness, and the warmth of the smile lingered after she had gone.

He knew she did not mean this aloofness to last between them. From the very first he was sure of that. When the time came she would make the opportunity to be alone with him. The thought was confusing and tremendously exciting. There was nothing he could do but wait, knowing she would see him when it suited her.

On the third day he lunched with Sue in a little downtown restaurant overlooking the great sweep of the metropolis across the river far below. Sue had shining brown curls and brown eyes, and her chin was a bit more prominent than is strictly accordant with beauty.

From childhood Sue had known what she wanted and how to get it, and it seemed to Oliver just now that she had never wanted anything quite so much as the sale of this house.

"It's such a marvelous offer for the old mausoleum," she said, breaking into a roll with a gesture of violence. "We'll never have a chance like that again, and prices are so high we'll need the money to start housekeeping. Surely you can do *something,* Oliver!"

"I'm trying," Oliver assured her uncomfortably.

"Have you heard anything more from that madwoman who wants to buy it?"

Oliver shook his head. "Her attorney phoned again yesterday. Nothing new. I wonder who she is."

"I don't think even the attorney knows. All this mystery—I don't like it, Oliver. Even those Sancisco people — What did they do today?"

Oliver laughed. "They spent about an hour this morning telephoning movie theaters in the city, checking up on a lot of third-rate films they want to see parts of."

"Parts of? But why?"

"I don't know. I think . . . oh, nothing. More coffee?"

The trouble was, he thought he did know. It was too unlikely a guess to tell Sue about, and without familiarity with the Sancisco oddities she would only think Oliver was losing his mind. But he had from their talk, a definite impression that there was an actor in bit parts in all these films whose performances they mentioned with something very near to awe. They referred to him as Golconda, which didn't appear to be his name, so that Oliver had no way of guessing which obscure bit-player it was they admired so deeply. Golconda might have been the name of a character he had once played—and with superlative skill, judging by the comments of the Sanciscos—but to Oliver he meant nothing at all.

"They do funny things," he said, stirring his coffee reflectively. "Yesterday Omerie—that's the man—came in with a book of poems published about five years ago, and all of them handled it like a first edition of Shakespeare. I never even heard of the author, but he seems to be a tin god in their country, wherever that is."

"You still don't know? Haven't they even dropped any hints?"

"We don't do much talking," Oliver reminded her with some irony.

"I know, but— Oh, well, I guess it doesn't matter. Go on, what else do they do?"

"Well, this morning they were going to spend studying 'Golconda' and his great art, and this afternoon I think they're taking a trip up the river to some sort of shrine I never heard of. It isn't very far, wherever it is, because I know they're coming back for dinner. Some great man's birthplace, I think—they promised to take home souvenirs of the place if they could get any. They're typical tourists, all right—if I could only figure out what's behind the whole thing. It doesn't make sense."

"Nothing about that house makes sense any more. I do wish—"

She went on in a petulant voice, but Oliver ceased suddenly to hear her, because just outside the door, walking with imperial elegance on her high heels, a familiar figure passed. He did not see her face, but he thought he would know that poise, that richness of line and motion, anywhere on earth.

"Excuse me a minute," he muttered to Sue, and was out of his chair before she could speak. He made the door in half a dozen long strides, and the beautifully elegant passerby was only a few steps away when he got there. Then, with the words he had meant to speak already half-uttered, he fell silent and stood there staring.

It was not the red-haired woman. It was not her dark companion. It was a stranger. He watched, speechless, while the lovely, imperious creature moved on through the crowd and vanished, moving with familiar poise and assurance and an equally familiar strangeness as if the beautiful and exquisitely fitted garments she wore were an exotic costume to her, as they had always seemed to the Sancisco women. Every other woman on the street looked untidy and ill at ease beside her. Walking like a queen, she melted into the crowd and was gone.

She came from *their* country, Oliver told himself dizzily. So someone else nearby had mysterious tenants in this month of perfect May weather. Someone else was puzzling in vain today over the strangeness of the people from the nameless land.

In silence he went back to Sue.

The door stood invitingly ajar in the brown dimness of the upper hall. Oliver's steps slowed as he drew near it, and his heart began to quicken correspondingly. It was the red-haired woman's room, and he thought the door was not open by accident. Her name, he knew now, was Kleph.

The door creaked a little on its hinges and from within a very sweet voice said lazily, "Won't you come in?"

The room looked very different indeed. The big bed had been pushed back against the wall and a cover thrown over it that brushed the floor all around looked like soft-haired fur except that it was a pale blue-green and sparkled as if every hair were tipped with invisible crystals. Three books lay open on the fur, and a very curious-looking magazine with faintly luminous printing and a page of pictures that at first glance appeared three-dimensional. Also a tiny porcelain pipe encrusted with porcelain flowers, and a thin wisp of smoke floating from the bowl.

Above the bed a broad picture hung, framing a square of blue water so real Oliver had to look twice to be sure it was not rippling gently from left to right. From the ceiling swung a crystal globe on a glass cord. It turned gently, the light from the windows making curved rectangles in its sides.

Under the center window a sort of chaise longue stood which Oliver had not seen before. He could only assume it was at least partly pneumatic and had been brought in the luggage. There was a very rich-looking quilted cloth covering and hiding it, embossed all over in shining metallic patterns.

Kleph moved slowly from the door and sank upon the chaise longue with a little sigh of content. The couch accommodated itself to her body with what looked like delightful comfort. Kleph wriggled a little and then smiled up at Oliver.

"Do come on in. Sit over there, where you can see out the window. I love your beautiful spring weather. You know, there never was a May like it in civilized times." She said that quite seriously, her blue eyes on Oliver's, and there was a hint of patronage in her voice, as if the weather had been arranged especially for her.

Oliver started across the room and then paused and looked down in amazement at the floor, which felt unstable. He had not noticed before that the carpet was pure white, unspotted, and sank about an inch under the pressure of the feet. He saw then that Kleph's feet were bare, or almost bare. She wore something like gossamer buskins of filmy net, fitting her feet exactly. The bare soles were pink as if they had been rouged, and the nails had a liquid gleam like tiny mirrors. He moved closer, and was not as surprised as he should have been to see that they really were tiny mirrors, painted with some lacquer that gave them reflecting surfaces.

"Do sit down," Kleph said again, waving a white-sleeved arm toward a chair by the window. She wore a garment that looked like short, soft down, loosely cut but following perfectly every motion she made. And there was something curiously different about her very shape today. When Oliver saw her in street clothes, she had the square-shouldered, slim-flanked figure that all women strove for, but here in her lounging robe she looked —well, different. There was an almost swanlike slope to her shoulders today, a roundness and softness to her body that looked unfamiliar and very appealing.

"Will you have some tea?" Kleph asked, and smiled charmingly.

A low table beside her held a tray and several small covered cups, lovely things with an inner glow like rose quartz, the color shining deeply as if from within layer upon layer of translucence. She took up one of the cups —there were no saucers—and offered it to Oliver.

It felt fragile and thin as paper in his hand. He could not see the contents because of the cup's cover, which seemed to be one with the cup itself and left only a thin open crescent at the rim. Steam rose from the opening.

Kleph took up a cup of her own and tilted it to her lips, smiling at Oliver over the rim. She was very beautiful. The pale red hair lay in shining loops against her head and the corona of curls like a halo above her forehead might have been pressed down like a wreath. Every hair kept order as perfectly as if it had been painted on, though the breeze from the window stirred now and then among the softly shining strands.

Oliver tried the tea. Its flavor was exquisite, very hot, and the taste that lingered upon his tongue was like the scent of flowers. It was an extremely feminine drink. He sipped again, surprised to find how much he liked it.

The scent of flowers seemed to increase as he drank, swirling through his head like smoke. After the third sip there was a faint buzzing in his ears. The bees among the flowers, perhaps, he thought incoherently—and sipped again.

Kleph watched him, smiling.

"The others will be out all afternoon," she told Oliver comfortably. "I thought it would give us a pleasant time to be acquainted."

Oliver was rather horrified to hear himself saying, "What makes you talk like that?" He had had no idea of asking the question; something seemed to have loosened his control over his own tongue.

Kleph's smile deepened. She tipped the cup to her lips and there was indulgence in her voice when she said, "What do you mean 'like that'?"

He waved his hand vaguely, noting with some surprise that at a glance it seemed to have six or seven fingers as it moved past his face.

"I don't know—precision, I guess. Why don't you say 'don't,' for instance?"

"In our country we are trained to speak with precision," Kleph explained. "Just as we are trained to move and dress and think with precision. Any slovenliness is trained out of us in childhood. With you, of course—" She was polite. "With you, this does not happen to be a national fetish. With us, we have time for the amenities. We like them."

Her voice had grown sweeter and sweeter as she spoke, until by now it was almost indistinguishable from the sweetness of the flower-scent in Oliver's head, and the delicate flavor of the tea.

"What country do you come from?" he asked, and tilted the cup again to drink, mildly surprised to notice that it seemed inexhaustible.

Kleph's smile was definitely patronizing this time. It didn't irritate him. Nothing could irritate him just now. The whole room swam in a beautiful rosy glow as fragrant as the flowers.

"We must not speak of that, Mr. Wilson."

"But—" Oliver paused. After all, it was, of course, none of his business. "This is a vacation?" he asked vaguely.

"Call it a pilgrimage, perhaps."

"Pilgrimage?" Oliver was so interested that for an instant his mind came back into sharp focus. "To—what?"

"I should not have said that, Mr. Wilson. Please forget it. Do you like the tea?"

"Very much."

"You will have guessed by now that it is not only tea, but an euphoriac."

Oliver stared. "Euphoriac?"

Kleph made a descriptive circle in the air with one graceful hand, and laughed. "You do not feel the effects yet? Surely you do?"

"I feel," Oliver said, "the way I'd feel after four whiskeys."

Kleph shuddered delicately. "We get our euphoria less painfully. And without the aftereffects your barbarous alcohols used to have." She bit her lip. "Sorry. I must be euphoric myself to speak so freely. Please forgive me. Shall we have some music?"

Kleph leaned backward on the chaise longue and reached toward the wall beside her. The sleeve, falling away from her round tanned arm, left bare the inside of the wrist, and Oliver was startled to see there a long, rosy streak of fading scar. His inhibitions had dissolved in the fumes of the fragrant tea; he caught his breath and leaned forward to stare.

Kleph shook the sleeve back over the scar with a quick gesture. Color came into her face beneath the softly tinted tan and she would not meet Oliver's eyes. A queer shame seemed to have fallen upon her.

Oliver said tactlessly, "What is it? What's the matter?"

Still she would not look at him. Much later he understood that shame and knew she had reason for it. Now he listened blankly as she said:

"Nothing . . . nothing at all. A . . . an inoculation. All of us . . . oh, never mind. Listen to the music."

This time she reached out with the other arm. She touched nothing, but when she had held her hand near the wall a sound breathed through the room. It was the sound of water, the sighing of waves receding upon long, sloped beaches. Oliver followed Kleph's gaze toward the picture of the blue water above the bed.

The waves there were moving. More than that, the point of vision moved. Slowly the seascape drifted past, moving with the waves, following them toward shore. Oliver watched, half-hypnotized by a motion that seemed at the time quite acceptable and not in the least surprising.

The waves lifted and broke in creaming foam and ran seething up a sandy beach. Then through the sound of the water music began to breathe, and through the water itself a man's face dawned in the frame, smiling intimately into the room. He held an oddly archaic musical instrument, lute-shaped, its body striped light and dark like a melon and its long neck bent back over his shoulder. He was singing, and Oliver felt mildly astonished at the song. It was very familiar and very odd indeed. He groped through the unfamiliar rhythms and found at least a thread to catch the tune by—it was "Make-Believe," from "Showboat," but certainly a showboat that had never steamed up the Mississippi.

"What's he doing to it?" he demanded after a few moments of outraged listening. "I never heard anything like it!"

Kleph laughed and stretched out her arm again. Enigmatically she said, "We call it kyling. Never mind. How do you like this?"

It was a comedian, a man in semi-clown make-up, his eyes exaggerated so that they seemed to cover half his face. He stood by a broad glass pillar before a dark curtain and sang a gay, staccato song interspersed with patter that sounded impromptu, and all the while his left hand did an intricate, musical tattoo of the nailtips on the glass of the column. He strolled around and around it as he sang. The rhythms of his fingernails blended with the song and swung widely away into patterns of their own, and blended again without a break.

It was confusing to follow. The song made even less sense than the monologue, which had something to do with a lost slipper and was full of allusions which made Kleph smile, but were utterly unintelligible to Oliver. The man had a dry, brittle style that was not very amusing, though Kleph seemed fascinated. Oliver was interested to see in him an extension and a variation of that extreme smooth confidence which marked all three of the Sanciscos. Clearly a racial trait, he thought.

Other performances followed, some of them fragmentary as if lifted out of a completer version. One he knew. The obvious, stirring melody struck his recognition before the figures—marching men against a haze, a great banner rolling backward above them in the smoke, foreground figures striding gigantically and shouting in rhythm, "Forward, forward the lily banners go!"

The music was tinny, the images blurred and poorly colored, but there was a gusto about the performance that caught at Oliver's imagination. He stared, remembering the old film from long ago. Dennis King and a ragged chorus, singing "The Song of the Vagabonds" from—was it "Vagabond King"?

"A very old one," Kleph said apologetically. "But I like it."

The steam of the intoxicating tea swirled between Oliver and the picture. Music swelled and sank through the room and the fragrant fumes and his own euphoric brain. Nothing seemed strange. He had discovered how to drink the tea. Like nitrous oxide, the effect was not cumulative. When you reached a peak of euphoria, you could not increase the peak. It was best to wait for a slight dip in the effect of the stimulant before taking more.

Otherwise it had most of the effects of alcohol—everything after awhile dissolved into a delightful fog through which all he saw was uniformly enchanting and partook of the qualities of a dream. He questioned nothing. Afterward he was not certain how much of it he really had dreamed.

There was the dancing doll, for instance. He remembered it quite clearly, in sharp focus—a tiny, slender woman with a long-nosed, dark-eyed face and a pointed chin. She moved delicately across the white rug—knee-high, exquisite. Her features were as mobile as her body, and she danced lightly, with resounding strokes of her toes, each echoing like a bell. It was a formalized sort of dance, and she sang breathlessly in accompaniment, making amusing little grimaces. Certainly it was a portrait-doll, animated to mimic the original perfectly in voice and motion. Afterward, Oliver knew he must have dreamed it.

What else happened he was quite unable to remember later. He knew Kleph had said some curious things, but they all made sense at the time, and afterward he couldn't remember a word. He knew he had been offered little glittering candies in a transparent dish, and that some of them had been delicious and one or two so bitter his tongue still curled the next day when he recalled them, and one—Kleph sucked luxuriantly on the same kind—of a taste that was actively nauseating.

As for Kleph herself—he was frantically uncertain the next day what had really happened. He thought he could remember the softness of her white-downed arms clasped at the back of his neck, while she laughed up at him and exhaled into his face the flowery fragrance of the tea. But beyond that he was totally unable to recall anything, for a while.

There was a brief interlude later, before the oblivion of sleep. He was almost sure he remembered a moment when the other two Sanciscos stood looking down at him, the man scowling, the smoky-eyed woman smiling a derisive smile.

The man said, from a vast distance, "Kleph, you know this is against every rule—" His voice began in a thin hum and soared in fantastic flight beyond the range of hearing. Oliver thought he remembered the dark woman's laughter, thin and distant too, and the hum of her voice like bees in flight.

"Kleph, Kleph, you silly little fool, can we never trust you out of sight?"

Kleph's voice then said something that seemed to make no sense. "What does it matter, *here?*"

The man answered in that buzzing, faraway hum. "The matter of giving your bond before you leave, not to interfere. You know you signed the rules—"

Kleph's voice, nearer and more intelligible: "But here the difference is . . . it does not matter *here!* You both know that. How could it matter?"

Oliver felt the downy brush of her sleeve against his cheek, but he saw nothing except the slow, smokelike ebb and flow of darkness past his eyes. He heard the voices wrangle musically from far away, and he heard them cease.

When he woke the next morning, alone in his own room, he woke with the memory of Kleph's eyes upon him very sorrowfully, her lovely tanned face looking down on him with the red hair falling fragrantly on each side of it and sadness and compassion in her eyes. He thought he had probably dreamed that. There was no reason why anyone should look at him with such sadness.

Sue telephoned that day.

"Oliver, the people who want to buy the house are here. That madwoman and her husband. Shall I bring them over?"

Oliver's mind all day had been hazy with the vague, bewildering memories of yesterday. Kleph's face kept floating before him, blotting out the room. He said, "What? I . . . oh, well, bring them if you want to. I don't see what good it'll do."

"Oliver, what's wong with you? We agreed we needed the money, didn't we? I don't see how you can think of passing up such a wonderful bargain without even a struggle. We could get married and buy our own house right away, and you know we'll never get such an offer again for that old trash-heap. Wake up, Oliver!"

Oliver made an effort. "I know, Sue—I know. But—"

"Oliver, you've got to think of something!" Her voice was imperious.

He knew she was right. Kleph or no Kleph, the bargain shouldn't be ignored if there was any way at all of getting the tenants out. He wondered again what made the place so suddenly priceless to so many people. And what the last week in May had to do with the value of the house.

A sudden sharp curiosity pierced even the vagueness of his mind today. May's last week was so important that the whole sale of the house stood or fell upon occupancy by then. Why? *Why?*

"What's going to happen next week?" he asked rhetorically of the telephone. "Why can't they wait till these people leave? I'd knock a couple of thousand off the price if they'd—"

"You would not, Oliver Wilson! I can buy all our refrigeration units with that extra money. You'll just have to work out some way to give possession by next week, and that's that. You hear me?"

"Keep your shirt on," Oliver said practically. "I'm only human, but I'll try."

"I'm bringing the people over right away," Sue told him. "While the Sanciscos are still out. Now you put your mind to work and think of something, Oliver." She paused, and her voice was reflective when she spoke again. "They're . . . awfully odd people, darling."

"Odd?"

"You'll see."

It was an elderly woman and a very young man who trailed Sue up the walk. Oliver knew immediately what had struck Sue about them. He was somehow not at all surprised to see that both wore their clothing with the familiar air of elegant self-consciousness he had come to know so well. They, too, looked around them at the beautiful, sunny afternoon with conscious enjoyment and an air of faint condescension. He knew before he heard them speak how musical their voices would be and how meticulously they would pronounce each word.

There was no doubt about it. The people of Kleph's mysterious country were arriving here in force—for something. For the last week of May? He shrugged mentally; there was no way of guessing—yet. One thing only was sure: all of them must come from that nameless land where people controlled their voices like singers and their garments like actors who could stop the reel of time itself to adjust every disordered fold.

The elderly woman took full charge of the conversation from the start. They stood together on the rickety, unpainted porch, and Sue had no chance even for introductions.

"Young man, I am Madame Hollia. This is my husband." Her voice had an underrunning current of harshness, which was perhaps age. And her face looked almost corsetted, the loose flesh coerced into something like firmness by some invisible method Oliver could not guess at. The make-up was so skillful he could not be certain it was make-up at all, but he had a definite feeling that she was much older than she looked. It would have taken a lifetime of command to put so much authority into the harsh, deep, musically controlled voice.

The young man said nothing. He was very handsome. His type, apparently, was one that does not change much no matter in what culture or country it may occur. He wore beautifully tailored garments and carried in one gloved hand a box of red leather, about the size and shape of a book.

Madame Hollia went on. "I understand your problem about the house. You wish to sell to me, but are legally bound by your lease with Omerie and his friends. Is that right?"

Oliver nodded. "But—"

"Let me finish. If Omerie can be forced to vacate before next week, you will accept our offer. Right? Very well. Hara!" She nodded to the young man beside her.

He jumped to instant attention, bowed slightly, said, "Yes, Hollia," and slipped a gloved hand into his coat.

Madame Hollia took the little object offered on his palm, her gesture as she reached for it almost imperial, as if royal robes swept from her outstretched arm.

"Here," she said, "is something that may help us. My dear—" She held it out to Sue—"if you can hide this somewhere about the house, I believe your unwelcome tenants will not trouble you much longer."

Sue took the thing curiously. It looked like a tiny silver box, no more than an inch square, indented at the top and with no line to show it could be opened.

"Wait a minute," Oliver broke in uneasily. "What is it?"

"Nothing that will harm anyone, I assure you." -

"Then what—"

Madame Hollia's imperious gesture at one sweep silenced him and commanded Sue forward. "Go on, my dear. Hurry, before Omerie comes back. I can assure you there is no danger to anyone."

Oliver broke in determinedly. "Madame Hollia, I'll have to know what your plans are. I—"

"Oh, Oliver, please!" Sue's fingers closed over the silver cube. "Don't worry about it. I'm sure Madame Hollia knows best. Don't you *want* to get those people out?"

"Of course I do. But I don't want the house blown up or—"

Madame Hollia's deep laughter was indulgent. "Nothing so crude, I promise you, Mr. Wilson. Remember, we want the house! Hurry, my dear."

Sue nodded and slipped hastily past Oliver into the hall. Outnumbered, he subsided uneasily. The young man, Hara, tapped a negligent foot and admired the sunlight as they waited. It was an afternoon as perfect as all of May had been, translucent gold, balmy with an edge of chill lingering in the air to point up a perfect contrast with the summer to come. Hara looked around him confidently, like a man paying just tribute to a stage-set provided wholly for himself. He even glanced up at a drone from above and followed the course of a big transcontinental plane half dissolved in golden haze high in the sun. "Quaint," he murmured in a gratified voice.

Sue came back and slipped her hand through Oliver's arm, squeezing excitedly. "There," she said. "How long will it take, Madame Hollia?"

"That will depend, my dear. Not very long. Now, Mr. Wilson, one word with you. You live here also, I understand? For your own comfort, take my advice and—"

Somewhere within the house a door slammed and a clear high voice rang wordlessly up a rippling scale. Then there was the sound of feet on the stairs, and a single line of song. *"Come hider, love, to me—"*

Hara started, almost dropping the red leather box he held.

"Kleph!" he said in a whisper. "Or Klia. I know they both just came on from Canterbury. But I thought—"

"Hush." Madame Hollia's features composed themselves into an imperious blank. She breathed triumphantly through her nose, drew back upon herself and turned an imposing façade to the door.

Kleph wore the same softly downy robe Oliver had seen before, except that today it was not white, but a pale, clear blue that gave her tan an apricot flush. She was smiling.

"Why, Hollia!" Her tone was at its most musical. "I thought I recognized voices from home. How nice to see you. No one knew you were coming to the—" She broke off and glanced at Oliver and then away again. "Hara, too," she said. "What a pleasant surprise."

Sue said flatly, "When did *you* get back?"

Kleph smiled at her. "You must be the little Miss Johnson. Why, I did not go out at all. I was tired of sightseeing. I have been napping in my room."

Sue drew in her breath in something that just escaped being a disbelieving sniff. A look flashed between the two women, and for an instant held—and that instant was timeless. It was an extraordinary pause in which a great deal of wordless interplay took place in the space of a second.

Oliver saw the quality of Kleph's smile at Sue, that same look of quiet confidence he had noticed so often about all of these strange people. He saw Sue's quick inventory of the other woman, and he saw how Sue squared her shoulders and stood up straight, smoothing down her summer frock over her flat hips so that for an instant she stood posed consciously, looking down on Kleph. It was deliberate. Bewildered, he glanced again at Kleph.

Kleph's shoulders sloped softly, her robe was belted to a tiny waist and hung in deep folds over frankly rounded hips. Sue's was the fashionable figure—but Sue was the first to surrender.

Kleph's smile did not falter. But in the silence there was an abrupt reversal of values, based on no more than the measureless quality of Kleph's confidence in herself, the quiet, assured smile. It was suddenly made very clear that fashion is not a constant. Kleph's curious, out-of-mode curves without warning became the norm, and Sue was a queer, angular, half-masculine creature beside her.

Oliver had no idea how it was done. Somehow the authority passed in a breath from one woman to the other. Beauty is almost wholly a matter of fashion; what is beautiful today would have been grotesque a couple of generations ago and will be grotesque a hundred years ahead. It will be worse than grotesque; it will be outmoded and therefore faintly ridiculous.

Sue was that. Kleph had only to exert her authority to make it clear to everyone on the porch. Kleph was a beauty, suddenly and very convincingly, beautiful in the accepted mode, and Sue was amusingly old-fashioned, an anachronism in her lithe, square-shouldered slimness. She did not belong. She was grotesque among these strangely immaculate people.

Sue's collapse was complete. But pride sustained her, and bewilderment. Probably she never did grasp entirely what was wrong. She gave Kleph one glance of burning resentment and when her eyes came back to Oliver there was suspicion in them, and mistrust.

Looking backward later, Oliver thought that in that moment, for the first time clearly, he began to suspect the truth. But he had no time to ponder it, for after the brief instant of enmity the three people from—elsewhere

—began to speak all at once, as if in a belated attempt to cover something they did not want noticed.

Kleph said, "This beautiful weather—" and Madame Hollia said, "So fortunate to have this house—" and Hara, holding up the red leather box, said loudest of all, "Cenbe sent you this, Kleph. His latest."

Kleph put out both hands for it eagerly, the eiderdown sleeves falling back from her rounded arms. Oliver had a quick glimpse of that mysterious scar before the sleeve fell back, and it seemed to him that there was the faintest trace of a similar scar vanishing into Hara's cuff as he let his own arm drop.

"Cenbe!" Kleph cried, her voice high and sweet and delighted. "How wonderful! What period?"

"From November 1664," Hara said. "London, of course, though I think there may be some counterpoint from the 1347 November. He hasn't finished—of course." He glanced almost nervously at Oliver and Sue. "A wonderful example," he said quickly. "Marvelous. If you have the taste for it, of course."

Madame Hollia shuddered with ponderous delicacy.

"That man!" she said. "Fascinating, of course—a great man. But—so *advanced!*"

"It takes a connoisseur to appreciate Cenbe's work fully," Kleph said in a slightly tart voice. "We all admit that."

"Oh yes, we all bow to Cenbe," Hollia conceded. "I confess the man terrifies me a little, my dear. Do we expect him to join us?"

"I suppose so," Kleph said. "If his—work—is not yet finished, then of course. You know Cenbe's tastes."

Hollia and Hara laughed together. "I know when to look for him, then," Hollia said. She glanced at the staring Oliver and the subdued but angry Sue, and with a commanding effort brought the subject back into line.

"So fortunate, my dear Kleph, to have this house," she declared heavily. "I saw a tridimensional of it—afterward—and it was still quite perfect. Such a fortunate coincidence. Would you consider parting with your lease, for a consideration? Say, a coronation seat at—"

"Nothing could buy us, Hollia," Kleph told her gaily, clasping the red box to her bosom.

Hollia gave her a cool stare. "You may change your mind, my dear Kleph," she said pontifically. "There is still time. You can always reach us through Mr. Wilson here. We have rooms up the street in the Montgomery House—nothing like yours, of course, but they will do. For us, they will do."

Oliver blinked. The Montgomery House was the most expensive hotel in town. Compared to this collapsing old ruin, it was a palace. There was no understanding these people. Their values seemed to have suffered a complete reversal.

Madame Hollia moved majestically toward the steps.

"Very pleasant to see you, my dear," she said over one well-padded shoulder. "Enjoy your stay. My regards to Omerie and Klia. Mr. Wilson—" she nodded toward the walk. "A word with you."

Oliver followed her down toward the street. Madame Hollia paused halfway there and touched his arm.

"One word of advice," she said huskily. "You say you sleep here? Move out, young man. Move out before tonight."

Oliver was searching in a half-desultory fashion for the hiding place Sue had found for the mysterious silver cube, when the first sounds from above began to drift down the stairwell toward him. Kleph had closed her door, but the house was old, and strange qualities in the noise overhead seemed to seep through the woodwork like an almost visible stain.

It was music, in a way. But much more than music. And it was a terrible sound, the sounds of calamity and of all human reaction to calamity, everything from hysteria to heartbreak, from irrational joy to rationalized acceptance.

The calamity was—single. The music did not attempt to correlate all human sorrows; it focused sharply upon one and followed the ramifications out and out. Oliver recognized these basics to the sounds in a very brief moment. They were essentials, and they seemed to beat into his brain with the first strains of the music which was so much more than music.

But when he lifted his head to listen he lost all grasp upon the meaning of the noise and it was sheer medley and confusion. To think of it was to blur it hopelessly in the mind, and he could not recapture that first instant of unreasoning acceptance.

He went upstairs almost in a daze, hardly knowing what he was doing. He pushed Kleph's door open. He looked inside—

What he saw there he could not afterward remember except in a blurring as vague as the blurred ideas the music roused in his brain. Half the room had vanished behind a mist, and the mist was a three-dimensional screen upon which were projected— He had no words for them. He was not even sure if the projections were visual. The mist was spinning wih motion and sound, but essentially it was neither sound nor motion that Oliver saw.

This was a work of art. Oliver knew no name for it. It transcended all art-forms he knew, blended them, and out of the blend produced subtleties his mind could not begin to grasp. Basically, this was the attempt of a master composer to correlate every essential aspect of a vast human experience into something that could be conveyed in a few moments to every sense at once.

The shifting visions on the screen were not pictures in themselves, but hints of pictures, subtly selected outlines that plucked at the mind and with one deft touch set whole chords ringing through the memory. Perhaps each beholder reacted differently, since it was in the eye and the mind of the beholder that the truth of the picture lay. No two would be aware of the same symphonic panorama, but each would see essentially the same terrible story unfold.

Every sense was touched by that deft and merciless genius. Color and shape and motion flickered in the screen, hinting much, evoking unbearable memories deep in the mind; odors floated from the screen and touched the heart of the beholder more poignantly than anything visual could do. The skin crawled sometimes as if to a tangible cold hand laid upon it. The tongue curled with remembered bitterness and remembered sweet.

It was outrageous. It violated the innermost privacies of a man's mind, called up secret things long ago walled off behind mental scar tissue, forced its terrible message upon the beholder relentlessly though the mind might threaten to crack beneath the stress of it.

And yet, in spite of all this vivid awareness, Oliver did not know what calamity the screen portrayed. That it was real, vast, overwhelmingly dreadful he could not doubt. That it had once happened was unmistakable. He caught flashing glimpses of human faces distorted with grief and disease and death—real faces, faces that had once lived and were seen now in the instant of dying. He saw men and women in rich clothing superimposed in panorama upon reeling thousands of ragged folk, great throngs of them swept past the sight in an instant, and he saw that death made no distinction among them.

He saw lovely women laugh and shake their curls, and the laughter shriek into hysteria and the hysteria into music. He saw one man's face, over and over—a long, dark, saturnine face, deeply lined, sorrowful, the face of a powerful man wise in worldliness, urbane—and helpless. That face was for a while a recurring motif, always more tortured, more helpless than before.

The music broke off in the midst of a rising glide. The mist vanished and the room reappeared before him. The anguished dark face for an instant seemed to Oliver printed everywhere he looked, like after-vision on the eyelids. He knew that face. He had seen it before, not often, but he should know its name—

"Oliver, Oliver—" Kleph's sweet voice came out of a fog at him. He was leaning dizzily against the doorpost looking down into her eyes. She, too, had that dazed blankness he must show on his own face. The power of the dreadful symphony still held them both. But even in this confused moment Oliver saw that Kleph had been enjoying the experience.

He felt sickened to the depths of his mind, dizzy with sickness and revulsion because of the superimposing of human miseries he had just beheld. But Kleph—only appreciation showed upon her face. To her it had been magnificence, and magnificence only.

Irrelevantly Oliver remembered the nauseating candies she had enjoyed, the nauseating odors of strange food that drifted sometimes through the hall from her room.

What was it she had said downstairs a little while ago? Connoisseur, that was it. Only a connoisseur could appreciate work as—as *advanced*—as the work of someone called Cenbe.

A whiff of intoxicating sweetness curled past Oliver's face. Something cool and smooth was pressed into his hand.

"Oh, Oliver, I am so sorry," Kleph's voice murmured contritely. "Here, drink the euphoriac and you will feel better. Please drink!"

The familiar fragrance of the hot sweet tea was on his tongue before he knew he had complied. Its relaxing fumes floated up through his brain and in a moment or two the world felt stable around him again. The room was as it had always been. And Kleph—

Her eyes were very bright. Sympathy showed in them for him, but for herself she was still brimmed with the high elation of what she had just been experiencing.

"Come and sit down," she said gently, tugging at his arm. "I am so sorry—I should not have played that over, where you could hear it. I have no excuse, really. It was only that I forgot what the effect might be on one who had never heard Cenbe's symphonies before. I was so impatient to see what he had done with . . . with his new subject. I am so very sorry, Oliver!"

"What was it?" His voice sounded steadier than he had expected. The tea was responsible for that. He sipped again, glad of the consoling euphoria its fragrance brought.

"A . . . a composite interpretation of . . . oh, Oliver, you know I must not answer questions!"

"But—"

"No—drink your tea and forget what it was you saw. Think of other things. Here, we will have music—another kind of music, something gay—"

She reached for the wall beside the window, and as before, Oliver saw the broad framed picture of blue water above the bed ripple and grow pale. Through it another scene began to dawn like shapes rising beneath the surface of the sea.

He had a glimpse of a dark-curtained stage upon which a man in a tight dark tunic and hose moved with a restless, sidelong pace, his hands and face startlingly pale against the black about him. He limped; he had a crooked back and he spoke familiar lines. Oliver had seen John Barrymore once as the crook-backed Richard, and it seemed vaguely outrageous to him that any other actor should essay that difficult part. This one he had never seen before, but the man had a fascinatingly smooth manner and his interpretation of the Plantagenet king was quite new and something Shakespeare probably never dreamed of.

"No," Kleph said, "not this. Nothing gloomy." And she put out her hand again. The nameless new Richard faded and there was a swirl of changing pictures and changing voices, all blurred together, before the scene steadied upon a stageful of dancers in pastel ballet skirts, drifting effortlessly through some complicated pattern of motion. The music that went with it was light and effortless too. The room filled up with the clear, floating melody.

Oliver set down his cup. He felt much surer of himself now, and he thought the euphoriac had done all it could for him. He didn't want to blur again mentally. There were things he meant to learn about. Now. He considered how to begin.

Kleph was watching him. "That Hollia," she said suddenly. "She wants to buy the house?"

Oliver nodded. "She's offering a lot of money. Sue's going to be awfully disappointed if—" He hesitated. Perhaps, after all, Sue would not be disappointed. He remembered the little silver cube with the enigmatic function and he wondered if he should mention it to Kleph. But the euphoriac had not reached that level of his brain, and he remembered his duty to Sue and was silent.

Kleph shook her head, her eyes upon his warm with
—was it sympathy?

"Believe me," she said, "you will not find that—important—after all. I promise you, Oliver."

He stared at her. "I wish you'd explain."

Kleph laughed on a note more sorrowful than amused. But it occurred to Oliver suddenly that there was no longer condescension in her voice. Imperceptibly that air of delicate amusement had vanished from her manner toward him. The cool detachment that still marked Omerie's attitude, and Klia's, was not in Kleph's any more. It was a subtlety he did not think she could assume. It had to come spontaneously or not at all. And for no reason he was willing to examine, it became suddenly very important to Oliver that Kleph should not condescend to him, that she should feel toward him as he felt toward her. He would not think of it.

He looked down at his cup, rose-quartz, exhaling a thin plume of steam from its crescent-slit opening. This time, he thought, maybe he could make the tea work for him. For he remembered how it loosened the tongue, and there was a great deal he needed to know. The idea that had come to him on the porch in the instant of silent rivalry between Kleph and Sue seemed now too fantastic to entertain. But some answer there must be.

Kleph herself gave him the opening.

"I must not take too much euphoriac this afternoon," she said, smiling at him over her pink cup. "It will make me drowsy, and we are going out this evening with friends."

"More friends?" Oliver asked. "From your country?"

Kleph nodded. "Very dear friends we have expected all this week."

"I wish you'd tell me," Oliver said bluntly, "where it is you come from. It isn't from here. Your culture is too different from ours—even your names—" He broke off as Kleph shook her head.

"I wish I could tell you. But that is against all the rules. It is even against the rules for me to be here talking to you now."

"What rules?"

She made a helpless gesture. "You must not ask me, Oliver." She leaned back on the chaise longue, which adjusted itself luxuriously to the motion, and smiled very sweetly at him. "We must not talk about things like that. Forget it, listen to the music, enjoy yourself if you can—" She closed her eyes and laid her head back against the cushions. Oliver saw the round tanned throat swell as she began to hum a tune. Eyes still closed, she sang again the words she had sung upon the stairs. *"Come hider, love, to me—"*

A memory clicked over suddenly in Oliver's mind. He had never heard the queer, lagging tune before, but he thought he knew the words. He remembered what Hollia's husband had said when he heard that line of song, and he leaned forward. She would not answer a direct question, but perhaps—

"Was the weather this warm in Canterbury?" he asked, and held his breath. Kleph hummed another line of the song and shook her head, eyes still closed.

"It was autumn there," she said. "But bright, wonderfully bright. Even their clothing, you know . . . everyone was singing that new song, and I can't get it out of my head." She sang another line, and the words were almost unintelligible—English, yet not an English Oliver could understand.

He stood up. "Wait," he said. "I want to find something. Back in a minute."

She opened her eyes and smiled mistily at him, still humming. He went downstairs as fast as he could—the stairway swayed a little, though his head was nearly clear now—and into the library. The book he wanted was old and battered, interlined with the penciled notes of his college days. He did not remember very clearly where the passage he wanted was, but he thumbed fast through the columns and by sheer luck found it within a few minutes. Then he went back upstairs, feeling a strange emptiness in his stomach because of what he almost believed now.

"Kleph," he said firmly, "I know that song. I know the year it was new."

Her lids rose slowly; she looked at him through a mist

of euphoriac. He was not sure she had understood. For a long moment she held him with her gaze. Then she put out one downy-sleeved arm and spread her tanned fingers toward him. She laughed deep in her throat.

"Come hider, love, to me," she said.

He crossed the room slowly, took her hand. The fingers closed warmly about his. She pulled him down so that he had to kneel beside her. Her other arm lifted. Again she laughed, very softly, and closed her eyes, lifting her face to his.

The kiss was warm and long. He caught something of her own euphoria from the fragrance of the tea breathed into his face. And he was startled at the end of the kiss, when the clasp of her arms loosened about his neck, to feel the sudden rush of her breath against his cheek. There were tears on her face, and the sound she made was a sob.

He held her off and looked down in amazement. She sobbed once more, caught a deep breath, and said, "Oh, Oliver, Oliver—" Then she shook her head and pulled free, turning away to hide her face. "I . . . I am sorry," she said unevenly. "Please forgive me. It does not matter . . . I *know* it does not matter . . . but—"

"What's wrong? What doesn't matter?"

"Nothing. Nothing . . . please forget it. Nothing at all." She got a handkerchief from the table and blew her nose, smiling at him with an effect of radiance through the tears.

Suddenly he was very angry. He had heard enough evasions and mystifying half-truths. He said roughly, "Do you think I'm crazy? I know enough now to—"

"Oliver, please!" She held up her own cup, steaming fragrantly. "Please, no more questions. Here, euphoria is what you need, Oliver. Euphoria, not answers."

"What year was it when you heard that song in Canterbury?" he demanded, pushing the cup aside.

She blinked at him, tears bright on her lashes. "Why . . . what year do you think?"

"I know," Oliver told her grimly. "I know the year that song was popular. I know you just came from Canterbury—Hollia's husband said so. It's May now, but it was autumn in Canterbury, and you just came from there, so lately the song you heard is still running through your head. Chaucer's Pardoner sang that song some time around the end of the fourteenth century. Did you see Chaucer, Kleph? What was it like in England that long ago?"

Kleph's eyes fixed his for a silent moment. Then her shoulders drooped and her whole body went limp with resignation beneath the soft blue robe. "I am a fool," she said gently. "It must have been easy to trap me. You really believe—what you say?"

Oliver nodded.

She said in a low voice. "Few people do believe it. That is one of our maxims, when we travel. We are safe from much suspicion because people before The Travel began will not believe."

The emptiness in Oliver's stomach suddenly doubled in volume. For an instant the bottom dropped out of time itself and the universe was unsteady about him. He felt sick. He felt naked and helpless. There was a buzzing in his ears and the room dimmed before him.

He had not really believed—not until this instant. He had expected some rational explanation from her that would tidy all his wild half-thoughts and suspicions into something a man could accept as believable. Not this.

Kleph dabbed at her eyes with the pale-blue handkerchief and smiled tremulously.

"I know," she said. "It must be a terrible thing to accept. To have all your concepts turned upside down— We know it from childhood, of course, but for you . . . here, Oliver. The euphoriac will make it easier."

He took the cup, the faint stain of her lip rouge still on the crescent opening. He drank, feeling the dizzy sweetness spiral through his head, and his brain turned a little in his skull as the volatile fragrance took effect. With that turning, focus shifted and all his values with it.

He began to feel better. The flesh settled on his bones again, and the warm clothing of temporal assurance settled upon his flesh, and he was no longer naked and in the vortex of unstable time.

"The story is very simple, really," Kleph said. "We —travel. Our own time is not terribly far ahead of yours. No. I must not say how far. But we still remember your songs and poets and some of your great actors. We are a people of much leisure, and we cultivate the art of enjoying ourselves.

"This is a tour we are making—a tour of a year's seasons. Vintage seasons. That autumn in Canterbury was the most magnificent autumn our researchers could discover anywhere. We rode in a pilgrimage to the shrine —it was a wonderful experience, though the clothing was a little hard to manage.

"Now this month of May is almost over—the loveliest May in recorded times. A perfect May in a wonderful period. You have no way of knowing what a good, gay period you live in, Oliver. The very feeling in the air of the cities—that wonderful national confidence and happiness—everything going as smoothly as a dream. There were other Mays with fine weather, but each of them had a war or a famine, or something else wrong." She hesitated, grimaced and went on rapidly. "In a few days we are to meet at a coronation in Rome," she said. "I think the year will be 800—Christmastime. We—"

"But why," Oliver interrupted, "did you insist on this house? Why do the others want to get it away from you?"

Kleph stared at him. He saw the tears rising again in small bright crescents that gathered above her lower lids. He saw the look of obstinacy that came upon her soft, tanned face. She shook her head.

"You must not ask me that." She held out the steaming cup. "Here, drink and forget what I have said. I can tell you no more. No more at all."

When he woke, for a little while he had no idea where he was. He did not remember leaving Kleph or coming to his own room. He didn't care, just then. For he woke to a sense of overwhelming terror.

The dark was full of it. His brain rocked on waves of fear and pain. He lay motionless, too frightened to stir, some atavistic memory warning him to lie quiet until he knew from which direction the danger threatened. Reasonless panic broke over him in a tidal flow; his head ached with its violence and the dark throbbed to the same rhythms.

A knock sounded at the door. Omerie's deep voice said, "Wilson! Wilson, are you awake?"

Oliver tried twice before he had breath to answer. "Y-yes—what is it?"

The knob rattled. Omerie's dim figure groped for the light switch and the room sprang into visibility. Omerie's face was drawn with strain, and he held one hand to his head as if it ached in rhythm with Oliver's.

It was in that moment, before Omerie spoke again, that Oliver remembered Hollia's warning. "Move out, young man—move out before tonight." Wildly he wondered what threatened them all in this dark house that throbbed with the rhythms of pure terror.

Omerie in an angry voice answered the unspoken question.

"Someone has planted a subsonic in the house, Wilson. Kleph thinks you may know where it is."

"S-subsonic?"

"Call it a gadget," Omerie interpreted impatiently. "Probably a small metal box that—"

Oliver said, "Oh," in a tone that must have told Omerie everything.

"Where is it?" he demanded. "Quick. Let's get this over."

"I don't know." With an effort Oliver controlled the chattering of his teeth. "Y-you mean all this—all this is just from the little box?"

"Of course. Now tell me how to find it before we all go crazy."

Oliver got shakily out of bed, groping for his robe with nerveless hands. "I s-suppose she hid it somewhere downstairs," he said. "S-she wasn't gone long."

Omerie got the story out of him in a few brief questions. He clicked his teeth in exasperation when Oliver had finished it.

"That stupid Hollia—"

"Omerie!" Kleph's plaintive voice wailed from the

hall. "Please hurry, Omerie! This is too much to stand! Oh, Omerie, please!"

Oliver stood up abruptly. Then a redoubled wave of the inexplicable pain seemed to explode in his skull at the motion, and he clutched the bedpost and reeled.

"Go find the thing yourself," he heard himself saying dizzily. "I can't even walk—"

Omerie's own temper was drawn wire-tight by the pressure in the room. He seized Oliver's shoulder and shook him, saying in a tight voice, "You let it in—now help us get it out, or—"

"It's a gadget out of your world, not mine!" Oliver said furiously.

And then it seemed to him there was a sudden coldness and silence in the room. Even the pain and the senseless terror paused for a moment. Omerie's pale, cold eyes fixed upon Oliver a stare so chill he could almost feel the ice in it.

"What do you know about our—world?" Omerie demanded.

Oliver did not speak a word. He did not need to; his face must have betrayed what he knew. He was beyond concealment in the stress of this nighttime terror he still could not understand.

Omerie bared his white teeth and said three perfectly unintelligible words. Then he stepped to the door and snapped, "Kleph!"

Oliver could see the two women huddled together in the hall, shaking violently with involuntary waves of that strange, synthetic terror. Klia, in a luminous green gown, was rigid with control, but Kleph made no effort whatever at repression. Her downy robe had turned soft gold tonight; she shivered in it and the tears ran down her face unchecked.

"Kleph," Omerie said in a dangerous voice, "you were euphoric again yesterday?"

Kleph darted a scared glance at Oliver and nodded guiltily.

"You talked too much." It was a complete indictment in one sentence. "You know the rules, Kleph. You will not be allowed to travel again if anyone reports this to the authorities."

Kleph's lovely creamy face creased suddenly into impenitent dimples.

"I know it was wrong. I am very sorry—but you will not stop me if Cenbe says no."

Klia flung out her arms in a gesture of helpless anger. Omerie shrugged. "In this case, as it happens, no great harm is done," he said, giving Oliver an unfathomable glance. "But it might have been serious. Next time perhaps it will be. I must have a talk with Cenbe."

"We must find the subsonic first of all," Klia reminded them, shivering. "If Kleph is afraid to help, she can go out for a while. I confess I am very sick of Kleph's company just now."

"We could give up the house!" Kleph cried wildly. "Let Hollia have it! How can you stand this long enough to hunt—"

"Give up the house?" Klia echoed. "You must be mad! With all our invitations out?"

"There will be no need for that," Omerie said. "We can find it if we all hunt. You feel able to help?" He looked at Oliver.

With an effort Oliver controlled his own senseless panic as the waves of it swept through the room. "Yes," he said. "But what about me? What are you going to do?"

"That should be obvious," Omerie said, his pale eyes in the dark face regarding Oliver impassively. "Keep you in the house until we go. We can certainly do no less. You understand that. And there is no reason for us to do more, as it happens. Silence is all we promised when we signed our travel papers."

"But—" Oliver groped for the fallacy in that reasoning. It was no use. He could not think clearly. Panic surged insanely through his mind from the very air around him. "All right," he said. "Let's hunt."

It was dawn before they found the box, tucked inside the ripped seam of a sofa cushion. Omerie took it upstairs without a word. Five minutes later the pressure in the air abruptly dropped and peace fell blissfully upon the house.

"They will try again," Omerie said to Oliver at the door of the back bedroom. "We must watch for that. As for you, I must see that you remain in the house until Friday. For your own comfort, I advise you to let me know if Hollia offers any further tricks. I confess I am not quite sure how to enforce your staying indoors. I could use methods that would make you very uncomfortable. I would prefer to accept your word on it."

Oliver hesitated. The relaxing of pressure upon his brain had left him exhausted and stupid, and he was not at all sure what to say.

Omerie went on after a moment. "It was partly our fault for not insuring that we had the house to ourselves," he said. "Living here with us, you could scarcely help suspecting. Shall we say that in return for your promise, I reimburse you in part for losing the sale price on this house?"

Oliver thought that over. It would pacify Sue a little. And it meant only two days indoors. Besides, what good would escaping do? What could he say to outsiders that would not lead him straight to a padded cell?

"All right," he said wearily. "I promise."

By Friday morning there was still no sign from Hollia. Sue telephoned at noon. Oliver knew the crackle of her voice over the wire when Kleph took the call. Even the crackle sounded hysterical; Sue saw her bargain slipping hopelessly through her grasping little fingers.

Kleph's voice was soothing. "I am sorry," she said many times, in the intervals when the voice paused. "I am truly sorry. Believe me, you will find it does not matter. I know . . . I am sorry—"

She turned from the phone at last. "The girl says Hollia has given up," she told the others.

"Not Hollia," Klia said firmly.

Omerie shrugged. "We have very little time left. If she intends anything more, it will be tonight. We must watch for it."

"Oh, not tonight!" Kleph's voice was horrified. "Not even Hollia would do that!"

"Hollia, my dear, in her own way is quite as unscrupulous as you are," Omerie told her with a smile.

"But—would she spoil things for us just because she can't be here?"

"What do you think?" Klia demanded.

Oliver ceased to listen. There was no making sense out of their talk, but he knew that by tonight whatever the secret was must surely come into the open at last. He was willing to wait and see.

For two days excitement had been building up in the house and the three who shared it with him. Even the servants felt it and were nervous and unsure of themselves. Oliver had given up asking questions—it only embarrassed his tenants—and watched.

All the chairs in the house were collected in the three front bedrooms. The furniture was rearranged to make room for them, and dozens of covered cups had been set out on trays. Oliver recognized Kleph's rose-quartz set among the rest. No steam rose from the thin crescent-openings, but the cups were full. Oliver lifted one and felt a heavy liquid move within it, like something half-solid, sluggishly.

Guests were obviously expected, but the regular dinner hour of nine came and went, and no one had yet arrived. Dinner was finished; the servants went home. The Sanciscos went to their rooms to dress, amid a feeling of mounting tension.

Oliver stepped out on the porch after dinner, trying in vain to guess what it was that had wrought such a pitch of expectancy in the house. There was a quarter moon swimming in haze on the horizon, but the stars which had made every night of May thus far a dazzling translucency, were very dim tonight. Clouds had begun to gather at sundown, and the undimmed weather of the whole month seemed ready to break at last.

Behind Oliver the door opened a little, and closed. He caught Kleph's fragrance before he turned, and a faint whiff of the fragrance of the euphoriac she was much too fond of drinking. She came to his side and slipped a hand into his, looking up into his face in the darkness.

"Oliver," she said very softly. "Promise me one thing. Promise me not to leave the house tonight."

"I've already promised that," he said a little irritably.

"I know. But tonight—I have a very particular reason for wanting you indoors tonight." She leaned her head against his shoulder for a moment, and despite himself his irritation softened. He had not seen Kleph alone since that last night of her revelations; he supposed he never would be alone with her again for more than a few minutes at a time. But he knew he would not forget those two bewildering evenings. He knew too, now, that she was very weak and foolish—but she was still Kleph and he had held her in his arms, and was not likely ever to forget it.

"You might be—hurt—if you went out tonight," she was saying in a muffled voice. "I know it will not matter, in the end, but—remember you promised, Oliver."

She was gone again, and the door had closed behind her, before he could voice the futile questions in his mind.

The guests began to arrive just before midnight. From the head of the stairs Oliver saw them coming in by twos and threes, and was astonished at how many of these people from the future must have gathered here in the past weeks. He could see quite clearly now how they differed from the norm of his own period. Their physical elegance was what one noticed first—perfect grooming, meticulous manners, meticulously controlled voices. But because they were all idle, all, in a way, sensation-hunters, there was a certain shrillness underlying their voices, especially when heard all together. Petulance and self-indulgence showed beneath the good manners. And tonight, an all-pervasive excitement.

By one o'clock everyone had gathered in the front rooms. The teacups had begun to steam, apparently of themselves, around midnight, and the house was full of the faint, thin fragrance that induced a sort of euphoria all through the rooms, breathed in with the perfume of the tea.

It made Oliver feel light and drowsy. He was determined to sit up as long as the others did, but he must have dozed off in his own room, by the window, an unopened book in his lap.

For when it happened he was not sure for a few minutes whether or not it was a dream.

The vast, incredible crash was louder than sound. He felt the whole house shake under him, felt rather than heard the timbers grind upon one another like broken bones, while he was still in the borderland of sleep. When he woke fully he was on the floor among the shattered fragments of the window.

How long or short a time he had lain there he did not know. The world was still stunned with that tremendous noise, or his ears still deaf from it, for there was no sound anywhere.

He was halfway down the hall toward the front rooms when sound began to return from outside. It was a low, indescribable rumble at first, prickled with countless tiny distant screams. Oliver's eardrums ached from the terrible impact of the vast unheard noise, but the numbness was wearing off and he heard before he saw it the first voices of the stricken city.

The door to Kleph's room resisted him for a moment. The house had settled a little from the violence of the —the explosion?—and the frame was out of line. When he got the door open he could only stand blinking stupidly into the darkness within. All the lights were out, but there was a breathless sort of whispering going on in many voices.

The chairs were drawn around the broad front windows so that everyone could see out; the air swam with the fragrance of euphoria. There was light enough here from outside for Oliver to see that a few onlookers still had their hands to their ears, but all were craning eagerly forward to see.

Through a dreamlike haze Oliver saw the city spread out with impossible distinctness below the window. He knew quite well that a row of houses across the street blocked the view—yet he was looking over the city now, and he could see it in a limitless panorama from here to the horizon. The houses between had vanished.

On the far skyline fire was already a solid mass, painting the low clouds crimson. That sulphurous light reflecting back from the sky upon the city made clear the rows upon rows of flattened houses with flame beginning to lick up among them, and farther out the formless rubble of what had been houses a few minutes ago and was now nothing at all.

The city had begun to be vocal. The noise of the flames rose loudest, but you could hear a rumble of human voices like the beat of surf a long way off, and staccato noises of screaming made a sort of pattern that came and went continuously through the web of sound. Threading it in undulating waves the shrieks of sirens knit the web together into a terrible symphony that had, in its way, a strange, inhuman beauty.

Briefly through Oliver's stunned incredulity went the memory of that other symphony Kleph had played there one day, another catastrophe retold in terms of music and moving shapes.

He said hoarsely, "Kleph—"

The tableau by the window broke. Every head turned, and Oliver saw the faces of strangers staring at him, some few in embarrassment avoiding his eyes, but most seeking them out with that avid, inhuman curiosity which is common to a type in all crowds at accident scenes. But these people were here by design, audience at a vast disaster timed almost for their coming.

Kleph got up unsteadily, her velvet dinner gown tripping her as she rose. She set down a cup and swayed a little as she came toward the door, saying, "Oliver . . . Oliver—" in a sweet, uncertain voice. She was drunk, he saw, and wrought up by the catastrophe to a pitch of stimulation in which she was not very sure what she was doing.

Oliver heard himself saying in a thin voice not his own, "W-what was it, Kleph? What happened? What—" But *happened* seemed so inadequate a word for the incredible panorama below that he had to choke back hysterical laughter upon the struggling questions, and broke off entirely, trying to control the shaking that had seized his body.

Kleph made an unsteady stoop and seized a steaming cup. She came to him, swaying, holding it out—her panacea for all ills.

"Here, drink it, Oliver—we are all quite safe here, quite safe." She thrust the cup to his lips and he gulped automatically, grateful for the fumes that began their slow, coiling surcease in his brain with the first swallow.

"It was a meteor," Kleph was saying. "Quite a small meteor, really. We are perfectly safe here. This house was never touched."

Out of some cell of the unconscious Oliver heard himself saying incoherently, "Sue? Is Sue—" he could not finish.

Kleph thrust the cup at him again. "I think she may be safe—for awhile. Please, Oliver—forget about all that and drink."

"But you *knew!*" Realization of that came belatedly to his stunned brain. "You could have given warning, or—"

"How could we change the past?" Kleph asked. "We knew—but could we stop the meteor? Or warn the city? Before we come we must give our word never to interfere—"

Their voices had risen imperceptibly to be audible above the rising volume of sound from below. The city was roaring now, with flames and cries and the crash of falling buildings. Light in the room turned lurid and pulsed upon the walls and ceiling in red light and redder dark.

Downstairs a door slammed. Someone laughed. It was high, hoarse, angry laughter. Then from the crowd in the room someone gasped and there was a chorus of dismayed cries. Oliver tried to focus upon the window and the terrible panorama beyond, and found he could not.

It took several seconds of determined blinking to prove that more than his own vision was at fault. Kleph whimpered softly and moved against him. His arms closed about her automatically, and he was grateful for the warm, solid flesh against him. This much at least he could touch and be sure of, though everything else that was happening might be a dream. Her perfume and the heady perfume of the tea rose together in his head, and for an instant, holding her in this embrace that must certainly be the last time he ever held her, he did not care that something had gone terribly wrong with the very air of the room.

It was blindness—not continuous, but a series of swift, widening ripples between which he could catch glimpses of the other faces in the room, strained and astonished in the flickering light from the city.

The ripples came faster. There was only a blink of sight between them now, and the blinks grew briefer and briefer, the intervals of darkness more broad.

From downstairs the laughter rose again up the stairwell. Oliver thought he knew the voice. He opened his mouth to speak, but a door nearby slammed open before he could find his tongue, and Omerie shouted down the stairs.

"Hollia?" he roared above the roaring of the city. "Hollia, is that you?"

She laughed again, triumphantly. "I warned you!" her hoarse, harsh voice called. "Now come out in the street with the rest of us if you want to see any more!"

"Hollia!" Omerie shouted desperately. "Stop this or—"

The laughter was derisive. "What will you do, Omerie? This time I hid it too well—come down in the street if you want to watch the rest."

There was angry silence in the house. Oliver could feel Kleph's quick, excited breathing light upon his cheek, feel the soft motions of her body in his arms. He tried consciously to make the moment last, stretch it out to infinity. Everything had happened too swiftly to impress very clearly on his mind anything except what he could touch and hold. He held her in an embrace made consciously light, though he wanted to clasp her in a tight, despairing grip, because he was sure this was the last embrace they would ever share.

The eye-straining blinks of light and blindness went on. From far away below the roar of the burning city rolled on, threaded together by the long, looped cadences of the sirens that linked all sounds into one.

Then in the bewildering dark another voice sounded from the hall downstairs. A man's voice, very deep, very melodious, saying:

"What is this? What are you doing here? Hollia—is that you?"

Oliver felt Kleph stiffen in his arms. She caught her breath, but she said nothing in the instant while heavy feet began to mount the stairs, coming up with a solid, confident tread that shook the old house to each step.

Then Kleph thrust herself hard out of Oliver's arms. He heard her high, sweet, excited voice crying, "Cenbe! Cenbe!" and she ran to meet the newcomer through the waves of dark and light that swept the shaken house.

Oliver staggered a little and felt a chair seat catching the back of his legs. He sank into it and lifted to his lips the cup he still held. Its steam was warm and moist in his face, though he could scarcely make out the shape of the rim.

He lifted it with both hands and drank.

When he opened his eyes it was quite dark in the room. Also it was silent except for a thin, melodious humming almost below the threshold of sound. Oliver struggled with the memory of a monstrous nightmare. He put it resolutely out of his mind and sat up, feeling an unfamiliar bed creak and sway under him.

This was Kleph's room. But no—Kleph's no longer. Her shining hangings were gone from the walls, her white resilient rug, her pictures. The room looked as it had looked before she came, except for one thing.

In the far corner was a table—a block of translucent stuff—out of which light poured softly. A man sat on a low stool before it, leaning forward, his heavy shoulders outlined against the glow. He wore earphones and he was making quick, erratic notes upon a pad on his knee, swaying a little as if to the tune of unheard music.

The curtains were drawn, but from beyond them came a distant, muffled roaring that Oliver remembered from his nightmare. He put a hand to his face, aware of a feverish warmth and a dipping of the room before his eyes. His head ached, and there was a deep malaise in every limb and nerve.

As the bed creaked, the man in the corner turned, sliding the earphones down like a collar. He had a strong, sensitive face above a dark beard, trimmed short. Oliver had never seen him before, but he had that air Oliver knew so well by now, of remoteness which was the knowledge of time itself lying like a gulf between them.

When he spoke his deep voice was impersonally kind.

"You had too much euphoriac, Wilson," he said, aloofly sympathetic. "You slept a long while."

"How long?" Oliver's throat felt sticky when he spoke.

The man did not answer. Oliver shook his head experimentally. He said, "I thought Kleph said you don't get hangovers from—" Then another thought interrupted the first, and he said quickly, "Where is Kleph?" He looked confusedly toward the door.

"They should be in Rome by now. Watching Charlemagne's coronation at St. Peter's on Christmas Day a thousand years from here."

That was not a thought Oliver could grasp clearly. His aching brain sheered away from it; he found thinking at all was strangely difficult. Staring at the man, he traced an idea painfully to its conclusion.

"So they've gone on—but you stayed behind? Why? You . . . you're Cenbe? I heard your—symphonia, Kleph called it."

"You heard part of it. I have not finished yet. I needed—this." Cenbe inclined his head toward the curtains beyond which the subdued roaring still went on.

"You needed—the meteor?" The knowledge worked painfully through his dulled brain until it seemed to strike some area still untouched by the aching, an area still alive to implication. "The *meteor?* But—"

There was a power implicit in Cenbe's raised hand that seemed to push Oliver down upon the bed again. Cenbe said patiently, "The worst of it is past now, for a while. Forget if you can. That was days ago. I said you were asleep for some time. I let you rest. I knew this house would be safe—from the fire at least."

"Then—something more's to come?" Oliver only mumbled his question. He was not sure he wanted an answer. He had been curious so long, and now that knowledge lay almost within reach, something about his brain seemed to refuse to listen. Perhaps this weariness, this feverish, dizzy feeling would pass as the effect of the euphoriac wore off.

Cenbe's voice ran on smoothly, soothingly, almost as if Cenbe, too, did not want him to think. It was easiest to lie here and listen.

"I am a composer," Cenbe was saying. "I happen to be interested in interpreting certain forms of disaster into my own terms. That is why I stayed on. The others were dilettantes. They came for the May weather and the spectacle. The aftermath—well why should they wait for that? As for myself— I suppose I am a connoisseur. I find the aftermath rather fascinating. And I need it. I need to study it at first hand, for my own purposes."

His eyes dwelt upon Oliver for an instant very keenly, like a physician's eyes, impersonal and observing. Absently he reached for his stylus and the note pad. And as he moved, Oliver saw a familiar mark on the underside of the thick, tanned wrist.

"Kleph had that scar, too," he heard himself whisper. "And the others."

Cenbe nodded. "Inoculation. It was necessary, under the circumstances. We did not want disease to spread in our own time-world."

"Disease?"

Cenbe shrugged. "You would not recognize the name."

"But, if you can inoculate against disease—" Oliver thrust himself up on an aching arm. He had a half-grasp upon a thought now which he did not want to let go. Effort seemed to make the ideas come more clearly through his mounting confusion. With enormous effort he went on.

"I'm getting it now," he said. "Wait. I've been trying to work this out. You can change history? You can! I know you can. Kleph said she had to promise not to interfere. You all had to promise. Does that mean you really could change your own past—our time?"

Cenbe laid down his pad again. He looked at Oliver thoughtfully, a dark, intent look under heavy brows. "Yes," he said. "Yes, the past can be changed, but not easily. And it changes the future, too, necessarily. The lines of probability are switched into new patterns—but it is extremely difficult, and it has never been allowed. The physio-temporal course tends to slide back to its norm, always. That is why it is so hard to force any alteration." He shrugged. "A theoretical science. We do not change history, Wilson. If we changed our past, our present would be altered, too. And our time-world is entirely to our liking. There may be a few malcontents there, but they are not allowed the privilege of temporal travel."

Oliver spoke louder against the roaring from beyond the windows. "But you've got the power! You could alter history, if you wanted to—wipe out all the pain and suffering and tragedy—"

"All of that passed away long ago," Cenbe said.

"Not—*now!* Not—*this!*"

Cenbe looked at him enigmatically for a while. Then —"This, too," he said.

And suddenly Oliver realized from across what distances Cenbe was watching him. A vast distance, as time is measured. Cenbe was a composer and a genius, and necessarily strongly empathic, but his psychic locus was very far away in time. The dying city outside, the whole world of *now* was not quite real to Cenbe, falling short of reality because of that basic variance in time. It was merely one of the building blocks that had gone to support the edifice on which Cenbe's culture stood in a misty, unknown, terrible future.

It seemed terrible to Oliver now. Even Kleph—all of them had been touched with a pettiness, the faculty that had enabled Hollia to concentrate on her malicious, small schemes to acquire a ringside seat while the meteor thundered in toward Earth's atmosphere. They were all dilettantes, Kleph and Omerie and the other. They toured time, but only as onlookers. Were they bored—sated—with their normal existence?

Not sated enough to wish change, basically. Their own time-world was a fulfilled womb, a perfection made manifest for their needs. They dared not change the past —they could not risk flawing their own present.

Revulsion shook him. Remembering the touch of Kleph's lips, he felt a sour sickness on his tongue. Alluring she had been; he knew that too well. But the aftermath—

There was something about this race from the future. He had felt it dimly at first, before Kleph's nearness had drowned caution and buffered his sensibilities. Time traveling purely as an escape mechanism seemed almost blasphemous. A race with such power—

Kleph—leaving him for the barbaric, splendid coronation at Rome a thousand years ago—*how had she seen him?* Not as a living, breathing man. He knew that, very certainly. Kleph's race were spectators.

But he read more than casual interest in Cenbe's eyes now. There was an avidity there, a bright, fascinated probing. The man had replaced his earphones—he was different from the others. He was a connoisseur. After the vintage season came the aftermath—and Cenbe.

Cenbe watched and waited, light flickering softly in the translucent block before him, his fingers poised over the note pad. The ultimate connoisseur waited to savor the rarities that no non-gourmet could appreciate.

Those thin, distant rhythms of sound that was almost music began to be audible again above the noises of the distant fire. Listening, remembering, Oliver could very nearly catch the pattern of the symphonia as he had heard it, all intermingled with the flash of changing faces and the rank upon rank of the dying—

He lay back on the bed letting the room swirl away into the darkness behind his closed and aching lids. The ache was implicit in every cell of his body, almost a second ego taking possession and driving him out of himself, a strong, sure ego taking over as he himself let go.

Why, he wondered dully, should Kleph have lied? She had said there was no aftermath to the drink she had given him. No aftermath—and yet this painful possession was strong enough to edge him out of his own body.

Kleph had not lied. It was no aftermath to drink. He knew that—but the knowledge no longer touched his brain or his body. He lay still, giving them up to the power of the illness which was aftermath to something far stronger than the strongest drink. The illness that had no name—yet.

Cenbe's new symphonia was a crowning triumph. It had its premiere from Antares Hall, and the applause was an ovation. History itself, of course, was the artist —opening with the meteor that forecast the great plagues of the fourteenth century and closing with the climax Cenbe had caught on the threshold of modern times. But only Cenbe could have interpreted it with such subtle power.

Critics spoke of the masterly way in which he had chosen the face of the Stuart king as a recurrent motif against the montage of emotion and sound and movement. But there were other faces, fading through the great sweep of the composition, which helped to build up to the tremendous climax. One face in particular, one moment that the audience absorbed greedily. A moment in which one man's face loomed huge in the screen, every feature clear. Cenbe had never caught an emotional crisis so effectively, the critics agreed. You could almost read the man's eyes.

After Cenbe had left, he lay motionless for a long while. He was thinking feverishly—

I've got to find some way to tell people. If I'd known in advance, maybe something could have been done. We'd have forced them to tell us how to change the probabilities. We could have evacuated the city.

If I could leave a message—

Maybe not for today's people. But later. They visit all through time. If they could be recognized and caught somewhere, sometime, and made to change destiny—

It wasn't easy to stand up. The room kept tilting. But he managed it. He found pencil and paper and through the swaying of the shadows he wrote down what he could. Enough. Enough to warn, enough to save.

He put the sheets on the table, in plain sight, and weighted them down before he stumbled back to bed through closing darkness.

The house was dynamited six days later, part of the futile attempt to halt the relentless spread of the Blue Death.

Footnote to *Shambleau* . . . and Others

One question is almost certainly asked of every professional writer more than any other: "Where do you get your ideas?" For the past forty-odd years I have had to admit I didn't know. But the answer has suddenly come to me as I look back over the origins of my first story, "Shambleau," and I am very happy indeed to pass it on to you.

Brace yourself now for some rather dull but necessary background: My name was Catherine Moore and I lived in a large midwestern city and the Depression of the 1930s was rampant over the land. So I was snatched from my sophomore year at the state university and crammed into a business school to learn the rudiments of shorthand and typing. By incredible good fortune, before I'd finished the course, a job opening in a large bank loomed up and I leaped at it, unprepared but eager. (In those days you didn't mess around. You bluffed, prayed, and grabbed.)

Well, I was adequate, but typing was something practiced in every spare moment. And this is where "Shambleau" began, halfway down a sheet of yellow paper otherwise filled up with boring quick-brown-foxes, alphabets, and things like "The White Knight is sliding down the poker. He balances very badly," to lighten the practice.

Midway down that yellow page I began fragments remembered from sophomore English at the university. All the choices were made at random. Keats, Browning, Byron—you name it. In the middle of this exercise a line from a poem (by William Morris?) worked itself to the front and I discovered myself typing something about a "red, running figure." I looked at it a while, my mind a perfect blank, and then shifted mental gears without even adding punctuation to mark the spot, swinging with idiot confidence into the first lines of the story which ended up as "Shambleau."

The red, running figure in the poem had been a young witch pursued by soldiers and townspeople in some medieval village. In my story they had perfectly sensible reasons for killing her as soon as possible.

I sat at the typewriter and heard distant bells ringing somewhere on the backstairs of my mind. The situation was wide open, and with no conscious mental processes whatever I surrendered myself to it and the typewriter. (This is among life's most luxurious moments—giving the story its head and just keeping your fingers moving. *They* know where they're going.)

Unfortunately, you can't expect your unconscious to carry on for very long unaided. So far I have only promised to reveal where the ideas come from, not the story itself. So stay with me, pay close attention, and I'll see what I can do.

First, you have to read a great deal of the works you enjoy most. Much of it will be useless. But the trusty unconscious can be relied on to make lots of unseen notes, just in case. Mine did not fail me.

I couldn't let my character Shambleau go on running forever, could I? I had the whole scene in hand now— medieval setting, red, running figure, pursuing soldiers and citizens. But then what?

Obviously she was going to need help—also a foil to set her off effectively and to give the story a shape it didn't yet have. So Northwest Smith strolled onstage without even a glance my way, perfectly sure of what he was going to do about this. (Northwest Smith? Well, once I had typed a letter to an N. W. Smith, and the name lingered tantalizingly in my mind, waiting for this moment. What would a man named Northwest Smith look like? Be like? Occupy himself with? I soon found out.)

To complete the triumvirate of lead characters to whom my typewriter introduced me that day long ago, a companion and foil for Smith slouched carelessly into view, thirsting for drink and women. His name was Yarol, and I cannot conceal from you that it is an anagram from the letters in the name of the typewriter I was using. But I like it anyhow.

Here we return to my conviction that you must read enough, enjoy it enough, to absorb unconsciously the structure of the fiction you like best. In this case Shambleau needed help urgently. There wasn't any yet. The story required a backbone strong enough to support the plot, and Northwest Smith arrived on cue. For contrast with the seemingly helpless fugitive, "Shambleau" needed a strong, tall, romantically steely-eyed male. I think it was along about here my mind got devious and I realized that after his use as a defender was over she might just possibly spring her trap and destroy him. You will note that this gave my still unfledged plot a way to go *after* the rescue.

So Smith himself was going to need help. Preferably from someone as antithetical to Smith as Smith was to Shambleau. (Who needs *two* Northwest Smiths?)

Therefore, Yarol.

And that's how it all began.

There are of course seven or eight other stories in this collection, which could be traced along much the same curve as I've just plotted for "Shambleau."

"No Woman Born," for instance. Given the basic idea —what would happen to the most beautiful and gifted dancer of her time if she were totally incapacited by a frightful accident? Well, you gear your mind to a technological solution, but the human element keeps intruding and you know you haven't really answered the question. How would being a quasi-robot, no matter how beautiful, affect her thinking and her feeling as a human being? How would *you* handle it?

"Vintage Season" was, I believe, the first science-fiction story to ask, "What if time travelers from the future visit epic events of our era simply as tourists, here to make a Roman Holiday of our personal disasters?" It's a challenging idea and has been dealt with often since.

If you have read past Shambleau to Jirel, you will probably have noticed what a close relationship the two women bear to one another. They set the keynote for a lot of my own (incessant) writing until I met and married Henry Kuttner. I realize now that, unconsciously, no doubt, both were versions of the self I'd like to have been. I'd never noticed this before. The unconscious works in a mysterious way, doesn't it? (I have just glanced at my Unconscious to see if the tribute was noticed. It wasn't. He has fitted himself into the image of a large black cat and is preening his left shoulder and ignoring me. A rebuke I should take to heart. The unconscious more than anything hates being dragged into public. He can't work under the inspection of the conscious mind.)

All but two of the stories in this collection ("No Woman Born" and "Vintage Season") were written before Henry Kuttner and I married, and there was not yet any melding of styles or even collaboration—beyond my asking helplessly now and then *"What* should come next?". All started out with some wild but malleable idea for which I had to choose a lead character strong enough to play the action against, which is what gives a story form.

Sometimes the stories went very fast and I had to cast around desperately when I outran the idea, until Unconscious himself came in dragging a rat or a bird and I could get on with it. (I always make him let the birds go—if possible.)

One last comment on "Shambleau." This is as good a time as any to clear up a misconception which has long crept about unchallenged. This story was not rejected by every magazine in the field before it crept humbly to the doorstep of *Weird Tales.* My own perfectly clear memory tells me that I sent it first to *WT* because that was the only magazine of the type I knew well, and that an answering acceptance and a check for the (then) fabulous amount of $100.00 arrived almost by return mail.

Actually, I was far too unsure of myself to have hammered on the door of every publisher in New York if my first opus had been so unkindly treated. I'd simply have given it up and turned to some other form of activity, and this book would not be in your hands now. (I'm glad it is, too.)

C. L. Moore
1975

MISCELLANEOUS

MODERN LIBRARY